# The Rover's Secret
## A Tale Of The Pirate Cays And Lagoons Of Cuba

*by*

Harry Collingwood

Double 9
BOOKS

# The Rover's Secret
## A Tale Of The Pirate Cays And Lagoons Of Cuba
## by Harry Collingwood

ISBN: 978-93-68093-08-4

**Published by**

# DOUBLE 9 BOOKS

2/13-B, Ansari Road
Daryaganj, New Delhi – 110002
info@double9books.com
www.double9books.com
Tel. 011-40042856

# ABOUT THE AUTHOR

Harry Collingwood was the pseudonym of William Joseph Cosens Lancaster (23 May 1843 - 10 June 1922), a British civil engineer and novelist who wrote over 40 boys' adventure tales, the majority of which were set on the sea. Collingwood was the eldest son of master mariner Captain William Lancaster (1813 - (1861 - 1871)) and Anne, née Cosens. According to his birth certificate, he was born on May 23, 1843 at 9:30 a.m. at Concord Place in Weymouth, Dorset. Collingwood was the first of the couple's three children. He was eight years old when his sister Ada Louise was born, and twelve when his sister Sarah Anne (1 June 1853 - 27 December 1941) was born. Both ladies were listed as draper helpers on the 1871 census. Collingwood's father had died by that time, and his mother lived with her daughters until her death. Ada never married and lived with her sister after leaving her family home. Sarah Anne married Mathew Smellie in St Michaels, Toxteth, Liverpool, Lancashire, on June 30, 1880. Harold Ernest Smellie, born on April 11, 1881, died on April 30, 1961. Harold, Collingwood's nephew, registered his death in 1922.

# CONTENTS

# Chapter One
# My Childhood

My father—Cuthbert Lascelles—was the great painter who, under a pseudonym which I need not mention here, was a few years ago well known in the world of art, and whose works are now to be found enshrined in some of the noblest public and private collections both at home and abroad.

He was a tall and singularly handsome man; with clear grey eyes, and a stern resolute-looking mouth shadowed by a heavy moustache which, like his short curly hair and carefully trimmed beard, was of a pale golden tint.

My mother died in giving me birth; and this, together with the fact that she was a native of Italy, was all I, for some years, knew concerning her.

One of the earliest impressions made upon my infant mind—for I cannot recall the time when I was free from it—was that my parents suffered great unhappiness during the latter part of their short married life; unhappiness resulting from some terrible mistake on the part of one or the other of them; which mistake was never explained and rectified—if explanation and rectification were indeed possible—during my mother's lifetime.

Having received this impression at so very early an age, I cannot, of course, say with certainty whence I derived it; but I am inclined to attribute it chiefly to the singularity of my father's conduct toward myself.

I was his only child.

He was a man to whom solitude and retirement appeared to be the chief essentials of existence. Though living in London, he very rarely mingled in society, yet I have since heard that he always met with a most cordial welcome when he did so—and it was seldom indeed that his studio doors unfolded to admit anyone but their master. If he went into the country, as of course was often the case, in search of subjects, he never by any chance happened to be going in the same direction as any of his brethren of the brush; his destination was invariably some wild spot, unfrequented— possibly even unknown—alike by painter and tourist. And there—if undisturbed—he would remain, diligently working all day in the open air during favourable weather; and, when the elements were unpropitious for work, taking long walks over solitary heaths and desolate mountain sides, or along the lonely shore. And when the first snows of winter came, reminding him that it was time to turn his face homeward once more, he would pack up his paraphernalia and return to town, laden with studies of skies and seas, of barren moorland, rocky crag, and foaming mountain torrent which provoked alike the envy and the admiration of his brother artists.

It will naturally be supposed that, to a man of such solitary habits as these, the society of his only child would be an unspeakable comfort. But, with my father, this did not appear to be by any means the case. He never took me out of town with him on his annual pilgrimage to the country; and, when he was at home, it often happened that I did not see him, face to face, for weeks together. As a consequence of this peculiar arrangement, almost the whole of the time which I spent indoors was passed in the nursery, where also my meals were served, and wherein my only companion was Mary, the nursemaid.

The only exceptions to this isolated state of existence were those rare occasions when my father, without the slightest warning, and apparently with as little reason, used to send for me to visit him in his studio. It was during these interviews that his peculiar treatment of me became most noticeable. As a general rule, when—after a vigorous cleansing of my face and hands and a change of my raiment had been effected by the nursemaid—I was introduced into the studio, my father would ensconce me in a roomy old easy-chair by the fire; provide me with a picture-book of some kind wherewith to amuse myself; and then take no further notice of me. This, however, seemed to depend to some extent upon the greeting which I received from him, and that proved to be a tolerably accurate index of the humour which happened to possess him at the moment. Sometimes the greeting would consist of a cold shake of the hand and an equally cold "I hope you are well, boy," accompanied by a single keen glance which seemed at once to take in every detail of my person and clothing. Sometimes the shake of the hand would be somewhat warmer, the accompanying remark being, perhaps, "I am glad to see you looking so well, my boy." And occasionally—but very rarely—I was agreeably surprised to find myself received with an affectionate embrace and kiss—which I always somewhat timidly returned—and the words, "Lionel, my son, how are you?"

When the greeting reached this stage of positive warmth, it usually happened that, instead of being consigned at once to the arm-chair and the picture-book, I was lifted to my father's knee, when, laying aside palette and brushes, he would proceed to ask me all sorts of questions, such as, What had I been doing lately; where had I been, and what had I seen worthy of notice; did I want any new toys? and so on; enticing me out of my reserve until he had coaxed me into talking freely with him. On these especial occasions he had a curious habit of wheeling round in front of us a large mirror which constituted one of his studio "properties," and into this, whilst talking to me, he would intently gaze at his own reflected image, and mine, laying his cheek beside mine so as to bring both our faces to the same level, and directing me also to look into the mirror. Sometimes this curious inspection terminated satisfactorily; in which case, after perhaps an hour's chat on his knee, I was tenderly placed in the easy-chair, in such a position that my father could see me without his work being materially interfered with; our conversation was maintained with unflagging spirit on both sides; and the day was brought to a happy close by our dining together, and perhaps going to the theatre or a concert afterwards. There were occasions, however, when this pleasant state of affairs did not obtain—when the ordeal of the mirror did not terminate so satisfactorily. It occasionally happened that, whilst gazing at my father's reflected features, I observed a stern and sombre expression settling like a heavy thunder-cloud upon them; and this always sufficed to speedily reduce me to silence, however garrulous I might before have been. The paternal gaze would gradually grow more intense and searching; the thunder-cloud would lower more threateningly; and unintelligible mutterings would escape from between the fiercely clenched firm white teeth. And, finally, I would either be placed—as in the last-mentioned instance—where my father could look at me whilst at work— and where he *did* frequently look at me with appalling sternness—or I was at once dismissed with a short and sharp "Run away, boy; I am busy."

Looking back upon the first eight years of my existence, and contemplating them by the light of my now matured knowledge, I am inclined to regard them as quite an unique experience of child-life; at all events I would fain hope that but few children have suffered so keenly as I have from the lack of paternal love. And yet I cannot say that I was absolutely unhappy, except upon and for a day or two after those chilling dismissals from my father's presence to which I have briefly referred; the *suffering*, although it existed, had by long usage become a thing to which I had grown accustomed, and it consisted chiefly in a yearning after those endearments and evidences of affection which I instinctively felt were my due. The conviction that *my father*—the one to whom my childish heart naturally turned for sympathy in all my little joys and sorrows—regarded me coldly—for his demonstrations of affection were indeed few and far between—exercised a subduing and repressive influence upon me from which, even now, I have not wholly recovered, and which will probably continue to affect me to the latest hour of my life. What made my position decidedly worse was that my father had, so far, not deemed it necessary to send me to school; and I had, therefore, no companions of my own age, none of *any* age, in fact, except Mary, the nursemaid aforementioned, and Mrs Wilson, the housekeeper; the latter—good motherly body—so far compassionating the state of utter ignorance in which I was growing up that, in an erratic, unmethodical sort of way, she occasionally devoted half an hour or so of her time of an evening to the task of forwarding my education. In consequence of this state of things I often found it difficult to effect a satisfactory disposal of the time left to lie somewhat heavily on my hands.

I have said that Mrs Wilson was kind enough to undertake my education; and very faithfully and to the best of her ability, poor soul, she carried on the task. But nature had evidently intended the old lady to be a housekeeper, and not an instructress of youth; for whilst she performed the duties of the former post in a manner which left absolutely nothing to be desired, it must be confessed that in her self-imposed task of schoolmistress she failed most lamentably. Not through ignorance, however, by any means. She was fairly well educated, having "seen better days," so she was possessed of a sufficiency of knowledge for her purpose had she but known how to impart it. Unfortunately, however, for me she did not; she was entirely destitute of that tact which is the great secret of successful instruction; she had not the faintest conception of the desirability of investing my studies with the smallest particle of interest; and they were in consequence dry as the driest of dry bones and unattractive in the extreme. She never dreamed that it might be advantageous to explain or point out the ultimate purpose of my lessons to me, or to illustrate them by those apposite remarks which are often found to be of such material assistance to the youthful student; if I succeeded in repeating them perfectly "out of book" the good woman was quite satisfied; she never attempted to ascertain whether I understood them or not.

Under such circumstances it is probable that I should have derived little or no advantage from my studies had not my preceptress possessed a valuable ally in my own inclinations. Writing I was fond of; reading I had an especial desire to master, for reasons which will shortly become apparent; but arithmetic I at first found difficult, and utterly detested—until I had mastered its rules, after which I soon reached a point where the whole became clear as the noonday light; and then I fell under the magical influence of that fascination which figures for some minds is found to possess. But geography was my favourite study. There was an old terrestrial globe in the nursery, the use of which my father had taught me in one of his rare genial moments; and over this globe I used to stand for hours, with my geography in my hand and a gazetteer on a chair by my side, finding out the positions of the various places as they occurred in the books.

It sometimes happened that Mrs Wilson went out to spend the evening with a married daughter who resided somewhere within visiting distance; and, when this was the case, my studies were of course interrupted, and other means of employing my time had to be found. Thanks, chiefly, to the fact that these occasions afforded Mary, my particular attendant, an opportunity of escape from the somewhat dismal lonesomeness of the nursery, these evenings were very frequently spent in the servants' hall, where I had an opportunity of enjoying the conversation of the housemaid Jane, the cook, and Tim, the presiding genius of the knife-board and boot-brushes. I always greatly enjoyed these visits to the lower regions, for two reasons; the first of which was that they were surreptitious, and much caution was needed, or supposed to be needed, in order that my journey down-stairs might be accomplished without "master's" knowledge; the remaining reason for my enjoyment being that I generally heard something which interested me. Whether the interest excited was or was not of a healthy character the reader shall judge.

The cook, of course, reigned supreme in the servants' hall, the other occupants taking their cue from her, and regulating their tastes and occupations in accordance with hers. Now this woman—an obese, red-armed, and red-visaged person of about forty years of age—was possessed by a morbid and consuming curiosity concerning all those horrors and criminal mysteries which appear from time to time in the public prints; and the more horrible they were, the greater was her interest in them. The evening, after all the work was done and there was opportunity to give her whole attention to the subject, was the time selected by her for the satisfaction of this curiosity; and it thus happened very frequently that, when I made my appearance among the servants, they were deep in the discussion of some murder, or mysterious disappearance, or kindred matter. If the item under discussion happened to be fresh, the boy Tim was delegated to search the newspaper and read therefrom every paragraph bearing upon it, the remainder of the party listening intently and open-mouthed as they sat in a semicircle before the blazing fire. And if the item happened to be so stale as to have passed out of the notice of the papers, the cook would recapitulate for our benefit its leading features, together with any similar events or singular coincidences connected with the case which might occur to her *memory* at the moment. From the discussion of murders to the relation of ghost stories is a natural and easy transition, and here Jane, the housemaid, shone pre-eminent. She would sit there and discourse by the hour of lonely and deserted houses, long silent galleries, down which misty shapes had been seen to glide in the pallid moonlight, gaunt and ruinous chambers, the wainscot of which rattled, and the tattered tapestry of which swayed and rustled mysteriously; gloomy passages through which unearthly sighs were audibly wafted; dismal cellars, with never-opened doors, from whose profoundest recesses came at dead of night the muffled sound of shrieks and groans and clanking chains; "of calling shapes, and beckoning shadows dire, and airy tongues that syllable men's names on sands, and shores, and desert wildernesses," until not one of the party, excepting myself, dared move or look round for fear of seeing some dread presence, some shapeless dweller upon the threshold, some horrible apparition, the sight of which, Medusa-like, should blast them into stone. Not infrequently the situation was rendered additionally harrowing by the cook, who would suddenly interrupt the narrative, send an icy thrill down our spines, and cause the unhappy Tim's scalp to bristle even more than usual, by exclaiming in a low startling whisper:

"*Hark*! didn't you hear something move in the passage just then?"

Whereupon Jane and Mary would spring to their feet, and, with pallid faces, starting eyes, and blanched lips, cling convulsively to each other, convinced that at last their unspoken fears were about to be dreadfully realised.

It will naturally be supposed that these *séances* would have a dreadfully trying effect upon my infantile nerves; but, strangely enough, they did not. I never looked beneath my cot with the expectation of discovering a midnight assassin; for, in the first place, the outer doors of the house were always kept so carefully closed that I did not see how such an individual could well get in; and, in the second place, admitting, for argument's sake, the possibility of his effecting an entrance, I did not for a moment believe he would give himself the wholly unnecessary trouble of murdering a little boy, or girl either, for that matter. Then, as to the ghosts, though it never occurred to me to doubt their existence, I entirely failed to understand why people should be afraid of them. I felt that, in regarding these beings as objects of dread and apprehension, the housemaid, the cook, and in fact everybody who took this view of them, entirely misunderstood them, and were doing the poor shadows a most grievous injustice. My own experience of ghosts led me to the conclusion that, so far from their being inimical to mankind, they were distinctly benign. There was one ghost in particular to whose visitations I used to look forward with the greatest delight; and I was never so happy as when I awoke in the morning with the vague remembrance that, at some time during the silent watches of the past night, I had become conscious of a sweet and gracious presence beside my cot, bending over me with eyes which looked unutterable love into mine, and with lips which mingled kisses of tenderest affection with softly-breathed blessings upon my infant head. At first I used to mention these visitations to Mary, my nurse, but I soon forbore to do so, noticing that she always looked uncomfortably startled for a moment or two afterwards, and generally dismissed the subject somewhat hurriedly by remarking:

"Ah, poor lamb! you've been dreaming about your mother."

Which remark annoyed me, for I felt convinced that so realistic an experience could not possibly result from a mere dream.

It sometimes happened that there were no tragedies or other horrors in the newspapers sufficiently piquant to tempt the cook's intellectual palate; and in the absence of these, if it happened also to be Jane's "evening out," Mary would occasionally produce a well-thumbed copy of the *Arabian Nights*, or some old volume of fairy tales, from which she read aloud.

How I enjoyed those evenings with the old Eastern romancist! How I revelled in the imaginary delights and wonders of fairydom! Of course I pictured myself the hero of every story, the truth of the most outrageous of which it never occurred to me to doubt. Sitting at Mary's feet, on a low stool before the fire, with the old cat blinking and purring with drowsy satisfaction upon my knee, I used to gaze abstractedly at the glowing coals, now thinking myself the prince in "Cinderella," now the happy owner of "Puss in Boots," and now the adventurous Sindbad. There was one story, however—I quite forget its title—which, in strong contrast with the others, instead of affording me gratification, was a source of keen annoyance and vexation to me whenever I heard it. It related to a boy who on one occasion had the good fortune to meet, in the depths of the forest, a little old man in red cap and green jerkin—a gnome or fairy, of course—who with the utmost good-nature offered to gratify any single wish that boy might choose to express. Here was a glorious chance, the opportunity of a lifetime! The boy's first thought was for ginger-bread, but before the thought had time to clothe itself in words the vision of a drum and trumpet flashed across his mind. He was about to express a wish for these martial instruments, and a real sword, when it occurred to him that the fairies were quite equal to the task of providing gifts of infinitely greater value and splendour than even these coveted articles. And then that unfortunate boy completely lost his head; his brain became muddled with the endless variety of things which he found he required; and he took so long a time to make up his mind that, when, in desperation, he finally did so, the unwelcome discovery was made that his fairy friend, disgusted at the delay and vacillation, had vanished without bestowing upon him so much as even one poor ginger-bread elephant. It was that boy's first and last opportunity, and he lost it. He never again met a fairy, though he wandered through the forest, day after day, week after week, and year after year, until he became an old man, dying at last in a state of abject poverty.

The moral of this story was obvious even to my juvenile mind. It plainly pointed to the necessity for being prepared to take the fullest advantage of every opportunity, whenever it might present itself; and I was resolved that, if ever I encountered a fairy, he should find me fully prepared to tax his generosity to its utmost limit. And, forthwith, I began to ask myself what was the most desirable thing at all likely to be within a fairy's power of bestowal. At this point I, for the first time, began to realise the difficulties of the situation in which the unhappy boy of the story found himself. I thought of several things; but none of them came quite up to my idea of a gift such as would do full honour and justice to a fairy's power of giving; the utmost I could imagine was a real ship full of real sailors, wherein I might roam the seas and perform wonderful voyages like Sindbad; and, in my efforts to achieve a still higher flight of imagination, I found myself so completely at a loss that I was fain to turn to Mary for counsel. Accordingly, as I was being escorted by that damsel upstairs to bed one night, I broached the subject by saying:

"Mary, supposing you were to meet a fairy, what would you ask him to give you?"

"Lor'! Master Lionel, I dun know," she replied. "That's a question I shouldn't like to answer just off-hand; I should want to think it over a good bit. I should read a lot of books, and find out what was the best thing as was to be had."

"What sort of books?" I asked.

"Oh! any sort," was the reply; "books such as them down-stairs in your pa's lib'ry; them's downright *beautiful* books—your pa's—full of all sorts of wonderful things such as you never heard tell of."

This reply afforded me food for a considerable amount of profound reflection before I went to sleep that night; the result of which was that on the following morning, as soon as I had taken my breakfast, I descended to the "lib'ry," opened the doors of one of the book-cases, and dragged down upon my curly pate the most bulky volume I could reach. With the expenditure of a considerable amount of labour I conveyed it to the nursery, and, flinging it and myself upon the floor, opened it hap-hazard, feeling sure that, in a book of such imposing dimensions, I should find something valuable wherever I might open it. It was an English work of some kind, I remember; but, alas for my aspirations! it might almost as well have been Greek. I was equal, just then, to the mastery of words of two syllables, but no more; and the result was that, though I occasionally caught a glimpse of the meaning of a sentence here and there, the subject matter of the book, as a whole, remained a profound mystery to me. My want of knowledge was at once made most painfully apparent to myself; I discovered that I had a very great deal to learn before the treasures of wisdom by which I was surrounded could be made available; and I forthwith bent all my energies to the task of perfecting myself in the art of reading as a first and indispensable step.

# Chapter Two
# My Mother's Portrait

Actuated by what was to me so powerful an incentive, my progress toward proficiency as a reader was rapid; and, in a comparatively short time, I felt equal to a renewed effort to sound the depths of the well of knowledge.

On this momentous occasion—momentous to me, at least, for I am convinced that it exercised a very material influence on my eventual choice of a career—I chanced upon an illustrated volume of *Travels by Land and Sea*. I opened it at the title-page, down which I patiently and conscientiously waded; then on to the preface—which, luckily, was a short one—and so into the body of the book. I of course encountered a great deal that I could only imperfectly understand; and I detected within myself a rapidly-growing disposition to skip all the hard words; but, notwithstanding these drawbacks, I contrived to catch a glimmering, if not something more, of the author's meaning. It was hard work, but I struggled on, down page after page, fascinated, my imagination vividly depicting the various scenes of which I read. I saw the deep blue tropic sea heaving and sparkling in the joyous sunshine, and the stout ship, with her gleaming wide-spread canvas, sweeping bravely over its bosom. I stood upon the deck of that ship, among the seamen, peering eagerly ahead, and saw a faint grey cloud gradually shape itself in the midst of the haze on the far western horizon. I heard the joyous shout of "Land ho!" break from the lips of the lookout at the mast-head; and watched the cloud gradually hardening its outlines and changing its tints until it assumed the unmistakable aspect of land; saw the distant mountains steal into view, and the trees emerge into distinct and prominent detail along the shore; saw, at length, the strip of sandy beach, dazzlingly white in the blazing sunlight; heard the deep hoarse roar of the breakers, and saw the flashing of the snow-white foam as the rollers swept grandly on and dashed themselves into surf and diamond spray upon the strand. Then I saw the natives launching their light canoes and paddling off through the surf to the ship; or leapt eagerly into the boat alongside; reached the strip of dazzling beach—strewn now with beautiful shells; plunged into the grateful shade of enticing groves rich with the prodigal luxuriance and fantastic beauty of tropical growth, ablaze with flowers of gorgeous hues, alive with birds whose plumage flashed like living gems, and breathed an atmosphere oppressive with perfume.

From that hour forward the entertainments of the servants' hall paled their ineffectual fires before the superior effulgence of those delightful visions which I now possessed the power of summoning at will; books or stories of travel and adventure alone had now any charm for me; and these I devoured with an appetite which grew by what it fed on. The natural consequence of all this will readily be foreseen: a desire sprang up, which steadily ripened into a resolve, that, when I should become a man, I too would be a traveller, and—like those of whom I was never tired of reading—would make my home upon the pathless sea.

Thus matters went on until the arrival of the eighth anniversary of my birthday, on the morning of which, soon after I had finished my breakfast, I was summoned to my father's studio. I was received somewhat coldly; and, after indicating to me the chair which he had placed for my occupation, my father resumed his work and continued it for some time without taking the slightest further notice of me.

A silence of perhaps half an hour ensued; when, laying down his brush, he said:

"I am glad to learn from Mrs Wilson that you are making very satisfactory progress with your studies; that, in fact, you are exhibiting a marked disposition to acquire knowledge. This is well; this is as it should be; and, to mark my appreciation of your conduct, I have resolved to further your desires and give you increased facilities for study, by sending you to school, where you will have the advantage of such guidance and assistance as only trained masters can give; and where you will also enjoy the companionship and association of lads of your own age. I hope the prospect is a pleasant one to you."

As this last remark seemed to partake somewhat of the form of a question, I replied that the prospect *was* pleasant, and that I felt very much obliged to him for his kind and thoughtful intentions. I wanted to say a great deal more by way of thanks; I wished him to understand how delightful to me would be the change which this arrangement involved; how I had longed for some one to take me by the hand, to guide my erratic footsteps and lead me by the shortest way to that fountain of knowledge for the waters of which I was just beginning to thirst; and I wished him to understand, too, how welcome would be the companionship of the other boys, after so lonely a life as mine had been. But to make all this clear to him through my imperfect method of expressing myself would have involved quite a long speech on my part; and, as my eager glance fell on his unsympathetic face, the words failed me, and I held my peace.

"The school I have selected is a large one," my father continued. "I am informed that the pupils at present number over two hundred; and it is quite in the country. The principal encourages every kind of innocent pastime, such as cricket, football, swimming, skating in the winter, and so on; so you will not lack amusements—the necessaries for joining in which I will take care that you shall be provided with. And I have arranged that, for the present, you shall receive from the headmaster sixpence a week as pocket-money—a sum which I consider quite sufficient for a boy of your age. With regard to your studies, I would urge you to make the most of your opportunities; as, on the completion of your education, you will have to make your own way in the world. My profession, as you will perhaps better understand later on, is somewhat a precarious one. As long as I retain my health and strength and the unimpaired use of all my faculties, matters will no doubt go well with me; but accident, disease, or the loss of sight may at any moment interrupt my labours or stop them altogether: in which case my income, which I derive solely from the use of my brush, would cease altogether. You will easily comprehend, therefore, that it would be unwise in the extreme for you to depend upon me in any way to provide for your future. Now, do you think you clearly comprehend what I have been saying?"

I replied, 'Yes, I believed I did.' I wanted to add that there was one thing, however, that I did *not* understand, which was, how a father could communicate to his only child so lengthy an explanation on a subject of so much importance without giving one word or sign of affection to that child, and that I was most earnestly anxious to know the reason, if any, for so marked an omission; but, whilst I was hesitating how to frame my remark in such a manner as to avoid the giving of offence, my father rose from before his easel, and, unlocking a cabinet which stood in the room, said:

"One word more. You will probably be asked by your companions all manner of questions about your home and your parents. Now, with regard to your mother, you know nothing about her beyond, possibly, the fact that she died when you were born; and that is quite as much as I consider it needful for you to know. But you may perhaps be glad to be made acquainted with her personal appearance; you may, possibly, at some future day—if you have not already experienced such a desire—be anxious to possess the means of bringing her before you as something more than a mere *name*. I will therefore give you this miniature, which is a correct and striking likeness of what your mother was when I painted it."

And, as he finished speaking, my father placed in my hand a small velvet case, to which was attached a thin gold chain by which it might be suspended from the neck.

I was about to open the case; but my father somewhat hastily prevented the action by throwing the chain round my neck, thrusting the miniature into the bosom of my dress, and dismissing me with the words:

"There! run away now and make your preparations. We shall set out for your school to-morrow, immediately after breakfast."

I hastened away to my play-room, and, once fairly within the bounds of my own domain, drew forth the miniature case and opened it. As the lid flew back at the pressure of my finger upon the spring a thrill of half joy, half terror, shot through me; for I instantly recognised in the features of the portrait a vivid presentment of that sweet dream-face whose visits to me during the silent and lonely night-watches had flooded my infant soul with such an ecstasy of rapture and delight. The portrait, which is before me as I write, was that of a young and beautiful girl. The complexion was clearest, faintest, most transparent olive; the face a perfect oval, crowned with luxuriant masses of wavy, deep chestnut hair, the colour almost merging into black; indeed it would have been difficult to decide that it was *not* black but for the lights in it, which were of a deep dusky golden tone. The eyebrows were beautifully arched, and the lashes of the eyes were represented as unusually long. The eyes themselves were very deep hazel, or black—it was impossible to say which; the nose perfectly straight; the lips, of a clear, rich, cherry hue, were full and slightly pouting; the mouth perhaps the merest shade larger than it ought to have been for perfect beauty; the chin round, with a well-defined dimple in its centre. Altogether, it was the loveliest face I had ever seen; and I stood for some time gazing in a trance of admiration on it, the feeling being mingled with one of deep regret that fate had, in snatching away the living original, deprived me of such rich possibilities of mutual love. I felt keenly that, had she continued to live, my life would, in all probability, have been widely different and very much happier than it ever had been. Musing thus, I turned the case over in my hand, and found that there was a contrivance for opening it at the back. I soon discovered the spring, upon pressing which the back flew open, disclosing a circlet of glossy chestnut hair reposing upon an oval of pale yellow silk, in the centre of which were painted the words "Maria Lascelles; aet. 18. C.L."

Closing the case again and placing it carefully in my bosom, I turned my thoughts to my new prospects; and whilst collecting together a few of my more treasured valuables to take with me, and packing the remainder away in a place of safety, I suffered myself to indulge in much pleasant speculation upon my immediate future.

On the following morning, about ten o'clock, my father and I left town in a post-chaise, and, stopping only for an hour about mid-day to dine at a pleasant little road-side country inn, arrived, at about seven o'clock in the evening, at our destination. This was a large brick-built edifice evidently constructed especially to serve the purposes of a scholastic establishment, standing in its own somewhat extensive grounds, and situated in a lonely spot about half a mile from the sea, and—though actually in Hampshire—some four miles only from the port of Poole in Dorsetshire. I was speedily presented to the principal, who at once made a favourable impression upon me, afterwards abundantly confirmed; and, after perhaps half an hour's conversation with him, my father formally delivered me over to his care and left me—his leave-taking, though somewhat hurried, being decidedly warmer than his abstracted manner during the journey had led me to expect.

At this school, let it suffice to say, I remained for the following seven years; enjoying, during that period of my life, such happiness as, up to then, my imagination had never been able to conceive; and devoting myself to my studies with a zest and enthusiasm which won the warmest encomiums from the several masters who had charge of my education. French, geography, mathematics, and navigation were my favourite subjects; and I also developed a very fair amount of talent with my pencil. Athletics I especially excelled in; and by the time I had been three years at the school I had become almost amphibious. It affords me particular pleasure to reflect that, notwithstanding my previous total want of training, I was, from the very outset of my school career, an especial favourite with my fellow-pupils, never having had more than one quarrel serious enough to result in a fight, on which occasion I succeeded in giving my antagonist—a great bully who had been cruelly tyrannising over a smaller boy—so severe a trouncing that a resort to this rough-and-ready mode of settling a dispute never again became necessary, so far as I was concerned. During this period there was only one thing that troubled me, which was, that I never saw my father. Owing to what at the time seemed to me an uninterrupted series of unfortunate coincidences, it invariably happened that when holiday-time came round my father had urgent business calling him away from home; and arrangements had accordingly to be made for my spending my holidays at the school. This, in itself, constituted no very great hardship; there were several other lads—Anglo-Indians and others whose friends resided at too great a distance to admit of the holidays being spent with them—who always remained behind to bear me company; and, as we were allowed to do pretty much what we liked so long as we did not misconduct ourselves or get into mischief, the time was passed pleasantly enough; but, notwithstanding his singular treatment of me, I loved my father, and regarded it as a positive hardship that so long a time should be permitted to elapse without my seeing him. I was continually in hopes that, as we were unable to meet at holiday-time, he would run down into the country and pay me a visit, but he never did, and this was another disappointment.

At length, however, an end came to my disappointment and to my school-days together; for, on the morning of my fifteenth birthday, I was sent for by the principal of the school, who, after complimenting me upon my diligence and the progress I had made whilst under his care, informed me that the day had arrived when my school-boy life was to cease, and when I must go out into the world and commence that great battle of life, which all of us have to fight in one shape or another. He added to his communication some most excellent advice, the value of which I have since had abundant opportunity of proving; and concluded with the announcement that my father would make his appearance that same evening and take me away with him.

Within a quarter of an hour of the time specified, the grinding sound of wheels upon the gravel drive in front of the building suggested the probability that the moment of my departure was at hand; and, a few minutes later, I was summoned to the library to meet my father. With my heart throbbing high with mingled feelings of joy and trepidation, I hastened to the spot, and, before I well knew where I was, found myself in the presence of the parent who had allowed seven full years to elapse without an attempt to see his only child. For an instant—which sufficed me to note that those seven years had left abundant traces of their passage on the once almost unwrinkled brow—we stood gazing with equal intentness in each others' faces; then my father grasped the outstretched hand which I offered, and said, somewhat constrainedly:

"So this is the once quiet dreamy little Leo, is it? I am glad to see you once more, my boy; glad to see you looking so strong and well—so wonderfully improved in appearance in every way, in fact; and glad, too, to hear that Dr Tomlinson is able to confirm so thoroughly the good reports of your conduct which he has sent me from time to time." He paused, and I was about to make a suitable answer to his greeting, when he continued— half unconsciously, it seemed to me, but with a quite perceptible ring of harshness in his voice:

"You are wonderfully like your mother, boy; no one who knew her would ever mistake you for anyone else than her son."

The words were simple, but were accompanied by such a regretful look, deepening into a baleful frown as he regarded me fixedly, that I was completely startled, and in fact so overwhelmed with astonishment that, for the moment, I was quite unable to make any reply; and before I could recover myself my father appeared to have become conscious of his singularity of manner, which he evidently overcame by a very powerful effort. Laying his hand somewhat heavily upon my shoulder, he said:

"Do not be frightened, Leo; I have been far from well lately, and my illness seems to have slightly affected my brain; sometimes I detect myself saying things which I had not the remotest intention of saying a moment before. If you should observe any little peculiarity of that kind in me, take no notice of it, let it pass. And now, if your boxes are all ready—as I suppose they are—let them be brought down and put on the chaise; we shall sleep in Poole to-night, and we can converse at the hotel, over a good dinner, as well as here."

An hour later we were discussing that same good dinner, and maintaining a tolerably animated conversation over it, too. My father put a few adroit questions to me relative to my school experiences, which had the effect of "drawing me out," and he listened to all I had to say with just that appearance of friendly interest which is so flattering and encouraging to a youthful talker. His treatment of me was everything that could be desired—except that he seemed to be rather taking the ground of an elder friend than of a parent. I should have preferred a shade less of the polite suavity of his manner and a more distinct manifestation of fatherly affection. He seemed anxious to efface the memory of the singularity which marked our first meeting; and yet I thought that, later on in the evening, when our conversation assumed a more general character, I could detect a disposition on his part to again approach the subject, these approaches being accompanied by a very perceptible nervousness and constraint of manner. But, though my father certainly led the conversation once or twice in that direction, he as often changed the subject again, and nothing more was said about it until our bed-room candles were brought to us and we were about to retire for the night. Then, as we vacated the chairs we had been occupying during the evening, and rose to our feet, he grasped me by the arm and planted me square in front of the chimney-piece, which was surmounted by a pier-glass, and, placing himself beside me, remarked, looking at our reflected images:

"You have grown tremendously, Leo, during the seven years you have been at school. I really believe you will develop into as tall a man as I am. But," (taking a candlestick in his hand and holding it so as to throw the light full upon our faces) "you are so like your mother, so painfully like your mother;" and again the frown darkened his face and for a moment he seemed almost to shrink from me.

"Well, sir," said I, "it seems to me that I have your forehead, your mouth, and your chin; we both possess considerable width between the eyes; and my hair, though dark, is curly, like your own."

"Ah, yes!" he answered, somewhat impatiently; "the latter, however, is a mere accident; and, as to the other points you have mentioned, I really *cannot* see any positive resemblance; I wish I could—I earnestly wish that my son resembled me rather than—Ah! there I go again, saying words which positively have *no* meaning. I really *must* take rest and medical advice; I have executed several very important commissions during the past year, and the strain upon my imagination and upon my nerves has been almost too much for me. Now, I'll be bound, Leo, that you have noticed more than once this evening that there are moments when I am not—well, not exactly my natural self."

"Well, sir," I hesitatingly replied, "I must confess that—that—"

"That you have," my father interrupted. "Very well; take no notice of it; forget it; it means nothing. Good night, boy; good night."

"Good night, sir," I replied. "I hope you will sleep soundly, and rise in the morning refreshed. And, oh father! I wish I could do anything to help you—"

"So you can, my son; so you can. Thank you, Leo, for your kind wish. You *can* help me very greatly, by taking no notice whatever of any little eccentricities you may observe in my behaviour, and by remembering that they are entirely due to overwork. Now, good night, once more; and remember that we must be stirring early in the morning, as we have a long journey before us."

And, with this very peculiar mode of dismissal, my father gently forced me out of the room, and closed the door upon me.

# Chapter Three
# I Join the "Hermione"

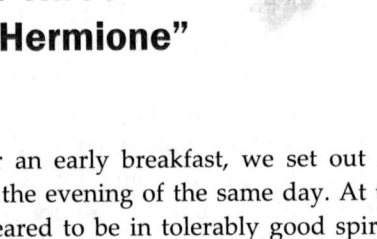

On the following morning, after an early breakfast, we set out for London; where we safely arrived on the evening of the same day. At the outset of the journey my father appeared to be in tolerably good spirits, conversing with much animation upon the subject—which he had introduced—of my future career. I explained to him that my great desire was, and had been for some time, to become a sailor; and that I hoped he would be able to see his way to forward my views. Contrary, I must confess, to my expectations, my father raised no objections, stipulating only that I should enter the naval service; and he promised me that he would use his best efforts to secure my nomination as a midshipman; but he cautioned me that, as he scarcely knew to whom to apply for this service, I might have to wait some time for the gratification of my wishes. The conversation which settled this, to me, important matter took place in the forenoon, the subject being finally disposed of and dismissed just as we alighted for luncheon. On the resumption of our journey the conversation was by no means so lively, and it distressed me much to observe that my father was gradually sinking back into the same strange moody state of mind which had possessed him on the previous day. I made several efforts to win him back to a more cheerful condition, but they were quite ineffectual; and, after receiving two or three increasingly impatient replies, I was compelled to abandon the attempt. For several days the same unsatisfactory state of affairs continued, my father and I only meeting at breakfast and dinner, and then exchanging scarcely half a dozen words beyond the ordinary courtesies; I was therefore not only considerably surprised but much gratified when he one morning informed me that he had succeeded in securing my appointment as midshipman on board the frigate *Hermione*, then about to sail for the West Indies. He added that there was no time to lose if I wished to go out in her; and that it would consequently be necessary for us to set out for Portsmouth on the following morning. This promptitude was rather more than I had bargained for; notwithstanding my father's very peculiar behaviour I was much attached to him, and had hoped to have enjoyed at least a month or two of his society; moreover, I felt very anxious as to his peculiar condition, and would fain have remained with him until I could have seen some improvement in his mental state; but, on my mentioning this, he seemed so singularly averse to any delay of my departure that I saw nothing for it but to acquiesce.

A week later I had joined my ship, and on November 18th, 1796, we were bowling down channel under double-reefed topsails.

We duly arrived at our destination—Port Royal, Jamaica—after a tedious passage of over two months' duration; and, having landed our despatches, were ordered to cruise between Cape Tiburon and the Virgin Islands.

By this time I had pretty well settled down into my proper place, had ceased to be the butt of the other midshipmen; and, having a real liking for my duties, had learned to perform them pretty satisfactorily. Mr Reid, the first lieutenant, had expressed the opinion that I "shaped well." But, even before our arrival at Jamaica, I had made the unwelcome discovery that the *Hermione* was by no means likely to prove a comfortable ship. The vessel herself there was no fault whatever to find with; she was a noble frigate of thirty-two guns, very fast, and a splendid sea-boat. But the skipper— Captain Pigot—was a regular tartar. He was a tall, powerful man, and would have been handsome but for his somewhat bloated features. Even to his officers he was arrogant, overbearing, and discourteous to an almost unbearable degree; to the men he was simply an unmitigated tyrant. There was certainly some excuse for severity of discipline and occasional loss of temper, had it gone no further than that, for our crew was, as a whole, the worst I have ever had the misfortune to be associated with, several of them being foreigners, and of the remainder a good sprinkling were men who had been *sentenced* by the magistrates *to serve the King*. Possibly in other and more patient hands they might have developed into a good smart body of men, and such it was doubtless the skipper's hope and intention to make them. But he most unfortunately went the wrong way to work. Punishment was his doctrine; the "cat" was his sovereign remedy for all evils. He flogged almost daily, even for the most trivial offences, and our "black list" was probably the longest in the navy for a ship of our size. As might be expected, with a captain of this kind, we poor unfortunate mids were constantly in trouble, and the greater part of our time was spent at the mast-heads.

One afternoon—it was on the 22nd of March, 1797—being off Zaccheo, the lookout aloft reported that a brig and several smaller vessels were at anchor inshore between that island and the larger one of Porto Rico. The first lieutenant thereupon at once went aloft with his telescope, where he made a thorough examination of the strangers and their position; having completed which to his satisfaction, he returned to the deck and made his report to Captain Pigot. The ship's head was immediately directed inshore; and the pinnace, first and second cutters, and gig were ordered away, under lieutenants Reid and Douglas, to go in, as soon as the ship had anchored, and cut out the vessels. Mr Reid, with whom, I think, I was somewhat of a favourite, kindly selected me to take charge of the gig; and young Courtenay, my especial chum, was fortunate enough to be chosen by Mr Douglas to command the second cutter. By Courtenay's advice, I procured from the armourer a ship's cutlass, to replace my almost useless dirk; and having carefully loaded and primed a very excellent pair of pistols with which my father had presented me, I thrust those useful articles into my belt and hastened on deck, just as the frigate was rounding to preparatory to anchoring. A couple of minutes later the anchor was let go abreast of and scarcely half a mile distant from a small battery, the guns of which commanded the vessels we were about to attack, and the canvas was very smartly clewed up and furled.

The men were still aloft when the battery, which had hoisted Spanish colours, opened fire upon us, the first shot severing our larboard main-topgallant back-stay. This damage, slight as it was, sufficed to effectually rouse Captain Pigot's hasty, irritable temper; and, hurrying the men down from aloft, he ordered the larboard broadside to be manned, and the guns to be directed upon the audacious battery. A couple of well-directed broadsides sufficed to silence its fire, and the boats were then immediately piped away.

"Mark my words, Lascelles," said Courtenay, as we trundled down the ship's side together, "we are going to have a tough time of it with those craft in there; three of them have boarding nettings triced up, and are evidently preparing to give us a warm reception. They look like privateers, and if so, I daresay they are full of men, who will have ample opportunity to bowl us over at their leisure whilst we are pulling in upon them. And we shall have no help from the frigate's guns, for the rascals are beyond their reach."

"Now then, Courtenay, no croaking, young gentleman, if you please, or I shall be under the painful necessity of sending you back on board, and taking Mr Maxwell in your place," said Mr Douglas, who was following us down the side, and who happened to overhear Courtenay's encouraging remarks.

"Oh, no, sir, you can't be so heartless as to do that; have some consideration for my feelings," laughed Courtenay; and flinging himself down in the stern-sheets of the boat, he drew his cutlass, and affected to be very cautiously feeling its edge, to the covert amusement of the men who happened to see him.

"It's a'most sharp enough for you to shave with, ain't it, sir?" demurely inquired the smart fore-topman, who was stroke-oar in Courtenay's boat, at which there was another grin; Courtenay's chin being as guiltless of hair as the back of a lady's hand, notwithstanding which it was whispered that he assiduously shaved every morning with his penknife.

"Now, are we all ready, Douglas?" asked Mr Reid, as he stood in the stern-sheets of the pinnace, and ran his eye critically over the boats. "Then, shove off; let fall and give way, lads. Lascelles and I will tackle the brig, Mr Douglas, whilst I must leave you and Mr Courtenay to give a good account of those two schooners which have hoisted their colours. We will take matters quietly, so as to spare the men as much as possible, until the shot begins to drop round us, when we must make a dash and get on board as quickly as we can."

Courtenay's assumption that the three vessels we had marked out for attack were privateers was speedily strengthened by the circumstance that boats were seen to put off from the smaller craft—doubtless prizes of the others—conveying what were probably the prize-crews back to their own ships, to assist in their defence. As we neared the land we made out that the people in the battery were still standing to their guns, and we momentarily expected them to open fire upon us; but they were wise enough to refrain, evidently having already had a sufficient experience of the frigate's broadsides, the destructive effects of which became distinctly visible as we pulled past.

Upon our arriving abreast the battery, the brig and the two schooners, for which we were heading, having got springs upon their cables and hoisted French colours, brought their broadsides to bear upon us, and commenced firing, whereupon we separated, taking "open order," as the marines say, so as to offer as small a mark as possible. It was the first time I had "smelt powder," and as the shot began to hum past us, I must plead guilty to having at the outset experienced a certain amount of nervous trepidation. I had an idea that every shot would find its mark, that "every bullet has its billet," and I momentarily expected to feel the crushing blow which would tell me that I had been hit. But on we swept, the shot flying close over our heads, or just past us on either side, occasionally striking the water within such near proximity as to dash a little shower of spray right over the boat, and presently the musketry bullets came whistling about our ears, yet we remained unscathed. This opened my eyes, and gave me a juster appreciation than I had had before of the perils of warfare. I saw that it was by no means the necessarily deadly thing I had hitherto imagined it to be, and my courage came back to me, my spirits rising momentarily higher in response to the increasing excitement of the occasion. For we were now dashing forward upon our several quarries at racing speed, the men straining at the oars until the stout ashen staves bent like willow wands, and the water buzzed and foamed and bubbled, hissing past us in a regular series of miniature whirlpools, whilst the boats seemed every now and then as though they were about to be lifted clear out of the water by the herculean efforts of their panting crews.

Once within musket-shot of the vessels, a very few minutes at this pace sufficed us to cover the remaining distance, when we dashed alongside— the first lieutenant ranging up on the brig's starboard quarter, whilst we in the gig took her in the larboard fore-chains—and a stubborn hand-to-hand fight immediately commenced. The craft we had attacked proved to be full of people; and upon our attempting to board, we found that they had been divided into two distinct parties, one of which was successfully opposing Mr Reid, whilst the other seemed determined at all costs to prevent my own little party from gaining a footing upon the deck. Twice were we forced back into the boat, and I saw that two or three of the men were bleeding from pike or bullet wounds. A third time we made the attempt, and as I was scrambling up into the brig's channels a Frenchman thrust his pike through a port at me. I grasped the weapon, and partly through my antagonist's efforts to wrench it away again, and partly with the aid of a friendly push behind from one of our own lads, I suddenly found myself shot in through the port, and safely landed on the brig's deck. Springing to my feet in an instant, I laid fiercely about me with my cutlass, and thus cleared a way for the gig's crew to follow me. In less than a minute the gigs were in possession of the fore part of the deck, and so quickly was the thing done, and with such good-will did our lads lay about them, that the party opposed to us recoiled in a sudden panic. Taking instant advantage of this, we charged them with a wild hurrah, whereupon they fairly turned tail and fled before us, rushing helter-skelter in among the other party. The whole body of defenders being thus thrown into disorder, the first lieutenant's party managed to make good their footing on deck; and then, after one desperate but ineffectual charge on the part of the Frenchmen, we had no further trouble, the defenders throwing down their weapons and calling for quarter. This was, of course, at once accorded them, and they were ordered below, the hatches being clapped over them, whilst the ship was subjected to an overhaul. She proved to be both empty and old, besides being apparently a particularly leaky tub; she was consequently valueless, and except for the purpose of destroying her, and thus putting a stop to her depredations, not worth the trouble of taking. This fact definitely ascertained, Mr Reid ordered the crew on deck again; and, giving them five minutes in which to collect their personal belongings, directed them to take the brig's boats and make the best of their way ashore. The crew thus got rid of, the vessel herself was effectually set on fire in three places, and as soon as the flames had taken such a hold as to prevent all possibility of their extinction we left her.

Meanwhile, the second lieutenant and Courtenay had been equally successful with ourselves, each having captured one of the schooners without very much difficulty. They proved, however, to be, like the brig, very old and weak, having evidently been strained all to pieces in the effort to make them perform services for which they were never built. They, therefore, were also set on fire. And as for their prizes, they consisted of half a dozen wretched little dirty coasters, the largest of which could not have measured over sixty tons. Their crews, we were informed, had been landed on various parts of the coast, so, their lawful owners not being there to take possession of them, these craft were likewise devoted to the flames. By the time that the Frenchmen had all been got rid of, and the little fleet effectually set on fire, it had fallen dark, and all hands being pretty well tired out, we made the best of our way back to the frigate. We had eight hands wounded in this skirmish, all the wounds proving fortunately of a very trifling character, so much so indeed that not one of the wounded was put on the sick list for even a single day.

The *Hermione* remained at anchor all night; and on the following morning Mr Douglas, with a boat's crew, went on shore, drove the small garrison out of the fort, and spiked and dismounted the guns.

Thus, harmlessly, so far at least as I was concerned, ended my first brush with the enemy; and though I never heard anything further of the affair, I received the gratifying information that the first lieutenant had spoken very highly of my conduct on the occasion when making his report to Captain Pigot.

# Chapter Four
# An Unsuccessful Chase

A fortnight later we fell in with and were ordered to join the squadron of Vice-admiral Parker.

This arrangement was, to the *Hermione's* officers at least, a source of intense gratification. For whereas, whilst we were cruising alone, our opportunities for social intercourse were limited to an occasional invitation to dine with the captain—and that, Heaven knows, was poor entertainment enough!—we now had frequent invitations to dine with the officers of the other ships, or entertained them in return in our own ward-room. But, though matters were thus made more pleasant for the officers of the *Hermione*, I cannot say that the change wrought any improvement in the condition of the ship's company—quite the reverse, indeed. For, so anxious was Captain Pigot that his ship should be the smartest in the fleet, that when reefing topsails at night, if any other ship happened to finish before us, the last man of the yard of the dilatory topsail was infallibly booked for a flogging next day. And so with all other evolutions. The result of which was, that while our crew became noted for their smartness, they daily grew more sullen, sulky, and discontented in their dispositions, shirking their work whenever there was a possibility of doing so undetected, and performing their duties with an ill-will which they took little pains to conceal. This, of course, only tended to make matters still worse. The skipper could not fail to notice his increasing unpopularity, and this wounded his self-love; added to which he soon got the idea into his head—and certainly not altogether without reason—that the men were combining together to thwart and annoy him. And this only made him still more irritable and severe. It seemed at length as though matters were steadily approaching the point when it would become an open and recognised struggle between the captain and the crew for supremacy in respect of dogged obstinacy and determination. What made it all the worse was that the officers, in the maintenance of proper order and discipline in the ship, were compelled—very much against their will—to support and countenance the skipper in his arbitrary mode of dealing with the crew; thus dividing the inmates of the frigate into two well-defined parties—namely, those on the quarter-deck and those on the forecastle. We were *all* unpopular in varying degrees, from the captain down to the midshipmen. I have good reason to believe that the first lieutenant on more than one occasion remonstrated with Captain Pigot upon his excessive harshness to the men, and strongly urged him to try the effect of more lenient measures with them; but, if such was the case, the remonstrances proved wholly unavailing. Added to all this there was, especially after we joined the squadron, incessant sail, gun, musketry, and cutlass drill, in addition to the daily combined evolutions of the ships; all of which made our poor lads pray for a change of some sort—they cared not what—it could scarcely be for the worse, and might very reasonably be hoped to be somewhat for the better.

Under such circumstances the joy of the men may be imagined when, one morning at daylight, the signal was made by the admiral to chase to the eastward. Nevertheless, our unfortunate lookout aloft was promptly booked for two dozen at the gangway that day because he had failed to be the first to discover the stranger.

We were cruising at this time in the Windward Channel, the squadron being at the moment of the discovery about midway between Points Malano and Perle. We were working to windward under double-reefed topsails on the starboard tack, the trade-wind blowing fresh at about east-nor'-east.

The strange sail was about ten miles dead to windward of us; and that she had sharp eyes on board her was manifest from the fact that, before we had time to acknowledge the admiral's signal, she had shaken the reefs out of her topsails and had set topgallant-sails. Every ship in the squadron of course at once did the same, and forthwith a most animated chase commenced. The *Hermione* happened to be the weathermost British ship, and, consequently, nearest the chase; and most anxiously did Captain Pigot struggle to maintain this enviable position; albeit we were closely pressed by the frigates *Mermaid* and *Quebec*, which were thrashing along, the one on our lee bow and the other on our lee beam, a distance of a bare cable's length separating the three ships from each other. It was an interesting and exhilarating spectacle to watch these two graceful craft leaping and plunging over the swift-rushing foam-capped emerald surges, spurning them aside with their swelling bows and shivering them into cloud-like showers of snowy spray which they dashed as high as their fore-yards; now rolling heavily to windward as they slid down into a liquid valley, and anon careering to leeward under the influence of wind and wave, as they mounted to the succeeding crest, until their wet gleaming sides and glistening copper flashed in the sun almost down to their garboard strakes.

Nor did our own ship present a less gallant spectacle as she careered madly forward through the hissing brine, now burying her bows deep in a fringe of yeasty foam, and next moment soaring aloft as though she meant to forsake the ocean altogether; her steeply-inclined deck knee-deep with the rushing cataracts of water which poured over her to windward, her canvas tugging at the stout spars until they bent and sprang like fishing-rods, and the wind singing through her tautly-strained rigging as through the strings of a gigantic Aeolian harp. The bearings of the chase were promptly taken by Mr Southcott, the master; and a single hour sufficed to show that we were not only fore-reaching, but also weathering upon her. By that time we had brought her a couple of points abaft our weather-beam, and the *Hermione* was then hove about, this manoeuvre temporarily bringing the chase fair in line with our jib-boom end; whilst the *Mermaid* lay broad away on our lee quarter fully a mile distant, with the *Quebec* half a mile astern of her. With the rising of the sun the breeze freshened still more; and it soon became evident, from the first lieutenant's manner, that he was beginning to feel anxious about his spars. Captain Pigot, however, who was on deck, would not allow the canvas to be reduced by so much as a single thread; so Mr Reid was at length compelled (at considerable risk to the men who executed the duty) to get up preventer back-stays fore and aft; and to this precaution was doubtless due the ultimate success which crowned our efforts. Another hour brought us fairly astern of the chase; and, the moment that her three masts were in line, we again tacked and stood after her, being now directly in her wake and about nine miles astern. Meanwhile the rest of the squadron had also tacked, and were now to be seen tailing out in a long straggling line on our lee quarter—the *Mermaid* leading, the *Quebec* next, and the rest—nowhere, as the racing men say.

Breakfast was now served, and by the time that I again went on deck we had so far gained upon the chase that the foot of her courses could be now and then seen as we rose upon the crest of a sea. She was evidently a very smart as well as a very fine ship; yet we were overhauling her, hand over hand, as our ships pretty generally did those of the French. It was freely admitted on all hands that the French were better shipbuilders than ourselves, yet our ships generally proved the faster in a chase like the present; and I had often wondered how it was. *Now* I saw and could understand the reason. It was because the British ships were better sailed and better *steered* than those of our enemies. Even at our then distance it was painfully apparent that the yards of the chase were trimmed in the most slovenly manner, and in the matter of steering she was sheering and yawing all over the place; whilst for ourselves, our canvas was trimmed with the utmost nicety; and we had a man at the wheel who never for a single instant removed his glance from the weather-leach of our main-topgallant—sail, which was kept the merest trifle a-lift—just sufficiently so, and no more, to show that the frigate was looking up as high as it was possible for her to go, whilst the remainder of her canvas was clean full and dragging her along at race-horse speed. The result was that, though our ship was possibly the slower of the two, her wake was as straight as though it had been *ruled* upon the heaving water; whilst that of the chase was so crooked that she must have travelled over nearly half as much ground again as ourselves, thus losing through faulty steering more than she gained through superiority in speed.

At 10 a.m., by which time we had neared the chase to within a distance of six miles, the stranger hove about for the first time and stood to the southward and eastward, close-hauled on the larboard tack. At 10:30 we followed suit, and half an hour later the high land behind Jean Rabel, Saint Domingo, was sighted from aloft Captain Pigot now came to the conclusion that the stranger was aiming to take refuge in Port au Paix; and, should she succeed in effecting her design, it might prove difficult if not impossible to capture her. His anxiety to speedily get alongside her and force her to action accordingly grew almost momentarily more intense, as also did his acerbity of temper, until at length he became so nearly unbearable that, had he just then happened to have been washed overboard, I believe not a single man in the ship—apart from the officers, that is, of course—would have raised a hand or joined in any effort to save him.

At noon, however, matters grew a little more tolerable; for it had by that time become apparent that, unless favoured by some unforeseen accident, the chase could not possibly escape us. At Jean Rabel the land begins to trend to the southward and westward, extending in that direction a distance of some four or five miles, when it bends somewhat more to the westward, thus forming a shallow bay. It was towards the bottom of this bay that the chase was now heading; and it speedily became apparent that, if she would avoid going ashore, there would soon be only two alternatives open to her; one of which was to go round upon the starboard tack and make a stretch off the land sufficient to allow of her fetching Port au Paix on her next board— in which event she would have to pass us within gun-shot; and the other was to bear up and run to the southward and westward, when she would have to run the gauntlet of the whole remaining portion of the squadron; in which case her fate could only be certain capture. We hoped and believed she would choose the first of these two alternatives.

We were both nearing the land very rapidly—the chase now only some three miles ahead of us—and at length Captain Pigot, feeling certain that the stranger must now very soon heave in stays, ordered our own people to their stations, resolved to tack simultaneously with the chase, and thus, by remaining some three miles further in the offing, retain the advantage of a stronger and truer breeze. Minute after minute lagged slowly by, however, and still the French ship kept steadily on, with her bows pointing straight toward the land. Suddenly, without warning or premonition, her three masts, with all their spread of canvas, were seen to sway violently over to leeward; and, before any of us fully realised what was happening, they lay prone in the water alongside, snapped short off by the deck. The next moment the ship swung round, broadside on to the land, and the sea began to break over her. Her captain had actually run her on shore to escape us.

Sail was at once shortened on board the *Hermione*, and the ship hove to, with her head off-shore. Captain Pigot then sent for his telescope, and, with its aid, made a thorough inspection of the stranded frigate; most of the officers following his example. Yes, there could be no possible mistake about it, she was hard and fast on shore, bumping heavily to all appearance, and with the sea breaking over her from stem to stern. Not satisfied, however, with this distant inspection, the skipper caused his gig to be lowered, and in her proceeded as near to the scene of the wreck as prudence would allow. He was absent two full hours, and on his return we learnt that the French ship was hopelessly lost; that the crew were with the utmost difficulty effecting a landing on the beach; and that the craft herself was already breaking up. He was highly exasperated, as indeed were we all, at this noble prize thus slipping through our fingers, at a moment, too, when escape seemed absolutely impossible; and in the heat of temper he denounced the French captain as a dastardly poltroon, a disgrace to his uniform; and swore that, could he but have got hold of him, he would have seized him to a grating and given him five dozen at the gangway. And I firmly believe he fully meant what he said. As for me, though I—youngster that I was—felt, perhaps, as keenly disappointed as the skipper himself, I yet thought that the French captain had more thoroughly performed his duty to his country than he would have done had he remained afloat and fought us. For, with the vastly superior force of an entire squadron on our side, escape would then have been for him impossible; his ship must inevitably have been captured; with the sequence that, in the hands of a British crew, she would have become a formidable foe to the country which had recently owned her. Whereas, now, though that country had lost her, her guns could at least never be turned against it.

Captain Pigot's inspection over, and the gig hoisted in, the *Hermione's* main-topsail was filled and we made sail for the offing, where the remainder of the squadron was now hove to awaiting the progress of events.

On the following day the hands were mustered to witness punishment, and, to the unspeakable surprise and indignation of everybody, officers as well as men, the whole of the poor fellows who had steered the ship during the unlucky chase of the preceding day were ordered to receive three dozen apiece, "for culpable negligence in the performance of their duty," Captain Pigot choosing to assert that, had the ship been properly steered, we should have overtaken and brought the French frigate to action. Now the manner in which the *Hermione's* helm had been manipulated on the occasion in question had excited the admiration of, and extorted frequent favourable comments from the officers; there was a stiff breeze blowing at the time; and the frigate, when heavily pressed upon a taut bowline, had a most unhandy knack of griping; notwithstanding which, as I have before stated, her wake had been as straight as though ruled upon the water. But Captain Pigot was bitterly chagrined at his want of success—quite unreasonably, for he and everybody else had done all that was possible to secure it—and he could not rest until he had vented his ill-humour upon some of the unfortunates placed in his power. Hence the cruel and unjust order; the issuing of which very nearly ended in results most disastrous, so far as I was personally concerned.

For, when the first man of the unfortunate batch had stripped and was seized up, seeing that the skipper actually intended to carry out his monstrous resolve—a fact which, until that moment, I had doubted—forgetting for the time everything but the cruelty and injustice of the action, I sprang forward and placing myself immediately in front of our frowning chief, exclaimed:

"No, no; do not do it, sir! I assure you that you are mistaken. The men do not deserve it, sir; they did their utmost, I am sure; indeed I heard Mr Reid remark to Mr Douglas that he had *never* seen the ship so beautifully steered before. Didn't you, sir?" I continued, appealing to the first lieutenant.

"Young gentleman, you have placed me in a very awkward position," replied poor old David, turning to me, very red in the face; "but I'll not deny it; I *did* say so, and I meant it, too."

Captain Pigot turned absolutely livid with fury; he was white even to the lips; his eyes literally blazed like those of a savage animal about to spring upon its prey; his hands were tightly clenched; and, for a moment, I felt that he would strike me. He did not, however; possibly even at that moment some instinct may have warned him that he was on the verge of committing a very grave imprudence; and, instead of striking the blow I had expected, he turned short on his heel and walked into his cabin. Then, and not until then—when I glanced about me and noted the universal consternation with which I was regarded—did I fully realise the enormity of the offence of which I had been guilty.

Captain Pigot was absent from the deck for perhaps ten minutes. When he returned the low hum of conversation which had set in on his disappearance abruptly ceased, and every eye was turned upon him in anticipation of the next act in this little drama.

He had evidently made a successful effort to subdue his excitement, for he was now, to all outward appearance, perfectly calm; this somewhat abrupt calmness seeming to me, I must confess, even more portentous than his recent exhibition of passion had been. Halting before me, he pointed sternly to the hatchway, and said:

"Go below, sir; and regard yourself as under arrest. I will consider your case by and by. So grave a dereliction of duty as that of which you have been guilty is not to be dealt with hurriedly."

I bowed, and turned to go below; and, as I did so, I heard him say to the first lieutenant:

"Since you, Mr Reid, appear to have taken a different view of these men's conduct from that which I had entertained, and have, moreover, seen fit to publicly express that view, I have no alternative but to give the fellows the benefit of our difference of opinion, and withhold that punishment which I still think they richly deserve. But I will take this opportunity of explaining to you, and to every other officer and man in this ship, that I reserve to myself the exclusive right of expressing an opinion as to the behaviour, individually and collectively, of those under my command; and, whatever any of you may choose to *think* upon such a matter, I shall expect that you will henceforward keep your opinion strictly to yourselves. Now, let the hands be piped down."

I had paused just below and under cover of the coamings long enough to hear this speech to its conclusion; now, as the boatswain's pipe sent forth its shrill sounds, I scurried off and made the best of my way to the midshipmen's berth. I felt that I had allowed my sympathy to get the better of my discretion, and in so doing had plunged myself into a very awkward predicament, out of which I did not at all clearly see how I was to extricate myself; but, whatever might be the result to myself of my imprudence, it had at least been the means of saving several men from an undeserved flogging, and this reflection served somewhat to comfort me. I was speedily joined by those of the midshipmen whose watch below it then happened to be; and with them came a master's mate named Farmer—a man of some thirty-five years of age, whose obscure parentage and want of influential friends had kept him back from promotion, and who in consequence of countless disappointments had grown chronically morose and discontented. My fellow-mids were very enthusiastic in their expressions of admiration for what they were pleased to term "the pluck with which I had tackled the skipper;" and equally profuse in the expression of their hopes and belief of a successful issue of the adventure. Farmer, however, speedily put a stopper upon their tongues by growling impatiently:

"Belay there with that jabbering, you youngsters; you don't know what you are talking about. The fact is that Lascelles there has made a fool of himself and an enemy of the skipper; and to do the latter, let me tell you, is no joke, as he will probably discover to his cost. He has, however, done a kindly thing; and perhaps, in the long run, he may have no reason to regret it."

I was suspended from duty for the remainder of that day, until late in the evening, when a marine made his appearance at the door of the berth, with an intimation that he had orders to conduct me to the captain's cabin; and in the custody of this man—who was armed with a drawn bayonet—I was accordingly marched into the presence of the skipper. On entering the cabin, I found Captain Pigot sitting over his wine, with the first lieutenant seated on the opposite side of the table. When I entered the apartment Mr Reid was leaning across the table, talking to his superior in a low earnest tone of voice, but upon my entrance the conversation abruptly ceased. The marine saluted, announced me as "The prisoner, sir!" and then, facing automatically to the right, took up a position just outside the cabin door. I approached until within a respectful distance of the table, and then halted; the first lieutenant rising as I did so and closing the door.

"Well, young gentleman," said the skipper when old David had resumed his seat, "have you anything to say by way of excuse for or explanation of your extraordinary and—and—insubordinate conduct this morning?"

"Nothing, sir," I replied, "except that I felt you were about—under the influence of a grave misapprehension—to inflict punishment upon men who had not deserved it; and that if you did so you would certainly regret the act most deeply. It was from no motive of disrespect that I acted as I did, I assure you, sir; it was done on the impulse of the moment, and because I felt that if the evil was to be prevented it must be done instantly. I acted as I should have wished another to act had I been in your place, sir."

This I felt was but a lame explanation, and not likely to help me to any great extent out of my difficulty; but there was really nothing else I could say without directly charging the skipper with wanton tyranny, which it was certainly not the place of a reefer on his first cruise to do; if Mr Reid and the rest of the officers were content with the position of affairs it was not for me to gainsay them.

"Very well, young gentleman," answered the skipper, after a somewhat lengthy pause, "I am willing to accept your explanation, and to believe that you acted upon a good motive the more readily that Mr Reid here has been most eloquent pleading your cause, and giving you the best of characters. But, hark ye, Mr Lascelles, never, for the future, presume to form *any* opinion—good or bad—upon your captain's conduct; nor, under any circumstances, attempt to put him right. You are too young and too inexperienced to be capable of forming a just judgment of the actions of your superiors; moreover, a midshipman's duty is to *obey*, not to judge or advise his superior officers. You may return to your duty, sir; and let the unpleasant incident of to-day be a warning to you throughout the remainder of your career."

Highly delighted, and, I must confess, equally surprised in so easy an escape from what threatened at the outset to be an exceedingly awkward scrape, I stammered out a few confused words of thanks and assurances of good behaviour for the future, bowed, and executed a somewhat hasty retreat.

# Chapter Five
# A "Cutting-Out" Expedition

On going on deck to stand my watch that night shortly after my dismissal by Captain Pigot, found the squadron heading to the northward on an easy bowline, under reefed topsails, with the island of Tortuga bearing southeast, about ten miles distant. We continued on the starboard tack during the whole of that night, tacking at eight o'clock on the following morning, and heading in toward the land once more, at the same time shaking the reefs out of our topsails. An hour later the lookout aloft reported a sail to leeward; and, on signalling the fact to the admiral, the *Hermione* received permission to chase.

We managed to approach within ten miles of the stranger without exciting his suspicions; but shortly afterwards a doubt appeared to enter his mind as to the honesty of our intentions, and he tacked, no doubt with the object of ascertaining whether our business had anything to do with him or not. He soon found that it *had*; for before he was fairly round our course had been altered so as to intercept him. This sufficed to thoroughly alarm him, and, wearing short round, he went square off before the wind, setting every stitch of canvas his little vessel—a schooner of some seventy tons— could spread to the breeze. The chase now showed herself to be a very smart little craft, staggering along under her cloud of canvas in a really surprising manner; indeed, had the pursuit lasted an hour longer we should probably have lost her, for she was within five miles of the harbour of Jean Rabel when we succeeded in bringing her to.

The obstinate craft having at length consented to back her topsail, Courtenay was sent away in the gig, with the crew fully armed, to give her an overhaul.

He remained on board nearly half an hour, and when he returned he brought the skipper of the schooner, a negro, with him. The little vessel, it now appeared, was a coaster, sailing under French colours, and was bound from Jean Rabel to Porto Caballo. She was consequently a prize, though utterly valueless to us; and Courtenay's instructions had been that, if such proved to be the case, he was to take her crew out of her and set her on fire. She, however, belonged to the negro who commanded her, and he had begged so earnestly that his property might be spared, and had backed up his petition by representations of so important a nature, that Courtenay had deemed it best, before carrying out his instructions, to bring the man on board the *Hermione*, and give him an interview with Captain Pigot. The skipper was in his cabin when the gig returned alongside, so Courtenay went in and made his report, the result being that the negro was speedily admitted to Captain Pigot's presence. The next thing that happened was the summoning of the first lieutenant to the cabin, Courtenay being at the same time dismissed. A conference of some twenty minutes' duration now ensued, at the termination of which Courtenay, with half a dozen men as a prize-crew, was sent away to take charge of the schooner; and on the return of the boat, both vessels filled away and stood off the land on a taut bowline, the negro owner of the schooner being detained on board the frigate.

Early the next morning the remainder of the squadron was sighted, and immediately after breakfast Captain Pigot boarded the commodore, taking the negro with him. He was absent for the greater part of the morning, and that something of moment was on the *tapis* soon became apparent, from the fact that the captains of the *Quebec, Mermaid, Drake,* and *Penelope* were signalled for. Everybody was now on the *qui vive*, a pleasant excitement taking the place of that stolid sullen indifference and apathy on the part of our crew which had gradually resulted from the skipper's ill-advised harshness to them. At length the boats were seen to push off on their way back to their respective ships; and, a few minutes later, Captain Pigot passed up the gangway and came in on deck. Everybody now waited in breathless expectation for the anticipated order which should convey to us an inkling of the nature of the work in hand; but, to our general disappointment, no such order was given. The skipper's face, however, wore a look of exultant satisfaction, and his demeanour was so much less unpleasant than usual that we felt convinced there was something in the wind; and all hands settled down accordingly to await, with what patience we could muster, the development of events.

It was not, however, until two days later, the 20th of April, that our curiosity was satisfied. A signal from the commodore requesting the captains of the *Hermione, Quebec, Mermaid, Drake,* and *Penelope* to repair on board him, was the first incident of the day; and this was followed by a conference so protracted that the gigs' crews only got back to their ships barely in time for dinner. A most careful and scrupulous inspection of the arm-chest consumed nearly the whole of the afternoon watch; and finally, at eight bells, or four o'clock p.m., after a considerable amount of signalling, the ships already named detached themselves from the rest of the squadron, and, under Captain Pigot's orders, made sail to the westward; the negro captain being at the same time restored to his command and allowed to proceed on his way.

Urged forward by a brisk trade-wind, to which we exposed every possible stitch of canvas, the little squadron made short miles of it, arriving, at three o'clock in the morning, off Port à l'Écu; where, at a distance of about a mile off the shore and some two miles from the harbour of Jean Rabel on the one hand, and Port au Paix on the other, the trade-wind encountering the land-breeze, we ran into a calm. A carefully-masked lantern was now exhibited on board the *Hermione*, the utmost caution being observed to prevent its light being seen from the shore, and at the same moment our launch, pinnace, and first and second cutters, the two former each carrying a boat's gun in the bows, were ordered away.

To Mr Reid, who, in conjunction with Lieutenant Burdwood of the *Penelope*, had been closeted with the skipper for at least two hours previously, was intrusted the command of one division of the boats which was about to be sent away, Lieutenant Burdwood being placed at the head of the other division. Mr Reid went, of course, in our launch; Mr Douglas commanded the pinnace; Farmer, a master's mate, was put in charge of the first cutter; and, to my supreme surprise and gratification, I was instructed to take charge of the second.

In less than five minutes, so well planned had been Captain Pigot's arrangements, our boats were joined by the rest of the flotilla; and, the whole having been quietly but rapidly marshalled by Mr Reid into two divisions, our muffled oars dropped simultaneously into the water, and we departed on our several ways.

Mr Burdwood, with his division, consisting of four boats from the *Mermaid*, two from the *Drake*, and two from his own vessel, pulled briskly away to the eastward, his destination being, as I shortly afterwards learned, Port au Paix, whilst the division to which I belonged headed west for Jean Rabel.

The night was fine, but very dark; a broad belt of dappled cloud overspreading almost the entire heavens, and permitting only an isolated star or two to twinkle feebly through it here and there. A couple of miles in the offing the trade-wind was blowing briskly, and inshore of us, at a distance of less than a quarter of a mile, the land-breeze was roaring down off the hills with the strength of half a gale. Where the two met there occurred a narrow belt of calm, broken into momentarily by an eddying puff of wind, now warm, as the trade-wind got slightly the better of the land-breeze, and anon cool, refreshing, and odoriferous with the perfume of a thousand flowers, as the land-breeze regained the ascendency and pushed forward in its turn on the domain of the trade-wind. Mr Reid availed himself of the opportunity afforded by our passage across this narrow belt of calm to rally the rest of the boats round the launch for a moment, in order to explain the object of the expedition, and to give a few brief directions respecting the movements of each boat. From this explanation we now learned that we were about to make an attack upon two privateer brigs, together with a ship and brig which had been captured by them, all of which were lying in Jean Rabel harbour, and were believed to be well protected and very strongly manned. The ship—a very fine vessel, which had recently been armed with eighteen 9-pounder brass guns, and manned by a crew of over one hundred men—our gallant "first" proposed to attack in person, the launch being supported by the first and second cutters. Mr Douglas, our second lieutenant, aided by the *Quebec's* launch, was to tackle the heaviest of the privateer brigs; the *Quebec's* first and second cutters were to attack the other; whilst the *Mermaid's* second cutter and the *Quebec's* gig were to make a dash at the remaining brig, a prize, and, having secured her, hold themselves in readiness to lend a hand wherever their presence might seem to be most required. Our work having thus been explicitly set out for us, Mr Reid gave the word for us to renew our advance, and we once more pushed ahead.

No night could well have been more favourable for such an attack as ours—which was meant to be a surprise, if possible—than the one selected; so dark, indeed, was it that, by a piece of the rarest good fortune, we had actually entered the harbour before we were able to completely identify our whereabouts.

It now became necessary for us to pause for a moment and look about us, in order to ascertain the locality of our game; and the word was accordingly quietly passed from boat to boat for the men to lay on their oars. At first it was simply impossible for us to distinguish anything—except the land, which loomed vague and dark, like a broad shadow, above the water. At length, however, one of the men in the launch announced, in a low cautious whisper, that he could make out the spars of a vessel directly ahead; and immediately afterwards, the clouds overhead breaking slightly away for a moment, we were able to distinguish the craft herself.

Feeling sure that this must be one of the vessels of which we were in quest, Mr Reid at once gave the order for the flotilla to again move cautiously forward; and the boats' oars immediately dipped into the phosphorescent water, causing it to gleam and flash brilliantly. There is no doubt that this vivid phosphorescence of the water—which must have been visible at a long distance in the intense darkness of the night—occasioned the premature discovery of our presence which now took place; for the men had not pulled half a dozen strokes before a startled hail came pealing out across the water; to which we of course paid not the slightest attention. Failing to get a reply, the hail was hurriedly repeated, a musket was fired, and a port-fire was burned on board the craft first sighted, which now proved to be the brig which our pinnace and the *Quebec's* launch were destined to attack. For the burning of this port-fire, though it rendered further concealment on our part impossible, we were very much obliged, as by its unearthly glare we were enabled to discern the whereabouts of the remaining vessels, at which, with a wild cheer, the crews of the boats at once dashed with the most commendable promptitude.

The ship happened to be moored in the innermost berth, or that which was farthest up the harbour; our contingent, therefore—consisting of the *Hermione's* launch, first, and second cutters—was the last to get alongside; and by the time that we reached the craft her crew were quite ready to receive us. She was, fortunately for us, riding head to wind, with her bows pointing up the harbour, and her stern directly towards us; consequently the only guns which she could bring to bear upon us were her two stern-chasers, each of which she fired twice, without effect. We were within twenty yards of her when the guns were fired for the second time; and immediately afterwards a most formidable volley of musketry was poured into us. Strange to say, though the bullets sent a perfect shower of splinters flying about our ears, not a man in either boat was hit; and before the Frenchmen had time to load again we were alongside—the launch on the port quarter, the first cutter under the main chains on the starboard side, and my boat under the bows. Luckily for us, they had not had time to trice up the boarding nettings, so that, with the aid of a volley from our pistols, we had not much difficulty in making our way in over the craft's low bulwarks. But when we gained the deck we found it literally crowded with Frenchmen, who met us with a most stubborn resistance; and had there been light enough for them to see what they were doing, we should probably have been driven back to our boats in less than three minutes. But the port-fire had by this time burnt itself out, or been extinguished, and the darkness, save for the intermittent flash of the pistols, was profound; so that, although there was a great deal of firing, of hacking, and hewing, and shouting, there was very little harm being done, at least to our side, so far as I could see. And if the French had the advantage of us in point of numbers, we had the advantage of them in an equally important matter; for whilst our men were dressed in their ordinary rig of blue-jackets and trousers, rendering them almost invisible in the darkness, the suddenness of our attack had compelled our enemies to turn out on deck in their shirts only, by which we were able to distinguish them pretty clearly.

The fight had been progressing in this unsatisfactory manner for about ten minutes, when suddenly the dash and rattle of oars was heard alongside, immediately followed by a ringing British cheer. In another instant a ghastly blue glare of light illumined the decks; and we saw Douglas, at the head of the pinnace's crew, fling himself in over the bulwarks, with a lighted port-fire held aloft in one hand, whilst he brandished his sword with the other. This timely reinforcement at once brought the fight to a conclusion, the Frenchmen forthwith flinging down their weapons and crying for quarter. The help came not a moment too soon, so far as Farmer was concerned; for the very first act of Mr Douglas, on reaching the deck, was to cleave to the chin a Frenchman whom he saw with both knees on Farmer's chest and with his sword shortened in his hand about to pin the unfortunate master's mate to the deck.

The Frenchmen were at once driven below and the hatches clapped over them; after which our lads were sent aloft to loose the topsails; and, the cable being cut, the ship was got under weigh. Whilst this was doing, I had time to question our gallant "second" as to the cause of his opportune appearance; and I then learned that so complete had been the surprise that the other craft had been taken almost without an effort; and that as soon as this was accomplished and the crews secured Mr Douglas had hastened to our assistance, rightly surmising that, from the longer warning given to the ship's crew and their great strength, we should have our hands pretty full with them. The moon, in her last quarter, and dwindled to the merest crescent, was just rising over the hills to the eastward of us as we swept before the land-breeze out of Jean Rabel harbour; and by her feeble light I was enabled with some difficulty to discern that, by my watch, it was just four o'clock in the morning. Thus satisfactorily terminated this cutting-out expedition; the most surprising circumstance connected with which was, perhaps, the fact that, when the hands were mustered, not one was found to have received a hurt worthy of being termed a wound.

We had scarcely got clear of the land with our prizes—consisting of one ship and three brigs—when we discovered three schooners and two sloops standing out from Port au Paix; and as they, like ourselves, were heading directly for the squadron in the offing, we conjectured—and rightly, as it afterwards proved—that they were the vessels which Lieutenant Burdwood had been sent in to attack.

Late in the evening of the following day we rejoined the remainder of the squadron, and Captain Pigot at once proceeded on board the admiral to report the complete success of the expedition. Nothing was settled that night as to the disposal of the prizes, but on the following forenoon it was arranged that, as both the *Quebec* and ourselves were getting short of provisions and water, we should escort the prizes into Port Royal, and at the same time avail ourselves of the opportunity to revictual.

We reached our destination in due time without adventure, and as it then seemed likely that there would be some delay in the matter of revictualling, Mr Reid improved the occasion to give the spars and rigging a thorough overhaul. This, with such repairs and renewals as were found necessary, kept all hands busy for four full days, at the end of which time the ship was once more all ataunto. Meanwhile, from some unexplained cause or other, the provisions were coming on board very slowly, much, it must be confessed, to the delight of the crew, who, having worked hard at the overhauling and repairs of the rigging—to say nothing of their behaviour at Jean Rabel—now confidently expected at least a day's liberty with its accompanying jollification ashore. But when the request for it was made Captain Pigot point-blank refused in language of the most intemperate and abusive character, stigmatising the whole crew as, without exception, a pack of skulking, cowardly ruffians. He added a pretty broad hint that in his opinion the officers were nearly, if not quite as bad as the men, and finished up by swearing roundly that not a man or boy, forward or aft, should set foot on shore, even though the ship should remain in harbour until she grounded upon her own beef-bones.

This was exasperating enough in all conscience, even for the hands forward, who, though there were certainly some rough characters among them, were by no means *all* bad—indeed a full half of the entire crew were really as smart willing fellows as one need wish to see; but it was even worse for the officers, for we had all been looking eagerly forward to a certain ball which was about to be given by the governor, to which every one of us had received an invitation. The disappointment was so keen and so general that good-natured "old David"—as our genial "first" was dubbed by all hands—took it upon himself to respectfully remonstrate with the skipper upon so arbitrary and high-handed a treatment of the ship's company, with no result, however, except that the first lieutenant received an unmitigated snubbing for his pains.

The revictualling of the ship was completed about five o'clock in the evening upon which the ball was to take place; there was plenty of time, therefore, for us aft to have availed ourselves of the governor's invitation had the skipper seen fit, but he remained obdurate, and we consequently had to content ourselves with watching the departure of the officers from the other ships, and framing such excuses as came uppermost at the moment in reply to the inquiries of such of them as passed near us as to why we were not going. This was made all the more difficult from the fact that, though we were under orders to sail at daybreak next morning, there were no less than three other ships in harbour similarly circumstanced, the officers of which were nevertheless going to be present at the ball. The only consolation we could find was in the reflection that, whereas the others would commence the duties of the next day fagged out with a long night's dancing, we should rise to them refreshed, with a more or less sound night's rest; and with this small crumb of comfort we were fain to go below and turn in.

When the hands were called next morning it was found that Captain Pigot was still absent from the ship, but as he was expected to turn up at any moment the messenger was passed and the cable hove short. A slight stir was occasioned by the crews of the other three ships making preparations to get under way; and as these craft one after the other let fall and sheeted home their topsails, finally tripping their anchors and making their way to sea with the last of the land-breeze, it became evident that something out of the ordinary course must have occurred to delay our skipper. It was close upon eight bells when the gig was sighted pulling down from the direction of Kingston, and when a few minutes later Captain Pigot came up over the side, it was noticed that he was ghastly pale and that his right arm was in a sling. He seemed to be suffering considerably, and it was in a somewhat wavering voice that he said to the first-lieutenant:

"Are you all ready, Mr Reid? Then get your anchor, sir, and let us be off at once. And, Mr Courtenay, be good enough to tell the surgeon I wish to see him in my cabin."

With which he turned short round and walked somewhat unsteadily away, not making his appearance on deck again for nearly a week.

It afterwards transpired that his awkward temper had led to a quarrel, during the progress of the ball, between himself and one of the soldier officers from Up-park Camp, which quarrel had terminated in a meeting on the Palisades, the soldier escaping unscathed, whilst Captain Pigot had emerged from the encounter with his arm broken by a bullet from his adversary's pistol.

Noon that day found us off Morant Point thrashing to windward under single-reefed topsails, with a sea running which every now and then made the frigate careen gunwale-to.

# Chapter Six
## A Remonstrance—and its Sequel

Our instructions, it seemed, were that we should cruise to the southward of Saint Domingo, from Cape Tiburon as far eastward as the Mona Passage, giving an occasional look into Port-au-Prince. We accordingly carried on all that day, taking a second reef in the topsails at sunset, and heaving the ship round on the starboard tack at midnight, which brought us well in under the lee of Cape Tiburon by daybreak next morning. We were then on our cruising ground; sail was shortened, and the frigate, being hove about, was allowed to jog along under easy canvas. Thenceforward, until Captain Pigot reappeared on deck, we had a pleasant and comfortable time of it; for although the discipline of the ship was never for one moment relaxed, there was an utter absence of all that worry and petty tyranny, and, above all, those daily floggings which the skipper seemed to consider essential to the maintenance of a proper degree of subordination and smartness on the part of the crew.

With the reappearance of Captain Pigot on deck, however, this brief period of rest and quietness came to an end. The pain and irritation of his wound, together, perhaps, with the reflection that he had been worsted in an encounter brought about by his own arrogant and overbearing demeanour, seemed to have chafed his temper almost to the point of madness. The floggings were resumed with greater severity than ever; and every time the hands were turned up a boatswain's-mate, armed with a colt, was stationed at each hatchway, with instructions to "freshen the way" of the last man on the ladder. And the same with shortening or making sail, the last man out of the rigging on each mast received a liberal application of the execrable colt to his shoulders. It certainly had the effect of making the men smart in a double sense, but it also made them, perhaps, the most discontented crew in the service.

Thus matters went on, steadily growing from bad to worse, until the month of September set in. We had been dodging off and on, carefully beating over every inch of our cruising ground and looking into every likely and unlikely spot, in the hope of picking up a prize or two, and our non-success had been simply phenomenal. It really seemed as though every craft worth the trouble of capture had deserted our part of the world altogether. This of course resulted, as was perhaps only natural, in a further accession of acerbity fore and aft, the brunt of which of course fell upon the hands forward, who—what with drill of one sort and another, perpetual making and shortening of sail, shifting of spars and canvas, overhauling and setting-up of the rigging, lengthy, tedious, and wholly unnecessary boat expeditions, in addition to the incessant floggings and coltings already referred to—at length found their lives a positive burden to them. This kind of treatment could, of course, produce but one result, and, by the period before-named, the crew had been wrought up to such a pitch of exasperation and revengeful fury, that I am convinced they would have refused to go to the guns had we encountered an enemy. It may easily be imagined how difficult and anxious a task it was for the officers to carry on the duty of the ship under such circumstances as these.

It had by this time become clear to everybody—excepting, apparently, Captain Pigot himself—that the existing state of affairs could not possibly last much longer; and at length the first lieutenant, recognising the gravity of the situation, took it upon himself to invite the second and third lieutenants and the master to a consultation in his own cabin, the result of which consultation was a resolve to adopt the extreme measure of making a collective representation and appeal to the skipper. This being decided, it was determined to carry out the resolve on that same evening, the time to be during the first dog-watch, it being Captain Pigot's habit to retire to his cabin after eight bells had been struck, and to devote an hour or so to reading before dinner.

Accordingly, no sooner had the skipper left the deck than I was despatched by Mr Reid to apprise Mr Douglas, Mr Maxwell, and Mr Southcott of the fact, and to state that the first lieutenant awaited them on the quarter-deck. We midshipmen had of course been left in the dark as to the proposed interview; but the message of which I was the bearer was of so very unusual a character that I at once suspected there must be something out of the common in prospect; and when, a few minutes later, I saw the four principal officers of the ship march with portentously solemn faces into the cabin, I determined that, right or wrong, I would know what was in the wind.

Fortunately for my purpose it was my watch below, and my absence from the deck would consequently not be noticed. It took me but a moment to form my plans, and not much more to execute them. The ship had a full poop, under which the captain's cabin was situated; the weather was warm, and all the ports were open. Slipping off my shoes and thrusting them beneath a gun, where they were not likely to be discovered, I made my way in my stockings up on to the poop, which was entirely deserted, and at once slipped over the side into the mizzen channels. The lid of one of the ports was then immediately beneath me, and I knew beforehand that there was just room for me to squeeze in upon it, where, though my attitude must be somewhat constrained, I should be perfectly concealed from every eye, whilst I should also be able to hear with tolerable distinctness every word which might be spoken in the cabin in an ordinary conversational tone of voice.

Now, I am not going to defend my conduct. I know, and I knew at the time, that I was doing what I had no business to do, but I was quite free from any feeling of absolute wrong-doing; I had an instinctive perception that the interview in which I was about to play the part of eaves-dropper was in some way connected with the critical state of affairs then prevailing on board, and I felt that whilst my cognisance of what was about to pass could be hurtful to nobody, the knowledge might be advantageous to myself, and possibly to others also. If I acted wrongly I must be content to bear the blame; the fact remains that I posted myself safely and undetected in the position I had fixed upon, and overheard almost every word which passed in the brief interview between the skipper and his visitors.

As I swung myself out over the channels and settled myself into my somewhat cramped quarters I heard Captain Pigot's strident voice speaking in a tone of surprised inquiry; but I was too busy just then to catch what he said. By the time he had finished, however, I was all ready to listen; and I presently heard Mr Reid reply:

"We have taken the unusual step, sir, of waiting upon you thus in a body, to direct your attention, in the most respectful manner, to the present condition and temper of the ship's company, the which we conceive to have resulted wholly from your excessive severity toward them. They are, almost to a man, in such an excited and dangerous frame of mind that we have the greatest difficulty in maintaining discipline, and keeping them under proper control. Indeed, to adequately carry on the duty of the ship has become almost an impossibility; and—to speak the truth frankly, sir—on comparing notes with my brother officers we have come to the conclusion that the men are no longer to be depended upon in case of an emergency. Matters cannot possibly remain much longer in their present state, a change of some sort is inevitable; and we would most respectfully suggest, sir, to your earnest and immediate consideration the desirability of adopting a more lenient and generous line of policy—"

"Great Heaven! man, do you know what you are saying?" gasped the skipper. And the crash of a falling chair together with the quiver in his voice seemed to indicate that he had started to his feet in a paroxysm of fury which he was ineffectually struggling to suppress. "How dare you," he continued—"how dare anyone or all of you presume to call in question my conduct, or dictate to me the line of policy which I shall pursue with regard to my crew—a lazy, skulking, cowardly set of vagabonds, three-fourths of whom are foreigners? Why, man, if it had not been for the severe discipline of which you complain they would have had the ship away from us ere now. I know the class of men I have to deal with, aboard here, and I also know how to deal with them; and you may take my word for it that I will never rest satisfied until I have made them the smartest crew in the service. As to the difficulty you profess to experience in carrying on the duty of the ship, I must confess I have not observed it, the rascals have always appeared active and willing enough whenever I have been on deck—thanks to that wholesome fear of the cat with which I have imbued them; and if the difficulty *really* exists, I cannot but think, gentlemen, the fault must be with yourselves, and it can easily be cured by a somewhat firmer maintenance, rather than a relaxation, of that rigid discipline which you deprecate. And I will take this opportunity of mentioning, whilst we are upon the subject, my very strong disapproval of the manifest tendency which I have observed in the officers of this ship to overlook and condone what I suppose *they* would term *trifling* infractions of duty. In so doing, gentlemen, you have made a most grievous mistake, which, however, I will do my best to remedy in the immediate future. There is nothing like plenty of flogging if you wish to keep such curs in proper order."

During the progress of this speech the skipper had gradually recovered the control of his temper; the tremulous tones of anger in his voice were succeeded by those of bitter sarcasm; and the manifest sneer with which he concluded made my blood boil.

There was a momentary pause, then I heard the first lieutenant say:

"With all submission, sir, permit me to say that I believe—nay, that I am *convinced*—you wholly misunderstand the character and disposition of the crew. Some of them—far too many of them, indeed—*are* foreigners, who have neither the strength nor the spirit to perform their duties as efficiently as Englishmen would, but I believe that, for the most part, they honestly do their best; and for honest service, faithfully performed, perpetual flogging seems to me but a poor reward. The jail-birds among our own countrymen are the most difficult subjects to deal with, and flogging only hardens them;

if I had to deal with them I should be far more disposed to look for a cure from the contempt and raillery of their shipmates. Besides, the rogues are so cunning that they frequently succeed in shifting the blame on to other shoulders; and when one man gets punished for another's offences we know that the tendency is to make him sullen and discontented. I could name at least a dozen men who, from being bright smart, active, reliable men at the commencement of the cruise, have degenerated into as many idle skulks, solely because their good qualities have received no recognition, and they have been punished over and over again for the faults of others. And as to our leniency toward the men—"

"There, that will do, Mr Reid; the less said on that head the better," interrupted the skipper impatiently. "This discussion has gone far enough," he continued, "and I must now request you all to withdraw. You have— relieved your consciences, let us say, by entering this formal protest and expressing your disapproval of my method of dealing with the hands forward; now let the matter drop. And hark ye, one and all, if there is any repetition of this impertinent interference with me, by the Heaven above us I will clap the presumptuous individual who attempts it in irons, and bring him to court-martial at the first convenient port we reach. Now go, and be hanged to you!"

"Very well, sir," said old David, "we *will* go; but, before we leave your presence, permit me to observe that—"

I heard no more, for, perceiving that the interview was about to somewhat abruptly terminate, I judged it best to effect an escape from my place of concealment whilst escape was still possible, and I forthwith proceeded hurriedly to do so. I managed to make my way back to the quarter-deck without attracting attention, and had barely secured my shoes and replaced them on my feet when the first lieutenant and his companions emerged from the poop cabin and began to pace the quarter-deck in apparently careless conversation, though I could tell, by the gloomy expression of their countenances, that they were discussing an anything but agreeable topic.

At length the westering sun approached the horizon; and Mr Douglas and Mr Southcott retired to their cabins in anticipation of Captain Pigot's appearance on deck to watch the nightly operation of reefing topsails, leaving Mr Reid and Mr Maxwell to slowly pace the quarter-deck side by side. It being now my watch on deck, I stationed myself in the waist on the larboard side of the deck and endeavoured to forget the gloomy forebodings which had arisen out of the conversation I had recently overheard by abandoning myself to the soothing influences of the glorious eventide.

It was indeed a glorious evening, such as is seldom or never to be met with outside the tropics. The wind had gradually fallen away during the afternoon until it had dropped stark calm; and there the ship lay, with her head to the northward, gently rolling on the long glassy swell which came creeping stealthily up out from the northward and eastward. The small islands of Mona and Monita—the latter a mere rock—lay broad on our larboard quarter about eight miles distant, two delicate purplish pink blots on the south-western horizon, whilst Desecho reared its head above the north-eastern horizon on our starboard bow, a soft grey marking in the still softer grey haze of the sky in that quarter. A great pile of delicately-tinted purple and ruby clouds with golden edges lay heaped up in detached fantastic masses along the glowing western horizon, shaped into the semblance of an aerial archipelago, with far-stretching promontories and peninsulas, and boldly jutting capes and headlands with deep gulfs and winding straits of rosy sky between. Some of these celestial islands were shaped along their edges into a series of minute gold-tipped projections and irregularities, which needed only the slightest effort of the fancy to become converted into the spires and pinnacles of a populous city or busy seaport; whilst certain minute detached flakelets of crimson and golden cloud dotted here and there about the aerial channels might easily be imagined to be fairy argosies navigating the celestial sea. Gazing, as I did, enraptured, upon that scene of magical beauty, it was not difficult to guess at the origin of that most poetical—as it is perhaps the oldest—nautical superstition, which gives credence to the idea that there exists, far away beyond the sunset, an enchanted region which poor storm-beaten sailors are sometimes permitted to reach, and wherein, during an existence which is indefinitely prolonged, they enjoy a complete immunity from all those perils and hardships with which the seaman's life is ordinarily environed; wherein life is one long day of ineffable peace and rest and tranquillity; and from whence every disagreeable influence is permanently banished.

I was abruptly aroused from my fanciful musings by the sound of the ship's bell, four strokes upon which proclaimed the end of the first dog-watch. The momentary bustle of calling the watch immediately followed, in the midst of which came the customary orders to reef topsails. Simultaneously with the appearance of the larboard watch, Captain Pigot issued from his cabin and, ascending the poop ladder, made his way aft to the taffrail, from which position he was able to command a view of the proceedings on each topsail-yard. The royals and topgallant-sails were very smartly clewed up and furled; and, as the topsail halyards were let run, I saw the skipper pull out his watch and, noting the time by it, hold it face upwards in his hand.

"Soho!" thought I, "that does not look very much as though the first lieutenant's remonstrance had produced any beneficial effect; there's trouble in store for some of those unfortunates on the yards if they are not exceptionally lively."

The hands themselves, who had not failed to mark the skipper's actions, seemed to think so too, and they set about their work with the activity of wild-cats. But "the more hurry the less speed" is an old adage; and so it proved in the present case, the men on the mizzen topsail-yard managing so to bungle matters that when, on the expiration of two and a half minutes — the outside limit of time allowed by the skipper for reefing a topsail — Captain Pigot closed his watch with a snap and replaced it smartly in his pocket, several of the reef-points still remained to be tied.

"Now," thought I, "look out for squalls." And as the thought passed through my mind the squall came, in the shape of a hail from the skipper himself.

"Mizzen topsail-yard, there!" he shouted, "what are you about, you lazy lubbers? Do you intend to spend the remainder of the watch in reefing that topsail? Wake up, and put some life into your motions, for (and here came an oath) I'll flog the last man off the yard."

The work was completed ere he had finished speaking, and the men began hurriedly and in some little confusion to lay in off the yard. There was a decided scramble for the topmast rigging, each man naturally striving to be off the yard before his neighbour, and thus exposing himself and those immediately about him to a very considerable amount of peril.

Mr Reid, who was also on the poop near the skipper, saw this, and hailed the men with:

"Steady, there, on the mizzen topsail-yard; steady, men, and take things quietly, or some of you will be meeting with a nasty accident."

The men's fear of an accident was, however, less than their dread of a flogging, and the hustling went on, much, apparently to the amusement of Captain Pigot, who smiled cynically as he silently watched the struggle. The two captains of the to were in the most disadvantageous position of all, as they, bent supposed to be the two smartest hands on the yard, had laid out, one to each yard-arm to pass and haul out the earrings and they would consequently, in the ordinary course of things be the last men off the yard. This, however, meant a flogging for at least one of them, which they were resolved to escape if possible. Instead, therefore, of laying in along the foot-rope like the rest of the men, they scrambled up on the yard, by the aid of the lifts, and standing erect on the spar, started to run in along it toward the mast. They managed very well until they reached the little struggling crowd about the topmast rigging, when, to avoid them, the two men made a spring simultaneously for the back-stays. How it happened can never be known, but, somehow or other, both overleaped themselves missed the back-stays, and came crashing down on the poop where they lay motionless upon the white planks which in another moment were crimsoned with their blood.

Captain Pigot turned ghastly pale as this sudden and terrible consequence of his tyrannical behaviour presented itself to him; but he never moved a single step to help either of the injured men. The first lieutenant, however, sprang forward and raised the head of one poor fellow, whilst I, springing up the poop ladder, went to the assistance of the other. The man to whom I went lay on his face, and, as I turned him over and raised his head, I turned sick and faint at the ghastly sight which met my horrified gaze. The features were battered out of all recognition, the lower jaw was broken, and from what appeared to be the crushed face the blood was spurting in a torrent which almost instantly drenched through my small-clothes and wetted me to the skin. Unable to endure the terrible spectacle, I turned my eyes in Mr Reid's direction, only to see that the unfortunate man whom he supported was in quite as bad a plight. It was evident not only that the poor fellow was dead, but also that death must have been instantaneous, the neck being broken, and the crown of the skull apparently crushed in such a way that the brain could be seen protruding, and the deck also was bespattered.

"Pass the word for the surgeon, there, somebody, and tell him to look smart!" gasped poor old David in a voice so hoarse and changed with horror and grief that I should never have recognised it as his had I not seen his lips move.

In a minute or two the surgeon made his appearance on the scene, and a very brief examination sufficed to enable him to pronounce both the men dead.

The first lieutenant undertook to announce the sad intelligence to the skipper, who still remained standing in the same position, apparently as unconcerned as if nothing had happened. I must confess that I, for one, fully expected to see some very decided manifestation of emotion on the captain's part when he learned the tragical nature of the disaster; but, instead of that, on being told the news, he—to the horror and indignation of everybody who heard him—simply said:

"Um! dead, are they? Then throw the lubbers overboard!" And this was actually done. Without the slightest pretence to ceremony or reverence of any kind, without so much as a single prayer to consecrate their dismissal to their final resting-place in the bosom of the deep, without even pausing to sew up the poor fellows in their hammocks, with a shot at their feet to ensure their safe arrival in the quiet and peaceful region of the ocean's bed, the bodies were straightway raised from the deck and, with a "One, two, three, *heave!*" were flung over the side, to be instantly fought over and torn to pieces by some half a dozen sharks which had put in an unsuspected appearance on the scene. Many a curse, "not loud but deep," was called down upon the skipper's head that night by the shipmates of the murdered men—for murdered they undoubtedly were—and many a vow of complete and speedy vengeance was solemnly registered. Insulted, scoffed at, derided, their last spark of self-respect—if indeed any such thing still remained to them—outraged and trodden under foot, the crew were that night changed from men to devils; and if, at the conclusion of those unceremonious obsequies, a leader had but stepped forward and placed himself at their head, they would have risen upon us and, all unarmed as they were, torn us to pieces.

No such thought or fear, however, appeared to present itself to Captain Pigot, for, instead of evincing or expressing any sorrow for what had occurred, he imperiously ordered the hands to be mustered in the waist, with the evident intention of "reading them a lecture," as he was wont to term his too frequent hectoring addresses.

The men, sullen, and with suppressed fury blazing in their eyes and revealing itself in their every gesture, swarmed aft and stood in reckless expectation of some further outrage. Nor were they disappointed.

"I have sent for you," the skipper began, in his most sneering and contemptuous accents, "not to express any hypocritical sorrow for the occurrence which has just taken place, but to point out to you the obvious lesson which is to be learned from it—a lesson which I fear your dense ignorance, your utter destitution of discernment and common-sense, would prevent your ever discovering for yourselves. Within the last half-hour two men have come to their deaths. How? Why, by a sneaking, cowardly attempt to evade the punishment justly due to the lazy, skulking, lubberly way in which they performed their duty. It would have been better for them had they listened to the first lieutenant's admonition and come quietly down from aloft, to receive at a proper time the punishment which they richly deserved. But they must needs attempt to shirk it, with the consequences which you have all witnessed; and, so far as I am concerned, I can only say that I think they have met with no more than their just deserts.

"But it is not of them I want to speak to you; it is of yourselves. The same shirking, idle, rebellious spirit which distinguished them is conspicuous in every one of you. It is little more than a couple of hours ago that your officers waited upon me in a body to make formal complaint of your idleness and insubordinate conduct. There was no necessity for them to do any such thing, for I am not altogether lacking in powers of observation, and I have not failed to notice that for some time past there has been a general disposition on the part of all hands to thwart and oppose me in every possible way; but I just mention the fact of this complaint to show you that I am not alone in my opinion as to your conduct. Now, my lads, you are a great many, and I am only one man; but if you suppose that on that account you will be able to get your own way, or successfully oppose me, you will discover that you never made a greater mistake in your lives. You may shirk your work, or perform it in a slovenly, unseamanlike manner as long as you please, but I warn you, one and all, that I have made up my mind to convert you from the lazy, skulking, mutinous set of tinkers and tailors you now are, into the smartest and best-disciplined crew in the service; and by Heaven I will do it too, even though it should be necessary to administer a daily flogging to every man in the ship. There are some few of you who are a shade worse—a shade more idle, and lubberly, and insubordinate—than the rest; you, Jones, are one; you, Hoskings, are another, and you, Thomson, Kirkpatrick, Davis, Morrison, I have my eye upon all of you; you are booked, every man of you, for an early taste of the cat; and I assure you that when it comes it will be a sharp one. You shall learn that, in laying yourselves out to oppose your captain, you have undertaken a task altogether beyond your strength. You shall have neither rest nor peace day or night, henceforward, until I have completely quelled your present rebellious spirit and brought you to a proper condition of subordination and smartness. So now, my lads, you know what you have to expect, and, whatever happens, you will never be able to say that I did not give you due warning. Pipe down!"

The men turned away and dispersed in perfect silence. Usually after the administration of a lecture, however severe, some irrepressible joker might be detected with his head cocked on one side and his face with a waggish grin upon it, turned toward his next neighbour, evidently giving utterance to some jocular comment upon the lately-delivered address, as he gave his breeches the true nautical hitch forward and abaft; but on this occasion there was nothing of the kind, the indignation and disgust aroused by the skipper's arrogant and threatening speech appeared to be altogether too overpowering to allow of the escape of a humorous idea to the surface.

The silence of the men was so complete as to be, to my mind, ominous, whilst their bearing was marked by that peculiar air of defiant recklessness which is to be observed in individuals who feel that Fortune has at length done her very worst for them. How much longer, I wondered, would they thus tamely suffer themselves to be hectored and browbeaten? how much longer go quietly to the gangway and submit to be severely flogged for the most trifling offences? Then, too, I felt indignant at the unscrupulous way in which the skipper had misrepresented the nature of the officers' recent interview with him, and had conveyed the impression that they were rather favouring than deprecating the severity of his discipline. Such conduct struck me as being not only barbarously tyrannical, but also in the highest degree impolitic; for what could any man of sense expect but that, by persistence in it, he would make good men bad, and bad men worse. And if the men were to turn restive in the presence of an enemy—which was, to my mind, not unlikely, though I never anticipated anything worse—what would be the result? The whole aspect of affairs looked unsatisfactory in the extreme, and when I turned into my hammock that night it was to indulge in sundry very gloomy forebodings before I finally dropped off to sleep; though Heaven knows how far I was from guessing at the scenes of horror of which the frigate was to be the theatre before another twenty-four hours had passed over my head.

# Chapter Seven
# The Mutiny

During the night a little air of wind sprang up from the eastward which carried us out clear of the Mona Passage, and when day dawned we found ourselves with a clear horizon all round the ship. At noon we wore round to retrace our steps, and by sunset we were within a dozen miles of the spot we had occupied at the same hour on the previous evening.

The day, for a wonder, had passed almost pleasantly; there had been no flogging; Captain Pigot had scarcely showed himself on deck, except for a few minutes after breakfast and again at noon; and the officers of the watches, glad to be freed from his obnoxious presence, had been careful not to unnecessarily hurry and badger the men whilst carrying on the duty of the ship. The only circumstance which, to my mind, seemed disquieting, was the unusual demeanour of the men, who performed their work, steadily enough indeed, but in a moody, unnatural silence, wearing, meantime, a gloomy, preoccupied air, whilst they at the same time—at least so it appeared to me—seemed to be, one and all, in a restless, anxious, watchful frame of mind, as though they were in momentary expectation of something happening. I could not at all understand this state of things, which was something quite new, for, notwithstanding the skipper's intolerable tyranny, there were a few of the men—and those among the best and smartest hands we had in the ship—who had hitherto contrived to maintain a fairly cheerful demeanour, and who seldom let slip such an opportunity as that afforded by the captain's absence from the deck to indulge in the exchange of a quiet bit of nautical humour or a harmless practical joke with their next neighbour. To-day, however, this sort of thing was conspicuously absent; and I was at first disposed to attribute the unwonted gloom to the men's horror and regret at the lamentable accident of the previous evening. But that, I felt again, would scarcely account for it; for, however sincere may be Jack's attachment to his shipmates whilst they are alive and with him, they are no sooner dead and buried than, from his quickly acquired habit of promptly casting behind him all disquieting memories, he forgets all about them and their fate.

At length, as the day wore on and drew to a peaceful close, my misgivings, such as they were—and they were, after all, so slight as scarcely to deserve mention—passed away; and at eight bells I retired to my hammock with a dawning hope that perhaps, after all, the collective remonstrance of the officers was about to bear good fruit.

My mind being thus at rest, I at once sank into a profound sleep, from which I was abruptly startled by a loud noise of some kind, though what it was I could not for the moment make out. Almost immediately afterwards, however, I heard it again—a loud furious combined shout of many voices from the fore part of the ship. Feeling instinctively that something was wrong, I leaped from my hammock—as also did Courtenay, my only companion in the berth—and began hurriedly to search for my clothes by the dim light of the smoky lamp which hung swaying from the deck-beam overhead. Before, however, I had time to do more than don my socks, a grizzled weatherbeaten main-topman named Ned Sykes made his appearance in the doorway of the berth, with a drawn cutlass in his hand and a pair of pistols in his belt. He looked intently at us both for a moment, and then said, in a gruff but kindly tone of voice:

"Muster Lascelles, and Muster Courtenay, ain't it? Ha! that's all right; I reckoned I should find you two young gen'lemen here, safe enough. Now, you two, just slip into your hammicks again as fast as you knows how, and stay there until I gives you leave to get out of 'em."

"Why, what is the matter, Ned? What is all the row about?" asked Courtenay, with wide-staring, horrified eyes. For, by this time, the shouting and yelling were tremendous, and accompanied by a loud thumping, rumbling sound, produced, as we afterwards ascertained, by the shot which the men were flinging about the decks.

"The matter is just this here, young 'un," replied Ned, entering the berth and seating himself on a chest, "The hands for'ard has made up their minds not to have no more such haccidents as them two that occurred last night; nor they ain't a-goin' to have no more floggin' nor bully-raggin', so they've just rose up and are takin' possession of the ship—Aha! I'm terrible afeard that means bloodshed," as a piercing shriek echoed through the ship. "Now," he continued, seeing that we evinced a strong disinclination to return to our hammocks, "you just tumble into them hammicks and lie down, *quick*; you couldn't do a morsel of good, e'er a one of yer, if you was out there on deck—you'd only get hurted or, mayhap, killed outright,—and I've been specially told off to come here and see as neither of yer gets into trouble; you've both been good kindly lads, you especial, Muster Lascelles—you've never had your eyes open to notice any little shortcomin's or skylarkin's on the part of the men, nor your tongues double-hung for to go and report 'em, so the lads is honestly anxious as you sha'n't come to no harm in this here rumpus."

"Then the men have actually mutinied," said I—and there I stopped short, for at that moment came the sound of a rush aft of many feet, with shouts and curses, mingled with which I heard the loud harsh tones of Captain Pigot's voice raised in anger. The *mêlée*, however, if such there was, quickly swept aft, and there was a lull for perhaps two or three minutes, followed by the sounds of a brief struggle on the quarter-deck, a few shrieks and groans, telling all too plainly of the bloody work going forward, and then silence, broken only now and then by the sound of Farmer's voice, apparently issuing orders, though what he was actually saying we could not distinguish.

During all this time Courtenay and I lay huddled up in our hammocks, too terrified and horror-stricken to say a word. At length, after the lapse of about an hour of quietness on deck, Sykes—after cautioning us most earnestly not, on any account, to move from where we were until his return—set out with the expressed intention of ascertaining how the land lay. He was absent about a quarter of an hour; and on his return he informed us in horrified accents that, out of all the officers of the ship, there remained alive only Mr Southcott the master, the gunner, the carpenter, Courtenay, myself—and Farmer, the master's mate, who, it appeared, had taken a leading part in the mutiny, and had been elected to the command of the ship. It was evident, from the scared and horrified appearance and manner of our informant, that he had never anticipated any of this awful violence and bloodshed, though he frankly admitted that he had been a consenting party to the mutiny—the general understanding being that the officers were all to be secured in the first instance, and afterwards handed over as prisoners to the enemy—and he hurriedly explained to us that, for his own safety's sake, it would now be necessary for him to leave us and join the rest of the mutineers without delay, but that he would return to us as soon as he possibly could; and that, in the meantime, we were on no account to leave the berth, or our lives would certainly be sacrificed.

After hearing such statements as these, no further warning was needed to keep us two unhappy mids close prisoners for the rest of the night. Further sleep was of course quite out of the question; so we hastily dressed, and, closing the door of the berth, seated ourselves on a sea-chest, where we passed the remainder of the night discussing the awful tragedy which had so suddenly been enacted, comparing notes as to our mutual forebodings of some such disaster, and, lastly, wondering what would be the ultimate fate of ourselves and the few other surviving officers.

At length, after what appeared to be a very eternity of suspense and anxiety, steps were heard approaching the berth; and, upon our throwing open the door, Sykes, somewhat the worse for liquor, made his appearance, hailing us, in tones of obviously forced joviality, with:

"Well, what cheer, my fighting cocks—my bully bantams? How goes it? Hope your honours has passed a comfortable night," with a ghastly grin at his own facetiousness. Then, with considerably more seriousness of manner, he continued:

"Well, young uns, Farmer—or *Mister* Farmer, I should say—has been axing arter you, and his instructions am that you may now go 'pon deck. But—hark 'e, my bullies, keep your weather eyes a-liftin' and a stopper upon your tongues. Whatsomever you may happen to see don't you be led away into indulgin' in any onpleasant remarks upon it; nor don't you go for to try and talk over any of the lads into 'returning to their duty,' or any rot of that sort; for so sure as either of you attempts anything like that, so surely will you get your brains blowed out. The ship's took—what's done is done—and neither you nor nobody else can make or mend the job; the men is in a mighty ticklish humour, I can tell 'e, and if you wants to save your precious carcasses you'll have to walk mighty carcumspect. And that's the advice and opinion of a friend, all free, gratis, and for nothink. Now, come along, my hearties; show a leg!"

We followed our well-meaning guide up the ladder to the quarter-deck, where we found Farmer apparently awaiting our appearance. He was standing or rather leaning in a wearied attitude against a gun on the starboard side of the deck; his cheeks were flushed and his eyes gleamed feverishly; he looked a good twenty years older than he had appeared to be on the previous day; and, like a good many of the other mutineers, he appeared to have been indulging somewhat freely in liquor. He roused himself at our approach, and, seating himself in a negligent, careless attitude on the breech of the gun, said:

"Good morning, young gentlemen. I am glad to see you both safe and sound. Sykes has of course informed you of what has taken place—he had my instructions to do so, as also to see that you were kept out of harm's way last night. Now, what I have to say to you is this. You two lads having invariably manifested kindness and sympathy for the men, they were especially anxious that whenever the rising might take place your lives should be spared. This has been done. You are alive and unharmed this morning, whilst others have gone to render an account of their manifold misdeeds—their countless acts of oppression and cruelty—before that Judge in whose sight their lives are not one whit more valuable than the lives of those whom they have goaded and driven to death—ay, and to *worse* than death—to such frantic desperation as can only be allayed by the shedding of blood like water. Now, mark me well, both of you; you have had neither part nor lot in this matter—those who wished you well have so managed that, whether or no, you should be kept strictly neutral throughout the affair; all those to whom you owed obedience are either dead or prisoners; you are not asked or expected to join us—we do not want you and should not care to have you even if you were willing—you are therefore relieved from duty; and all that is asked of you is that you shall interfere in no way, either by word or deed, with the working of the ship or with our plans. If you are agreeable to abide by this proposal, well and good; you will be welcome to come and go as you like until we find it convenient to land you; you will be allowed to occupy your former quarters, and your rations will be regularly served out to you. But if on the other hand you make the slightest attempt to communicate with the prisoners, or endeavour in any way to seduce any of the men from their loyalty to the rest, I will hang you both that same hour, one from each yard-arm. That is understood and agreed to, is it not, men?" he continued, raising his voice and appealing to the crowd of mutineers who had gathered round us.

"Ay, ay, that's agreed; that's fair enough," was the unanimous reply.

With that, Farmer waved his hand to us by way of dismissal; and considerably thrown off our balance by the address to which we had just listened, and by the terrible turn affairs had taken generally, we slunk off to the poop, so as to be as far away as possible from the murderous gang and from the ghastly puddles of coagulated blood about the quarter-deck, which still bore witness to heaven against them.

At this moment a man on the forecastle electrified all hands by shouting:

"Sail ho!"

I saw Farmer start from his seat on the gun as if shot, his flushed features turned ashen pale, and for a moment his palsied lips refused to give utterance to a sound.

"Sail ho!" repeated the man in a louder hail, thinking, I suppose, that his first intimation had passed unnoticed. This second hail fairly startled the men, and in a moment everything was bustle and confusion and panic. It aroused Farmer too; he pulled himself together sufficiently to respond to the hail with the usual question, "Where away?" and, on receiving the reply, "Two points on the larboard bow," walked forward to personally inspect the stranger. We, of course, likewise directed our glances in the specified direction; and there she was, sure enough, a large ship, on the starboard tack, with every stitch of canvas set that would draw, and steering a course which would take her across our bows at a distance of about a mile.

"Bring me the spy-glass out of the cabin, somebody!" hailed Farmer from the forecastle. The glass—a very powerful one and a favourite instrument with the murdered captain—was handed him by one of the quarter-masters, and he applied it to his eye. A breathless silence now prevailed fore and aft for the stranger had all the look of a British man-of-war, and everybody was waiting to hear what Farmer's verdict would be. The inspection was a long-sustained and evidently anxious one. At length, dropping the glass into the hollow of his arm Farmer turned and said:

"Bring Mr Southcott on deck, and let us hear his opinion of yonder hooker."

In a few minutes the master was escorted on deck by a couple of armed seamen, and led forward to where Farmer was standing.

"Mr Southcott," said the mutineer, turning toward the individual addressed, and perceptibly shrinking as their glance met, "be good enough to take this glass, and let me know wha' you think of the stranger yonder."

"Stranger!" ejaculated Southcott. "Where away? Ah, I see her!" and he took the glass from Farmer's extended hand.

"Well, what think you of her?" asked Farmer impatiently, after the master had been silently working away with the glass for some two or three minutes.

"One moment, please," answered Southcott with his eye still glued to the tube; "I think—but I am not quite sure—if she would only keep just the merest trifle more away—so as to permit of my catching a glimpse—"

"Sail ho!" shouted a man in the fore-top; "two of 'em, a brig and a ship on the starboard beam, away in under the land there!"

Farmer unceremoniously snatched the glass away from the master and levelled it in the direction indicated.

"Ay, ay, I see them," said he. "That is the *Drake* nearest us, and the *Favourite* inshore of her. They are all right; we have nothing to fear from them. It is this stranger here ahead of us that bothers me. Come, Mr Southcott," he continued, "you ought to know something about her by this time—you have been looking at her long enough; do you think you ever saw her before?"

The master took the glass, had another long squint at the ship ahead, then handed the instrument back to Farmer, with the answer:

"I decline to say whether I have or not."

"That is enough," said Farmer; "your answer but confirms me in my conviction as to the identity of yonder frigate. It is the *Mermaid*. Speak, sir, is it not so?"

"You are right, Farmer, it *is* the *Mermaid*, thank God! and you cannot escape. See! she is already hauling up to speak us; and in another twenty minutes will be alongside. Now, sir, resign to me the command which you have with so much violence and bloodshed usurped; and you, men," he continued, turning round and in a loud voice addressing the rest of the crew, "return at once to your duty. Support and assist me in recovering the command of the ship, and I promise—"

"Silence!" roared Farmer, striking the master a heavy blow full in the mouth with his clenched fist. "Seize him, you two," he continued to the men who had charge of the prisoner, "and if he offers to speak again to the men clap a belaying-pin between his teeth. My lads, you now know the truth; yonder frigate is our old acquaintance the *Mermaid*. Mr Southcott proposes that I should surrender the command of this ship to him; and if I do so we all know what will follow. Most of us will dangle at the yard-arm; and though, *through the royal clemency*," (with a bitter sneer), "a few may be allowed to escape with a flogging through the fleet, with left-handed boatswains' mates to cross the lashes—think of that, men, and compare it with the mere two or three dozen at the gangway which most of you have tasted since you joined the *Hermione*—where is the man among you, I ask, who can point to himself and say, 'I shall be one of the *fortunate* few?' No, no, my lads! after last night's work there must be no talk of surrender; the ropes are already round our necks, and as surely as we ever find ourselves beneath the British flag again, so surely will those ropes be hauled taut and ourselves bowsed up to the yard-arm. And, even if our lives could be assured to us, what inducement is there to us to serve under British bunting again? I say there is *none*. We must choose, then, between two alternatives; we must either fight or fly. Which is it to be?"

The rest of the mutineers huddled together, evidently irresolute; each man eagerly sought his neighbour's opinion, the *pros* and *cons* of Farmer's question were hurriedly discussed, and I saw with inexpressible delight that a good many of the men were more than half disposed to fall in with the master's suggestion.

Mr Southcott must have seen this too, for he wheeled round upon Farmer and exclaimed:

"Surely, Farmer, you are not mad enough to entertain the idea of fighting the *Mermaid*? Why, man, you could not stand up before her for five minutes with the men in their present undisciplined state and no one but yourself to direct operations. Your defeat under such circumstances is an absolute certainty; and think what would be the fate of yourself and your misguided followers if taken in arms against the flag under which they have sworn to serve. At present some at least of them may hope for mercy if they will but—"

"Away with him! Take him below!" shouted Farmer, "and if he attempts to open his mouth again put a bullet through his brains. Now, shipmates," he continued, as the master was hurried below, "make up your minds, and quickly too; which will you have, the yard-rope or a pitched battle?"

"What occasion is there for either?" inquired a burly boatswain's-mate. "There's more ways of killing a cat than choking of her with cream. Let's square dead away afore it and set stunsails alow and aloft, both sides. I'll lay my life we run far enough away from the *Mermaid* afore sunset to dodge her in the dark."

"No good," dissented Farmer. "The *Mermaid* could beat us a couple of knots off the wind in this breeze."

"Ay, ay; that's true enough; she could so," assented a topman. "But we have the heels of her on a taut bowline; so why not brace sharp up on the starboard tack, pass between the islands, and then make for Porto Rico?"

"What! and run the gauntlet of those two cruisers inshore there, as well as take our chance of falling in with the *Magicienne* and the *Regulus*, which we know are knocking about somewhere in that direction! Is that the best counsel you can give, Ben?"

"Well, then, let's haul close in with the land, set fire to the ship, and take to the boats," answered Ben.

"And what then?" sneered Farmer.

"Why, land, to be sure, and take sarvice with Jack Spaniard," was the reply.

"Why, man, do you suppose they would welcome us if we went to them empty-handed?" asked Farmer. "No, no, that will never do. If we join the Spaniards we must take the ship with us to ensure a welcome; and I'm half inclined to think that will be the best thing we can do. But not now; that must be thought over at leisure. Meanwhile, what is to be done in the present emergency? We have no time for further argument. Will you stand by me and obey my orders?"

"Ay, ay, we will, every man Jack of us, sink or swim, fight or fly," was the reply from a hundred throats.

"That's well, my lads," exclaimed Farmer exultantly; "it shall go hard but I will bring you through somehow. Starboard your helm, there," to the man at the wheel; "let her come to on the larboard tack; to your stations, men; let go the larboard sheets and braces, and round in on the starboard. Smartly, my bullies; let's have no bungling, now, or Captain Otway there will at once suspect that something is amiss. That's well; ease up the lee topgallant and royal-braces a trifle; well there of all; belay! Afterguard, muster your buckets and brushes and wash down the decks. Roberts, go below with a gang and rouse the hammocks on deck; and quarter-masters, see that they are snugly stowed. Where's the signal-man? Bend the ensign on to the peak-halliards and our number at the main; and main-top, there I stand by to hoist away the pennant. Gunner, muster your crew; go round the quarters with them; and see that everything is ship-shape in case we should have to make a fight of it."

I was surprised to see how, as Farmer issued his orders in a tone of authority, the instinct of discipline asserted itself; the men sprang to their stations as nimbly and executed their several duties as smartly as though Captain Pigot himself had been directing their movements. The *Hermione* was braced sharp up on the larboard tack and heading as near as she would lay for the *Mermaid*, which was now about a point and a half on our weather bow, about four miles distant, and nearing us fast; whilst the *Favourite* and the *Drake* were stretching out from under the land to join her.

Presently a string of tiny balls went soaring aloft to the *Mermaid's* mainroyal mast-head, to break abroad as they reached it and stream out in the fresh morning breeze as so many gaily coloured signal flags.

"There goes the *Mermaid's* bunting, sir!" sang out the signal-man, "she is showing her number."

"Ay, ay, I see it," exclaimed Farmer. "And, by Heaven," he added, "it never struck me until this moment that Pigot was senior captain. Hoist away your ensign and pennant! up with the number! We are all right, my hearties; I know how to trick them now."

He raised the telescope to his eye and brought it to bear upon the *Mermaid*.

"All right," he exclaimed a few seconds later, "she sees our number—haul down! Now signal her to chase in the north-eastern quarter. Hurrah, my hearties, that's your sort! There goes her answering pennant; and there she hauls to the wind on the starboard tack. That disposes of her at all events. Now signal the *Favourite* and *Drake* to chase to the nor'ard; that will send them through the Mona Passage, and leave us with a clear sea."

A quarter of an hour later the three cruisers which had caused the mutineers so much uneasiness were thrashing to windward under every rag they could spread; when Farmer bore up and ran away to the southward and westward with studding-sails set on both sides of the ship.

# Chapter Eight
# La Guayra

After breakfast that morning the men were mustered on the quarter-deck; and Farmer, with some half a dozen of the other mutineers, discussed in their presence and hearing the question of what should be done with the ship now that they had her. There was, of course, a great deal of wild talk, especially among the foreigners — of whom, most unfortunately for the ill-fated officers of the ship, there were far too many on board — and at one period of the discussion it seemed by no means improbable that the frigate would be converted into a pirate, in which event there can be no doubt but that, for a time at least, she would have proved a terrible scourge to all honest navigators in those seas. Farmer, however, was strongly in favour of going over to the Spaniards; and in the end his counsels prevailed, though he met with a great deal of opposition.

This point settled, the ship's head was laid to the southward; and sunrise on the fourth morning succeeding the mutiny found us off La Guayra, with a flag of truce flying. The signal was duly observed and answered from the shore; upon which the gig was lowered, and, with a white flag floating from her ensign staff, her crew in their holiday rig, and Farmer with three other ringleaders of the mutiny in her stern-sheets, she shoved off for the harbour. She was absent for the greater part of the day, it being seven bells in the afternoon watch before she was observed pulling out of the harbour again; and when she made her appearance it was at once observed that she was accompanied by several heavy launches full of men. It took the flotilla fully an hour to pull off to us, and when they reached the frigate it was seen that the occupants of the shore-boats were Spanish seamen, with a sprinkling of officers among them. On coming alongside the entire rabble at once boarded; the ship was formally handed over by Farmer to an officer in a resplendent uniform, whose first act was to direct one of his aides to strike the white flag and hoist the Spanish ensign at the peak; and the surviving officers — five of us in number — were then mustered and ordered into one of the boats alongside. We were compelled to bundle down over the side just as we were, without a single personal belonging, or article of clothing except what we stood in; and, the boat being manned by some twenty as bloodthirsty-looking desperadoes as I ever clapped eyes on, we were forthwith pulled ashore and at once marched off to prison.

It was dark by the time that we reached the harbour; we were consequently unable to see much of the place that night beyond the fact that it lay at the base of a lofty range of hills. We were received at the landing-place by a party of soldiers with fixed bayonets, who had evidently been awaiting our arrival, and, escorted by them, we arrived—after a march of about a mile—at the gates of a most forbidding-looking edifice constructed of heavy blocks of masonry, and which had all the appearance of being a fortress. Passing through the gloomy gateway—which was protected by a portcullis—we found ourselves in a large open paved courtyard, across which we marched to a door on the opposite side. Entering this door, we wheeled to the right and passed along a wide stone passage which conducted us to a sort of guard-room. We were here received by a lanky, cadaverous-looking individual with a shrivelled yellow parchment skin, hands like the claws of a vulture, piercing black eyes, and grizzled locks and moustache, who, with but scant courtesy, took down the name and rank of each of us in a huge battered volume; after which we were conducted through another long echoing passage, and finally ushered into a sort of hall, about sixty feet long by forty feet wide, with a lofty stone groined roof, and six high, narrow, lancet-shaped windows in each of the two longer walls. These windows we subsequently found were closely grated on the outside with heavy iron bars. The moment that we crossed the threshold the heavy oaken door was closed and barred upon us, and we were left to shift for ourselves as best we could.

The first thing of which I was distinctly conscious on entering the hall was the volume of sound which echoed from the walls and the groined roof. Singing, laughter, conversation, altercation were all going on at the same moment at the utmost pitch of the human voice, and apparently with the whole strength of the assembled company, which, after winking and blinking like an owl for several moments, I succeeded in dimly making out through the dense cloud of suffocating smoke which pervaded the place, and which appeared to emanate from a wood fire burning on the pavement at the far end of the hall, and from some three or four flaring oil lamps which were suspended from nails driven into the walls between the joints of the masonry.

It was a minute or two before any of the noisy company appeared to notice us. At length, however, one man, rising to his feet and shading his eyes with his hand as he looked in our direction, ejaculated:

"Who have we here? More companions in misfortune?"

Then advancing with outstretched hand he exclaimed uproariously:

"What cheer, my hearties? Welcome to Equality Hall!"

Then, as he for the first time noticed our uniforms, he muttered:

"Why, dash my old frizzly wig if they ain't navy gents!" adding in a much more respectful tone of voice: "Beg pardon, gentlemen, I'm sure, for my familiarity. Didn't notice at first what you was. Come forward into the range of the light and bring yourselves to an anchor. I'm afraid you'll find these but poor quarters, gentlemen, after what you've been used to aboard a man-o'-war. And you'll find us a noisy lot too; but the fact is we're just trying to make the best of things here, trying to be as happy as we can under the circumstances, as you may say. Here, you unmannerly lubbers," he continued, addressing a group who were sprawling at full length on a rough wooden bench, "rouse out of that and make room for your betters."

The men scrambled to their feet and made way for us good-naturedly enough; and we seated ourselves on the vacated bench, feeling—at least I may answer for myself—forlorn enough in the great dingy, dirty, comfortless hole into which we had been so unceremoniously thrust. Our new friend seated himself alongside Mr Southcott, and, first informing that gentleman that the company in which we found ourselves were the crews of sundry British merchantmen which had been captured by the Spaniards, and that he was the ex-chief mate of a tidy little Liverpool barque called the *Sparkling Foam*, proceeded to inquire into the circumstances which had led to our captivity. The account of the mutiny was received by the party, most of whom had gathered round to listen to it, with expressions of the most profound abhorrence and indignation, which were only cut short by the appearance of a sergeant and a file of soldiers bearing the evening's rations, which were served out raw, to be immediately afterwards handed over to a black cook who answered to the name of "Snowball," and who had good-naturedly constituted himself the cook of the party. The rations, which included a portion for us newcomers, consisted of a small modicum of meat, a few vegetables, a tolerably liberal allowance of coarse black bread, and water *ad libitum*. The little incident of the serving out of rations having come to an end, and the sergeant having retired with his satellites, our friend of the *Sparkling Foam*—whose name, it transpired, was Benjamin Rogers—resumed his conversation with us by proceeding to "put us up to a thing or two."

"I've no doubt, gentlemen," he said, "but what you'll be asked to give your parole to-morrow, if you haven't already—you haven't, eh? well, so much the better; you'll be asked to-morrow. Now, if you'll take my advice you won't give it; if you do, you'll simply be turned adrift into the town to shift for yourselves and find quarters where you can. If you've got money, and plenty of it, you might manage to rub along pretty well for a time; but when your cash is gone where are you? Why, simply nowheres. Now, this is a roughish berth for gentlemen like you, I'll allow; but within the last few days we've been marched out every morning and set to work patching up an old battery away out here close to the beach, and we've been kept at it all day, so that we get plenty of fresh air and exercise, and merely have to ride it out here during the night. There's only some half-a-dozen soldiers sent out to watch us; and it's my idea that it might be no such very difficult matter to give these chaps the slip some evening, and at nightfall make our way down to the harbour, seize one of the small coasting craft which seem to be always there, and make sail for Jamaica. At least that's my notion, gentlemen; you are welcome to it for what it's worth, and can think it over."

We thanked our new friend for his advice, which we followed so far as to think and talk it over before stowing ourselves away for the night upon the bundle of straw which constituted the sole apology for a bed and covering allowed us by the Spaniards.

Mr Southcott, the master, was indignant beyond measure at the scurvy treatment thus meted out to us as prisoners of war, and talked a great deal about the representations he intended to make to the authorities with regard to it; but in the meantime he decided to give his parole, in the hope of a speedy exchange, and strongly recommended us to do the same. He was possessed of a little money, it seemed, which he had taken the precaution of secreting about his person immediately on the ship making the land, in anticipation of his speedily finding a use for it; and this money he most generously offered to share with us as far as it would go. To this, however, none of us would listen; and as we were wholly without means the only alternative left to us was to refuse our parole, and put up as best we could with such board and lodging as the Spaniards might be disposed to give us, and to bend all our energies to the accomplishment of a speedy escape. As for me, I still held in vivid remembrance the statement which my father had made to me on the eve of my departure for school, and the caution he had given me against expecting any assistance from him after I had once fairly entered upon my career; and I resolved to endure the worst that could possibly befall me rather than act upon a suggestion which the master threw out, to the effect that possibly someone might be found in the town willing to cash (for a heavy premium) a draft of mine upon my father.

Rogers' expectation that we should be asked for our parole was verified next morning; and Southcott, giving his, bade us a reluctant farewell after a further ineffectual effort to persuade us to reconsider our decision. Finding that we were not to be persuaded he bade us take heart and keep up our spirits, as his very first task should be to make such representations to the authorities as must result in a very speedy and considerable amelioration of our condition. We parted with many expressions of mutual regret; and that was the last any of us ever saw of the poor fellow, nor were our subsequent inquiries as to what had become of him in the slightest degree successful.

As for us who remained, upon our explaining, through the medium of a very inefficient interpreter, that the lack of means to support ourselves precluded the possibility of our giving our parole upon the terms offered us, we were brusquely informed that we must then be content to be classed among the common prisoners, to put up with their accommodation, and to take part in the tasks allotted to them. We were then abruptly dismissed, and, without further ceremony, marched off to the scene of our labours, which we found to be the fort mentioned by Rogers—an antiquated structure in the very last stage of dilapidation, which it was the task of the prisoners to repair.

To be obliged to work was, after all, no very great hardship. We were in the fresh open air all day, which was infinitely better than confinement between four walls, even had those walls inclosed a far greater measure of comfort than was to be found within the confines of our prison-house. The physical exertion kept us in a state of excellent health, and consequently in fairly good spirits; the labour, though of anything but an intellectual character, kept our minds sufficiently employed to prevent our brooding over our ill fortune; we were allowed to take matters pretty easily so long as we did not dawdle too much, and thus entail upon our lounging guard the unwelcome necessity of scrambling to their feet and hunting up our whereabouts; our daily labours brought with them just that amount of fatigue which ensured sound sleep and a happy oblivion of the dirt and manifold discomforts of our night quarters; and finally, there was the prospect that at any moment some lucky chance might favour our escape.

Four days from the date of our incarceration the muster-roll of the prison was increased by the addition of the names of half a dozen Spanish smugglers, who had been captured a few miles up the coast by one of the guarda-costas and brought into La Guayra. They were a rough, reckless-looking set of vagabonds; but their looks were the worst part of them, for they all turned out to be gay, jovial spirits enough, taking their reverse of fortune with the utmost nonchalance, and having a laugh and a jest for everything and everybody, the guards included, with whom they soon became upon the most amicable terms. One of these men, a fellow named Miguel—I never learned his other name—was attached to the gang of labourers to which I belonged; and though I fought rather shy of him for a time his hearty good-nature and accommodating disposition soon overcame my reserve, and I gradually grew to be on the best of terms with him. He could speak a word or two of English, and, seeming to have taken a fancy to me, he would strike up a conversation with me as often as the opportunity offered, much to his own amusement and mine, since we rarely succeeded in comprehending each other. These efforts at conversation, however, inspired me with the idea that this man's companionship afforded me an opportunity to acquire a knowledge of Spanish, which could not fail to be of service to me; and this idea I at length with some difficulty succeeded in conveying to my smuggler friend. He pantomimically expressed himself as charmed with the suggestion, which he intimated might be improved upon by my undertaking in return to teach him English; and, a satisfactory understanding being arrived at, we commenced our studies forthwith. We were of course utterly destitute of all aid from books, and we were therefore compelled to fall back upon the primitive method of pointing out objects to each other and designating them alternately in English and Spanish, each repeating the word until the other had caught its proper pronunciation. From this we advanced to short simple sentences, the meaning of which we conveyed as well as we could by appropriate gestures; and though we sometimes made the most ridiculous mistakes through misunderstanding the meaning of those gestures, yet on the whole we managed tolerably well. The first steps were the most difficult, but every word mastered cleared the way to the comprehension of two or three others; so that by the time we had been a couple of months at our studies we found ourselves making really satisfactory progress. And when seven months had been thus spent, though neither could speak the language of the other like a native, each could converse in the other's language with tolerable fluency and make himself perfectly understood. I had, long before this, however, after considerable hesitation and cautious feeling of my ground, broached to Miguel the question of escape, and had been considerably chagrined to learn from him that, unless aided by friends outside the prison, there was hardly the remotest chance of success. The only way in which it could be done was, in his opinion, to obtain shelter and concealment for, say a month, in some family in the immediate neighbourhood; and *then*, when the scent had grown cold and the zeal of the pursuers had died away, a dark night and some assistance might enable one to get safely off the coast. If *he* were free now, he was good enough to say, the thing might be managed, for a consideration, without any very great difficulty; but—a shrug of the shoulders and a glance at the prison dress which he was condemned to wear for more than a year longer eloquently enough closed the sentence.

About this time—or, to speak more definitely, some eight months from the date of our landing at La Guayra—a change in our fortunes occurred, which, whilst it had the immediate result of considerably ameliorating Courtenay's and my own condition, was destined to ultimately—but avast! I must not get ahead of my story. It happened in this way. One morning after we had been out at work about a couple of hours the military engineer who was in charge of our operations rode up to the battery, accompanied by a very fine, handsome, middle-aged man, evidently also a soldier, for he was attired in an undress military uniform.

"Hillo!" exclaimed Miguel, as he noticed the new arrivals, "what is in the wind now? That is the commandant of the district with Señor Pacheco."

The appearance of such a notability naturally created a profound sensation; but we were of course obliged to go on with our work all the same. The commandant dismounted, and, accompanied by Señor Pacheco, proceeded to make an inspection of the battery, which by this time was beginning to assume the appearance of a tolerably strong fortification. That done, the sergeant of the guard was summoned, and something in the nature of a consultation ensued, which terminated in Courtenay and myself being ordered to drop our tools and step forward to where the commandant was standing.

The great man regarded us both fixedly for a moment or two, and then said, of course in Spanish:

"I understand that you are two of the officers who were landed here from the British frigate *Hermione*?"

I replied that we were.

"Well," he said, "I suppose, in that case, you know all about ships, or, at all events, sufficient to be able to construct and rig a few models?"

I answered that we certainly did.

"Very well," said he, turning to Señor Pacheco, "in that case they will serve my purpose very well, and you may send them up to the castle at once. And, as they are, after all, merely a couple of boys, I think we shall run no very great risk of losing them if we arrange for them to stay about the place altogether; what say you?—it will be much more convenient for me; and I will find rations and quarters for them; and they can report themselves periodically at the citadel, if need be."

Señor Pacheco expressed himself as perfectly satisfied with the proposed arrangement; and we were forthwith instructed to leave work there and then and make the best of our way to a chateau which was pointed out to us, and which lay embosomed in trees some three miles to the westward of the town and about a mile from the shore. We had no packing to do, as we possessed nothing in the world but the clothes we stood up in—and which, by the way, were now in the very last stage of "looped and windowed raggedness"—so we simply nodded a "good-bye" to such of our envious acquaintances as happened to be within saluting range, and at once set off up the road which we were informed would conduct us to our destination.

Once fairly away from the scene of our late labours, Courtenay and I gave full rein both to our tongues and to our imaginations, discussing and wondering what in the world the commandant could possibly want with ship-models; but that, after all was a question which we did not greatly trouble ourselves to solve; the dominant thought and reflection in our minds that we were likely to be, for some time at least, absentees from the prison and all the discomfort and wretchedness connected with it, and which I have not dwelt upon or attempted to describe for the one simple reason that it was wholly undescribable. We never thought of escaping, although we soon found ourselves passing through a thinly-inhabited country where our abandonment of the high-road and concealment in the neighbouring woods could have been accomplished without the slightest risk of observation; but we had learned by this time that escape was no such easy matter; it was a something which would have to be carefully planned beforehand and every possible precaution adopted to ensure success, and had we been foolishly tempted to try it then and there our non-arrival at the chateau would speedily have been reported, with the result that a search would have been instituted, followed by our speedy recapture and ignominious return to the abhorred prison. No; we were very thankful for and very well satisfied with the sudden change in our fortunes which had been so unexpectedly wrought, for, though we could of course form no very clear idea of what our lot would be in the service of the commandant, we felt pretty certain it would be much easier than what we had been obliged to put up with since our landing from the frigate; and, for the rest, we were content to wait and see what time had in store for us, whilst we were fully resolved to keep a bright lookout for and to take the utmost advantage of any opportunity for escape which might be opened out to us.

We had just arrived at a handsome pair of park gates which we conjectured gave admittance to the castle grounds when we were overtaken by the commandant, on horseback. He nodded to us; remarked, "I see you have found your way all right;" shouted for the ancient custodian to open the gates; and then, as the heavy iron barriers swung back, dismounted, threw the bridle over his arm, and walked up the long avenue with us.

We now had an opportunity to observe him a little more closely than at our first interview; and we found him to be a tall and strikingly handsome man, somewhere about fifty years of age, as we judged; with piercing black eyes which seemed to read one's very thoughts, yet which were by no means devoid of amiable expression, and black hair and moustache thickly dashed with grey. Somewhat to our surprise, we found that he could speak English very fairly. His demeanour to us was characterised by that lofty stately courtesy peculiar to the old nobility of Castile (of which province he was a native); and we subsequently learned that he was as gallant a warrior as he was a polished gentleman, having served with much distinction in various parts of the world. His style and title, we afterwards ascertained, was El Commandant Don Luis Aguirre Martinez de Guzman; and we speedily found that he had a very strong predilection for the English, attributable to the fact—which ultimately leaked out—that his first and deepest love had been won by an English girl, whom, however,—the course of true love not running smoothly—he never married.

As we walked up the noble avenue side by side he questioned us as to our names, ages, and rank, how long we had been prisoners, and so on; and expressed his astonishment at the harsh treatment which we had received at the hands of the prison authorities. Upon this I thought it advisable to mention to him our refusal to give our parole, stating as our reason our total lack of funds.

"Oh, well," he said laughingly, "that need no longer influence you, you know. You will have free quarters and rations at the castle, in addition to the remuneration to which you will be entitled for your services, so you can give your parole when next you report yourselves at the citadel, and that will end the matter."

This, however, would not suit our views at all, though we did not choose to say so; we therefore changed the subject by asking him what more particularly were the services which we should be asked to perform. His answer was to the effect that his especial hobby was the study of fortification, respecting which, it seems, he had several rather novel theories, in the working out and testing of which—and also by way of amusement—he had constructed the model of a fortified town on the shores of a small lake within the castle grounds; and he had sought our assistance to enable him to place a fleet of ship-models before this town, to illustrate his method of overcoming the difficulties attendant upon a state of siege and blockade. By the time that this fancy of his had been fully explained we had reached the castle—a noble building as to size but of no very great pretensions from an architectural point of view—and, the major-domo having been summoned, we were handed over to him with the necessary instructions for our proper housing and so on.

# Chapter Nine
# Inez De Guzman

We were conducted by our guide—an ancient and somewhat pompous individual—to a large and very pleasantly situated room in the north wing of the castle, from whence, through an opening between the trees, a glimpse of the sea was to be obtained; the foreground being occupied by a kitchen-garden. This room, it seemed, was to be our sleeping apartment. It was somewhat meagrely furnished, according to our English ideas, and there was only one bed in it—our guide informing us, however, that the commandant had ordered another to be placed there forthwith—but what little furniture the apartment contained was good, and everything was scrupulously clean, so that, in comparison with our recent quarters, those we were now to occupy seemed absolutely palatial. And our gratification was considerably increased when we were informed that another very large and handsomely furnished room, through which we had passed to gain access to our sleeping quarters, was to be devoted to our exclusive use and occupation during the day at such times as we were not engaged in the park. We voted the commandant a trump, there and then, and mutually resolved to do all that in us lay to retain our exceedingly comfortable berths until we should find opportunity to quit them of our own accord for good and all.

Having duly installed us, and suggestively directed our attention to the toilet gear—of which in truth we both most grievously stood in need—the major-domo left us, first informing us, however, that if, when we were ready, we would ring a bell, the cord of which he pointed out to us, a servant would bring us some refreshment.

We lost no time in freshening ourselves up and making ourselves as presentable as circumstances would permit, and then sat down to a plain but substantial meal, which, after our meagre and coarse prison fare, seemed a veritable banquet. At the conclusion of this meal we were informed that the commandant awaited us below, upon which we followed our informant down a sort of back staircase, and issuing from a little side door found ourselves in the garden before mentioned. It was walled in on all sides, but a door in the wall adjoining the house was pointed out to us, and issuing through it we found ourselves on the noble terrace which stretched along the whole front of the castle. Here we discovered the commandant pacing up and down with a cigar in his mouth, and joining him he proposed to conduct us to the scene of our future labours.

With all his stateliness, which he never laid aside, Don Luis de Guzman knew how to be very affable when he chose, and he chose to be so with us. Commencing a long conversation by courteously expressing a hope that our apartments were to our liking, and kindly informing us that, if they were not, a hint to the major-domo would be sufficient to secure the rectification of whatever might be amiss, he then went on to speak of "the unnecessary haste" with which we had been removed from the ship, and of the inconvenience which we must have experienced from the scantiness of our wardrobe, an inconvenience which, he said, he would "take the liberty" of having remedied as speedily as might be. This, of course, was very kind of him, and we ungrudgingly credited him with the most generous of motives; at the same time I have no doubt that the stately don was as heartily ashamed of the two scarecrows who accompanied him as we were of our own appearance.

Having thus cleared the ground, as it were, our benefactor proceeded to question us closely as to the circumstances connected with and which led up to the mutiny, at which he expressed the most unqualified reprobation; and when we had told him all we knew about it he informed us that the British government had made a formal demand for the restitution of the frigate and the surrender of the mutineers, as well as the captive officers, a demand which, he said, the Spanish government had seen fit to refuse; and I thought, from his manner of speaking upon the subject, that he by no means favourable regarded the action of his countrymen in the matter. This conversation, and indeed all that we subsequently held with him, was, I ought to say, conducted in English. He asked us questions innumerable— indeed more than we were able to fully answer—respecting the habits and customs of our nation, our mode of government, and what not; and it was not long before we were able to perceive that his liking for the English was as strong as it was possible for a thorough-bred Spanish noble to entertain.

A walk, or rather a saunter, of about a mile and a half through the park brought us to the scene of our future operations—a lake of, I should say, some four or five acres in extent - and here the subject of our conversation was diverted to the theme of the commandant's requirements of us.

The lake, it appeared, was a natural feature of the landscape, with a stream some twenty feet in width flowing through it. A walk had been constructed right round it, crossing the stream by a couple of rustic bridges; and for about one-half its length the banks had been most beautifully laid out as a flower-garden. For the remaining half of its length, however, nature had been allowed to have pretty much her own way, except at the point where the stream entered the lake. There the ground had been carefully cleared of trees, and trimmed so as to present the aspect of a low flat shore, with hills in the rear. And on this shore, covering an area of some fifty feet square on each side of the stream, the commandant had caused to be constructed an exceedingly pretty and carefully finished model of a town, with streets, houses, public buildings, squares, and even monuments, with a harbour, including moles, piers, lighthouses, batteries, etcetera, complete down to the minutest detail. It had evidently been a labour of love with him, as could be seen at a glance from the care and finish lavished upon the work; and we afterwards learned that it had occupied him and a staff of a dozen workmen for more than a year. It was to blockade this miniature town and port that the fleet of ships which we were to construct was required, the trenches and investing earthworks and batteries on the land side being already finished. It was surprising to see how this most dignified Spaniard unbent, and how enthusiastic he became as he described his plans to us and gave us instructions respecting the dimensions and number of his pigmy fleet. He was evidently much pleased with the admiration we expressed at the care and skill exhibited in working out his quaint idea; and when we had minutely inspected every part of it he led us to a comfortable airy little workshop, concealed in a kind of brake among the trees, where we found a good stock of wood, with a capital supply of tools and everything necessary to the proper carrying out of our task. We did not do anything in the way of work on that day, however, for by the time that we had seen everything and had taken a walk to the seaward extremity of the park the sun was getting low, and the time had arrived for us to see about getting back to the castle.

Oh, how we enjoyed the luxury of that first dinner at the castle!—the only decent meal of which we had partaken since our landing—with the quiet evening which followed it, spent in a large, lofty, well-furnished apartment, lighted up by a massive silver lamp of elaborate workmanship, and cooled by the light evening breeze which floated in through the widely-opened casements. Stretched luxuriously in a couple of low comfortable sloping-backed chairs, we sat at one of these open casements discussing a bottle of excellent wine, and looking out upon the dark woods which surrounded the building, watching the full moon soar into the cloudless sky from behind the gently-swaying foliage, and listening to the song of the nightingale, amidst which we once or twice thought we detected the tinkling sounds of a guitar apparently issuing from one of the open windows in another wing of the castle.

We retired early to rest that night, after a bath, not so much because we were tired, but rather to enjoy the unwonted luxury of rest in an actual bed, with the pleasant accompaniment of clean sweet-smelling linen.

We were disappointed, however, in our anticipations of a sound night's sleep. After making shift for so long with a heap of straw spread on a hard pavement, the beds seemed too soft and yielding to our unaccustomed limbs, and we lay tossing to and fro for a long time before we eventually dropped off to sleep. This trifling inconvenience disappeared, however, after a few nights' experience.

We were up and stirring by daybreak next morning, and a few minutes later we might have been seen scudding across the park on our way to a certain rocky pool on the beach, which the commandant had pointed out to us the day before as a place where we might safely venture to indulge in a swim without fear of the sharks. Taking his word for it we plunged in and swam off, until we found ourselves almost among the breakers, then returned to the shore, dressed, and made our way back to the castle, which we reached in good time for breakfast. That meal over we set out for the workshop, Pedro—the servant who seemed to have been appointed to wait upon us—informing us as we started that he had orders to have luncheon ready for us by one o'clock. Arrived at the scene of our labours we each selected a suitable block of wood, and whilst Courtenay set to work upon a model of the *Hermione*, I, with greater ambition, devoted all my energies to the hewing out of a line-of-battle ship. Thus occupied the time passed swiftly away, and almost before we were aware of it the commandant, who had looked in upon us to see how we were progressing, announced that it was time for us to see about returning to the castle. He walked back with us, chatting most affably all the way; and on reaching our rooms we found a tailor awaiting us, by his orders, to take our measures for a new outfit of rigging. The first instalment of this, in the shape of a loose white nankin suit apiece, with shirt, stockings, light shoes of tan-coloured leather, crimson silk sashes—to serve instead of braces—and broad-brimmed cane-hat, all complete, awaited us on our waking a couple of mornings later, much to our gratification, as the idea grew upon us that the castle contained other inmates besides the commandant, and we were anxious to avoid a rencontre with these so long as we retained our ragged, scarecrow appearance.

We had been at work about a week; Courtenay had completed the hull of his frigate, and was busy about her spars, whilst I was putting the finishing touches to a figure-head for my seventy-four, when, about four o'clock in the afternoon, our workshop suddenly became darkened to such an extent that we could no longer see to work. Looking up and glancing out of the window, we observed that, unnoticed by us, a heavy thunder-storm had been gathering over the sea, and the clouds, setting shoreward, were now hovering immediately overhead. That it was likely to be a severe storm was manifest, the sky being blacker than I had ever seen it before. We were debating upon the advisability of effecting an immediate retreat to the castle, and taking our chance of reaching it before the storm should burst, when a vivid flash of lightning, green and baleful, quickly succeeded by a most deafening peal of thunder, decided us to remain where we were. Another flash and another rapidly followed, and then down came the rain in a perfect deluge. It fell, not in drops but in regular *sheets* of water, lashing the surface of the lake into a plain of milky foam, and so completely flooding the ground that in five minutes the water everywhere, as far as we could see from the window at which we had taken our stand, must have been ankle-deep. The storm gained in intensity with startling rapidity, the lightning blazing and flashing about us so uninterruptedly that the whole atmosphere seemed a-quiver with the greenish-blue glare; whilst the rattling crash and roar of the thunder went on absolutely without any intermission, filling the firmament with one continuous chaos of deafening sound and causing the very earth beneath our feet to tremble. This had been going on for some eight or ten minutes, perhaps, when we caught sight, through the streaming deluge outside, of a couple of white-clad flying figures making their way down the path from the rustic bridge toward the workshop. I sprang to the door and threw it open; and in another moment two young women plunged through the doorway—their light flimsy garments streaming with water and clinging about their limbs—and flung themselves breathlessly down upon a bench, the taller and darker of the two panting out:

"A thousand thanks, señors! Madre de Dios, what a storm!"

"It is indeed terrible," I replied in my best Spanish, as I closed the door again. "And you have been fairly caught in it. Have you come from a distance?"

"Only from the castle. I am Inez de Guzman, the commandant's daughter, and this," pointing to her companion, "is Eugenia Gonzalez, my foster-sister. We left home about two hours ago to walk through the park as far as the beach; and it was not until we had emerged from among the trees near the shore that we noticed the gathering storm. Then we hastened back homeward as quickly as possible, but were overtaken before we could gain shelter anywhere. I hope you will excuse our bursting in so unceremoniously upon you. You are the young English officers who have come to assist my father, I presume?"

Courtenay and I bowed our affirmatives with all the grace we could muster.

"Poor papa!" she continued. "Are you not amused at his having taken so much, so *very* much trouble just to work out and illustrate his pet theories?"

"By no means," we hastened to assure her. "On the contrary," said I, "I regard it as an evidence of the thoroughness with which the commandant carries out all his undertakings."

"Ah, yes!" said she, evidently well pleased, "I see you understand my father. He is just the same in everything. Heavens, what a flash! Will the storm *never* cease!"

"There is no present indication of its ending," said I as I glanced through the window at the blackness outside illumined only by the quivering lightning flashes. "However, it surely *cannot* last very much longer. Meanwhile you are both wet to the skin, and I fear we are utterly destitute of means to remedy the disaster. I am afraid you will be chilled sitting there in your drenched garments; and indeed—if you will forgive me for saying so—I think that, since you cannot possibly be made more wet than you now are, you would run less risk of taking cold if you were to proceed home to the castle at once, even though you would have to walk through the storm. We would of course accompany you if you would permit us that honour."

"But," said she with a little shudder indicative of incipient chill, "you are both of you dry and comfortable."

"That is nothing," said I. "It is evident that we shall have to go through it sooner or later; so perhaps the sooner the better."

After a little more persuasion on our part and protestations on theirs our fair companions acceded to our suggestion, and we set out, I leading the van with the commandant's daughter, and Courtenay following with the foster-sister.

We stepped out briskly, so as to avert, if possible, any evil consequences of the drenching already received; and as we picked our way along the partially submerged footpath, giving the trees as wide a berth as possible for fear of the lightning which still played vividly about us, my fair companion informed me that the commandant on returning from his visit to us that morning had found an urgent summons to Cartagena awaiting him, and that he had started in obedience thereto within half an hour of its receipt, mentioning, as he hastily bade her farewell, that he could not get back in less than a fortnight at the earliest. We discussed this subject and her father's probable present whereabouts for a few minutes, and then the young lady asked me to detail to her the particulars of the mutiny on board the *Hermione*, which I did as fully as I possibly could, exciting thereby her keenest anger against the mutineers and her tenderest commiseration for the sufferers.

"Poor boy!" said she as I concluded my narrative, "what a dreadful experience for you to pass through!"

After that we seemed to get along capitally together; and in due time—an incredibly short time it seemed to me—we reached the castle without misadventure; and, parting with our charges at the chief entrance, Courtenay and I repaired to our own quarters to take a bath and don dry clothing preparatory to sitting down to dinner.

Courtenay, it seemed, had been as favourably impressed with his companion as I had been with mine; and for the next two or three days we could talk of little but the two charming girls who had burst in upon us so unexpectedly on the afternoon of that, for us, lucky thunder-storm, reiterating our hopes that the soaking had done them no harm, and wondering whether we should ever be favoured with another meeting, and, if so, when. And, indeed, trivial as the incident may seem, it exercised an important and beneficial influence on our lives after the eight months of hardship and misery unspeakable which we had so recently experienced; it gave us something fresh and pleasant to think about, and prevented our dwelling for ever upon the subject of our escape, which event seemed every day to assume a more thoroughly impossible aspect.

On the fourth day after the eventful one of the storm, and just when we were beginning to despair of ever seeing our fail acquaintances again, we were agreeably surprised by seeing them enter the workshop one afternoon, about half an hour after we had returned from luncheon.

They paused just within the threshold, and Dona Inez, glancing somewhat shyly at me, said:

"Will you allow us to come in and sit down for a little while? We should like to watch you at your work."

We replied, as coherently as our fluster of delight would allow us, that nothing would give us greater pleasure; and, flinging down our tools, Courtenay and I hastened to dust down a bench, place a tool-box in such a position that it would serve for a footstool, and in other ways arrange as far as we could to make our visitors comfortable.

Our preparations completed, the young ladies sat down, and, Courtenay and I pairing off as before, an animated conversation ensued which lasted for the remainder of the afternoon, during which I am ashamed to say that very little work was done.

If we were charmed at our first interview with these young ladies, when they appeared under all the disadvantages incidental to a condition of utter limpness of soaked and draggled clothing, I fear I should lay myself open to the charge of indulging in unbridled rhapsody were I to attempt a description of the effect produced upon our rather susceptible hearts on the occasion of this their second visit. Not that on the present occasion their charms were very greatly enhanced by the adventitious aid of dress; far from it—but the present opportunity is as good as any to describe their appearance.

Dona Inez Isolda Aurora Dolores Maria Francesca de Guzman was a little above the average height of her countrywomen, with a somewhat slender yet perfectly-proportioned figure. Her skin was dazzlingly fair; her luxuriant hair, which floated unconfined in long wavy tresses down her back, was of so deep a chestnut hue that it might easily have been mistaken for black; and her eyes—well, they sparkled and flashed so brilliantly that it was difficult for a stranger to determine their precise colour. Her features were perhaps scarcely formed with sufficient regularity to warrant her being termed strictly *beautiful*, but she was most assuredly, at least in my eyes, bewitchingly lovely. She possessed just sufficient colour in her cheeks and lips to give assurance of her being in the most perfect health, and the music of her voice and laugh was nothing short of a revelation to me. I could see that, being an only child, she had not wholly escaped being spoiled; but the slight touch of hauteur and imperiousness which was noticeable in her manner was only just sufficient to add to it another piquant charm. Like her foster-sister she was attired in white, the bodice being fastened with a white silken lace or cord, and having no sleeves, a couple of shoulder-straps trimmed with lace taking their place. That was the fashion of the country, and was doubtless adopted for the sake of coolness and comfort. Neither of the girls wore a hat or head-gear of any description, a most graceful and picturesque substitute therefore being a lace mantilla folded over the crown of the head with the ends brought down over the shoulders and knotted across the bosom. A handsome feather fan fastened to the loose silken girdle or sash about the waist was both useful and ornamental, and gave the only finishing touch required to as piquant and graceful a costume as I ever saw.

Courtenay's companion, little Eugenia Gonzalez, was a striking contrast to her foster-sister. She was a couple of inches shorter in stature, and less slender in figure; a blonde, with blue eyes and just the faintest suggestion of ruddiness in the tints of her hair; a merry, good-humoured expression of countenance; and altogether, though of humble parentage, as dainty, piquant a little beauty as anyone would wish to see.

As may be supposed, with such visitors as these to entertain, our work that afternoon did not progress very rapidly; but Courtenay and I quieted our consciences by entering into a mutual compact to exercise such increased diligence in the future as should fully make up for lost time. But when, an afternoon or two later, we overtook our fair friends in the park as we were making our way back to the workshop after our mid-day meal, and they seemed again inclined to favour us with their company, our good resolves took flight and we once more neglected our work in the enjoyment of their society.

This, however, I saw would never do. It seemed pretty evident that, being so strictly secluded within the confines of the castle demesne as these two girls were, our appearance upon the scene had assumed almost the importance of an event in their lives, and had wrought so interesting a change in the somewhat monotonous daily routine of their existence that the unsophisticated creatures had each inwardly resolved to make the most of the novelty whilst the opportunity to do so remained. And in that case our work was likely to suffer both in quality and quantity. This, I felt, ought not to be allowed. At the same time the pleasure to be derived from their society was a thing not to be lightly given up; and so the end of it all was that we prevailed upon the two girls to walk with us in the park after dinner instead of visiting the workshop. This arrangement was rendered all the more easy by the arrival of a letter from the commandant announcing his detention at Cartagena, and the probable delay of a month in the date of his return.

# Chapter Ten
## Our Flight—And Subsequent Mystification

I am fully aware *now* that in thus persuading the commandant's daughter and her companion to meet us in the park we were quite inexcusable, and that the fact that they were members of the family of a man who had very materially befriended us should have deterred us from tempting them to act in a clandestine manner such as the father of Inez would certainly have disapproved. And if we had been honourable *men* it would doubtless have done so. But we were not men, we were simply *boys*, and thought only of the pleasant companionship. I frankly plead guilty to the charge of deplorable *heedlessness*. We were as heedless as lads of our age usually are; and, thinking no harm, we at once succumbed to the temptation to neglect the task on which we were employed and to devote ourselves to the society of Inez and her companion. The consequences were, almost as a matter of course, such as an older and more experienced head would at once have foreseen—so far, at least, as Dona Inez and I were concerned—for we discovered that we were as desperately in love as ever boy and girl believed themselves to be.

But at length our rosy dream was rudely broken in upon and our souls filled with consternation by the news that in three days' time the commandant hoped to be once more at home. We knew at once what that meant. We felt instinctively that, blameless as our love for each other might be, it would meet with no sympathy from Don Luis, nor would he tolerate its continued indulgence for a moment. At first a wild hope sprang up within my heart that such might not be the case; that the fact of my being a British officer might have some weight with the haughty don. But Inez dispelled that hope in a moment.

"No," she sobbed, "you do not know my father or you would understand that nothing of that kind would influence him in the slightest degree in our favour. He loves me; oh, yes! he loves me more than anything else in the world; and I believe he would do almost anything to secure my happiness— but not *that*. My father is proud—*very* proud—of his birth and lineage; and whenever the idea of my marriage may suggest itself to him I am certain he will wish me to wed some noble of at least equal rank with himself. Of you, my poor Leo, he knows nothing save that you are a prisoner; and were you to go to him and plead our cause, not only would he refuse to listen to you, but I greatly fear his anger would fall heavily upon us both. Our only hope, dear Leo, lies in your speedily recovering your freedom, and gaining such distinction in your profession as shall justify you in asking him for my hand."

"And that is precisely what I *will* do," I exclaimed in an ecstasy of mingled hope and despair; "Courtenay and I will make good our escape before your father's return, even if we have to take to the sea in an open boat."

"And where would you go in your open boat, supposing that you could secure one, and could make good your escape from the shore?" asked Inez.

"We should head for Jamaica, and take our chance of being picked up by a friendly craft," I replied.

"And supposing that you were *not* picked up by a friendly craft?" persisted my fair questioner.

"In that case," said I rather ruefully, "we should have to push on, taking our chance as to wind and weather, and also as to our being able to hit Jamaica. It is only some twelve hundred miles or so across, and with favourable weather and a good boat we might accomplish the run in from ten days to a fortnight."

"*A fortnight! in an open boat!*" exclaimed Inez. "Oh no, Leo, that would never do! You must not attempt it; the risk is far too great. It were better that you should remain here prisoners than that you should lose your lives in any such desperate attempt as that. Let me think. You want to get to Jamaica, do you not? And to get there safely you must be conveyed there in a vessel. Ha! I have it. Eugenia, when does your brother sail?"

"In about a week hence, so he told me yesterday," was the answer.

"A week hence! that is too late," exclaimed Inez. "Send for him, and tell him to call at the castle early to-morrow morning, without fail."

I inquired who and what this brother of Eugenia's might happen to be, and was informed that he was the owner and master of a small felucca which traded regularly between La Guayra and Santiago de Cuba, and that by a lucky chance his vessel happened at that moment to be lying in the former port. This was eminently satisfactory, as I did not doubt for a moment that an arrangement might be come to whereby we could get him to run us directly across to Port Royal, we of course undertaking to insure him and his craft against capture during the run and on arrival there. There was a fair amount of prize-money due to us from the Jean Rabel affair; and even if it had not yet been awarded I felt certain that we could raise cash enough upon it to defray the expenses of the trip.

On the following morning, whilst we were at the workshop, the two girls made their appearance, accompanied by a hearty, honest-looking young fellow, who was introduced to us as Juan Gonzalez, Eugenia's brother.

In answer to our inquiries he informed us that he would be quite willing to convey us to Port Royal, and to land us safely there, in consideration of the sum of one hundred dollars, to be paid to him within six hours of our arrival, with the proviso that we should guarantee him against capture during the entire trip, the said sum of one hundred dollars to cover everything, provisions included, and to entitle us to the sole use of the felucca's cabin during the passage across. These terms we considered exceedingly reasonable, and upon inquiring of him when he would be ready to sail, and being informed that he could start at any moment, we at once closed the bargain. That matter satisfactorily settled we determined upon leaving forthwith, since there was nothing to detain us; and it was then arranged, upon Juan's suggestion, that instead of making our way into town and boarding the felucca in harbour, we should avoid all risk of capture by taking our departure from a little cove about three miles to the westward of the castle, the felucca calling off the place about nine o'clock that night and sending her boat ashore for us.

As may be supposed, the conclusion of these arrangements threw us all into a state of such excitement that it was quite impossible to think further of work. Courtenay and I therefore hastily put the workshop into something like decent order, wrote a joint note to the commandant—which we left conspicuously displayed on the workshop table—wherein we expressed our most sincere thanks for all the kindness he had shown us, and begged that he would not think too hardly of us for seizing upon an opportunity which had presented itself for our escape.

Now I am painfully aware that—keeping in view our exceeding youthfulness—any reference which it may be necessary for me to make to the mutual attachment subsisting between myself and Dona Inez is liable to be received with a certain amount of gentle ridicule and incredulity. But in deprecating any such reception of my confidential communications I will only say that we ourselves were thoroughly in earnest, and that the prospect of our speedy separation reduced us both to a condition of the keenest anguish and despair. The luncheon hour passed unheededly by, and it was not until the deepening shadows warned us of approaching night that we reluctantly turned our steps castleward, to complete the very trifling preparations necessary for the coming flight.

Courtenay, I was glad to see, was so completely heart-whole that he was in the highest possible spirits; and he did such ample justice to the dinner set before us as in some degree to make up for my own shortcomings in that respect. The meal over we dismissed Pedro for the night, and then proceeded to pack up our dilapidated uniforms in a small parcel, to assist in our identification as British officers should such prove necessary. This brought the time on to about half-past seven, at which hour we had arranged to meet again in the park, Inez having insisted—much against my wish—in accompanying us to the cove and satisfying herself as to the fact of our actual escape.

The walk to the cove was not a long one, only some three miles or so, but it occupied us a full hour and a half, and a very wretched time it proved for both of us.

We reached the place fixed upon as the point for our embarkation at nine o'clock, and a few minutes later a small wavering black blotch appeared through the intense darkness off the entrance. We heard the sound of a coil of rope being flung upon a deck, followed by a creaking of blocks; then a scraping sound and a splash such as would be caused by the launching of a boat over the low gunwale of a small craft, an indistinct murmur of voices for a moment, and then the plash of oars in the water. The distance to be traversed by the boat was not more than three or four hundred feet; I therefore had time only to breathe a hurried and inarticulate word or two of final farewell to Inez, during which I slipped on to her slender finger the only ring I possessed, when a grating sound down by the water's edge told us that the boat had grounded, and we hurried away down the beach.

The boat was a tiny cockle-shell of a craft, with only one man in her, and he was just hauling her nose up out of the water as we reached him.

"Oh, you are here, excellencies!" he exclaimed in a tone of some little surprise, I thought. "So much the better. Jump in, caballeros, and let us be off; there is another craft creeping down under the land, only a mile or so astern of us, of which el capitano feels somewhat suspicious, and he will be glad to make a good offing before she comes up."

"All right, my man!" said Courtenay as we tumbled into the stern-sheets of the small craft; "shove off as soon as you like."

The man placed his shoulder against the stem of the boat and gave her a powerful shove, scrambling in over the bows as she slid stern-foremost into the deep water, and thereby nearly capsizing all hands. However we managed, between us, to keep the boat right side up, and the man seating himself at the oars the craft was slewed round by one powerful stroke until her nose pointed seaward, and away we went, a faint clear silvery cry of "*A mas ver! A Dios!*" floating after us into the darkness, accompanied by a ghostly flutter of scarcely discernible handkerchiefs. "*A Dios!*" we shouted back as the two lingering forms vanished in the gloomy shadow of the precipitous slope leading down to the shore; and in another minute or so we shot alongside the felucca and sprang in over her low bulwarks.

"Welcome, gentlemen!" exclaimed the figure who received us. "This is better than I expected. I was afraid we should have been obliged to wait for you; and there is a craft creeping down alongshore there whose movements I do not like. I fear she has been watching us, since she can have no other business down here so close in with the land. However, here you are, so we will bear away at once, if you please; and if he wants to watch us let him follow. It will take a smart craft to overhaul the little *Pinta*. Perhaps you would like to go below at once and inspect your berths?"

We replied that we should, whereupon he ushered us aft to the small companion, and, cautioning us against the almost perpendicular ladder and the lowness of the beams, shouted to some unseen "Francisco" to show a light below and to attend generally to our wants.

We dived below and entered the small cabin; a gruff order or two on deck, accompanied by a creaking of blocks and gear bearing testimony to the fact that the *Pinta* was bearing away for the open sea, and that our escape was actually an accomplished fact.

"Francisco" proved to be a bright intelligent lad of some thirteen or fourteen years of age, jauntily rigged in a picturesque costume somewhat similar to that of the Neapolitan fishermen in "Masanielo;" but his shapely features were somewhat marred by the long white cicatrice of an ugly wound across his forehead which showed up with startling distinctness against the somewhat dusky hue of his skin. The wound must have given him a rather narrow squeak for it when it was inflicted; and I was about to question him as to the particulars concerning it when he bustled away, and in a few minutes returned with a couple of bottles of wine and the materials for an excellent supper, which he laid out upon the table and then with a graceful bow invited us to fall to. This diverted our thoughts in another direction. We seated ourselves, and in a very few minutes—I, at least, having eaten scarcely anything at dinner—were thinking of nothing beyond the satisfaction of our appetites.

Before the meal was over the little vessel began to roll and tumble about in such a lively manner as to satisfy us that she was hauling out fast from under the lee of the land, and presently we heard the sharp patter and swish of rain upon the deck overhead. It was by this time past ten o'clock; the two standing berths, one on each side of the small cabin, looked tolerably clean and inviting; so, instead of going on deck as we had originally intended, we turned in, and tried to lose remembrance of the somewhat exciting events of the day in a sound sleep.

The sun was shining brightly down through the diminutive sky-light when I awoke next morning, and the lad Francisco was busy sweeping out the cabin. Seeing me astir he inquired at what time we would choose to have breakfast, to which I answered that we would have it as soon as it could be got ready; but that in the meantime we should be glad to be supplied with water, soap, and towels. These he scuttled away to get, whilst I tumbled out of my bunk and began to dress, calling out at the same time to rouse Courtenay, who was snoring away most melodiously in his berth on the opposite side of the cabin. The little *Pinta* was lying over a good deal, and the loud gurgling rush of the water past her sides seemed to indicate that she was travelling through it at a fairish speed, whilst the long regular heel to leeward, the steady buoyant soaring motion of the little vessel, with the succeeding recovery and weather-roll and rapid drop as she settled away down into the trough, informed us that we were favoured with a fresh breeze, accompanied by quite a respectable beam-sea. With the exception of an occasional footstep, or a word or two from the vicinity of the binnacle, everything, save for the singing of the wind in the rigging and the hissing of the surges past our lee side, was quiet enough on deck; but below Courtenay and I could scarcely hear each other speak for the noise and clatter; bulk-heads creaking, the crockery in the pantry rattling, the weapons in the rack abaft the table clanking and jarring, and Heaven knows how many other sounds beside.

By the way, those same weapons had attracted my notice on the previous evening, though my thoughts were at the time so much preoccupied with other things that I made no remark about them. Now, however, their persistent clank and clatter forced them so prominently upon our attention that we both burst simultaneously into some exclamation respecting the incongruity of so small a craft being so well provided with arms. So well-furnished indeed was the *Pinta* in this respect that anyone entering her cabin might naturally have supposed himself to have been on board a privateer, or something worse. In the first place there was a rack stretching right athwart the aftermost bulkhead, in which were stacked a dozen good serviceable-looking muskets, their barrels brightly polished, the stocks carefully oiled,

The Rover's Secret | 93

and new flints in every one of the locks. These were flanked on each side by a sheaf of some half a dozen boarding-pikes, the points of which had been ground almost to the sharpness of a needle. Above the muskets, forming a star-shaped trophy, which occupied almost the whole remaining surface of the bulkhead, were a dozen brace of sturdy pistols, their muzzles pointing inward, whilst their butts, all turned one way, formed the outer extremities of the star-rays. These, too, were as bright and clean as it was possible for them to be; and I noticed that, fancifully as they were arranged, they were merely suspended from nails, from which they could be snatched at a moment's notice. And, finally, over each stand of pikes was arranged another star formed of sheathed cutlasses, with belts and cartridge-pouches attached, all ready, in short, for instant service.

"I cannot for the life of me imagine why our friend Juan should arm his cock-boat like this," I remarked; "why, there must be enough weapons here for twice the number of men the *Pinta* carries."

"Who can tell!" returned Courtenay. "For my part I fancy all Spaniards have very lax notions of commercial morality, and Master Juan may perhaps amuse himself, as opportunity offers or when times are bad, with a little quiet smuggling. Although, even in such a case," he continued, "I can scarcely see the need for such a formidable armoury; for I should hardly suspect him of the inclination to undertake the risk of running a cargo worth fighting for. Well, shall we go on deck and take a look round before sitting down to breakfast?"

"By all means," said I; and we were in the very act of ascending the companion-ladder when Francisco made his appearance at its head, coming down stern-foremost, with a coffee-pot in one hand and a smoking dish of broiled fish in the other, so we had to give way for him or run an imminent risk of being scalded.

"El capitano kisses your hands, excellencies," said the lad, as he laid his double burden on the table, "and he hopes you have both slept well."

"Admirably," I answered, adding, as I looked at the appetising dish which sent up its grateful odours from the table, "Put out another plate, knife and fork, and so on; and tell 'el capitano' that we shall be very pleased if he will join us at breakfast."

The lad stared at us in mute astonishment for a moment, flushing like a bashful girl meanwhile. Then, recovering himself, he muttered: "I will tell him, gentlemen; he will feel himself highly honoured."

"That is all right," laughed Courtenay, as the lad slid up the companion; "a very right and proper feeling, though I scarcely know why he should experience it."

A minute later a heavy tramp was audible coming along the deck. The sunlight streaming down through the open companion suffered a temporary eclipse; a pair of legs, encased in enormous sea-boots, presented themselves to our admiring gaze, and finally a huge fellow of fully six feet in height, and broad in proportion, came towards us, bowing and stooping in the most awkward manner, partly by way of salutation and partly to avoid striking his head against the low deck-beams. He was dark-complexioned, bushy whiskered, with keen restless black eyes, and a shock of ebon hair very imperfectly concealed by a black-and-red-striped fisherman's cap of knitted worsted, which he removed deferentially the moment his eye fell upon us. He wore large gold ear-rings in his ears, and was attired in a thick dreadnought jacket over a black-and-red-striped shirt, which was confined about his waist by a broad leather belt, to which was attached a sheath-knife of most formidable dimensions. The skirts of the shirt were worn *outside* his trousers, so that his *tout ensemble* was exactly that of a dashing pirate or smuggler bold, as that interesting individual is presented on the boards of a third-rate transpontine theatre of the present day. He was a picturesque-looking person enough, *but he certainly was not Juan Gonzalez*, to whom he bore no more resemblance than I did.

Courtenay and I glanced at each other in surprise, but neither of us said a word.

"*Muchisimos gracias* for your honoured invitation, excellencies," said our friend, again bowing awkwardly, as he slid into a seat at the head of the table, leaving Courtenay and me to stow ourselves on the lockers, one on each side of him. "I am gratified to learn from Francisco that you rested soundly during the night I was afraid the motion of the felucca would prove disagreeable to you. We have had a fine breeze from the eastward all night, and La Guayra is now nearly a hundred miles astern of us."

"That is good news," I remarked. "But why should you have anticipated any evil results to us from the motion of the craft? Are you not aware that we are pretty well seasoned sailors?"

"No," said our companion; "I was not aware of it. When I urged the captain-general to send naval officers I understood him to say that he had none available for the service, but that he would send two officers of marines. I did not like his proposal, and I am very glad to find that he has thought better of it. What can a soldier—even though he be a marine—know about soundings, and bearings, and sea-marks? And the entrance to the place is very difficult indeed, as you will see, gentlemen, when we come to it."

"What in the world is the man talking about?" thought I, glancing across the table at Courtenay to see what he thought of it. That irrepressible young gentleman elevated his eyebrows inquiringly, tipped me a wink of preternatural significance with his left eye—our host was sitting on Courtenay's starboard hand—and then devoted himself most assiduously to the red snapper off which he was breakfasting.

"How long do you reckon it will take us to make the run?" I asked, with the view of maintaining the conversation rather than because of my comprehension of it.

"Well," said our picturesque friend, "let me reckon. To-day is Thursday. If this breeze holds steady we ought to be off Cape Irois about daybreak next Wednesday morning. Then, unless the wind heads us, we may hope to weather Cape Maysi about sunset the same day; after which we may expect to have the breeze well on our starboard quarter, which will enable us to complete the run in good time to pass through the Barcos Channel and reach our anchorage before nightfall on the following Friday evening."

"Ah!" remarked Courtenay, as coolly as though he fully understood the whole drift of this singular conversation, "a little over a week, if the weather remains favourable. When you say that the entrance is difficult, do you refer to the Barcos Channel more particularly or to—?"

"Oh no!" was the reply; "that is easy enough—for a small vessel of light draught, that is to say—although there are one or two awkward places there which I will point out to you; but it is the entrance to the lagoon itself which will give you the most trouble."

"Precisely; that is what we have been given to understand," said Courtenay, addressing himself to us both. "I presume you have a chart of the place?"

"No," said our friend; "the place has never yet been surveyed, and Giuseppe will not permit anyone to sound anywhere within the entrance to the lagoon. I told the captain-general this when he asked me the same question. Did he not mention this to you?"

"No, he did not," said Courtenay, with all the seriousness imaginable; "he never said a word to me about it. Did he mention it to you?" with a glance across the table at me.

"Not a word," said I. "I suppose he forgot it in his hurry. You must understand," I continued, turning to the unknown one, "that so far as *we* are concerned, this business has been arranged in the most hurried manner, and we must look to you for enlightenment upon any points which the captain-general may have omitted to explain to us."

"Oh, yes! assuredly, señors, assuredly," was the satisfactory reply. "It is part of my bargain, you know."

"Quite so," chimed in Courtenay. "And if, as my friend and I talk the matter over, we happen to come to something which is not altogether clear, we will not fail to apply to you. By the by, do you happen to have such a thing as a decent cigar on board this smart little felucca of yours?"

Our interlocutor glanced from one to the other of us with a merry twinkle in his eye, as though Courtenay's innocent inquiry veiled the best joke he had heard for a long time.

"A decent cigar!" said he. "Ha! ha! if I have not, then I don't know where else you should look for one, gentlemen. Allow me." And, pushing past me to the after part of the locker, he raised a lid and produced a box of weeds which he laid upon the table. Then, with an awkward bow, he said, as he made for the companion-ladder:

"If you have finished breakfast, gentlemen, I will send Francisco down to clear the table."

# Chapter Eleven
## Captain Carera imparts some interesting Information

Not a word was said by either of us until the unknown one had emerged from the companion and removed himself well out of ear-shot. Then, as Courtenay pushed the cigar-box across the table to me, after selecting a weed for himself, he looked me in the face and, with a mischievous twinkle in his eye, remarked:

"Well, Lascelles, what is your interpretation of this riddle? What is the character of this felucca? Who and what is her skipper? And whither are we bound?"

"Hush!" said I, "here comes the boy. We shall find ourselves in an exceedingly awkward fix unless we keep a very bright lookout."

Here Francisco entered the cabin and began to clear away the wreck of the breakfast.

"Why, Francisco, my lad, you look pale. You surely do not feel sea-sick, do you?" exclaimed Courtenay.

"Sea-sick! oh, no!" said the lad. "I got over all that long ago."

"Ah, indeed!" remarked my fellow-mid in his usual off-hand manner. "And, pray, what may 'long ago' mean? Last voyage, or the voyage before—three months ago—six months—a year?"

"More nearly two years ago, señor. I shall have been to sea two years come next month," was the reply.

"Two years, eh! Why, you are a perfect veteran, a regular old sea-dog, Francisco," continued Courtenay as he exhaled a wreath of pale-blue smoke from his pursed-up lips and watched it go curling in fantastic wreaths up through the open sky-light. "And have you been all that time in the *Pinta*?"

"Yes, señor, all that time. Captain Carera is my uncle, you know. He adopted me when my mother died, and has promised to make a sailor of me."

"Ah! very good of him; very good, indeed," went on Courtenay. "A very worthy fellow that uncle of yours, Francisco. And has the *Pinta* been engaged in the same trade ever since you joined her?"

"The same trade, señor? I—I—"

"There, don't be alarmed at my question, my lad," interrupted Courtenay. "You need not answer it unless you choose, you know; but there is no occasion for secrecy with *us*. You understand that, do you not?"

"Well, I don't know, I am sure, excellency. I suppose it is all right, however, or you would not be here, so I do not mind answering. We *have* been engaged in the same trade—for the most part—ever since I joined the *Pinta*."

"And a pretty profitable business your uncle must have found it," remarked Courtenay.

"I don't know so much about that, señor," was the reply. "It *used* to be profitable enough at first, I believe, when el capitano had it all in his own hands. But now that Giuseppe has admitted other traders, we not only have to pay higher prices for the goods, but we also have to take our turn with others for a cargo. Then, too, Giuseppe has not been so very fortunate of late; the British cruisers have given him a great deal of trouble."

"Ah, yes, they are a pestilent lot, those British—always thrusting their noses into other people's business!" agreed my unabashed chum. "Well," he continued to me, "shall we go on deck and take a look round? Uncommonly good cigars these of your uncle's, Francisco. Leave the box on the table, my lad, will ye?"

On reaching the deck we were now, for the first time, able to take particular note of the vessel on board which we, by some inexplicable blunder, thus found ourselves—for that a blunder had been perpetrated by somebody we now fully realised. The craft proved to be a sturdy little felucca of some sixty tons or so; very shallow and very beamy in proportion to her length; stoutly built, with high quarters, and low but widely-flaring bows, which tossed the seas aside in fine style and enabled her to thrash along with perfectly dry decks. She was rigged with a single stout, stumpy mast, raking well forward, upon which was set—by means of an immense yard of bamboos "fished" together, and twice the length of the craft herself—an enormous lateen or triangular sail, the tack of which consisted of a stout rope leading from the fore-end of the yard to a ring-bolt sunk into the deck just forward of the mast, whilst the sheet travelled upon an iron hawse well secured to the taffrail. There were five hands on deck when we made our appearance, namely, the skipper and the helmsman—who were having a quiet chat together—and three men in the waist, on the weather side of the deck, who were busy patching a sail. The weather was gloriously fine, with scarcely a cloud to be seen in the clear sapphire vault overhead; and a fresh cool breeze from about east-north-east was ruffling up the white-caps to windward, straining at the huge sail until the yard bent like a fishing-rod, and careening the gallant little craft to her covering-board, whilst it drove her along at the rate of a good honest nine knots in the hour. There was no other sail anywhere in sight, nor indeed anything to distract attention from the little vessel herself, save the shoals of flying-fish which now and then sparkled out from under our forefoot and went skimming away through the air to leeward, until they vanished with a flash, only to reappear, perhaps, next moment, with their inveterate foe, a dolphin, in hot pursuit. The moment we showed ourselves above the companion the skipper rose to his feet—he had been sitting cross-legged on the deck, under the weather bulwarks—and joined us, evidently under the impression that it was an essential part of his duty to make himself agreeable. He made some commonplace remark about the weather, to which we both vouchsafed a ready and gracious response, very fully realising by this time the peculiarity and perilous nature of our position on board the felucca—a position from which it was, of course, utterly impossible for us then to effect a retreat— and being especially anxious not only to avert any possibility of a suspicion as to our *bona fides*, but also to extract such further hints as might tend to the elucidation of that position. For some time the conversation was of a general and utterly unimportant character; at length, however, Carera, evidently reverting to the topic which was uppermost in his mind, remarked:

"I have thought it best, señors, to mention to Manuel, my mate there," nodding his head toward the helmsman, "and the rest of the hands, the fact that you are both seamen, and they are as pleased as I was to hear it. It has made matters much easier for us all round, and very much less dangerous for you; indeed, Manuel thinks that if you will only consent to act as part of the crew whilst we are in harbour there, and rig accordingly, neither Giuseppe nor any of his people will suspect anything, and you will thus be able to freely look about you and make such observations as will enable you to subsequently carry out your part of the scheme with success. If it can only be carried through it will make all our fortunes, for they must have doubloons stored away by the caskful by this time. Why, I am taking across two hundred doubloons this time to trade with, and I have never taken less in any one of my trips."

"And how many trips do you consider you have made altogether?" asked Courtenay.

"Oh, well, let me see—not less than sixty, I should suppose," was the answer.

"Sixty times two hundred gives twelve thousand. Twelve thousand doubloons—that is a goodly sum indeed," murmured I.

"Yes," answered Carera; "and to that you must add what the other traders have taken across, which will perhaps amount to at least as much more. And there is also the specie which he has captured, and which of course he has had no need to barter away."

"Whew!" I involuntarily whistled, a great light suddenly bursting in upon my hitherto darkened understanding. Courtenay frowned a warning to me, and I hastened on to say: "That will be a big haul, certainly. Why, Carera, you will be able to retire from the sea altogether, and live like a gentleman for the rest of your days."

"Yes," he responded somewhat gloomily, "if the secret is well kept. If not—if it ever gets abroad that any of us on board here have been the means of—of—well, of betraying Giuseppe and his gang, our lives will not be worth a maravedi; for were all hands over there,"—nodding ahead—"to be taken, there would still be the traders to reckon with. We shall completely spoil their game, you know, señors, and where there is so much money to be made out of it they would never forgive us."

"Pooh!" exclaimed Courtenay reassuringly, "have no fear about that; they will never get to know how the thing has happened. If you can only depend upon your own people keeping close you may rely upon *our* so managing affairs that no suspicion shall rest upon you."

"I hope so—I fervently hope so!" murmured Carera anxiously. "Riches would be of little value if one had to go about in constant dread of the assassin's knife."

We gave a cordial affirmation to this sentiment, and then noticing that our worthy and most estimable skipper seemed somewhat indisposed for further conversation just then, Courtenay and I retired to the cabin to talk matters over, having at length extracted sufficient information to show us pretty nearly how the land lay.

On getting below Master Courtenay's first act was to carefully select another cigar from the box on the table, cut off the point with mathematical regularity, light the weed, and then push the box over to me with the cheerful invitation:

"Help yourself, old fellow. Really superb weeds these—wonder what was the name of the ship these were taken out of, eh?"

Then he seated himself upon the lockers, planted his elbows squarely on the table, rested his chin in the palms of his hands, and, in this by no means elegant attitude, puffed a long thin cloud of smoke at me. He intently watched the tiny wreath for a moment or two, and then broke ground by saying:

"Well, Lascelles, old boy, do you happen to know whereabouts we are?"

"Certainly," I answered, in perfectly good faith; "we are now just about one hundred and twenty miles to the northward and westward of La Guayra."

"Precisely. And we are—also—in—the—centre—of—a—hobble!" retorted the lively youth, nodding his head impressively at every word to give it additional emphasis. "In the centre of a hobble—that's where you and I happen to be at the present moment," he continued more soberly. "Let us look at the facts of the case. To start with, we are manifestly on board the wrong ship. The crew of that ship, or *this* ship—it is all the same in the present case—take us to be, not two unfortunate fugitive British midshipmen yearning to return to their duty, but two officers of the Spanish navy told off by that no doubt most respectable old gentleman—whose acquaintance I regret I have not yet had the honour of making—the captain-general, to execute a certain duty which we may perhaps make a rough guess at, but as to the precise nature of which we are at present without any definite information. Do you agree with me so far?"

"Yes," said I. "But why can't you discuss the matter seriously? It may prove serious enough for us both at any moment, Heaven knows!"

"True for you, O lovelorn youth with the solemn visage. But wherefore this emotion? *Becoje tu heno mientras que el sol luciere* is as sound a bit of wisdom as any that I have happened to pick up during our exceedingly pleasant sojourn at La Guayra. 'Make hay whilst the sun shines!'—make the most of your opportunities—have all the fun you can during your enforced absence from the jurisdiction of the first luff—is a proverb which ought to command the most profound respect of every British midshipman; and I am surprised at you, Lascelles, and disappointed in you, that you so little endeavour to live up to it," remarked Courtenay. "However," he resumed, "there is a certain glimmering of truth in what you say; this hobble—I like the word 'hobble,' don't you, so expressive, eh?—this hobble, then, in the centre of which we find ourselves, may prove a serious enough matter for us both at any moment, so let us go carefully over the ground and ascertain exactly how we stand. To start once more. I suppose you are prepared to accede to my proposition before stated, that we have by some unaccountable mistake blundered on board the wrong craft; and that on board her we have, in the same unaccountable way, established in our two respectable selves a most interesting case of mistaken identity, eh?"

"Yes," said I, "I agree with you there. Go on," seeing that it was quite hopeless to think of diverting him from his ridiculous mood.

"That is all right," resumed Courtenay. "Now, judging from the fragmentary information we have been able to acquire thus far in our interesting conversations with that amiable old traitor, Carera, on deck there, I imagine our position to be this. We are two youthful but intelligent Spanish naval officers commissioned by the captain-general at La Guayra to accompany Carera on a little trading voyage he is making to certain lagoons lying somewhere inside the Barcos Channel. Now where *is* the Barcos Channel? Do you know?"

"Haven't the slightest idea, beyond the exceedingly hazy one I have been able to form from what Carera said," answered I.

"Neither have I," acknowledged Courtenay. "But I think we know enough to identify its position very nearly. If I understood our friend aright we are now heading for Cape Irois, the most westerly point of Saint Domingo. From thence he intends to shape a course for Cape Maysi, which we both know to be the easternmost point of Cuba. Then, having weathered that point, he informed us that we might expect to have the wind well on our starboard quarter, which—knowing as we do that the prevailing wind in that latitude is from about east-north-east—means that we shall be steering a westerly course, or say from west to north-west. That would take us up along the northern coast of Cuba. Now, how long did you understand Carera to say it would take us to complete the run to the Barcos Channel?"

"Something like forty-eight hours," I replied.

"Exactly," acquiesced Courtenay. "That was what I understood. Now I should say that, with the wind on her quarter, this little hooker may be expected to run about ten knots per hour, which, for forty-eight hours, gives a run of four hundred and eighty miles, at which distance, there or thereabouts, from Cape Maysi, I imagine the Barcos Channel to be. That, then, seems to indicate approximately the locality of the spot to which we are bound. Do you agree with me?"

"I do," said I. "That is precisely how I have reasoned it out in my own mind."

"That is well," resumed Courtenay. "Now, why are we going there? Manifestly to assist in the betrayal of one Giuseppe something—I don't happen to know his other name. From a hint dropped by Carera I have formed the opinion that this Giuseppe must be an industrious, hard-working, and, withal, somewhat canny gentleman of the piratical profession; a man who seems to have made the business pay pretty well, too, for does not our friend on deck estimate that he has accumulated the tidy little sum of close upon twenty-five thousand doubloons? Now, however, that fickle goddess, Fortuna, appears to have withdrawn her smiles from him. Those pestilent British cruisers are interfering with him, and we know that when *they* meddle with a business of that kind it means simple ruination for the honest people who are trying to make a livelihood out of it; consequently, our amigo Carera is no longer able to depend upon finding a rich cargo, at a low figure for cash, awaiting him at Giuseppe's snug little stronghold. Carera, the honest and faithful, therefore proposes to become virtuous. He has, doubtless, of late experienced certain qualms of conscience respecting the trade he is at present engaged in, and he has made up his mind to abandon it. He has also resolved to reform his friend Giuseppe; and, in order that the reformation of that estimable person may be made thoroughly effectual, he has undertaken—for a consideration, most probably a share of the plunder—to point out to us, the captain-general's deputies, the various rocks, shoals, and other impediments which obstruct the fairway to the pirates' anchorage, and to indicate the several sea-marks which will enable us to safely and successfully pilot an expedition into such a position as will enable it to knock Giuseppe's stronghold into a cocked hat. How does that accord with your view of the situation?"

"Yes," said I, "I think you are about right. That is pretty much the idea I have formed of it."

"Good, again!" ejaculated Courtenay. "Let us go a little further. We now come to the 'hobble,' or dilemma, if you prefer the latter word, in which we find ourselves. The unfortunate hitch in this business, as I look at it, is this. It so happens that we are *not* the captain-general's deputies, but two British midshipmen, and we want to go, not to the Barcos Channel, but to Port Royal. How are we to get to the latter place?"

"That is a question which will demand our most serious consideration; but we need not worry about it for a few days," I replied. "And, as to our not wanting to go to the Barcos Channel, why should we not want to go there?"

"Why, because we want to go to Port Royal instead, I suppose. What d'ye mean, Lascelles?—hang it, man, I—what are you driving at?" stammered Courtenay, thoroughly taken aback.

"Ah!" said I, with a certain air of triumph, I am afraid, "I see that my plan has not yet dawned upon your benighted understanding. What is to prevent our going to this Barcos Channel, seeing everything that is to be seen there, and then making our way to Port Royal—the difficulty as to that will be no greater then than it is now—and reporting the whole affair to the admiral, who will doubtless send an expedition on his own account, and send us with it as a reward for our—"

"That will do," interrupted Courtenay enthusiastically. "By George, Lascelles, you are a trump! a genius! a—a—in fact I don't know what you are not, in the line of 'superior attainments,' as my schoolmaster used to say. And I—what a *consummate* idiot I must have been not to think of it too! I say, old fellow, would you be so kind and obliging as to kick me *hard* once or twice. No? Well, never mind; I daresay somebody else will, sooner or later, so I will excuse you. But, I say, Lascelles," he continued, as serious now as myself, "it is an awful risky thing to do; do you think we have nerve and—and—*impudence* enough to carry it through without being found out? We are only two against ten, you know, on board here; and if we are detected it will be a sure case of,"—and he drew his hand suggestively across his throat—"eh?"

"No doubt of that, I think," said I. "But why should we be found out? I feel as though my nerve would prove quite equal to the task; and as for impudence, you have enough and to spare for both of us."

"All right, then," said he, "we'll chance it; and there's my hand upon it, Lascelles. You make whatever plans you may consider necessary, and I'll back you up through thick and thin. A man can but die once; and if we fail in this we shall at least have the consolation of feeling that we fell whilst doing our duty—for there can be no mistake about its being our duty to bring about the destruction of that gang of pirates who, I now feel convinced, are lurking among those lagoons inside the Barcos Channel."

"Yes," said I, "I think there can be no doubt about that. And now, having arrived at a clear understanding as to what we are about to do, I think it is all plain sailing up to the time of our arrival in those lagoons. We must carefully note every particular which Carera may point out to us, and make a sort of chart, if possible, wherewith to refresh our memories; after which it only remains for us to find our way to Port Royal; and *that*, it seems to me, is the only item in our programme which is likely to give us any very serious difficulty."

This closed the discussion for the time being, and we went on deck, where Carera once more obsequiously joined us, much to our disgust; for it seemed probable that, if this sort of thing was to continue, we should find the fellow far too attentive to suit our ulterior plans. We, however, made the best of the matter, and, finding that his thoughts were wholly occupied with the trip and its object, we simply let him talk about it to his heart's content, merely interjecting a remark here and there with the object of directing his conversation into such channels as would afford us the information in which we still happened to be deficient. In this way we gradually—and with some little skill, we flattered ourselves—acquired full particulars of the plot in the carrying out of which we were supposed to be important agents, and which turned out to be very much the sort of thing we had already pictured to ourselves. The man Giuseppe was, we found, an Italian, who had made his appearance in West Indian waters some five or six years previously, first in the character of a slaver, and afterwards as an avowed pirate. He was, according to Carera's account, a man of exceptional daring, as wily as a fox, and a thorough seaman; and these excellent qualities had not only raised him to the position of head or chief of the powerful gang with whose fortunes he had identified himself, but had also enabled him to carry on his nefarious business so successfully that he had gradually acquired an almost fabulous amount of booty, and had at the same time gained for himself—at all events among the Spaniards—the somewhat sensational title of "The Terror of the Caribbean Sea." He had established a sort of head-quarters for himself in a snug spot at the head of the Conconil lagoons, where he had erected buildings for the accommodation of his entire gang—part of which always remained on shore to look after the place—and where he had gradually surrounded himself with every convenience for repairing and refitting his craft. It was to this secluded, and indeed almost unknown spot, that he was in the habit of running for shelter when hard pressed by the cruisers who were always on the lookout for him; and, from Carera's description of the difficulties of the navigation, it would seem almost impossible to devise or hit upon a place better suited for such a purpose. It was here, also, that he first stored his plunder, and afterwards bartered it for gold or such necessaries as he might happen to require, with the three or four favoured individuals who, with the most extreme precaution, he had invited to trade with him. And it was the key to the navigation of these lagoons and their approaches which Carera had undertaken to sell to the Spanish authorities in consideration of his receiving, as the price of his treachery, one-half the amount of the captured spoil.

For the remainder of that day our minds were chiefly occupied with the question of how, after our visit to the Conconil lagoons, we were to make our way to Port Royal; and the more carefully we considered the question the more numerous and insurmountable appeared to be the difficulties in our way. It was not as though we were going to touch at a civilised port; in that case, if it came to the worst, we might have run away from our craft and taken our chance of getting another to suit us. But this, under the circumstances, was out of the question. Moreover, directly we began to consider the matter, it seemed imperative that the *Pinta* and her entire crew should be detained at least until our expedition should have sailed, otherwise Carera, finding himself duped, might endeavour to make the best of a bad matter by hurrying off to warn Giuseppe of the possibility of our beating up his quarters. The situation eventually resolved itself into this: that whereas, on the completion of our ostensible trading errand, the *Pinta* would, in the ordinary course of events, return to La Guayra, taking us with her—when on her arrival the whole fiasco would come to light and the least misfortune we might expect would be a return to our loathsome prison quarters—it was necessary for the success of our plan that the craft and her crew should, by some means or other, find their way to Royal Port. How was the affair to be managed? The outlines of a scheme at length arranged themselves in my mind; and, although it was of so desperate a character that we agreed it was almost impossible that we should be able to carry it through, we nevertheless took immediate steps to further its accomplishment. It was not much that we could do just then; all that was possible for us was to assume extreme pleasure at being allowed to steer the little craft; and we so managed affairs that in the course of a few days it came to be an understood thing among the hands that whenever either of them happened to be too lazy to take his "trick" at the tiller he could always get relief by appealing to one or the other of us—if we happened to be on deck at the time.

The breeze continued to hold from the eastward; but as we drew over toward the coast of Saint Domingo it softened down a trifle; so that, on our arrival off Cape Irois, we found ourselves just about twelve hours behind the time reckoned on by Carera. That, however, was a matter of no very great moment, being rather an advantage than otherwise, since it enabled us to slip across the Windward Channel with less risk of being sighted and overhauled by a British cruiser, an incident which—now that Courtenay and I had quite made up our minds to go through with the adventure—we were folly as anxious as any of the *Pinta's* regular crew to avoid. We were fortunate enough to make the passage without molestation, though not wholly without an alarm, for a large ship was made out, about the end of the middle watch, coming down before the wind and heading right for us, with a whole cloud of flying kites aloft and studding-sails set on both sides. She proved, however, to be a merchantman, apparently British; and, from the course she was steering, we judged her to be bound to Kingston. She swept magnificently across our stern at a distance of about a couple of miles; and in little more than an hour from the time of our first sighting her she was hull-down again upon our larboard quarter.

With sunrise we found ourselves hauling in under the high land about Cape Maysi; and here we ran into the calm belt dividing the land and sea-breezes, and lay for an hour rolling gunwale under, our great sail flapping noisily and sending the dew pattering down on deck in regular showers with every roll of the little vessel, whilst the huge yard swayed and creaked aloft, tugging at the stumpy mast and tautening out the standing rigging alternately to port and starboard with such violence that I momentarily expected to see the whole affair go toppling over the side. "Hold on, good rope-yarns!" was now the cry; and they *did* hold on, fortunately, though, during that hour of calm, there was more noise aloft than I had ever before heard on board a vessel. At length the sea-breeze came creeping down to us; a cat's-paw filled the lofty tapering sail, and passed, causing the canvas to flap heavily ere it filled to the next. Another flap; then the sail swelled out gently and "went to sleep," the nimble little hooker turned her saucy nose into the wind's eye; a few bubbles drifted past her side as she gathered way, a long smooth ripple trailed out on each side of her sharp bows, then she heeled gracefully over to larboard as the languid breeze freshened upon us, and presently down it came, half a gale of wind, burying us half bulwark deep and making everything crack again as the boat gathered way and darted off like a startled dolphin. And here Carera was within an ace of making a mess of the whole business; for whilst we had been tumbling about becalmed a current had got hold of us and had set us so close in with the land that whilst rounding the point we actually passed *through* the breakers beating on the reef; and I am convinced that had we been a couple of fathoms further to leeward the hooker would have laid her bones there. However, the danger was come and gone in less than a minute; it was the extreme point of the reef we had grazed so very closely, and, once past it, we had a clear sea ahead and were out of the reach of all further danger. It was Courtenay, however, who actually saved the felucca; for at the supreme moment when the little craft plunged into the breakers, and when, if ever, there was the utmost need for coolness and self-possession, what must all hands do but plump down upon their knees, calling upon Saint Antonio and Heaven knows how many other saints to come and help them, Carera himself being one of the foremost to do so, abandoning the tiller meanwhile, and leaving the vessel to take care of herself, at the very moment of all others when she most needed looking after. She of course shot into the wind's eye in an instant, and in another minute the craft would have been on the rocks, stern-foremost, and beating her bottom in, had not Courtenay—who happened to be standing close by—sprung to the tiller and jammed it hard a-weather, thus causing her to pay off and forge ahead before losing steerage-way altogether.

Once fairly clear of the point, Carera put his helm up, and away we went, with a flowing sheet, upon a north-west by west course; arriving off Mangle Point about noon. From thence we began to haul somewhat off from the land, the wind drawing further aft and freshening somewhat as we did so; so that by sunset the lively little craft had brought Lucrecia Point fairly on her larboard beam. As the sun went down the wind manifested a disposition to drop; and for a couple of hours we crept along at a speed of scarcely five knots; but it breezed up again just after the first watch came on deck; and by two bells we were smoking through it faster than I had ever before seen the craft travel. In accordance with the plan which Courtenay and I had arranged, we took the tiller between us during the whole of the first watch, the two hands whose places we had taken coolly going below and turning in. When the watch was called at midnight we felt that we had done enough for our purpose, so we retired below and spent the remainder of the night in our bunks.

# Chapter Twelve
# A Narrow Escape

At daybreak next morning we were awakened by a terrific hubbub overhead, and going on deck to ascertain what was the matter we found that the felucca, having been allowed to draw in too close with the land during the night, was becalmed off Guajaba Island, whilst a sail, some nine miles distant in the offing—evidently a British man-of-war from the cut of her canvas, and apparently a frigate from her size—was heading straight for us, close-hauled on the larboard tack, with a rattling breeze, as we could see by the way she was laying over to it and the rapidity with which her sails rose above the horizon. There could be no doubt that they had seen us with the first approach of daylight and were determined to give us an overhaul, hence the confusion which had aroused us from our peaceful slumbers. It was laughable to witness the agonised dismay with which the Spaniards viewed the approach of this craft, and to listen to the prayers, vows, and maledictions which issued indiscriminately from their lips as she swept relentlessly down toward us. They anticipated nothing less than the capture and destruction of the felucca, and the detention of themselves as prisoners, which catastrophe, bad enough in itself as it must have appeared to them, was doubtless rendered infinitely more disagreeable by the reflection that to this mishap must be added the total collapse of their pretty little plan for the betrayal of their friends the pirates, and the subsequent division of the spoil. And even to us the prospect was by no means inviting. It was true that here was a chance for us to rejoin our own countrymen, and so escape from the dilemma in which we foresaw that we should be placed after leaving the Conconil lagoons; but we were not altogether without hopes that we might in any case be able to escape from that dilemma; and having resolved to go through with the adventure we were now by no means disposed to have it nipped in the bud. We were consequently quite as averse to a visit from the frigate as was Carera himself, and we at once set our wits to work to see if it might not be possible to devise some means of escape. The breeze was blowing fresh to within a mile of where we lay, and I felt convinced that the frigate, with the way she had on her, would shoot far enough ahead, even after she had entered the calm belt, to reach us with her guns; it was therefore evident that whatever was to be done would have to be done quickly, if it was to be of any use at all. I looked around and saw, by the colour of the water, that there was a shoal at no great distance inshore of us. I called Carera aft and said to him:

"Look here, Carera, do you happen to know this coast pretty well?"

"Every inch of it, señor," was the reply.

"I see there is shoal water over there," said I, indicating the direction with a nod of the head. "Now, what is to hinder you from rigging out your sweeps and sweeping the felucca into such shallow water as will prevent the frigate yonder from approaching you near enough to reach you with her guns? The *Pinta* is in light trim, and with all hands at the sweeps you ought to be able to move her pretty smartly through the water. And even should the frigate send her boats after us, we might be able to keep out of their way until the breeze comes."

"Excellent, señor!" he exclaimed rapturously. "I had never thought of that. Ah, it is you gentlemen of the navy who, after all, have the ideas! Out sweeps, forward there!" he continued; "we will escape that accursed Englishman yet."

The crew, aroused by the hopeful tone in which Carera spoke, scrambled up off their knees, and rigging out the sweeps soon had the little craft heading direct for the shore and moving through the water at the rate of some four knots. The frigate seeing this hoisted her ensign and fired a gun as a signal for us to heave to, of which we took not the slightest notice. I placed myself at the tiller, Carera took up a position on the stem-head, conning the felucca, and Courtenay devoted all his energies to the encouragement of the men as they laboured at the sweeps. Meanwhile, the breeze was gradually creeping nearer to us every minute, which, whilst an advantage in so far as it lessened the time during which the men would have to toil at the sweeps, was more than counterbalanced by the disagreeable fact that it would enable the frigate to approach so much the nearer to us before she in her turn became becalmed.

At length the noble craft shot across the outer boundary of the calm belt, and the instant that her canvas flapped to the masts her helm was gently ported until she headed straight for us, when another gun was fired; and before the smoke had cleared away she had swept round until her whole broadside—numbering eighteen guns—was bearing upon us.

"Now," shouted Courtenay, "look out for squalls!"

The words had scarcely left his lips when *bang*! went another gun, and we saw the shot come skipping and ricochetting across the glassy surface of the water straight toward us, ploughing up long steamy jets of spray at every bound, and finally, with a skurrying splash, disappearing about a dozen yards astern of us. After this there was a pause of about half a minute, apparently to see whether we were really foolhardy enough to persist in attempting our escape—and also, probably, to give the muzzles of their guns a little more elevation—when, seeing that the sweeps were still kept steadily going, she let fly her whole broadside at us with a rattling crash, which caused the Spaniards with one accord to let go their hold upon the sweeps and drop flat on their faces on the deck. Another moment and the shot came hurtling about us, some overhead and a very fair dose on each side of the little craft, so close too that the spray flashed in over the deck in a regular shower, whilst one shot came crashing in through the taffrail, flying close past me where I was standing at the tiller, smashing through the head of the companion and then flying out over the bows, passing through the sail on its way and missing Carera's head by a hair's-breadth.

"Eighteen-pounders, by the powers!" ejaculated Courtenay, turning to me. "A narrow squeak that for you, old boy? Now, then, my hearties," to the Spaniards, "tail on to those sweeps again, and look sharp about it. Remember, if we are caught away goes your chance of making a fortune out of friend Giuseppe yonder."

This suggestion aroused anew their courage, or their cupidity, and with a shout they sprang once more to their feet and to the sweeps.

Meanwhile, the breeze had crept in until it had overtaken the frigate, which at once filled on the starboard tack, keeping her luff until she had gathered good way, when she squared away and once more came booming into the calm belt, nearing us almost half a mile by this manoeuvre.

"It is no good, excellencies; we shall have to give up!" exclaimed Carera, coming aft. "We are now as close in as we dare go; and if that diabolical frigate fires another broadside at us she will blow us out of the water. Port your helm, señor—hard a-port! the coral is close under our keel."

"Hard a-port!" I responded. "But why give up, my good fellow? The frigate is as close now as she dare come to us. You may take my word for it that her captain will not run the risk of plumping his ship ashore for the sake of such an insignificant craft as the *Pinta*. Ha, look out! here comes another broadside."

How we escaped that second storm of shot I am sure I cannot tell, for we were now almost within point-blank range; but escape we did, although for a single instant the whole air around us seemed filled with iron, so thick and close did the shot fly about us. The sail was pierced in three places, but beyond that no harm was done.

"He is after us with the boats! He will waste no more powder and shot upon us," exclaimed Courtenay; and sure enough on looking astern I saw two boats just dropping into the water.

"We must give up—we must give up," cried our crew as they saw this; and leaving their sweeps they came aft in a body with the request that Carera would hoist the Spanish ensign and haul it down again in token of our surrender.

"No, no," I exclaimed; "see how the breeze is creeping down to us; it will be here as soon as the boats—or sooner, if you stick to the sweeps—and then I will engage that we scrape clear somehow. Is there no place, Carera, that we can run into, and so dodge the frigate! We can laugh at the boats if we once get the breeze."

"Place! of course there is!" exclaimed the skipper, his courage again reviving; "there is the Boca de Guajaba, not half a mile from us on our larboard bow. Once in there we can run up at the back of Romano—I know the channel—and so effectually give the frigate the slip. Back to your sweeps, children! we will never yield until we are obliged."

Again the crew manned the sweeps, and again—animated by another judicious reminder from Courtenay of the treasure awaiting them in the Conconil lagoons—they bent their backs and lashed the water into foam as they gathered way upon the felucca; and once more Carera went forward to con the craft through the dangerous channel we were now fast approaching. Meanwhile the two boats—a gig and a cutter—were tearing after us, going two feet to our one, and evidently quite alive to the fact that, unless they kept ahead of the breeze and reached us before it, we still stood a fair chance of escape.

Presently a narrow opening revealed itself in the shore about a quarter of a mile away, among the trees which clustered close to the water's edge; and Carera, directing my attention to it, informed me that was the channel. The surf was breaking heavily all along the shore, and to attempt a passage through it seemed, from the point of observation we then occupied, to be simply courting destruction. I said nothing, however, trusting in Carera's assertion that he knew the place, and presently a narrow band of unbroken water appeared in the midst of the foam, toward which a minute later the felucca was headed.

The boats were now closing with us fast, the gig, which was leading, being within about three cables' length of us, whilst the cutter was not more than fifty feet astern of her. Three or four minutes at most would suffice to bring them alongside of us, fast as we were moving through the water, unless the breeze came to our aid. The sea was ruffled all astern of them, and a cat's-paw now and then would come stealing along the glassy surface between us and them, but so far they had managed to keep ahead of the breeze. The measured roll of the oars in their rowlocks could now be distinctly heard and the sound reaching the ears of the Spaniards made them strain and tug at the sweeps more desperately than ever, Courtenay not only cheering them on but now actually tailing on to a sweep which the lad Francisco was manfully tugging away at with the best of them. The perspiration was pouring off the poor fellows' faces and bare arms in streams, but they still worked away, looking eagerly at me every time I shot a hasty glance astern, as if anxious to gather from my expressive countenance what hopes of escape still remained.

At length we reached the mouth of the channel, and I dared no longer withdraw my eyes for a single instant from Carera. The passage was exceedingly narrow, so confined, indeed, that a man might have leaped from either rail into the seething breakers on each side of us. The little craft bobbed and pitched as she glided into the troubled water, the huge sail rattled and flapped, and we seemed to visibly lose way. At this juncture a voice hailed us in execrably bad Spanish from the gig astern, peremptorily exclaiming:

"Heave to, you rascally pack of piratical cut-throats, or I will fire into you!"

"Pull, men, *pull!*" I urged. "Here is the breeze close aboard of us."

At the same instant our great lateen sail swelled heavily out, wavered, jerked the sheet taut, and collapsed again. The Spaniards greeted the sight with a joyous shout, and, whereas they had hitherto been toiling in grimmest silence, they now burst out with mutual cries of encouragement and a jabber of congratulatory remarks which were almost instantly cut short by the crack of a musket, the ball of which clipped very neatly through the brim of my straw hat. Again the sail flapped, collapsed, flapped again, and then filled steadily out.

"Hurrah, lads!" I exclaimed. "Half a dozen more strokes with the sweeps and the breeze will fairly have got hold of us. See how the sheet tautens out!"

"In bow-oar, and stand by to heave your grapnel!" I heard a voice say in English close underneath our counter; and the next instant came the rattle of the oar as it was laid in upon the thwart. Courtenay too heard the words, and knowing well what they meant left his sweep and sprang aft.

"Give way, men, give way!" now came up from the boat. "Spring her, you sodjers, *spring her*, and take us within heaving distance, or they will get away from us yet. See how the witch is gathering way! Bend your backs, now; lift her! *well* pulled! another stroke—and another—that's your sort; *now* we travel—hang it, men, *pull*, can't ye! heave there, for'ard, and see if you can reach her."

Courtenay was crouching low behind the bulwarks on the watch for the grapnel, and in another second it came plump in over the taffrail. Before it had time to catch anywhere, however, my chum had pounced upon it, and, tossing it into the air just as the bowman in the boat was bringing a strain upon the chain, the instrument dropped overboard again.

"You lubberly rascal!" exclaimed the officer in charge of the gig, addressing the unfortunate bowman, "you shall get a couple of dozen at the gangway as soon as we get back to the ship for that. And if you miss next time I'll make it five dozen. We've lost a good fathom of distance through your confounded stupidity. *Pull*, men! D'ye mean to let the hooker slip through your fingers after all?"

Then a thought seemed suddenly to strike this exasperated individual; his boat was too close under our counter to enable him to use his own muskets, so he hailed the cutter and inquired if there was "no one in her clever enough to pick off that rascally Spaniard at the felucca's tiller?"

"Come," thought I, "this is pleasant! A pretty pass the service is coming to when a man is coolly fired upon by his own countrymen. However, let us hope the 'cutters' are as bad shots with the musket as the average of our blue-jackets!"

Just then *crack!* went a musket from the cutter, and I heard the thud of the bullet in the planking somewhere behind me.

"A miss is as good as a mile," thought I; whilst the lieutenant in the gig astern relieved his feelings by alternately anathematising the poor marksmanship of the 'cutters,' and urging his own crew to increased exertions. By this time, however, the breeze had fairly caught us; we were in smooth water, and slipping so rapidly through it that it was evident the sweeps were no longer rendering us the slightest effective service; whilst, from the more subdued sounds issuing from the pursuing gig, I could tell that we were distinctly drawing away from her; I therefore took it upon me to order the sweeps to be laid in, an order which was obeyed with the utmost alacrity. This action of ours seemed to inspire the gigs with renewed hope and they put on such a determined spurt that for the next ten minutes it was an even chance whether after all they would no catch us. They *did* gain upon us decidedly for the first five minutes of the spurt; but their desperate and long-continued exertions were now beginning to tell pretty severely upon the oarsmen, and by the end of that time it became evident that they were completely pumped out, for we rapidly ran away from them. The cutter, meanwhile, had been manfully following her lighter consort all this while, the midshipman in charge of her amusing himself by blazing away at me as fast as he could load and fire even after we had run out of range. Fortunately he was an outrageously poor shot, his first attempt being his best, so I escaped unhurt; but I inwardly vowed that if ever I happened to meet him in the future I would have my revenge by telling him pretty plainly what I thought of him as a marksman. At length, the felucca having distanced the gig about a mile, we saw both boats give up the chase and lay upon their oars; and a few minutes later they turned tail, and made their way slowly back toward the channel. We had escapee—so far.

Meanwhile, having passed safely through the narrow channel we found ourselves in an extensive lagoon, some ten miles wide, and so long that we had a clear horizon to the southward and eastward, whilst on our starboard hand was a cluster of perhaps a dozen islands, large and small, some almost awash, whilst others rose to a height of from fifty to sixty feet above the water's edge at their highest points, all of them being wooded right down to the water. To the northward and westward of us the lagoon narrowed down to about a mile in width, forming a sort of strait between the largest of the islands above-mentioned and a bold projecting promontory; and beyond this strait the horizon was again clear save for certain faint grey blots which our experienced eyes told us were the foliage crowning another group of islands. It was an enchanting prospect for a man to gaze upon; the broad sheet of water upon which we were sailing was perfectly smooth save for the slight ruffle of the breeze upon it; every spot of dry land, large or small, within sight of us, was completely hidden by the luxuriant tropical vegetation which flourished upon it, the foliage being of every conceivable shade of green, from the lightest to the darkest, and thickly besprinkled with flowers and blossoms of all the hues of the rainbow. Nor was animate life wanting to add its charm to the scene; for aquatic birds of various kinds were to be seen stalking solemnly about the shallows busily fishing, or skimming with slowly-flapping pinions close along the surface of the water; whilst, as we shot between two of the contiguous islands, butterflies of immense size and gorgeous colouring were distinctly visible flitting to and fro among the blossoms of the plants and trees; a flock of gaily painted parroquets, startled by our sudden appearance, took to flight with discordant screams; humming-birds hovered and darted here and there, their brilliant metallic-like plumage flashing in the sun so that they resembled animated gems; and lizards of various kinds, including an immense iguana, could be seen lying stretched out at full length on some far-reaching branch, basking in the broiling sun. It was all very beautiful; and I should have liked nothing better than to spend a week with my gun and sketch-book in so charming a spot, but this was of course impossible; and it was also impossible for me, posted as I still was at the tiller, to take more than a hasty glance now and then, for the water was extremely shallow everywhere but in the channel, which was so intricate that, with the fresh breeze then blowing, it taxed me to the full extent of my ability to follow Carera's quick motions and keep the little hooker from running bodily ashore with us.

This novel species of inland navigation lasted until four bells in the forenoon watch, by which time we had cleared the second group of islands. The channel then became wider, deeper, and less difficult to follow; the land receding on either hand so far that all details were lost; the trip consequently began to grow somewhat monotonous; so I resigned the tiller to Manuel, the mate, and joined Courtenay below for a quiet chat. At one o'clock Carera called down through the sky-light that we were about to make for the open sea again, whereupon we proceeded on deck to watch the passage of the felucca out through the northern channel. This was simply a pleasant repetition of our morning's experience for a run of about three miles; after which we found ourselves at sea again, indeed, but with still a very awkward passage of some nine miles to make over an extensive shoal before we could reach deep water. We had a most disagreeable time of it for the first half-hour, for, though we were under the lee of a couple of islands, a heavy swell was setting in from seaward, the white water was all round us in every direction, and a very sharp eye was needed at the con, and an equally quick hand at the tiller, to prevent the little craft from beating her bottom in on the coral. After that, however, the water gradually deepened; and about two o'clock, to everybody's intense relief, we found ourselves once more in open water, with no sign of the frigate, or indeed of a sail of any kind, anywhere within sight.

For the remainder of that day and during the ensuing night our course led us to the northward and westward close along the northern edge of the great shoal, dotted with its multitudinous *cayos* and *cays*, which commences some thirty miles to the eastward of the Boca de Guajaba, through which we had run to escape the frigate's boats, and extends right along the north-eastern coast of Cuba to its most northerly point, terminating at Maya Point at the entrance to Matanzas Bay. These cays lie so thickly scattered along the coast, and are so close to each other, that they afford innumerable places of shelter with snug anchorage for small craft; whilst, from the fact that they are all situated well within the outer limit of the shoal, they are unapproachable except by vessels of exceedingly light draught; I was therefore not at all surprised to learn from Carera that they were infested by a perfect nest of pirates, who, in feluccas and schooners of great speed and shallow draught of water, were wont to sally forth for a few days' cruise in the Gulf of Florida, or among the Bahamas, to prey upon the shipping bound into and out of the Gulf of Mexico; returning to their dépôts after every successful raid, and landing their booty there, so that, in the event of their encountering a man-of-war, nothing of an incriminating character might be found on board them. I asked Carera whether he was never afraid that some of these free-and-easy gentlemen might some time or another take it into their heads to overhaul the *Pinta*, on the chance of her happening to have on board something worth taking; to which he replied, with a laugh, that he had no fear whatever of any such thing; the pirates always respected such traders as happened to be engaged in dealing with any of the fraternity, these traders having a means of making their characters known to any suspicious-looking craft which might happen to manifest a too curious interest in their movements. And, indeed, we had a verification of this statement that same evening, whilst we were lying becalmed off the Cristo cays; for a noble felucca, which we had sighted an hour or so before, came foaming down toward us, with sails furled and ten sweeps of a side lashing the glassy surface of the water into foam, evidently determined to know the why and the wherefore of our being there. Carera, seeing there was a chance of his being boarded, dived below and routed out a small square red flag, with a black diamond in the centre, which he hoisted at the end of the yard; whereupon the felucca swerved slightly from her course, and, passing close under our stern, inquired whither we were bound; to which Carera replied: "The Conconil lagoons," an answer which appeared to be perfectly satisfactory. This felucca was quite a formidable craft of her class, measuring, I should say, close upon two hundred tons. She was very low and very broad on the water—due, as I could distinctly see when she swept so closely past us, to the extreme shallowness of her hull; there was no scale on her stern-post to show her draught of water; but it could not have been more than eight feet, if as much; her water-lines were the finest I had ever seen, and she must have been a wonderfully smart vessel under canvas, judging from the ease and the speed with which her crew swept her through the water. There were fully sixty men on her roomy decks as she passed us—and possibly others below—as ruffianly-looking a set of wretches as I ever wish to see; and her armament consisted of eight long brass nines—four in each battery—with a long eighteen between her fore and main mast. She was rigged with three masts; and, from the great length of her graceful tapering yards, she must have been capable of showing an enormous spread of canvas to the breeze. With an eye to future business, I not only noted the direction in which she was steering, but also questioned Carera about her; but that individual was—or professed to be—totally unacquainted with her.

Next morning at daybreak we were aroused by Carera, who requested us to put in an appearance on deck as soon as possible, as we were off the mouth of the Barcos Channel and he wished to run in with the first of the sea-breeze. We accordingly dressed with all expedition and hurried on deck, to find ourselves becalmed off a cluster of low mangrove-covered islets, so numerous that the whole sea inshore of us seemed to be completely covered with them. A single glance sufficed to convince us that no more suitable spot than this for a pirate's head-quarters could well be found, for any attempt on the part of the uninitiated to penetrate the intricacies of these multitudinous cays must inevitably have resulted in failure. Channel there was none—so far as we could see—or rather, there were hundreds of them, each more hopelessly impracticable than the other, for there appeared to be only a very few feet of water in any of them. Had we been able to ascend to any such elevation as, say, a frigate's mast-head, it might indeed have been possible to pick out the true channel; but, viewed from the low deck of the felucca, they all appeared pretty much alike. That there *was* a channel, however, and that a fairly good one, Carera assured us, pointing out at the same time an island fully a mile in length, and lying about due east and west, which he informed us marked the western boundary of the entrance.

Soon afterwards the sea-breeze set in, and, squaring away before it, we ran straight for a tiny islet with a single tree upon it, which lay some distance within the mouth of the channel, and which had been brought exactly midway between the long island above-mentioned and a much smaller one about a quarter of a mile to the eastward of it. Courtenay now set to work to take soundings throughout the whole length of the channel, whilst I noted down upon a piece of paper the particulars and bearings of the numerous marks. The Barcos Channel itself was some two miles in length, as nearly as I could guess at it, curving slightly to the eastward from its entrance, and by no means difficult to navigate when once one had fairly hit off its mouth, but so narrow that a passage through it in either direction could only be accomplished with a leading wind. Once through this passage we found ourselves in an extensive sheet of water—an immense lagoon, in fact—which Carera informed me was known as Santa Clara Bay; and it is at the bottom of this bay that the Conconil lagoons, to which we were bound, is situated.

And here our difficulties may be said to have fairly commenced. The wide expanse of water upon which we were now sailing is exceedingly shallow, a fathom and a quarter of water being its average depth everywhere, except at its south-eastern extremity, where it dwindles down to one fathom only. The *Pinta*, from her exceedingly light draught, might, with careful management, have made a tolerably straight run of it from the inner extremity of the Barcos Channel to the entrance to the lagoons; but this of course would not do for us; a deeper, though very intricate passage to the last-named point existed, and it was of the utmost importance to us to have it pointed out to us; it was, in fact, supposed to be the chief object of our journey with Carera. Accordingly, away we went for it, stretching across the lagoon, now to one side, now to another; bearing away for a few yards, then hauling close to the wind; twisting and doubling like a hunted hare, and changing our course so rapidly that it was all I could do to jot down the various marks as they were pointed out to me. The distance to be traversed was, in a straight line, about ten miles, so Carera told me; but we must have passed over fully forty miles of ground in following the windings of this exasperating channel, for it was two o'clock in the afternoon when we reached the entrance to the Conconil lagoons. These lagoons extend about six miles in length, and vary in breadth from perhaps half a mile in their widest part, to less than a hundred feet at their narrowest. They run pretty nearly east and west and are formed by a remarkable spit, shaped like an inverted L, jutting out from the mainland, and some eight or nine islands of various sizes. Some of these islands stand fair in the middle of the lagoon, as regards its width, and where these occur the channel is exceedingly narrow, and consequently can be very easily defended. The lagoons, in fact, constitute a stronghold within a stronghold; and as we wound our way slowly along, the breeze coming to us only light and fitfully through the dense and lofty vegetation crowning the islands outside of us, my admiration for Signor Giuseppe's sagacity in selecting such a place of refuge grew momentarily more profound. At the same time I could not but think, as my gaze rested for a moment upon the black turbid water upon which we floated, whilst my offended nostrils sniffed the very unfragrant odours which it exhaled, that the possible unhealthiness of the place more than compensated for its exceeding safety in other respects. However, when we reached the head of the lagoon, I found, contrary to my expectations, that a very capital and apparently healthy site had been pitched upon for the depôt at the higher extremity of the last lagoon—an irregular triangular-shaped piece of water about a mile long by half a mile wide, with four small islands pretty evenly distributed over its surface. The largest of these rose somewhat precipitously from the water's edge to a height of about fifty or sixty feet—quite high enough, at all events, to be above the level of the miasmatic fogs which gather on the surface of the water toward evening—and on the very summit of this island, deliciously embowered with noble trees, were placed the various buildings appertaining to the piratical community. A narrow strip of firm sandy beach fringed the island on its eastern side; and as we opened it out from behind a projecting point of land, we saw a fine smart-looking schooner hauled close in to it and hove down for repairs. We anchored about a quarter of a mile distant from her, in four fathoms of water; and as Courtenay joined me he made the gratifying announcement that he had never met with less than two and a half fathoms of water in all the soundings he had taken.

# Chapter Thirteen
# The Conconil Lagoons

No sooner was our anchor down than the boat was launched over the side; the felucca's hatches were whipped off, and Carera, diving below, drew forth from some mysterious recess in the little cabin a stout canvas bag containing the two hundred doubloons which he had brought with him for the purpose of trading, whilst the crew, including Courtenay and myself, who were appropriately rigged for the occasion, roused up out of the hold sundry bales of canvas and clothing, coils of rope, casks of provisions, and other etceteras which had been purchased on Giuseppe's account and to his especial order, and for which he would pay in booty. These articles were at once passed over the side into the boat, and as soon as she was loaded with as much as she could safely carry, Carera and a couple of his most trusted hands jumped into her and pulled ashore. As Courtenay and I were strangers, whilst all the other hands belonging to the felucca had frequently visited the place before and were pretty well known to the whole gang, it was deemed advisable that we should remain on board, so as to obviate as far as possible the propounding of perhaps awkward questions as to who and what we were, with the contingent probability of arousing suspicion in the minds of the pirates. To this arrangement we had no objection whatever to make, as Carera assured us there was nothing in the least likely to interest us on shore—nothing whatever, in fact, that we could not just as well see from the felucca's deck with the aid of a telescope. We therefore remained on board, busying ourselves by putting our notes into shape whilst everything was still fresh in our minds, and making as thorough an examination of the island, with the various buildings upon it, as was possible without running the risk of attracting attention. The latter part of our task was an easy one, there being only four buildings altogether on the island; the largest, a kind of general storehouse, being built upon the beach just above high-water mark, so as to be easy of access from the water; whilst the remaining three, consisting of a dwelling for Giuseppe and his principal officers, a long, rambling barrack-like structure for the men who might happen to be left on shore, and a cook-house, were all erected on the top of the hill. The schooner naturally attracted a great deal of attention. She was dismantled, all to her lower masts, and was hove right down on her beam-ends, so as to bring her keel out of the water, so that we could not see as much of her as we should have liked; but, judging of her size from the boats alongside, and the men working about her, we estimated her to measure about one hundred and fifty tons. Her bottom was turned in our direction, and the men were busily engaged in stripping off a quantity of her sheathing and removing several of her planks below the water-line, which, in conjunction with the fact that we detected what looked uncommonly like a couple of shot-holes through her bottom, led us to believe that she, like ourselves, had recently had a very narrow escape of being sunk. The position she was in afforded us an excellent opportunity of inspecting her lines, and I must say I never before saw any nearly so perfect. Looking at them from where we were, they seemed to be absolutely faultless; and as we critically examined them the conviction forced itself upon us that, in moderate weather and with not too much sea on, there was nothing flying British bunting in West Indian waters—or elsewhere, for that matter—which would stand the slightest chance of catching her.

After an absence of about an hour the felucca's boat came off again, without Carera, but loaded down to the gunwale with the most heterogeneous assortment of goods it is possible to imagine, including bales of silk and other valuable stuffs, casks of wine and spirits, and a considerable quantity of handsome silver plate; the latter alone being worth, according to my estimation, considerably more than Carera's bag of doubloons and the rest of his cargo to boot. These goods were passed on deck and from thence down into the hold; the remainder of our own small cargo was loaded into the boat, and away she went on shore again. When she came off the second time it was nearly sunset; Carera came with her, bringing off the remaining price of his barter, consisting of half a dozen bales of tobacco and fifty boxes of prime cigars. The rascal seemed thoroughly well pleased with the result of his bargaining, as indeed he very well might be, for he must have secured fully four times the value of the money and goods he had brought with him to the lagoons. He informed us that, if we had seen all we considered necessary to the successful issue of our projected expedition, he would be off again at daybreak next morning, as Giuseppe was in a most unamiable, and indeed dangerous temper, having been badly mauled a week previously by a British frigate—most probably the one which had manifested such a very marked interest in the *Pinta's* movements—and that he had only scraped clear of her and made good his escape at last by the happy accident of being close to shoal water, into which he had retreated, with his schooner half unrigged and seven eighteen-pound shot-holes through her sides and bottom, which he had inefficiently plugged with the utmost difficulty, reaching the lagoons at last in a water-logged and sinking condition. Carera further informed us that, by a lucky combination of circumstances, he had not only discovered the locality of but had actually been permitted to enter the pirates' treasure-house—a cellar hollowed out of the earth beneath Giuseppe's dwelling—and that there was a considerably larger accumulation of treasure in it than even he had imagined; and that, further, there was no time to be lost in organising the expedition against the pirates, as it had transpired that many of them were growing anxious to enjoy the fruit of their nefarious labours, and serious thoughts were entertained of a speedy general division of the spoil and dispersion of the gang. I may as well mention, *en passant*, that it appeared to be the fashion for everybody visiting the lagoons to speak of Giuseppe, whenever they had occasion to mention him, as "Captain Merlani," whilst within the limits of Santa Clara Bay. I have not the least idea why it was so, but such is the fact; and as the use of a man's Christian name seems to imply a closer degree of intimacy with, and personal friendship for, him than we could rightfully claim, I will, with the reader's kind permission, refer to him henceforward as "Merlani" The reason why I have not done so earlier in my story is, that it was not until our arrival within his territory, so to speak, that we became acquainted with the fellow's surname. This by the way.

As night closed down upon the lagoons with that rapidity which is peculiar to the tropics and the regions immediately adjacent thereto, our ears were assailed by that babel of sound which prevails with scarcely a moment's intermission all through the hours of darkness wherever there is a patch of land large enough to support a few trees with their almost invariable attendant undergrowth, and which emanates from the countless myriads of insects which find their home in the ground, the long grass, the foliage, and the bark of the trees, the chorus being swelled in the present instance by the cries of countless lizards—from the diminutive and harmless grass-lizard up to the alligator, the weird sounds uttered by the nocturnal birds which flitted on noiseless wing from bough to bough, and the rattling *chirr* of a whole army of frogs. And very soon, too, we discovered that we were in one of the favourite haunts of the mosquito, for the cabin lamp was scarcely lighted when the pests made their appearance below in absolute clouds, and so tormented us that we were fain to beat a hasty retreat to the deck, in the vain hope of avoiding them.

We had no sooner set foot on deck, however, than we felt almost thankful to the pertinacious little wretches for having driven us there, for a scene at once burst upon us of such singular and bewitching beauty as I certainly had never up to that time looked upon. The moon, nearly full, and tinted a pale but rich crimson by the atmosphere of miasmatic fog which overhung the lagoon, was just rising into view above the tree-tops and flinging a long tremulous trail of blood-red colour athwart the almost stagnant water. The trees near at hand stood up black as ebony, and motionless as if painted upon the deep soft violet of the cloudless sky, whilst, as they receded to the right and left, their forms gradually became merged with and lost in the fog, which floated not in one uniform mass but in wreaths of ever-changing and most fantastic shape, with their upper edges here and there delicately tinged in faintest rainbow hues as the slanting moonbeams fell upon them. Fireflies, visible only as tiny sparks of light, flitted and glanced and whirled hither and thither against the black shadows of the foliage, whilst the black water, so highly phosphorescent that every tiniest ripple was edged with its own individual and separate line of silvery fire, glowed and darkened, sparkled and flashed, and at times seemed to fairly throb with liquid lightning as the countless living creatures within it stirred its sleeping depths. So insignificant a disturbance even as the falling of a leaf into the water sufficed to evolve a slowly-widening circle of silver light, whilst a frog, a lizard, or a water-rat, making an aquatic excursion, revealed his form and presence much more distinctly than would have been the case at noonday.

Our attention, however, was soon distracted from this witching scene—the exquisite beauty of which is not to be described in mere words—by a noise of singing and shouting on Merlani's island. Presently a feeble flickering fame became visible on the sandy beach, which, quickly increasing in brilliancy, revealed the evident fact that a party of the buccaneers were intent upon a carouse. With the aid of a telescope we could see that these men, some twenty in number, had seated themselves round the fire—which they had probably kindled for the twofold purpose of providing themselves with light and smoking away the mosquitoes—and were industriously passing round a bulky jar, presumably containing spirits, from which, as it came round, each man scrupulously replenished his pannikin; the intervals not devoted to the more important business of drinking being occupied in the singing, or rather *shouting*, of ribald songs, in the performance of which every man's aim appeared to be to out-yell everybody else. This lasted for rather more than an hour, when a temporary lull occurred, and we were in hopes that the orgy was about over and that the hubbub had ceased for the night, when a large boat full of men was seen to be pulling off in our direction. I did not like the look of this at all; the idea of being boarded there in that out-of-the-way spot by a score of desperadoes, half crazy with drink, and, even at the best of times, ripe for any deed of diabolical mischief, was so uninviting that I suggested to Carera the advisability of at once arming all hands, so as to be in readiness for any emergency. I could see that Carera was even more discomposed than ourselves at the approach of the boat, but he would not for a moment listen to my proposal to arm the felucca's people, hastily explaining—and possibly he was right—that the display of weapons would be only too likely to further excite our coming visitors and lead to some overt act productive of a terrible disaster. He expressed the opinion—his teeth chattering with fear, meanwhile, to such an extent that he could scarcely articulate—that the visit would probably prove to be no more than a drunken frolic, and that if it were received and treated as such all would doubtless turn out well; but he very earnestly urged upon Courtenay and me the desirability of our retiring and keeping out of sight so long as our visitors remained on board, which I thought good enough advice to be acted upon, and we accordingly retreated below forthwith. At first sight this retreat of ours smacked a little, I will admit, of slinking off out of possible harm's way; but after all what good could we have done by remaining on deck? And having thus far carried our somewhat foolhardy adventure prosperously through, it was scarcely worth while to endanger its ultimate success by courting risks in which the remarks or questions of a drunken desperado might at any moment involve us.

We had barely made good our retreat when the boat arrived alongside, and her occupants were in another moment in possession of the felucca's deck. A torrent of ribald banter and raillery—of the sort which, coming from a drunken man, is expected to be received as jovial humour, but which a chance word or inadvertent glance of misappreciation may in a moment cause to be exchanged for expressions and acts of the most diabolical ferocity—was at once discharged by these ruffians at Carera and his crew, who, anxious to propitiate their most unwelcome visitors, did their best to retort in kind; and for the next twenty minutes or so the little vessel fairly rang with the most foul, blasphemous, and blood-curdling language it has ever been my misfortune to listen to. Fortunately for us our knowledge of the Spanish tongue, though it had proved sufficiently thorough to deceive Carera and his crew into the belief that we were their fellow-countrymen, was not equal to the comprehension of one-half of the utterances to which we were just then compelled to listen, or I have no doubt we should have been even more thoroughly shocked and disgusted than we were.

And here let me break the thread of my story for a moment to speak an earnest word of kindly caution to my youthful readers. Avoid the use of foul, obscene, or blasphemous language, my lads, as you would avoid the most deadly pestilence. I am grieved to notice that it is sometimes the fashion among lads, ay, even in some cases those of respectable parentage, to freely *garnish*, as they think, their conversation habitually with language of the most vile and disgusting description. They perhaps think it *manly* to do so, and imagine that a bold reckless style of conversation, freely besprinkled with obscenity and profanity, will excite admiration. But if they think this they are making as great and grievous a mistake as they are ever likely to make in the whole course of their lives. The feeling excited is not admiration; it is utter loathing and disgust. Can you think of any man the victim of this horrible vice, for whom you entertain the smallest spark of admiration or respect? Would you like to hear such words from the lips of your own father or mother, your brother or your sister? Or would you like either of them to hear you making use of such language? After all, who and what are the men who thus habitually indulge in obscenity and profanity? Are they not the vicious and disreputable, the brutal drunken ruffians, the scum of the slums, the lowest of the low, the very outcasts and pariahs of society? And is it for one of these that you would like to be mistaken? is it with this repulsive brotherhood that you would choose to ally yourself? Hardly, I would fain hope. No, boys, it is *not* manly—still less is it *gentlemanly*—to be ribald and profane. No true gentleman—let his position in life be what it may—ever degrades himself by the use of foul language, and don't you do it, unless you are anxious to gain for yourself the loathing and utter contempt of your fellows.

To resume. In this horrible interchange of filthy banter the pirates appeared to have forgotten, for the time being, the object of their trip off to the felucca, but at length one of them exclaimed, with a profusion of oaths, that Carera had secured an unfair advantage of them during the afternoon's bartering transactions, and that they had come off to demand a cask of rum with which to square the account Carera, on his part, tried to laugh off the whole affair as an excellent joke, and proposed to mix them a tub of grog there and then as an appropriate finish to it; but this would by no means satisfy the ruffians, who were firm in their demands. So at length, recognising that longer refusal would prove dangerous, he reluctantly ordered the hatches to be lifted. The cask of rum was hoisted out and lowered into the boat, the pirates tumbled in after it, and, finally, with more profanity mingled with snatches of sea-songs, which were bellowed forth at the top of their voices in the style usual with half-tipsy men, away they went for the shore, followed by the smothered imprecations of Carera and his fervent prayers that the boat might capsize and drown them all.

This visit had evidently discomposed Carera's nerves to a very considerable extent, for the boat was no sooner fairly away from the felucca's side than our host presented himself in the cabin, to inform us that, the land-breeze having sprung up and the night being fine and clear, he proposed to go to sea at once instead of waiting until morning. We accordingly went on deck again instead of turning in, as had been our original intention; and a few minutes later—the boat being by this time close to the beach, and so thoroughly within the circle of the brilliant firelight that her occupants were not likely to observe our movements—the canvas was loosed and all hands went cheerily to work to get the anchor. This, the water being shallow, was not a long job, and a quarter of an hour later we were stealing noiselessly away down the lagoon; the land-breeze, which was rustling cheerily among the tree-tops, just reaching us in a languid zephyr, mingled now and again with fitful puffs, which sent us along at a speed of about three knots.

It was now nearly ten o'clock at night; the moon rode high in the heavens, which were flecked here and there by small patches of fleecy scurrying cloud; the fog had drifted away, leaving the atmosphere delightfully pure and clear, so that, narrow as was the channel down which we were winding our way, we had no difficulty in steering clear of all obstruction. As we crept down the lagoon we gradually got a truer breeze and more of it, so that by midnight we found ourselves just passing out of the Conconil lagoons and entering Santa Clara Bay.

We now had a fine rattling breeze, which we expected would carry us across the bay and out through the Barcos Channel within the next hour, but, to Courtenay's and my own inexpressible chagrin, Carera now informed us that, in order to escape the possibility of a second rencontre with the frigate we had fallen in with on our passage up, he had determined to go to the westward, returning round Cape San Antonio instead of by way of Cape Maysi.

This was horribly disconcerting, for, to tell the truth, we had to a large extent been hoping for and depending upon such a rencontre as a means whereby we might effect our escape from the felucca. We thought that, in the event of such a meeting, as we had on the former occasion afforded such material assistance to the felucca's crew in their evasion of capture, so now by a little judicious manoeuvring on our part we might be the means of effecting it; and it was a severe disappointment to us to find that this—the most promising opening we had so far been able to think of—was going to slip through our fingers. We urged upon Carera the importance of time, and reiterated, as often as we dared, our (assumed) belief that the frigate was by that time far enough away from the Bahama Channel; but it was all in vain, the fellow was not to be dissuaded from his purpose, and accordingly, on leaving the Conconil lagoons, instead of stretching away before the wind straight for the Barcos Channel, the felucca was headed to the westward, on the larboard tack, for the Manou Channel, leading from Santa Clara Bay into Cardenas Bay.

As this course would take us over new ground, Courtenay and I determined to remain on deck to pick up any information likely to be of use to us in the future; and I went to the helm, whilst my companion busied himself with the sounding-line. An hour's run brought us to the inner end of the channel, which we found to be somewhat serpentine in its course, but trending generally in a north-north-west direction, with a minimum depth of two and a half fathoms. A run of about twenty minutes carried us clear of this channel and we found ourselves in Cardenas Bay, an almost landlocked sheet of water nearly double the area of Santa Clara Bay and with slightly deeper water, though even here navigation was only possible for vessels of very light draught. Stretching across the bay we, half an hour later, passed through a group of small cays, after which the water began to deepen somewhat. At two o'clock a.m. we passed Molas Point, and, hauling sharp round it, found ourselves a quarter of an hour later fairly out at sea and clear of all dangers. After which, thoroughly tired out by our long and busy day, Courtenay and I went below and turned in.

By noon next day—or rather, *the same* day, to speak with strict accuracy— we were off Havana; and I was in hopes that Carera would put in there, as he seemed at first to have some idea of doing; for our whole thoughts were now bent on effecting our escape from the felucca as early as possible, and I considered it not improbable that in so important a harbour some neutral ship might be found, on board which we might succeed in taking refuge, and with the master of which we might be able to effect an arrangement by which he would be willing to convey us to Port Royal. But to our intense, though secret, mortification, Carera at length resolved to keep straight on; and thus another of our cherished hopes was disappointed. We found, however, on inspecting Carera's well-worn chart, that the route he had adopted would take us within some ten miles of West Point, Jamaica; and shaving the island so closely as that there was just a possibility that we might be pounced upon by one of our own cruisers, so that we were, after all, not exactly in despair. Still, there was, on the other hand, the chance that the felucca might scrape clear; and it was just this chance that we had to provide against, the attempt to do which cost us an infinite amount of anxious and almost fruitless thought. It was, indeed, the only thing now left us to think about. By a curious combination of fortuitous circumstances we had not only tumbled blindfold, as it were, into this singular adventure, but had also been enabled to successfully avoid awakening the suspicions of the people we were so unexpectedly associated with, as well as to see our way clearly all through the adventure, except to its successful ending; and, having carried the thing smoothly forward so far, we did not intend to be beaten at last, if there was any possibility of avoiding it. We racked our brains perpetually on the subject, separately and together, and numerous enough were the schemes which we evolved; but, alas, they were all so nearly impracticable that only under the most exceptionally favourable circumstances could we hope to carry them through successfully. The two least impracticable were Courtenay's proposal to scuttle the felucca when within a few miles of Jamaica, trusting to all hands being able to make the island, as the nearest place of refuge, in the boat; and my own scheme, which was that we should secure possession of the armoury in the cabin, and, seizing upon the first favourable opportunity which might present itself, arm ourselves to the teeth, and, driving the watch on deck into the forecastle, take possession of the felucca and endeavour to navigate her into Port Royal by our own unaided exertions. The chief objections to the first scheme were the difficulty of obtaining the tools necessary to the effectual performance of the scuttling, in the first place, and, in the next, the still greater difficulty of performing the operation undetected. As regards my own scheme, the difficulty lay in the fact that, unless the watch could be driven below without alarming that portion of the crew already in the forecastle, our case was utterly hopeless; for, should these last be disturbed and come on deck, what could two slender lads, even fully armed, do against ten stout, sinewy, full-grown men? We might possibly shoot down three or four; but unless the rest happened to be cowed by this—which we decided was not by any means to be depended upon—we must then be quickly overpowered by sheer force of numbers. This scheme was justly regarded by us both as being of so exceedingly desperate a character, that only as a very last resource would its adoption be justifiable. Nevertheless, we determined to take such measures as were possible for the carrying out of either scheme in the event of nothing better occurring to us.

Meanwhile, day succeeded day without the slightest opportunity occurring for us to initiate Courtenay's scheme. We required a good-sized auger with which to bore the necessary holes in the ship's bottom, and some soft wood out of which to fashion plugs wherewith to plug up those holes until the proper moment should arrive for withdrawing them and letting the water into the hull. The wood there was no difficulty about, and we secured enough for a dozen or more plugs; but no such thing as an auger could we lay hands upon. We even went the perilous length of inventing a pretext for gaining access to the carpenter's tool-chest, without success; and we were at length driven to the conclusion that, strange as it might seem, there was no such thing on board the felucca.

To add to our chagrin and discomfiture, we were no sooner round Cape San Antonio than we discovered that Carera, quite as acute as ourselves, had also foreseen the possibility of a British cruiser being fallen in with if Jamaica were shaved too closely; and he had provided against this contingency by laying off a course for Cartagena, which would enable him to give the island a wide berth. This move on our worthy skipper's part we were, however, able to a large extent to frustrate; for we found that he was no navigator, sailing his vessel by dead-reckoning only, so that by each of us taking long spells at the tiller, as was now indeed our regular custom, we were able to edge the felucca considerably to windward of her course and in toward Jamaica without Carera being any the wiser.

In this exceedingly unsatisfactory manner time progressed—and we with it—until the sixth morning after our abrupt departure from the Conconil lagoons; when, as day broke and the sun rose, clearing away a light bank of grey cloud on the eastern horizon, a soft, delicate purplish hummock-like protuberance was seen rising out of the sea broad on our larboard bow, which was at once recognised as *land*, and so reported to Carera. Courtenay and I were in our berths and asleep at the moment; but the cry of "*Land ho!*" at once aroused us, and, slipping on our clothes, we hurried on deck to see what it looked like. We found Carera there, staring in the utmost perplexity at the small grey shape—only discernible when the felucca rose on the crest of a sea—and audibly wondering what on earth it could be. *We* knew pretty well what it was; Carera kept his small stock of charts in the after cabin, and always spread them out on the cabin table to lay off his course and distance run, so that we had had abundant opportunity to refer, as often as we pleased, to the particular chart he was using on that trip, and had met with no difficulty whatever in keeping a private dead-reckoning of our own, from which we were already aware that we might expect to make Dolphin Head, the highest point of land at the extreme westernmost end of Jamaica, on this particular morning. The report that other land had just become visible about a point further to the southward—and which we judged to be the lofty hill behind Blewfields Bay—confirmed us in our belief that our calculations had proved correct. Carera, in his perplexity, went aloft as far as our stumpy mast-head—a thing we had never known him do before—to get a clearer view of the land, the bearings of which were then taken, after which our skipper, accompanied by Courtenay and me, descended to the cabin to consult the chart. On reference to this, there was of course only one conclusion to be arrived at, which was that the land in sight was none other than Jamaica. It now turned out that he had never visited the island, had never indeed sighted it from the westward before; hence his difficulty in identifying it; but whilst we were all three discussing the matter down below Manuel came to the open sky-light in great trepidation to report shoal water all round the ship. This of course caused us to rush straightway on deck again, though Courtenay and I, knowing that we must be just about crossing the edge of the Pedro bank, felt no apprehension whatever. With Carera and the rest of the felucca's people the matter was very different; they were all out of their reckoning, and confused accordingly; and the sudden sight of the bright-green water all about us, and the shorter, more choppy character of the sea, whilst only a short time before the water had been as purely blue as the heaven above us, and the sea long and regular, completed their discomfiture. For a minute or two disorder reigned supreme on board the little craft; everybody had an opinion to express and advice to give, everybody was jabbering excitedly at the same moment; no man paid the slightest attention to his neighbour; and as all hands were by this time on deck the result may be imagined. Even the helmsman deserted his post at last to join in the general clamour; a circumstance of which Courtenay took immediate advantage by springing to the tiller and ramming it hard down. The lively little craft at once shot into the wind with her canvas loudly flapping; and this stilled the tumult in a moment.

"'Bout ship!" shouted Courtenay, as every man stopped short in the midst of his gabbling; "'bout ship! there is blue water away there to windward of us, and if we can once reach it we are safe."

The men sprang at once like cats to their stations, and the immense lateen sail was trimmed over on the other tack with an amount of alacrity which showed how intense was their relief at finding somebody on board equal to the occasion.

So far, this was well; the felucca was now heading about north-north-east and straight for the land, so that our chance of falling in with a British cruiser was a shade better than before. But, alas, no cruiser, or sail of any kind, was just then in sight; for, giving way to my anxiety, I in my turn shinned aloft to take a good look round. But the land was there, plainly enough, not only the two peaks already reported—the second of which was

now directly ahead—but also five others, ranging from three to five points on our weather bow.

We stood on as we were going for a couple of hours, so as to get well to windward of the shoal—though, as a matter of fact, there was plenty of water over it everywhere to have floated us, or even a frigate, for that matter—going about again when the men had taken their breakfast. The high land was by this time well in sight all along our larboard beam, being certainly not more than forty miles distant; and the circumstance that Carera was afraid of the shoal and determined to keep off it was greatly in our favour, since in order to clear Portland Rock, at its north-eastern extremity, we should have to draw even closer still in with the island. I was at first terribly afraid that some suspicion would attach to my comrade and myself as the authors of the error in the course we had been steering, but I was agreeably disappointed; so far, indeed, was Carera from suspecting anything that he confided to us at breakfast—to which we had invited him—that, though he could not in the least account for our being so far to windward, he was most heartily glad of it, since we appeared to have the sea all to ourselves. He was still a trifle uneasy, however, at being so near the very stronghold and head-quarters of the dreaded British in those waters; and when we all went on deck after breakfast, his first act was to order a hand aloft to the mast-head to keep a bright lookout. It was just ten o'clock in the forenoon, and the man at the mast-head was in the very act of descending the rigging—another man getting ready meanwhile to relieve him—when he uttered an excited exclamation which at once attracted all eyes toward him.

"Look over there, captain, broad on our weather bow. Do you see that turtle lying there asleep on the water?"

Carera sprang on to the weather rail, and, steadying himself with one hand by the shroud whilst he shielded his eyes with the other, peered eagerly to windward. The rest of the watch also dropped whatever they happened to be busied with, and, exclaiming "A turtle! a turtle!" unceremoniously ranged themselves alongside their skipper.

"No," said Carera, after a long look in the direction indicated, "I don't see anything of him; where is—"

"There he is; I see him!" exclaimed one of the men. "Ah! now he is gone again, settled into the trough. Look a bit further out in that direction, captain—there he is again; Madre de Dios, what a monster! don't you see him?"

"Yes, yes; I see him now," answered Carera excitedly; "down with your helm, my man, and let her shoot into the wind. We will have that fellow. Get the boat into the water, smartly now, men. Give the watch below a call."

"To what purpose?" I interposed: "No, no, let the poor fellows finish their sleep in peace; my friend and I will look after the felucca whilst you are away in the boat."

"To be sure we will," said Courtenay, with a quiet wink at me; and springing aft to the tiller, he laid his hand upon it, saying to the man who held it:

"Away with you, José, my fine fellow, into the boat, and lend a hand to secure that turtle; it is not every day we sailors get such a chance."

Meanwhile, the rest of us unshipped the lee gangway, and getting the boat athwart the deck, sent her stern first overboard with a splash which I was in an agony of fear would awake the turtle, and so frustrate the scheme which had darted into my brain—and Courtenay's also, I fancied, by the knowing wink he had bestowed upon me—when it was proposed to go away in the boat after the creature. But no; there he was still, apparently fast asleep, rising and falling upon the surface of the restless waters, his capacious shell glistening brightly as the sunbeams flashed upon it.

The four men constituting the watch stepped as quietly as possible into the boat, and, followed by Carera, took their places at the oar; Carera standing up in the stern-sheets to look out for the quarry and to direct his men how to pull. I was in a perfect fever of anxiety lest the flapping of the sail and the bustle on deck should awaken the watch below and bring them out of the forecastle to see what was the matter; but seamen seldom pay any attention to these things, so far at least as to leave their bunks in their watch below; and when at length the boat shoved off and paddled gently round the felucca's quarter, Courtenay and I found ourselves most unexpectedly in the very situation for which we had so long been ineffectually scheming, namely, in undisputed possession of the little craft's deck.

Without wasting a single moment in watching the progress of the boat, I at once slipped forward, and, gently drawing over the slide of the fore-scuttle, slipped the hasp over the staple, stuffed a few doubled-up rope-yarns through the latter to keep the former in position, and then quietly walked aft.

"Well, old boy," said I, as I joined Courtenay at the tiller, "the felucca is ours; and that, too, without a single particle of all that trouble which we anticipated. If we had planned the thing ever so elaborately we could not

have managed half so well. Up stick, my hearty, fill on her; and hey for Port Royal, which I hope we shall see to-morrow morning."

"Ay, ay," said Courtenay with a puzzled air, "that is all very well. But what about those poor beggars adrift there in the boat? What are they to do without food and water?"

"Well," said I, "to tell you the truth I never thought about that. It is true they are only forty miles from the land, with fine weather and every prospect of its lasting, but I suppose we ought not to leave them without a mouthful of bread or a drop of water. Just jog the felucca gently along, taking care that the boat is not allowed to come alongside again, and I'll see what I can do. I wonder how they are getting on in the matter of the turtle!"

I jumped on the rail in the wake of the rigging and looked out to windward. Apparently they were too much engrossed with their chase to take any notice of us, for I could see them paddling warily along, evidently purposing to get to windward of their sleeping prey and then drift with the wind noiselessly down upon him. Carera was still standing up in the stern-sheets peering eagerly over the boat's larboard bow; and the men were all intently looking over their right shoulders. Presently I saw them lay their oars cautiously inboard, and then all hands ranged themselves along the larboard side of the boat, careening her almost gunwale-to as they stretched their arms over her side. Then followed a short pause of evidently breathless suspense, succeeded by a simultaneous *grab*! and in another instant I saw that they had secured the turtle—and a splendid fellow he was—and were dragging him inboard by main strength.

"All right!" I exclaimed; "they have caught him. Now, I will see what I can do toward providing them with some food and water."

As I turned away to do this a large wash-deck tub caught my eye; and it immediately struck me that this would be a capital thing to turn adrift with a supply of food, as it was sufficiently capacious to hold as much as would last them, with care, two or three days, instead of the twenty hours or so which it would take them to reach the land. The tub was quite dry inside and perfectly water-tight, as I happened to know, so I dragged it to the lee gangway for convenience in launching, and then hurried away to the cabin in search of provender. Opening the store-room door, I rummaged about until I found a bread-bag half full. I turned the bread out of this until there was only enough left to serve them amply for the time they were likely to be afloat, and in on top of this I popped half a cheese, together with a cooked ox-tongue, which we had only cut into that morning at breakfast, and a piece of boiled salt beef. This cargo I conveyed on deck and deposited in the tub,

which I considered was then loaded as fully as was desirable, considering that we intended to set it afloat in a roughish sea for a craft of that build. I then went below again for an empty vinegar keg which I had stumbled over in the store-room; and, taking it on deck, I filled it with water from the scuttle-butt, bunged it securely, and my preparations were complete.

Meanwhile Courtenay had been very cleverly dodging the felucca along almost in the wind's eye, so that she had made but little progress, and the boat, which had been tearing after us as hard as the oarsmen could pull her through the water, was not more than half a mile astern. I told Courtenay what I had done, and what I proposed to do; and whilst I passed a couple of rope's ends through the handles of the tub, in readiness to launch it overboard at the proper moment, my companion wore the felucca round and stood back toward the boat.

Seeing us returning directly toward them, the men laid upon their oars, possibly imagining that we were about to pick them up. Straight as a line for them we ran until they were only about a cable's length distant, when Courtenay sprang his luff, and we darted away considerably to windward of them, upon which they took to their oars once more, and began to force the boat heavily ahead against the sea. Seeing that we had ample time to launch the tub, I now signed Courtenay to shoot the felucca into the wind, when, waiting until she had all but lost her way, we very cleverly launched the tub and the keg over the side without causing the former to ship so much as a drop of water, and then filled away once more. The occupants of the boat, by this time thoroughly mystified, paddled quietly up to the floating tub, and transferred its contents to the boat. Meanwhile we in the felucca, having stood on to a sufficient distance, once more wore round, and again made for the boat, luffing and shaking the wind out of our sail when within hailing distance of her. Then, whilst Courtenay narrowly watched the boat, and held himself ready to fill on the felucca again in good time to avoid being boarded, I sprang into the lee rigging and hailed:

"Boat ahoy! We are sorry to take the felucca from you, but circumstances, which we have now no time to explain, oblige us to do so. We are going to take her to Port Royal. Yonder is the land, not more than forty miles away; the weather is fine and settled, so you will have no difficulty in reaching the shore by this time to-morrow. When you land make at once for Port Royal. We will arrange that, on reaching there, you shall be properly cared for until such time as the *Pinta* can be restored to you. You will find provisions in the tub and fresh water in the keg, which we have dropped overboard. And now, adieu! we wish you a pleasant passage."

Carera and his comrades seemed to take in my meaning even before I had finished speaking, for, with a whole torrent of sonorous Spanish maledictions, they once more dashed their oars into the water and made for the felucca. But Courtenay promptly kept her away and filled the sail, and we slid foaming past the boat at a distance of some five-and-twenty feet; and of course, once fairly moving in such a breeze and sea, no boat that was ever built would have had the slightest chance with the *Pinta*. They pulled desperately after us for fully half an hour, however, and then we lost sight of them.

We were hardly well clear of the boat when a hammering and shouting at the fore-scuttle told us that the watch below had awakened to the suspicion that something was amiss on deck, and that they were anxious to know why they were battened down. I accordingly went forward and, without opening the scuttle, shouted to them that the felucca had been surprised and captured by the British, which in a sense was quite true, and that, unless they wished to be treated as pirates, the best thing they could do would be to remain perfectly quiet and give no trouble whatever. That the vessel was being taken into Port Royal, and that on our arrival there I would make it my business to see the proper authorities and so explain matters to them that the worst thing likely to befall the felucca's crew would be their temporary detention only. It is very likely that this communication puzzled them considerably, but if so, it also had the effect of keeping them quiet, for we never heard another sound from them. Indeed, had they tried to give us trouble, it is probable we should have mastered them before they could all have gained the deck, for our first act, after quieting them, was to arm ourselves each with a whole beltful of loaded pistols and the best of the swords in the felucca's armoury, after which we pitched the whole of the remaining weapons overboard.

Next morning, at daybreak, we took on board a black pilot off Portland Point, reaching Port Royal just in time to hear eight bells struck on board the various ships lying at anchor in the harbour.

# Chapter Fourteen
# A Packet of Disturbing Letters

The first task was to send by shore-boat a brief note on board the admiral, informing him of our capture, and requesting him to send a few hands on board to take care of the vessel. A prompt reply, in the shape of a somewhat dandified mid, with a dozen stout seamen to back him, was vouchsafed to this request, the midshipman bringing with him also a verbal message to the effect that the admiral would be glad to see us on board to breakfast with him. This condescension, of course, merely meant that he was curious to hear full particulars of the capture, but we nevertheless felt much gratified at the invitation; and, detaining the gig alongside only long enough to enable us to make ourselves presentable, we jumped into her, and five minutes later found ourselves on the quarter-deck of the old *Mars*.

Admiral J— himself happened to be on deck at the moment when we stepped in through the entering port, and the look of mingled astonishment and anger with which he regarded us as we presented ourselves before him at once told us that something was wrong.

"How now, young gentlemen!" he testily exclaimed; "are you the two midshipmen who sent me this note, informing me that you had captured yonder cock-boat of a felucca?" We respectfully intimated that we were. "Then how comes it, sirs, that you have presumed to come on board me in those 'longshore togs? Away with you back at once, and when next you venture to appear in my presence, see to it that you come in a proper uniform."

The murder was out. We were, of course, dressed in the clothes with which Don Luis de Guzman had so generously supplied us, and we had been for so long a time out of uniform that it had never occurred to us that our costume would be regarded as in the slightest degree inappropriate. We explained in as few words as possible that we were two of the surviving officers of the *Hermione*, that we had been for some time prisoners in La Guayra, and that we had only very recently effected our escape therefrom; and that put the whole affair straight in a moment, the admiral, who, peppery as was his temper, was a thoroughly kind-hearted old fellow in the main, actually condescending to apologise for his hasty speech; and, the steward at that moment announcing that breakfast was on the table, we all—that is to say, the admiral, Captain Bradshaw, Courtenay, and myself—trundled into the cabin and took our places at the table. Then, for the first time, as we found ourselves once more in the society of our own countrymen, with good wholesome English fare sending forth its grateful odours to our nostrils, with the table covered with its snowy linen, and laden with the handsome, yet home-like breakfast equipage, did we fully realise all that we had passed through since we had last found ourselves so placed, and for my part the revulsion of feeling almost overcame me. The emotions of a midshipman are, however, proverbially of a very transient character, and I soon found myself prosecuting a most vigorous attack upon the comestibles, and, between mouthfuls, relating in pretty full detail all our adventures from the moment of the mutiny, excepting, of course, my love passages with Dona Inez, which I kept strictly to myself.

The story of the mutiny naturally excited a very lively interest, and Courtenay and I were questioned and cross-questioned upon the subject until we were absolutely pumped dry, it transpiring that we were the first survivors of that dreadful tragedy who had reappeared among our own countrymen. The narrative of our sojourn in La Guayra did not, I regret to say, prove one-tenth part so attractive; but when we reached the subject of the Conconil lagoons, Merlani's treasure hoard, and the scheme of the Spanish authorities to at once possess themselves of it and suppress the piratical band, the interest again revived, and we were questioned almost as closely on this subject as we had been about the mutiny.

Before the meal was concluded, it had been settled that a schooner— lately a French privateer—recently captured, and then in the hands of the dockyard people undergoing the process of refitting, should be hurried forward with all possible despatch, and commissioned by a certain lieutenant O'Flaherty, with Courtenay and myself as his aides, her especial mission to be the destruction of Merlani's stronghold, and the capture of as many members of the piratical gang as we could lay hands upon. As, however, it seemed that the *Foam*—as the schooner had been re-christened—could not possibly be got ready under eight or ten days at the earliest, we were informed that we might take a week to look about us, a permission of which we most gladly availed ourselves. We were also informed that the prize-money for the Jean Rabel affair had been awarded, and the admiral was good enough to advise us to put our business affairs into the hands of his own agent in Kingston, to whom he gave us a letter of introduction.

Our first business on leaving the *Mars* was to take passage to Kingston in one of the many sailing-boats which, owned by negro boatmen, are always obtainable at Port Royal, and in her we managed, with the aid of a fine sea-breeze, to make the passage in an hour, being badly beaten, however, in a race with a gig belonging to the frigate *Volage* which happened to be lying at Port Royal at the time.

Arrived in Kingston we made our way, in the first instance, to the post-office, where we each found several letters awaiting us. There were nine for me, of which eight were from my father, and one—heaven only knows how it had found its way across in so short a time—from Dona Inez. I *ought*, I suppose, to have first opened those from my father; but I did not. With the ardour that might have been expected I first tore open the envelope superscribed by Inez. The letter was dated the day after our flight from La Guayra; and the poor girl, who had already learned from the faithful Juan that our plans had somehow been capsized, had written in an agony of apprehension as to our safety. It appeared that Juan—whose arrival at the cove had been delayed about half an hour by the suspicious manoeuvres of a felucca ahead of him, undoubtedly the *Pinta*—had hung about the spot for something like an hour and a half, at the expiration of which time two Spaniards had presented themselves on the beach and had inquired whether he belonged to the *Pinta*. On his saying that he did not he had been very sharply cross-questioned as to who he was, and the reasons for his presence there at that hour, which cross-questioning he was sensible enough to evade and cut short by retreating to his felucca and returning to La Guayra, from whence he, the first thing next morning, made his way to the castle to report and to seek further instructions. Having actually witnessed our departure, and knowing from the time at which it had occurred that we must have made our way on board the wrong felucca—which Juan was subsequently able to say with almost absolute certainty *must* have been the *Pinta*—my lady-love was painfully anxious as to our fate; for it appeared that the *Pinta* and her crew bore a somewhat evil reputation among those who professed to know her best at La Guayra; and the only hope or consolation which Dona Inez could find lay in her somewhat too favourable estimate of our ability to take care of ourselves. She most earnestly entreated that I would not lose a moment, after the receipt of her letter, in writing to set her mind at rest. She added that her father had returned home in excellent health; and that, though he had at first betrayed some vexation at the loss of our services, he had soon cooled down, and had then acknowledged that he was glad, for our sakes, that we had succeeded in effecting our escape.

Having read and re-read this most cherished epistle some half a dozen times over, I refolded and put it carefully into my pocket, next turning to the letters from my father, which I arranged and opened according to the dates of the postmarks.

The first of these letters—being the third written by my father since the date of my leaving England (I had received the other two on the occasion of our former visit to Port Royal, in the *Hermione*)—was very similar to all others which had ever reached me from the same writer; brief, cold, and evidently strained and artificial as to the one or two expressions of affection contained therein—altogether a painful and unsatisfactory letter to receive, in fact. The second was somewhat similar, except that therein my father condescended to inform me that he was by no means well; that he thought he had perhaps been overworking himself, and that unless his health speedily mended he feared he should be obliged to call in medical advice. This was sufficiently alarming; but the third letter was even more so, for in it he informed me that he had suffered a complete break-down in health and spirits; that he had placed himself under the care of Doctor Wise, one of the most eminent physicians of the day, and that he had not only been strictly enjoined to entirely lay aside his brush for at least six months, but that he had also been ordered to travel. This, however, was evidently not the worst of it; for the letter, a long, rambling, and somewhat incoherent epistle this time, went on to hint mysteriously at the causes which had brought this lamentable state of affairs about; but so obscurely was the letter worded that, on its first perusal, the only information I could definitely gather from it was that my father was then suffering from the effects of many years of mental anguish resulting from some matter which, if I understood him aright, seemed to be in some way connected with my poor dead mother. The letter concluded with the extraordinary words, "Lionel, the shadow of deception and falsehood rests upon us both, and from no fault of ours.— Yours distractedly, Cuthbert Lascelles."

"The shadow of deception and falsehood!—no fault of ours!—yours distractedly!" Whatever could it all mean? The closing words of the letter, "yours distractedly," puzzled me most of all. Hitherto my father's communications to me, however lacking in affection they might otherwise have been, had all terminated with the orthodox "your affectionate father." Why, then, this departure from the rule? Was it intentional, or was it merely to be regarded as an indication of the terribly disturbed state of the writer's mind?

I read and re-read this most singular epistle at least half a dozen times without gathering any additional light upon the obscure and mysterious hints which it contained, and I then turned to the remaining letters, thinking I might possibly find in them a solution to the enigma. And at the first reading I imagined I *did* find it; the conclusion at which I arrived being that my poor unfortunate father must have gone mad! I patiently went through the whole packet a second time, seeking in them some additional evidence of insanity; but no, saving on this one particular matter the writer had evidently been in full possession of all his faculties. The fourth letter contained the information that the news of the mutiny on board the *Hermione* had reached England, and that it was believed some of the officers had escaped massacre and had been landed at La Guayra. Touching this matter he had written: "I can scarcely say, at this moment, whether I hope you are among the living or among the dead. If the latter, I shall at least enjoy the melancholy satisfaction of knowing that I have seen the last of one who, though I could have dearly loved him, and have been proud of him for his own sake, was, nevertheless, although my own son, almost hateful to me, because of his marked resemblance to one whose duplicity has been the curse of my life. But if, on the other hand, you are living, Lionel—as something whispers to me that you are—I shall perhaps be disposed to accept your preservation as a token from Heaven that I may, after all, have been mistaken, and that your mother could, had I given her the opportunity, have explained those circumstances which, unexplained, completely shattered her own happiness and mine."

The next letter, the fifth, was dated from Rome, in which city my father informed me that he had then been staying for about three weeks; but that he was about to leave it again, for what destination he could not then say, as he had derived no benefit whatever from the change—was rather worse, in fact—since the city was so full of associations connected with my mother that his trouble was then harder than ever to bear. He added that he was still strongly impressed with the idea of my being alive, and that this idea, with the excuse it afforded him for continuing to write to me, gave him some small comfort. He said he had been exceedingly gratified at the very favourable report which had reached him of my conduct at Jean Rabel, and he most earnestly besought me, if indeed I were still alive, to comport myself in such a manner that my glorious deeds might in some measure, if not wholly, atone for the suffering my mother had caused him. The remaining letters were dated from Naples. They all dwelt upon the same theme; but the last closed with the request that, if it ever reached me, I would at once write in reply, addressing my letter to his lawyer in London, who would be kept advised of his whereabouts and would forward it on to him. There was also an assurance that he had no desire to visit my mother's heartless deception of him upon me, since, whatever were *her* faults, I was his son, and he had no intention of disowning the relationship; so that, if ever in need of money, I was without hesitation to draw upon him for any reasonable amount. "In want of money, indeed!" Luckily, I was not; but, as I crushed the letters back into my pocket, I solemnly vowed that, rather than touch a penny of that man's money, at least whilst his state of mind remained what it then was, I would perish of starvation in a ditch. Then bewildered, stunned, and utterly crushed in spirit, I hastily excused myself to Courtenay upon the plea of having received distressing news from England, and, obeying the same impulse which impels a wounded animal to rush away and hide itself and its suffering in the deepest solitudes, I turned my back upon Kingston, with its busy bustling streets, and hastened to bury myself among the hills. I pushed forward without rest or pause until I found myself on the crest of a lofty eminence overlooking the town and harbour; when, flinging myself down beneath the grateful shade of a gigantic cotton-wood, I gave free vent to my feelings of suspense, indignation, and sorrow, and burying my face in my hands wept as if my heart would break. I will not attempt to describe or enlarge upon the feelings which then harrowed my soul; the words have never yet been coined which could adequately express my anguish. No merely mortal pen could depict it; nor can anyone, save those unfortunates who have passed through such an ordeal, imagine it. Moreover, the subject even now, when I am old and grey-headed, is still so painful to me that I care not to dwell unduly upon it. Let me, therefore, pass on to the moment when, relieved, yet exhausted by the passage of that terrible outburst of tears, I had so far regained composure as to be able to look my position fairly in the face.

My first act was to draw forth the fatal bundle of letters and reperuse them patiently from beginning to end, still clinging to the desperate hope that I had after all, in some unaccountable way, misunderstood my father's meaning, and that I was under some hallucination. But no; there were the words all too plainly written for any possibility of mistake. His was the hallucination—not mine. *False?* A dissimulator? I thrust my hand into my bosom, and dragged forth the velvet case containing my mother's portrait, which I had worn next my heart throughout all the vicissitudes of fortune encountered by me since the moment it had first been placed in my hands, and, pressing the spring, threw back the cover, and allowed my eyes to rest upon the loveliness it had concealed. Deceitful! If falsehood lurked within the liquid depths of those clear, calm, steadfast eyes, or was hidden behind that smooth and placid brow, then I thought must the very angels be false! If falsehood could shroud itself behind a mask of such surpassing loveliness, such an aspect and personification of all that is pure, and innocent, and faithful, and true, "where," I asked myself, "oh! where is truth to be found?" That my mother had, all unwittingly, and in some inexplicable manner aroused my father's suspicions, I could not doubt; but, after all, the matter was manifestly, to my mind, merely one of fancied or implied duplicity or deceit capable of easy explanation; it would probably have had no lasting effect on any but a diseased mind; and, knowing him as well as I did, I could understand how, with his reserved temperament and in his wounded pride, my father would silently withdraw himself from his wife, nor deign to stoop so far as to seek an explanation. I could discern only too clearly that he had taken as proof of dissimulation some circumstance that would only appear suspicious until the opportunity for explanation had passed away for ever—hence the unhappiness of which I had gained an inkling during my nursery days—and that it was probably not until his heart had been softened by bereavement that he had coolly and dispassionately enough reviewed the circumstances to arrive at the conclusion that he might, after all, have been mistaken. My father had written of his "doubts and misgivings," and I felt confident that it was nothing in the world but the tenacious hold of these doubts and misgivings upon his mind which had in the first instance made him so unfatherly in his treatment of me, and had now reduced him almost to a condition of insanity. It was the horrible uncertainty which was killing him, soul and body—the uncertainty whether, on the one hand, his suspicions had been well founded; or whether, on the other hand, he had been hideously cruel and unjust to the one being who, above all others, ought to have been the object of his most tender solicitude. *I* had no doubt whatever upon the subject; there was a conviction, amounting to absolute certainty in my mind, that my unhappy father had all too easily allowed himself to be deceived, and I there and then solemnly vowed and resolved that henceforward it should be the great object and aim of my life to demonstrate this to him to the point of positive conviction. "Yes," I exclaimed, springing to my feet with renewed hope, "I had already one incentive—my love for Inez—to spur me forward to great and noble achievements: I have now another—the justification of my dead mother's memory; and henceforward these shall be the twin stars to guide me onward in my career. 'For Love and Honour' shall be my motto; and, with these two for guerdon, what may a man not dare and do?"

An hour later saw me back in Kingston and comfortably ensconced in the bay-window of a private room in the — hotel, inditing a long epistle to my father in collective reply to the entire budget I had that morning received from him. In this letter I summarily disposed of the mutiny and my subsequent adventures in half a dozen brief sentences, feeling that such a matter could well wait until my father was in a more congenial mood for the communication of particulars; devoting my entire energies to the combating of those doubts which I now saw had been for years insidiously sapping his happiness, ay, and his very intellect as well I thanked him for taking me into his confidence, fully entered into my reasons for regarding his suspicions as groundless, and besought him first to communicate to me fully all the facts of the case—which, I pointed out to him, I ought to be made acquainted with, in order that I might be enabled to take the fullest advantage of any opportunity which might offer, in my wanderings, to sift the matter to the bottom—and then to dismiss all thought of it from his mind. This letter cost me three or four hours of severe study; but I contrived to bring it to a satisfactory conclusion at last; and then, with a considerably lighter heart, I began and finished a letter to Inez, in which, mingled with the usual lover-like protestations, I gave her full details of our adventure from the parting moment on the beach to our arrival in Port Royal harbour. I further told her that I found myself at that moment possessed of a tidy little sum in prize-money, and that, inspired by my love for her, I had resolved to fight my way to the top of the ladder with the utmost possible expedition, with a great deal more of the same sort, which would no doubt appear the most arrant nonsense to *you*, dear reader, so I will not inflict it upon you.

These two important tasks completed, I felt very much more easy in my mind, and was able to sit down to my dinner, which was shortly afterwards served, with a tolerable appetite. Whilst I was engaged in discussing the meal Courtenay came in. He informed me that he had accepted an invitation for himself and me to spend a week with Mr Thomson (the admiral's, and also our own, agent) at his country house, some fifteen miles off in the heart of the Blue Mountain range; and that, as he had been unable to find me in time for us to go out there that evening, our host had promised to send in a couple of saddle-horses and a negro guide for our accommodation next morning, and that we should find them awaiting us at Mr Thomson's store at nine o'clock. This was good news, for though I had pulled myself pretty well together after the shock occasioned by the perusal of my father's letters, I felt that a little change and amusement would be most acceptable under the circumstances.

On the following morning, punctual to the moment, we presented ourselves at the rendezvous; where we found, as had been promised, a couple of excellent saddle-horses awaiting us in charge of a grinning, happy-looking negro groom, who was mounted on a stout mule. Our guide, who informed us that his name was Pompey, promptly took charge of our valises, which he slung one on each side of his own saddle; we then mounted, and without loss of time got under weigh for our destination. The first six or seven miles of our journey was uninteresting enough, but when we plunged into the mountain road and found ourselves environed on each side by a thick growth of luxuriant tropical vegetation, the foliage and flowers of which bore all and more than all the hues of the rainbow, whilst gorgeous butterflies, gaudy insects, and birds of the most brilliant plumage flitted hither and thither about us, with an occasional opening in the dense growth revealing the most enchanting little views of the distant harbour and sea, or perchance a passing glimpse of some quiet vale, with its cane-fields, boiling-house, and residential buildings, our journey became an enjoyable one indeed. We reached our destination—an extensive and somewhat straggling one-storied building, with large lofty rooms shrouded in semi-darkness by the "jalousies" or Venetian shutters which are used to carefully exclude every ray of sunlight—about noon; and received a most cordial and hearty welcome from our host, a most hospitable Scotchman, and his family, and here—not to unnecessarily spin out my yarn—we spent one of the most pleasant and enjoyable weeks I had up to that time passed. The family, in addition to our host and his charming wife, consisted of a son and three daughters, who did everything that was possible to make our visit pleasant, and they were a musical family throughout; so that what with shooting, riding, visiting our somewhat distant neighbours, and receiving visits in return, when singing and dancing became the order of the evening, our short holiday passed all too quickly. These most excellent people were the first, as they were the warmest, friends I ever made in the island; and when, late in the afternoon of the eighth day of our visit, Courtenay and I, with Pompey again for our pilot, mounted to return to Kingston, we received a very warm and evidently sincere invitation from the whole family to make their house our home whenever opportunity would afford. We slept at our hotel that night, and, bright and early next morning, made our way to Port Royal, where almost the first object which met our view was our new ship, the *Foam*, at anchor close under the stern of the flag-ship, with the hands on board busy bending a new suit of canvas.

Directing our boatman to run alongside, a minute or two later saw us on deck shaking hands with Mr Neil O'Flaherty, our new commander, who proved to be a regular typical Irishman—genial, high-spirited, and full to overflowing with fun and humour. We took to him in a moment; and I think the favourable impression was mutual, for we never had the ghost of an unpleasantness with him during the short but eventful period which we served under him. We had been thoughtful enough to bring our chests along with us in the boat, so that we could join at once, if need were; these were accordingly hoisted up over the side, and the boatman dismissed; after which, at O'Flaherty's invitation, we descended to the cabin to cement our new friendship over a glass of wine, and to have a chat about the cruise upon which we were about to enter, leaving the boatswain to superintend the operations on deck. The admiral, it seemed, had only given our new skipper a very general set of instructions, leaving him to arrange all details as to the armament and manning of the schooner after a conference with us, as we were supposed to be the persons best posted on the question of these requirements. The whole of the morning was devoted to a full and particular recital on our part of everything which had transpired from the moment of our boarding the *Pinta* until that of our leaving her; after which we formed ourselves into a committee to discuss the outfit of the craft; and we now learned, somewhat to our chagrin, that Carera and his boat's crew, having duly turned up at Port Royal, had made such representations to the admiral as had induced that distinguished officer to release them and the felucca forthwith, upon the understanding that they were to return at once to La Guayra, and were not to attempt to communicate, either directly or indirectly, with Merlani or any of the other pirate gangs on the Cuban coast which it was proposed that we should attack. This, of course, was all very well; and would do no harm whatever *if* the rascals only adhered to their agreement; but of this I confess I felt somewhat doubtful. The mischief, however, if mischief there were, was done, and it was therefore no use to worry about it; but I saw that it would need even greater circumspection than ever in the carrying out of our difficult enterprise, and for that, heaven knows, the necessity ought never to have been created.

Our palaver over, we all adjourned to the deck, and from, thence into the gig, which had been ordered alongside to convey us on shore to the dockyard. We took advantage of this opportunity to make a thorough inspection of the outward appearance of the craft which was to be our future home; and, so far as I at least was concerned, I cannot say that the impression produced was an altogether satisfactory one. In the first place, the *Foam* was, to my mind, rather small for the work she had to do, measuring only eighty tons register. She was, it is true, a very fine beamy little vessel for her size, of shallow draught of water, with sides as round as an apple, and beautifully moulded; indeed, I judged, from the look of her, that she had evidently been specially built for privateering purposes, her carrying capacity being very small, whilst no effort seemed to have been spared to render her exceedingly fast and stiff under her canvas. She was very strongly built of oak, with massive timbers, copper fastened throughout, and heavily coppered up to her bends; so that, as far as her hull was concerned, there was not much, beyond its size, to find fault with. But, in the matter of spars and rigging, those heathens the dockyard riggers had completely ruined her, as O'Flaherty admitted, almost with tears in his eyes. Her lower masts had been left in her intact and untouched, as they had been when she first fell into our hands, and two handsomer sticks I never saw; but, in place of the tall slim willowy topmasts which she then carried, they had sent up a couple of heavy, clumsy sticks which, with the yards on her foremast, were stout enough for a vessel of at least twice her tonnage. And, not content with this, they had further hampered the poor little craft with a regular maze of heavy shrouds, stays, and back-stays, all of which had been set up until they were as taut as harp-strings; so that we had only too much reason to fear that, in a fresh breeze and a choppy sea, we should find the little craft cramped and her sailing powers completely spoiled. There was one comfort, however, the rigging was all new; and we trusted that a few hours at sea would stretch it sufficiently to restore in some measure the spring and play of her spars; but the heavy top-hamper with which she was burdened was an evil which could only be cured in one way; and I resolved that it *should* be cured as soon as we got out of harbour, if I could bring O'Flaherty to my way of thinking.

Our inspection completed, we pulled ashore to the dockyard, where O'Flaherty made out and handed in his requisition for such further stores as we considered would be necessary; and from thence we wended our way to the gun wharf, where arrangements were made for the substitution of six brass long sixes in place of the nine-pound carronades with which it had been proposed to arm the little hooker. These, with the long eighteen which was already mounted on a pivot on the forecastle, would, we considered, make us as fit to cope with the pirates as we could hope to be in so small a craft. The guns came alongside and were hoisted in that same afternoon; and the following day witnessed the completion of our preparations for sea, including the shipping of our ammunition and the filling up of our water-tanks, etcetera. O'Flaherty was able to report himself ready for sea late that afternoon, upon which all three of us were invited on board the *Mars* to dine with the admiral. The captain of the *Emerald* frigate, which had arrived the previous day, and his son, a midshipman belonging to the same ship, were also among the guests; and, in the latter, I thought I recognised the young gentleman who had amused himself by popping away at me with a musket during the pursuit of the *Pinta* through the Boca de Guajaba. I was not quite certain about the matter at first; but the conversation which ensued upon the admiral making mention of the *Foam's* destination and mission soon convinced me that I was correct in my surmise. The *Emerald*, it then turned out, was the identical frigate from which we had so narrowly escaped; and Captain Fanshawe at once waxed eloquent upon the unparalleled audacity and effrontery of the Cuban pirates, and the urgent necessity for their prompt suppression, instancing the escape of the *Pinta* as a case in point. His son, too, as one of the actual participators in the pursuit, had a great deal to say upon the subject, and seemed somewhat disposed to draw the long-bow when narrating his own share of the exploit, which tendency I thought it only kind to nip in the bud by giving our version of the affair. Both father and son at first appeared to be considerably nettled when they found that it was to us they owed their discomfiture; but their better sense speedily prevailed, and they joined as heartily as the rest in the laugh against themselves. On parting at the gangway that night, however, as we prepared to leave for our respective vessels, young Fanshawe laughingly remarked, as he gave our hands a cordial farewell grip:

"You have the laugh on your side at present, Lascelles; but I warn you that you will not get off so easily the next time I have an opportunity of taking a pot-shot at you."

We reached the *Foam* about midnight; and next morning at daybreak weighed and worked out of the roadstead with the first of the sea-breeze, nipping sharp round the point as soon as we could weather it and keeping close along to windward of the Palisades until we were abreast of Plum Point; when, being fairly clear of the shoals, we braced sharp up for Yallah's Point. Once abreast of this, we were enabled to check our weather-braces a trifle and ease off a foot or two of the main-sheet, when away we went for Morant Point through as nasty a short choppy sea as it has ever been my luck to encounter; the schooner jerking viciously into it and sending the spray flying from her weather bow right aft into the body of the mainsail and out over the lee quarter. But the discomfort to which we were thus subjected was amply compensated for by the magnificent panorama of wooded mountain, brawling stream, sweeping bay, landlocked inlet, frowning cliff, and white sandy beach, as we skirted the shores of this most beautiful island of Jamaica.

# Chapter Fifteen
# A Brush with a Piratical Felucca

We had not been three hours at sea before the unwelcome conviction forced itself upon us that our apprehensions respecting the injury to the *Foam's* sailing powers were only too well founded; whatever they might originally have been the bungling dockyard riggers had effectually destroyed them. The breeze was blowing so strongly that we had been compelled to furl the topgallant—sail, and, steering as we were with the wind abeam, we ought, with the shapely hull we had beneath us, to have been going at least nine knots, whereas, so cramped were the little vessel's movements by her tautly set-up rigging and the consequent rigidity of her spars, that she was going little more than six. This was anything but satisfactory; O'Flaherty's first action, therefore, was to order a general easing-up of lanyards, fore and aft, aloft and alow; and no sooner was this done than we felt the advantage of the change; the swing and play of the spars being restored, and the rigging eased up until they were merely *supported* without their pliancy being interfered with, the little craft at once recovered her elasticity, and not only went along faster, but also took the seas much more buoyantly, riding lightly over them instead of digging through them as before, so that she no longer threw the spray over and over herself, but went along as light and dry as an empty bottle. But it was still evident that her top-hamper was too heavy; we therefore set the carpenter to work to reduce a couple of spare topmasts we had on board, with the view to shifting them upon the first favourable opportunity; and, this done, we hoped to have the hooker once more at her best.

Nothing of importance occurred until we arrived off the Cristo Cays, when—the time being about three bells in the forenoon watch, and the larger island bearing about two miles on the larboard bow, a couple of miles distant—O'Flaherty brought a chart on deck and, spreading it out on the companion slide, beckoned me to him.

"Look here, Lascelles," said he, making a mark on the chart with his pencil-point, "there is where we are, and that," pointing away over the larboard bow, "is Cristo Cay. Now, whereabouts is the channel that you saw that big felucca going into?"

"It is further on to the westward; you cannot see it from here. But why do you ask?" I inquired.

"Because, me bhoy, I intind to take a look in there and see what there is to be seen," he replied.

"If you will excuse my saying so, I think you had better not," said I. "In my opinion it would be wiser to meddle with these other places as little as possible until we have beaten up Merlani's quarters. From all that we could learn from Carera his gang is far and away the most formidable all along this coast; and it seems to me that it would be only prudent on our part to create as little alarm as possible among these fellows until we have polished him off. His snuggery is strong enough and difficult enough of approach as it is, and it might be made infinitely more so if an alarm were given along the coast, as it easily might be if one of their craft happened to escape us; my advice, therefore—if you ask it—is to interfere with nobody until we have been into the Conconil lagoons."

"Why, Lascelles, you surely are not *afraid*?" he asked, looking me surprisedly in the face.

"No, sir, I am *not*," I answered, rather nettled, "I am only prudent; and—"

"Pooh!" he interrupted lightly, "prudent! Me dear bhoy, prudence is a very good thing—sometimes, but it does not do for such business as ours. A bould dash and have done wid it is the motto for us. Anyhow, I intind to go in, so there's an end av it, and I'll thank ye, young gintleman, to point out the channel as soon as we open it."

"But," I remonstrated, "I know nothing whatever of the place beyond what I saw of it in passing. Do you?"

"Not a wan ov me; but what matther?" was his characteristic reply.

"Simply this," said I. "The navigation is doubtless difficult, and the water shallow. We should find ourselves in a pretty pickle if we plumped into a hornet's nest and on to a shoal at the same moment."

"How big did you say that felucca was that you saw going in there?" he asked.

"Nearly or quite two hundred tons," said I, "but—"

"And we are eighty," said he. "Where she could float we can—"

"By no means," I interrupted. "I do not believe she drew an inch more than eight feet, whilst we draw nine; and an extra foot of water, let me tell you, Mr O'Flaherty, makes all the difference in these shallow inlets."

"Say no more," was the answer. "In we go, even if we never come out again."

That, I thought, was scarcely the resolution to which a wise commander would have come; but after such an expression I could, of course, only hold my peace, and I did so until a few minutes later when we opened the entrance to the channel, which I pointed out to him.

"Then you will clear for action and send the crew to quarters, av ye plaise, Mr Lascelles," said O'Flaherty; which done, we hauled our wind and reached in for the narrow opening.

It was a foolhardy undertaking, to my mind; but I must do. O'Flaherty the justice to say that, having entered upon it, he neglected no precaution to ensure our success. Thus, his first act, after the mustering of the crew, was to furl the square canvas, to facilitate the working of the schooner; after which he requested Courtenay to go aloft to the topgallant-yard to search out from that elevation the deepest water and to con the ship accordingly.

On entering the channel it was discovered to be very narrow, so much so indeed that at one point there was not width enough to work the ship, and it was only by means of a very smartly executed half-board, under Courtenay's directions from aloft, that we avoided plumping the schooner ashore on the projecting spit. The water, too, was so shallow that, on looking over the taffrail, it was seen to be quite thick and clouded with the sand stirred up by the vessel's keel; whilst so close aboard of us was the land on either hand that a couple of batteries, of, say, four twenty-four pounders each, one on either side of the channel, would have inevitably blown us out of the water. Most fortunately for us, it had not occurred to the frequenters of the place to plant batteries at this spot; so we passed in unmolested. The channel was about a mile in length, on emerging from which we found ourselves in a landlocked lagoon about four and a half miles wide at its broadest part, and so long that neither extremity could be accurately defined even from the elevated perch occupied by Courtenay. No sign whatever of anything like a settlement could be anywhere seen from the deck; but Courtenay hailed us to the effect that he could see something like a vessel's mast-head over the middle island of a group of three on our starboard beam. He further reported, on the question being put to him, that the water was very shoal all round the ship, but that there were indications of something like a channel to the southward and eastward; upon which sail was shortened to lessen the schooner's speed through the water, and her head was put in the direction indicated. This course was held for about two miles, when, by Courtenay's direction, it was changed to south-south-west. Another run of two miles enabled us to open the southern sides of the three islands before referred to; and there, sure enough, in a snug bight between the two most distant islands, and completely concealed from to seaward by the lofty trees with which the ground was densely overgrown, we discovered three feluccas at anchor, two of them being small, one-masted craft, of about the same tonnage as the *Pinta*, whilst the third carried three masts, and looked very much like the identical craft we had seen when last we passed up the coast. They were about four miles distant from us; and for the first minute or two after sighting them not the slightest sign of life could we discover about them. As we now had a trifle more water under our keel sail was once more made upon the schooner, and we headed straight for the strangers; but we were hardly round upon our new course before we saw four very large boats, full of men, push out from among the bushes and make in all haste for the craft at anchor; two of them going alongside the big felucca, and one each to the smaller craft. They remained alongside only about a minute, and then returned to the shore with two men in each. Watching the craft through our glasses, we could see the crews bustling about the deck in a state of extraordinary activity; and, in less time than it takes to describe it, the enormous lateen yards—which had, evidently for the purpose of concealing the whereabouts of the craft, been lowered down on deck—were mastheaded, the canvas loosed, and the feluccas got under weigh. The two small craft at once made sail to the westward, heading for a passage between the mainland and a long mangrove-covered spit which jutted out from the larger and more westerly of the three islands; but the large felucca boldly headed for us direct under every inch of canvas she could spread.

"Now," said I to O'Flaherty, "if that is the same felucca that passed the *Pinta* when we were up here before, we shall have our hands full, for she carries two more guns than we do, and hers are nines whilst ours are sixes; moreover, she has half as many men again as we have, and if they are anything like as tough as they appeared to be they will fight desperately. However, it will never do to turn tail now, so please say how you mean to engage her, and I will take the necessary steps."

"We will run her aboard, me bhoy, throw all hands on her decks, and dhrive her cut-throat crew below or overboard in less than two minutes, or I'm very much mistaken. So be good enough, Misther Lascelles, to have the guns loaded wid a couple ov round shot and a charge ov grape on the top ov thim," said O'Flaherty, rubbing his hands gleefully.

I was in the act of issuing the necessary orders when Courtenay hurriedly hailed from aloft—what he said I could not distinguish—and the next moment the schooner gave a sort of upward surge and stopped dead. We were aground!

"Loose and set the topsail and topgallant-sail, and throw them aback!" shouted O'Flaherty. "Lower away the quarter-boat; get the stream-anchor into her with a hawser bent on to it, and run it away astern; be smart, my lads; we must get afloat again before that felucca reaches us."

These orders were obeyed with that smartness and promptitude which distinguishes the disciplined man-of-war's-man; but the operation of laying out the anchor astern necessarily occupied some little time. The boat had only just dropped the anchor overboard, and the men on board the schooner were gathering in the slack of the hawser preparatory to taking it to the capstan, when the felucca came foaming down upon us, and a hasty turn had to be taken with it, and the men at once sent back to their guns, as the manoeuvres of our antagonist seemed to threaten that she was about to turn the tables upon us by laying us aboard, as we had contemplated doing with her.

"Boarders prepare to repel boarders!" exclaimed O'Flaherty, drawing his sword. I whipped out my toasting iron, and at the same moment down came Courtenay on deck by way of the back-stays. "Give me a musket, somebody," exclaimed he, as he alighted on the rail and sprang nimbly from thence to the deck.

"Here you are, sir, all ready primed and loaded," responded the captain of one of the guns, promptly thrusting the required weapon into my chum's hands.

The felucca was within one hundred feet of us, foaming along at the rate of about seven knots, and apparently aiming to strike us stem on directly amidships, when Courtenay sprang on the rail again, and, steadying his body against the fore-topmast back-stay, raised the musket steadily to his shoulder.

"Stand by, men, to fire, but wait until I give the word, and then fire only when you are certain of your shot taking effect!" exclaimed O'Flaherty. "Mr Courtenay, the helmsman is your mark, if you can—"

Crack! went Courtenay's musket, interrupting O'Flaherty's speech; a cry was heard on board the felucca, and her bows began to fly into the wind as Courtenay jumped down off the rail again, and, requisitioning a cartridge, began to hastily reload his piece.

"Now, men—now is your time to rake her! Fire!" exclaimed O'Flaherty, and our broadside of three six-pounders rang sharply out, followed by the crashing and rending sound of timber as the shot entered through the felucca's starboard bow, and a hideous outburst of shrieks, groans, yells, and shouts of defiance as the grape tore obliquely along her deck almost fore and aft. In another moment, still flying up into the wind, the felucca crashed into our starboard quarter with a shock which made us heel to our covering-board, and caused our antagonist to rebound a full fathom from us. Then, as the schooner recovered herself and rolled heavily to windward, the felucca poured in her broadside, and whilst the sharp ring of her brass pieces, mingled with the crash of timber, was vibrating in my ears, I felt a sharp stunning blow on the head which momentarily rendered me unconscious.

"Hurrah, sir, we're afloat, we're afloat!" were the first sounds I heard as my scattered senses came back to me; and, clearing away with my pocket-handkerchief the blood which was streaming down into my eyes and blinding me, I found that I had been knocked up against the mainmast, to one of the belaying-pins in the spider-hoop of which I was clinging with one hand; and I further observed that the shock of the collision, coupled no doubt with the action of our square canvas, which had been laid aback, had caused the schooner to back off the shoal on which she had grounded, and that she now had stern-way upon her. A hasty glance round the deck showed that our bulwarks and deck-fittings had been considerably damaged by the felucca's fire; and some eight or nine prostrate forms—O'Flaherty's among them—bore still further witness to its destructive effect.

The boatswain came up to me and said:

"Poor Mr O'Flaherty's down, sir; and you're hurt, yourself. Who is to take command of the schooner, sir?"

"I will," said I, rallying at once as a sense of the responsible position in which I thus suddenly found myself rushed upon me.

The boatswain touched his forelock and remarked:

"We've got starn-way upon us, sir, and if we don't look out we shall drive over that there stream of ours and perhaps send a fluke through our bottom."

"Yes," said I. "Have the goodness, Mr Fidd, to muster all hands aft here; let them tail on to the hawser and rouse it smartly inboard; then man the capstan and lift the anchor."

"Ay, ay, sir," was the reply, and the man turned away to see the order executed. At that moment Courtenay came aft.

"Why, Lascelles, old man," he exclaimed, starting back as I turned my face toward him, "what have the rascals done to you? You're an awful sight, old fellow; are you hurt much?"

"I can scarcely say yet," I replied; "not very much, I think; but my head is aching most consumedly. I wish you would kindly get a couple of hands and have Mr O'Flaherty taken below. I must remain here and look after the ship."

"Is O'Flaherty wounded?" gasped Courtenay. I pointed to the prostrate body of the lieutenant, upon which my chum at once hurried away, and, raising the wounded man in his arms, called one of the men to help in conveying him below.

We were lucky enough to trip and recover our anchor without accident; the quarter-boat was hoisted up, and we then wore round after the felucca, which was hovering irresolutely about a mile away, apparently undecided whether to renew the attack or not. On seeing, however, that we were afloat again and after her, she bore up and stood to the eastward, close hauled on the larboard tack.

We cracked on after her under every stitch of canvas we could spread, but she walked away from us hand over hand, at the same time looking up a couple of points nearer the wind than we did, so that it soon became evident we might as well hope to catch the Flying Dutchman as to get alongside the chase. And in the midst of it all we plumped ashore again, this time with such violence that our fore and main-topmasts both snapped short off at the caps, like carrots, and hung dangling by their gear to leeward.

We were now in a very tidy mess, and had our late antagonist chosen to retrace her steps and renew her attack upon us we should, in our disabled condition, have found her an exceedingly awkward customer to tackle. Fortunately for us she seemed to have had as much as she wanted; and a quarter of an hour later she slid out through one of the numerous channels between the islands and disappeared.

Setting one watch to clear away the wreck and the other to furl all canvas, I requested Courtenay, who was now again on deck, to take the quarter-boat and a sounding-line and to go away in search of the deepest water. This was found at about fifty fathoms distant from and directly to windward of the ship; and in this direction we accordingly ran away our stream-anchor and cable as before, the cable this time, however, being led in through one of the chocks on the larboard bow, from whence it was taken to the capstan. The men hove and hove until everything creaked again, whilst the schooner careened fully a couple of streaks to port; but it was all to no purpose, not an inch would she budge; and finally the anchor began to come home pretty rapidly. The stream was evidently of no use, so I sent away the boat to weigh it, giving orders at the same time to get the larboard-bower ready for slinging between the quarter-boat and the launch, which

I also ordered to be hoisted out. Presently the quarter-boat came alongside with the stream-anchor hanging over her stern; and then the reason for its coming home became evident—we had hove upon it until one of the flukes had been torn off.

By the time that the stream-anchor was out of the boat the bower was hanging at the bows ready for slinging, and it was then run away by the two boats directly to windward. As soon as it was let go we began to heave away once more, but with no better result—the schooner was hard and fast, and no efforts of ours were equal to the moving of her.

We now found ourselves in a very pretty pickle; and to add to my annoyance I made the discovery that we had grounded just about high-water, and that the tides, such as they were, were "taking off;" that is to say, each high tide would be a trifle lower than the preceding one until the neaps were reached and passed. There was nothing for it then but to lighten the ship; and getting the remaining boat into the water, all three were brought alongside, and the iron ballast was then hoisted out of the hold and lowered into the boats until they were as deeply loaded as they could be with safety, even in that perfectly smooth water. This lightened the schooner so considerably that I felt sanguine of getting her afloat when the tide next rose; but, not to neglect any means at my disposal to secure this very desirable end, I ordered all our spare spars to be launched overboard, and with them, some empty casks, and a quantity of lumber from the hold, a raft was constructed capable of supporting three of the guns, though they sank it so deep that I was at first afraid we should lose them altogether. I could then do no more until it was again high-water—which would not be until an hour past midnight—unless I sent the boats ashore to discharge their cargoes on the beach and then come alongside again to further lighten the ship; and this I was very loath to do, as I felt convinced that the process of handling and re-handling the heavy pigs of ballast would consume so much time that we should lose rather than gain by it, to say nothing of the exhausting labour which would thus devolve upon the men. Leaving Courtenay, therefore, who was uninjured, in charge of the deck, I retired to the cabin, which was at that moment serving for a cockpit, and, finding the surgeon disengaged, submitted myself to his tender mercies.

His first act was to bathe my head with warm water until the dry blood with which my hair was matted was cleared away as much as possible, and then the hair itself was shorn away until the wound was fairly exposed. The injury was then found to consist of a scalp wound some six inches in length, extending from a point above my right eye, just where the hair commenced, obliquely across the skull toward the back of the left ear, the scalp itself, for a width of about four inches, being torn from the skull and folded back like a rag. It burned and throbbed and smarted most horribly, particularly when the sponge was applied to my bare skull to clear away the blood preparatory to replacing the scalp; and I was informed by the medico that it was a very ugly wound, probably inflicted by a piece of langridge which, if it had been deflected a couple of inches to the right, would in all probability have killed me. And I was warned that I should have to exercise the greatest caution in the matter of exposing myself to the night air, or inflammation might set in, with very serious results. During the tedious and exceedingly painful operation of dressing the wound, I learned that O'Flaherty's injury consisted of a contusion on the head, whereby he had been struck senseless to the deck, and a very badly lacerated right shoulder, the bone of which was also broken, so that he would probably be quite unfit for duty for the remainder of the cruise. When at length I was fairly coopered up and made tolerably comfortable, I sent word to Courtenay that I intended to lie down for a while, but that he was to have me called the moment that my presence on deck might be necessary, and then retired to my berth and stretched myself, dressed as I was, upon my bed, where, though I was in too much pain to get sound sleep, I soon dozed off into a kind of half-delirious stupor which, unpleasant as was the sensation, still afforded me a certain measure of relief.

From this I was aroused by the clatter of plates and dishes in the cabin, which, as it was quite dark in my berth, I rightly assumed must indicate the forwarding of preparations for dinner. I now felt very much more comfortable than when I had lain down; the violent splitting headache had almost entirely passed away; the cool soothing salve which had been liberally applied to my wound had greatly modified the burning, smarting sensation; and I experienced a feeling of by no means unpleasant languor, which produced an almost irresistible repugnance to move. I remembered, however, that the ship was now in my charge—unpleasant as it might be I could now less than ever afford to neglect my duty—so, though the effort produced a sudden giddiness and momentary lapse into almost total insensibility, I staggered to my feet and cautiously groped my way to the door of my berth, through which I passed into the close and stuffy cabin, and from thence up the companion-way and out on deck.

Here everything was so perfectly silent, save for the gentle lap and gurgle of the water alongside, that I was for a moment startled into the belief that the ship had been deserted; and it was so intensely dark that I could see absolutely nothing. Glancing aft, however, I detected a tiny glowing spark away in the neighbourhood of the taffrail, and at the same moment I heard Courtenay's voice saying:

"Is that you, Mr O'Flaherty?"

"No," I responded, "it is I, Lascelles. What has become of the hands, Courtenay?"

"They are below getting their suppers," he answered. "And I told them that, when they had finished, they might turn in for an hour or two. They must be pretty well done up with their hard day's work, and we can do nothing more now until after half-flood. How are you feeling now, old fellow? Sanderson tells me you got a very ugly clip over the head to-day in our little boxing match with the felucca. It has been rather an unfortunate business altogether—two killed and seven wounded at a single broadside from only four guns is pretty hard lines."

"Do you mean to say that we have lost two men?" I exclaimed, for I had not heard this before.

"Yes," was the answer. "Jones—that comical fellow who used to play the violin on the forecastle during the dog-watches, and poor Tom Cotterel have both lost the number of their mess; and there are five more in their hammocks hurt more or less severely; though I believe O'Flaherty and yourself are the worst sufferers in that respect."

I was greatly concerned to hear this; and more than ever regretted the fool-hardihood—as I could not help thinking it—which had induced O'Flaherty to rush headlong, as it were, into a lagoon so shallow that there was scarcely water enough in it in the deepest part to float the schooner, and abounding, moreover, as we had found to our cost, in shoals, of the position of which we knew absolutely nothing. The mischief, however, had been done, and nothing now remained but to make the best of it; with which reflection we made our way below to dinner in obedience to the steward's summons.

As we entered the cabin Sanderson, the surgeon, emerged on tiptoe from O'Flaherty's state-room, and requested us, in a whisper, to make as little noise as possible, as the lieutenant, under the influence of a soothing draught, had just dropped off to sleep.

"I want to keep him as quiet as possible," continued Sanderson, "for if he is disturbed or excited I am afraid I shall have a deal of trouble with him. What I am principally afraid of in his case—as in yours, Lascelles—is an access of fever, which, with its resulting restlessness, may retard the healing of the wound, or even bring on mortification."

"And what about the others?" I asked, "are any of their injuries severe?"

"No; chiefly lacerations, painful enough, but not serious," was the reply. "Those rascals must have fired nothing but langridge, or canister."

"Ay," said Courtenay; "and had they fired a little earlier, and so allowed the charges to scatter more, they would have made a clean sweep of our decks. As it was the charges took effect almost like solid shot, as may be seen by the marks in the planking and bulwarks where they struck."

"Ah, well! it's a good job it was no worse," remarked Sanderson. "It has had one good result, in that it has let some of the wild Irish blood out of O'Flaherty, and has taught us the lesson, let us hope, to be a trifle more cautious in future. And, by the by, in the meantime, whilst he is on his beam-ends, which of you youngsters is going to be skipper?"

"Oh, Lascelles, of course," answered Courtenay quickly. "We joined the service together, you know; but he is a few months my senior in point of age. Moreover, he is ever so much the better navigator of the two; indeed I am ashamed to say I am so shaky in my navigation that I should really be almost afraid to take sole charge of a ship. I *might* manage all right, but I am not absolutely sure of myself, and that is an awfully unpleasant feeling to have, let me tell you, when you are occupying a position of responsibility."

The land-breeze, meanwhile, had sprung up, and was by this time blowing pretty strongly; so, as I was a trifle anxious about the raft with the guns alongside, we hurried our meal to a conclusion; and, whilst Sanderson first took another peep at O'Flaherty, and then went forward to look after the rest of his patients, Courtenay and I went on deck, where we found the gunner keeping a lookout. "Well, Mr Tompion," said I, as the man approached, "how are matters looking here on deck?"

"All quiet, sir," was the reply, "leastways as far as one can be sartain on sich a pitch-dark night as this. It's lightnin' a little away down there to the west'ard, and durin' one o' the flashes I sartaintly *did* think I see some objek a-movin' away over there in the direction where the felucca came from, but when the next flash took place there weren't a sign of anything."

"Oh, indeed!" said I, "what did the object look like?"

"Well, sir, it might ha' been a boat—or a raft—or it might only ha' been the trunk of a tree struck adrift; but if it had been a tree I don't think as it would ha' wanished quite so quick."

"How long ago was this, Mr Tompion?"

"Just a minute or two afore you came on deck, sir."

"Well," said I, "we must keep a sharp lookout, that is all we can do at present Is there anybody on the lookout on the forecastle?"

"Yes, sir, Jack Sinclair and Bob Miles."

"Thank you, that will do, Mr Tompion," said I, and the man turned away to his former post at the gangway.

Whatever the mysterious object might have been it was invisible on the occurrence, not only of the next, but also of several succeeding flashes of the bluish summer lightning which quivered up from behind a heavy bank of cloud low down on the western horizon, momentarily lighting up with a weird evanescent radiance the lagoon, the mainland, the distant islands toward which our suspicious glances were directed, and the ship herself, which, partially dismantled as she was, looked in the faint and momentary illumination like the ghost of some ancient wreck hovering over the scene of her dissolution; the incident was therefore soon forgotten as Courtenay took me round from point to point explaining what further steps he had taken, after my retirement below in the afternoon, to facilitate the floating of the ship.

The tide was now again making, and at length, about two bells in the first watch, we became conscious that the schooner, which had been lying somewhat over on her port bilge, was gradually becoming more upright. Meanwhile the lightning had ceased, and the darkness had become, if possible, more profound than ever, whilst the only sounds audible were the rippling splash of the water alongside, the melancholy sough of the wind, and the faint *chirr* of insects ashore which the breeze brought off to us on its invisible wings.

As the tide made so the schooner continued imperceptibly to right herself, and at length she was so nearly upright that I thought we might set about the attempt to get her afloat. The wind, being now off-shore, was in our favour, as the deepest water was to leeward or to seaward of us, and the canvas, had I dared to set it, would have materially assisted us; but I did not care to set it, as, once off the bank, we should have perforce to remain at anchor where we were until morning, any attempt at navigating those shallows in darkness being the most utter madness. I therefore left the canvas stowed, resolving to seek its aid only as a last resort, and in the event of all other means failing, and ordered the messenger to be passed and the capstan manned. The anchor was already laid out to leeward, so the slack of the cable was soon hove in, and a steady strain brought to bear upon it, after which came the tug of war. The capstan bars were now fully manned; the tars pressed their broad chests against the powerful levers, planted their feet firmly upon the deck, straightened out their backs, and slowly pawl after pawl was gained until the schooner was once more heeling over on her bilge, this time, however, in consequence of the intense strain upon her cable.

"That's your sort, my hearties," exclaimed the boatswain encouragingly, as he applied his tremendous strength to the outer extremity of one of the bars, "heave with a will! heave, and she *must* come! *heave*, all of us!! now— one—*two*—three!!!"

The men strained at the bars until it seemed as though they would burst their very sinews; another reluctant click or two of the pawl showed that something was at length yielding; and then, first with a slow jerky motion which quickened rapidly, and ended in a mighty surge as the men drove the capstan irresistibly round, the bows of the schooner swerved to seaward, the vessel herself righted, hung for a moment, and then glided off the tail of the bank, finally swinging to her anchor, afloat once more.

"Well done, lads!" I exclaimed joyously, for it was a great relief to me to have the schooner afloat again—a sailor feels just as much out of his element in a stranded ship as he does when he personally is on *terra firma*—and in the exuberance of my gratification I gave orders to "splice the main brace" preparatory to the troublesome and laborious task of getting the guns and ballast on board once more.

# Chapter Sixteen
# The Pirates attempt a Night
# Attack upon the "Foam"

The men were busily discussing their "nip" of grog when, mechanically glancing over the black surface of the water which lay spread out on all sides of the ship, my gaze was arrested by a sudden phosphorescent flash on our starboard beam, which was now turned in the direction of the islands we had been watching so suspiciously earlier on in the night. Looking intently I caught it again, and yet again, three or four times.

The gunner at that moment approached me to report that the men were all ready to turn-to once more, upon which I directed his attention to the point at which I had noticed the mysterious appearance, and asked him if he could see anything.

Shading his eyes with his hand, he looked earnestly in the direction indicated.

"N–o, sir, I can't say as I can," replied he, after a good long look; "you see, sir, it's so precious dark just now that there's no—eh, what was that? I thought I seed something just then, sir," as another flash appeared, this time sensibly nearer the ship than before.

"So did I," I replied; "and it is my belief, Tompion, that what we saw is neither more nor less than the phosphorescent flash of oars in the water. If I am not mistaken there is a boat out there trying to steal down and catch us unawares. Just go to the men, please, and pass the word for them to go *quietly* to quarters, and see that the starboard broadside guns are loaded with grape."

Courtenay just then emerged from the companion with a lighted cigar in his mouth, which he had helped himself to in the brief interval of rest following the floating of the schooner. The spark at the end of the weed glowed brightly in the intense darkness, and could probably be seen for a considerable distance.

"Dowse that cigar, Courtenay, *quick*!" I exclaimed, as I moved to his side, "and tell me if you can hear or see anything over there."

Instinctively guessing at an alarm of some kind from the quarter I had indicated, my shipmate stepped to the opposite side of the deck, dropped his cigar over the rail, and rejoined me.

"Now then, what is it, Lascelles?" he asked; "is there anything wrong? and why are the men mustering at quarters?"

"Look over in that direction, and see if you can find an explanation," said I.

Unconsciously imitating Tompion in the attitude he assumed, Courtenay stood intently gazing into the darkness for a full minute or more, without result. He had turned to me and was about to speak when a faint *crack*, like the breaking of a thole-pin, was heard, the sound being accompanied by a very distinct luminous splash of the water.

"Ha!" exclaimed Courtenay, "there is a boat over there at no great distance from us!" and at the same moment Fidd came barefooted and noiselessly to my side with the question:

"Did ye see and hear that, sir?"

"Ay, ay, Mr Fidd, I saw it. Are the starboard guns loaded?"

"Yes, sir."

"Then kindly pass along the word to the captain of each gun to watch for the next splash and then to train his gun upon it."

"Ay, ay, sir," was the reply; and Fidd turned away to execute his mission as I sprang upon the rail and, grasping one of the shrouds of the main rigging to steady myself, hailed in Spanish:

"Boat ahoy! who are you, and what do you want? Lay on your oars and answer instantly, or I will fire upon you."

I waited a full minute without eliciting any response or sign of any description from the direction in which our enemies were supposed to be lurking, and then ordered a port-fire to be burnt and a musket to be fired in their direction.

A brief interval elapsed, and then the darkness was suddenly broken into by the ghastly glare of the port-fire, with which one of the men nimbly shinned up the fore-rigging in order to send the illumination as far abroad as possible, and at the same instant a musket was fired. For a moment or two nothing whatever was to be seen but our own decks, with the men standing stripped to the waist at their guns—a row of statues half marble, half ebony, as the glare lighted up one side of each figure and left the other side in blackest shadow—the spars and rigging towering weird and ghostly up into the opaque blackness above us like those of a phantom ship; whilst the water shimmered like burning brimstone under the baleful light. Then, evidently under the impression that the boat had become visible in the gleam of the port-fire—though at that instant we could see nothing—a voice was heard from out the darkness on our starboard beam exclaiming in Spanish:

"Give way with a will, my heroes! one smart dash now and we shall be alongside yet before they can load their guns."

The dash of oars in the water instantly followed, the whereabouts of the boat being at once made manifest by the flash of the port-fire upon the wet oar-blades, and upon the foaming ripple which gathered under the bows of the boat; and by the time that half a dozen strokes had been pulled the boat herself—a very large craft, apparently, and crowded with men—became dimly visible like a faint luminous mist driving along the surface of the inky water.

"Steady now, men," I cried. "Take your time, and aim straight. Say when you are ready."

"All ready with the midship gun!"

"All ready aft!"

"Ready for'ard!"

The replies were uttered almost simultaneously, and I instantly gave the word "*Fire!*"

The three guns rang out as one, the triple flash not only illuminating vividly, for a fraction of a second, the boat against which they were discharged, but also revealing for the same brief space of time a second and similar boat a few yards in the rear of the first. Fatally sped those three terrible charges of grape. The guns had been aimed with such deadly precision, and discharged so exactly at the right moment, that the leading boat was literally torn to pieces; so utterly destroyed, indeed, that she seemed to have vanished instantly from the surface of the lagoon, leaving in her stead only a few fragments of shattered planking, and a broad patch of phosphorescent foam in the midst of which floated her late crew, a ghastly array of *corpses*, save where, here and there, some wretch, less fortunate than his comrades, still writhed and splashed feebly as the life reluctantly left his torn and mutilated body. The spectacle of this catastrophe, so suddenly and completely wrought, this instant destruction of some thirty or forty human beings, was absolutely appalling; and its effect was intensified by the extraordinary circumstance that not a single shriek, or groan, or outcry of any description, escaped the victims of our murderous fire. So dreadful was the sight that, for perhaps half a minute, the entire crew of the schooner, fore and aft, stood motionless and dumb, petrified with horror, staring with dilated eyeballs at the spot where the bodies, now all motionless, lay faintly defined in the last rays of the almost burnt-out port-fire.

But there was no time to be lost; another boat was lurking out there somewhere, in the impenetrable gloom; so, rallying my faculties by a powerful effort, I managed to exclaim in a tolerably steady voice:

"Load again, men, smartly! there is another boat out there somewhere, and she must be prevented from coming alongside at all costs. Light another port-fire forward, there!" as the man in the fore-rigging dropped the fag-end of the first into the water alongside and the blackness of darkness once more enshrouded us as with a pall.

There was, apparently, to be no more fighting just then, however; the crew of the remaining boat had evidently seen enough to completely damp their ardour, for the time being at least, for before the operation of reloading the guns had been completed, the splash and roll of oars in their rowlocks could be heard in fast diminishing cadence, conveying to our experienced ears the fact that our enemies were beating a precipitate retreat.

But the horrors of the night were not yet quite over, for, whilst we were busily preparing to hoist in the guns from the raft alongside and to get the ballast back into its proper place in the hold, a loud, confused, splashing sound was suddenly heard away on our starboard beam, and, on looking in that direction to ascertain what this new disturbance might portend, we saw that the water was literally alive with hundreds of sharks, distinctly visible by the phosphorescent glow which shone from their bodies, which were tearing and snapping at the floating corpses of the pirates, rending them limb from limb, and rushing off in all directions with the dismembered fragments as the monsters succeeded in securing them.

Such a sight was not calculated to inspire the men with any relish for the somewhat perilous task of going down upon the submerged raft and into the deeply-laden boats to sling the guns and ballast; but the work had to be done, and the boatswain and the gunner volunteering to go down first, we soon had the work well under weigh, finishing it satisfactorily off and bringing a toilsome night of labour to an end about two o'clock the next morning.

By daybreak all hands were once more astir, notwithstanding the arduous character of their previous day's and night's work; the anchor was weighed; and under short canvas, with Courtenay once more on the topgallant-yard to con us, and a leads-man in the fore-chains on each side of the ship, we cautiously felt our way to the northward and westward until, about seven bells, we managed to reach the anchorage which the feluccas had vacated on the previous day. A hurried breakfast was then scrambled through; after which the long-boat and the gig, under the command of Courtenay and the boatswain, with their crews fully armed, pulled away for the shore, to see whether they could discover anything like a dépôt, of which no sign whatever could be detected from the deck of the schooner.

They pulled inshore about a quarter of a mile, after which we suddenly lost sight of them among the mangroves which thickly fringed the shores of the island. Three or four minutes later the sound of musketry firing, at first in whole volleys and then intermittingly, floated off to us from the direction where the boats had disappeared, and very soon we saw the light wreaths of pale-blue smoke floating up and out from among the trees. The firing soon ceased; and then nothing more was heard or seen for nearly two hours, at the end of which time a thin volume of light brownish smoke rose into the sky from about the spot where we had before seen the indications of musketry firing; the smoke, rapidly increasing in volume and deepening in colour until, thickly besprinkled with sparks, it poured across the bay in one vast dense black cloud which swept right over us where we lay, half suffocating us with its pungent fumes, and almost hiding the islands from sight. Then, when the smoke-cloud had become almost intolerable, the boats were seen approaching; upon which the schooner was hove short and the canvas set in readiness for a speedy retreat from our uncomfortable berth. The moment that they came alongside the anchor was tripped, and, by the time that the boat's crews were once more on the schooner's decks, we had run out clear of the nuisance. The *Foam* was then hove to; seven singularly heavy kegs were hoisted in from the long-boat; the boats themselves next followed; and then away we went, groping our way as before, back toward the main channel from the sea. This channel was successfully traversed and the open sea reached about three bells in the afternoon watch, when I turned over the command of the schooner to Courtenay and went below to my berth, not only dead tired, but also suffering dreadfully from the wound in my head, which had not been dressed for nearly twenty-four hours, and which was certainly none the better for the excitement and exposure of the preceding night. Previous to this, though, I had been fully informed of what had transpired on shore; and which may be related in a very few words.

It appeared that the sudden evanishment of the boats from our sight was due to the fact that they had discovered and pushed into a narrow channel running to the northward and eastward between the two westernmost islands of the group; along which channel they had proceeded for about half a mile when they suddenly opened a tiny bay, on their starboard hand, from the shore of which projected a long wooden jetty of rough mangrove piles decked over with ship timber. This jetty they at once headed for, and were immediately saluted with a volley of musketry from a long black wooden building which stood close to the shore. Luckily, nobody was hit; and the same good fortune befell them when, whilst landing on the jetty, a second volley was fired at them. The tars, headed by Courtenay and the boatswain, then charged up to the building, and, without very much difficulty, burst in the door, just in time to see some twenty Spaniards effecting a hasty retreat through an opening in the opposite side of the building. Our lads at once crowded sail in chase, shouting and laughing like a parcel of schoolboys out for a holiday, and occasionally stopping to pop away at the enemy with musket or pistol as opportunity offered. The Spaniards, however, were lighter in the heels than our own men, and they possessed the further advantage of knowing the country, so they quickly hauled out of sight, nor was anything further seen of them, though Courtenay maintained the pursuit for about half an hour. The party then returned to the shed by the beach; and whilst Courtenay with three or four hands gave the place a thorough overhaul, Fidd, with the remainder of the men, turned to and broke up a very large yawl-built boat which was lying alongside the jetty, afterwards carrying her dismembered planking and timbers up to the shed, to be still more effectually destroyed with it by fire. A quantity of ship's stores, such as rope, canvas, pitch, tar, paint, etcetera, was found, evidently showing that this was one of the many pirates' rendezvous which were known to be in existence along this coast; but there was nothing in the shape of plunder except the seven heavy kegs before mentioned, one of which, upon being opened, proved to be filled with Spanish dollars (as did the rest, eventually), so they were promptly tumbled down to the jetty and put on board the long-boat. It had evidently been a place of some little importance; but, from Courtenay's account, it was not to be compared for a moment with Merlani's establishment. At last, the place having been thoroughly rummaged, a bonfire was built on the weather side of the shed, which, being well fed with tar, etcetera, soon set the entire building in a blaze, after which they retreated to the boats, firing the jetty also before shoving off. Altogether it was a very satisfactory morning's work, since, with their limited facilities, it would be a long time before the pirates could make good the loss and damage inflicted upon them, if indeed they would have the heart to attempt it at all. The Barcos Channel being only some five hours' sail distant from the Cristo Cays, near which we had emerged once more into open water, and as it would be quite impossible for us to traverse the intricate channel through Santa Clara Bay during the hours of darkness, Courtenay stretched off the land under easy canvas, and employed the remainder of the afternoon in getting up the two topmasts which the carpenter had reduced, in place of the spars expended on the previous day. This job was completed and the schooner made all ataunto again by sunset; at which hour the *Foam* was hove to with her head toward the land; and all hands, with the exception of the officer of the watch and two men on the lookout, were allowed to go below and get as much rest as possible, in order that they might not only recover from the fatigue of the previous night, but also prepare for what would probably prove an equally fatiguing day on the morrow.

On sitting down to the dinner-table that evening we were much gratified to learn from Sanderson that poor O'Flaherty was doing remarkably well; so well indeed, that the doctor had yielded a somewhat unwilling assent to a wish the lieutenant had expressed to see me after dinner. But I was strictly enjoined to make the interview as brief as possible; and to be cautious above all things not to engage in conversation of an exciting character. Accordingly, as soon as dinner was over, I knocked at the door of O'Flaherty's state-room, and, in response to his feebly spoken "Come in," entered. Notwithstanding what Sanderson had previously told us about his appearance, I was shocked to see how terribly loss of blood and the torture of his wound had pulled the poor fellow down. His swarthy, sunburnt features were now sallow, bloodless, and shrunken; contrasting strongly with his dark curly hair, which hung in long elf-locks over his forehead and about his face, dripping with perspiration caused partly by the excessive heat of the cabin and still more by the anguish from which he was suffering. A sheet was his only covering, his body being bare from the chest upwards, for greater convenience in dressing his wound; and his right shoulder and arm down to the elbow was closely swathed in bandages through which the blood still oozed here and there. There was a restless feverish gleam and glitter in his eyes which told all too plainly how acutely he was suffering; and there was an occasional nervous twitching of the fingers of the right hand which I did not like to see, and which he said had come on within the last half-hour. But his spirits were excellent; and his voice became stronger almost with every word he spoke as he questioned me about our doings since the moment of his being struck down. He expressed himself as highly satisfied with all that we had done, and especially so at the watchfulness which had defeated the pirates' attempt at a night attack; but he intimated his expectation that, although he was unable to actually command the schooner, I would keep him fully acquainted with everything which might transpire, and consult him with regard to every proposed movement of an important character. This I, at the time, thought reasonable enough; but I soon had cause to regret that he had imposed any such condition upon me.

Daybreak next morning found us some eight miles off the mouth of the Barcos Channel, and in such a position that we should be dead to windward of it upon the springing up of the sea-breeze. We were, consequently, as well placed for the run down to it as heart could wish. But, on the boatswain calling me—I had remained in my berth all night—I was greatly annoyed to learn that there was a small craft of some kind, apparently a one-masted felucca, hovering about the entrance of the channel and manoeuvring in such a way as to lead to the belief that she was enacting the part of lookout. Courtenay and I had both been called at the same time; but he was the quicker of the two in his movements; and upon my reaching the deck I discovered him on the topsail-yard scrutinising the stranger through his telescope.

The craft was then becalmed, though *we* had a nice little breeze from about east-north-east; but on our filling upon the schooner and edging away in her direction, the felucca—for such she was—at once rigged out six sweeps of a side and headed direct for the mouth of the channel. Now this, I was afraid, indicated first, that the felucca was enacting the part of lookout; and second, that our late antagonists had effected a retreat to the Conconil lagoons, where they had probably united themselves temporarily with Merlani's gang; and I anticipated that, if this surmise of mine should prove correct, we should have our hands more than full in the forthcoming attack. So heavy, indeed, would be the odds against us in such a case that I thought it would be more prudent to defer the attack for a day or two, merely passing through the channel and affecting to make an examination of the cays on each side of it, previous to retiring again and pursuing a course to the westward, thus throwing our adversaries off their guard; when I considered it might be possible to effect a descent upon them by way of Cardenas Bay, through which we might perhaps be able to so nearly approach them, unobserved, as to take them in a great measure by surprise. This plan, however, in consequence of the injunction O'Flaherty had laid upon me at our interview of the previous evening, I dared not put into effect without first submitting it for his approval; and I accordingly went down to his state-room to speak to him about it. To my surprise and chagrin I found him utterly opposed to it. He argued that my plan would *not* throw the pirates off their guard, whilst it would allow them a great deal more time in which to complete their preparations for an effective defence; moreover, he disliked the idea of our making our approaches through Cardenas Bay because of our having originally passed through it during the night, when, as he said, we had had no opportunity to take careful note of the landmarks, etcetera. I reminded him of the fact that the water in Cardenas Bay was deep enough to float the schooner everywhere about the track over which we should have to pass, and that that track was, moreover, so nearly straight that, with a good breeze, we could traverse it in an hour, thus materially lessening our chance of discovery; but it was all of no avail, he *would* have his own way; so I was perforce compelled—with, I must confess, somewhat serious misgivings—to return to the deck and give the necessary orders for running in through the Barcos Channel as soon as the sea-breeze should spring up.

At length, after what appeared to me an unusually long delay, a cat's-paw reached us; and presently the true sea-breeze came creeping along the water, freshening as it came. We allowed it to reach the mouth of the channel, when the *Foam* bore up; and a quarter of an hour later we were rattling through the passage at the rate of eight knots. On clearing the channel and opening up the bay we discovered the felucca some four miles ahead, or about half-way across, foaming along with her enormously long tapering yard square across her deck and the sheet eased well out, running down dead before the wind, straight for the entrance of the lagoons, apparently in the hope that we would follow her and thus ground upon one of the numerous shoals which lay between her and us. But if they hoped this they were speedily disappointed, as the moment we had cleared the end of the channel, all concealment being then impossible, we hauled our wind and headed the schooner for the first of the marks which were to pilot us safely on our difficult way. Before we had completed our first reach the felucca had arrived at the entrance to the lagoons, and had disappeared. It was half an hour after noon when we reached the same spot.

Two miles further on lay the narrowest passage in the whole length of the lagoons, and here I fully expected our progress would meet with a check. Nor was I disappointed, for on reaching the spot our further progress was suddenly interrupted, and the schooner brought up all standing, by a heavy chain which had been thrown athwart the channel, just far enough beneath the surface of the water to catch our forefoot, the ends being artfully concealed among the bushes on either side.

"Down, flat on your faces on the deck, every man of you, fore and aft!" I shouted, for I guessed what would follow; and scarcely was the order obeyed when the flash of artillery blazed out from among the mangroves on either hand, and a perfect hailstorm of grape and langridge struck us, riddling our bulwarks, and tearing the foot of the mainsail and foresail to shreds, but, luckily, not hitting a soul of us; though how Courtenay and I escaped—it not being etiquette for either of us to seek the shelter of the bulwarks—heaven only knows; but we did. The guns were pointed so as to sweep the ship from stem to taffrail at about the level of the top of the bulwarks; and, had the men been standing erect, we must have lost half of them.

"Starboard your helm! hard a-starboard!" cried I to the man at the wheel, as the schooner rebounded from the chain; "let fly your starboard braces!

Gigs and quarter-boats away! Mr Courtenay, have the goodness to take the gig and silence that battery on the north side of the channel; Mr Fidd, go you in the quarter-boat and do the same with the battery on the south side. Take a hammer and a bag of nails each, and spike the guns before you leave them. Flatten in, forward there, the larboard sheets, and help her head to pay round; we must go outside again and seek a passage elsewhere."

The men, fully realising the peril of the situation in which we now found ourselves, sprang like wild-cats to execute the orders I had given; and in an incredibly short time both boats were in the water, with their crews in them, fully armed.

They were in the very act of shoving off when the sound of a sudden commotion in the cabin reached me, quickly followed by cries for help from Sanderson; and, before I had time to reach the sky-light to see what was amiss, up through the companion dashed poor O'Flaherty closely followed by the doctor, the former naked as when he was born, his hair bristling, his eyes aflame with fever, his teeth clenched, and the blood streaming from the disarranged bandages about his right shoulder. He glared round the deck for an instant, a single horrible unearthly cry escaped from between his clenched teeth, and then—before any of us had sufficiently recovered from our astonishment to lay a preventing hand upon him—with one bound he reached the rail, sprang upon it, and, steadying himself with his left hand by grasping the main-topmast back-stay, waved his bleeding right arm frantically to Courtenay, who by this time was a hundred yards away. At this moment the hidden battery on the north side of the channel again opened fire, this time with round shot. We felt a jar which told us that the schooner had been hulled; and, at the same moment, heard a sickening thud and saw poor O'Flaherty's body, doubled-up like a pair of compasses, dashed lifeless and bloody to the deck by one of the shot, which had struck him fair in the stomach and cut him almost in two. It was a ghastly sight; but there was no time just then to inquire of Sanderson what the sudden escapade meant, or even to have the body removed, for the schooner was at that moment head to wind, and I was most anxious to get her round, which in that cramped channel was no very easy matter. We managed to box her off, however, in the right direction, when the topsail was backed, and we lay motionless on the half stagnant water waiting for the return of the boats.

We had not very long to wait. A loud, confused shouting, intermingled with a ringing British cheer from our own lads now and then, accompanied by the clash of steel and the popping of pistols, told us, whilst we were manoeuvring the schooner, that the boats' crews had effected a landing; and about ten minutes later Courtenay's boat reappeared, emerging from among the mangroves with another boat in tow, which, being captured from the enemy, was stove and sunk directly she was brought alongside the schooner. Fidd's boat followed almost immediately afterwards; and I then had the gratification of learning that both batteries had been captured, the guns spiked and capsized into the mud, and the men who manned them driven off into the swamps, where they were perfectly powerless to work us further harm, for some time to come at all events, in consequence of the destruction of the boat, which constituted their only means of escape from the situation they then occupied. And this, too, without injury to a man on our side, though the pirates had suffered pretty severely.

This was eminently satisfactory. There was now nothing to prevent the removal by us of the chain which barred our passage up the lagoon; but I had a shrewd suspicion that other snares and pitfalls had been prepared for us further on, and I had made up my mind to see if these could not be evaded by passing out of the lagoons and making our way to the westward, close along the northern shore of the chain of islands which formed them. I thought it quite possible that a navigable channel for the schooner might be found somewhere between these islands, giving access to the lagoons so near their head as to be beyond the range of whatever other barriers to our upward progress might have been prepared; and, if we failed in this, I felt confident that we should at least be able to push through with our boats. As soon, therefore, as the boats had been hoisted up, we filled on the schooner and made the best of our way back again.

I judged that it would take us a full hour or more to reach the spot which I had in my mind's eye; advantage was therefore taken of this brief period of peace and quietness to let the men get their dinners, with a glass of grog afterwards. They were thus rested, refreshed, and ready to do anything or go anywhere when, about three bells in the afternoon watch, we arrived at a spot distant something like five miles from the entrance to the lagoons, where we found a narrow but apparently deep channel trending to the southward, and promising to give access to the lagoons.

The schooner was at once hove to, and Courtenay, in the gig, with his crew fully armed, went away to take soundings and to reconnoitre. Twenty minutes later the boat returned with the gratifying intelligence that the channel was scarcely a quarter of a mile in length; that it communicated, as anticipated, with the lagoon, and that, too, so advantageously that, with due caution and by taking advantage of the cover afforded by a small island, it might be possible for the boats to approach undetected so closely to our enemies as to take them in a great measure by surprise. It was further discovered that there were three feluccas—one large three-masted craft and two small one-masters, surmised to be our recent acquaintances of the Cristo Cays—lying in the anchorage, with springs on their cables and apparently all ready for immediate action; but the schooner which we saw on our last visit was now absent, and Merlani—presumably—with her. The channel upon which we had so fortuitously chanced was found to be of ample depth throughout almost its entire length to float the *Foam*; but, unhappily, there was a sort of bar, with only four feet of water upon it, stretching entirely across its inner extremity; and we should thus be compelled to make the attack with the boats. This was peculiarly unfortunate, as it would necessitate the division of our forces, a certain number of hands being required to look after the schooner—and this we could ill afford to do in view of the strength of those opposed to us. There was, however, evidently no help for it; we therefore manned all three of the boats, a six-pounder being placed in the bows of the long-boat, or launch as our people had got into the way of calling her; and I decided, after considerable reflection, to personally lead the attack, leaving the schooner under weigh and with all her guns loaded with round and grape, with six hands and the quarter-master on board to take care of her. I was, heaven knows, wretchedly unfit for service of so arduous a character as that involved in a boat attack; but the consciousness that upon the result of this action depended the success or failure of the main object of the expedition, coupled with the anxiety attendant upon my responsible position, overcame for the time being the feeling of illness resulting from my wound, and created a restless excitement and eagerness for which I feared I should afterwards suffer severely, but which impelled me at all risks to be present and to take the direction of affairs. The men, encouraged by the report of the gig's crew, tumbled into the boats with alacrity and in high spirits; Courtenay retained the command of the gig; Fidd, the boatswain, again assumed the command of the quarter-boat; and, snatching a cutlass from the arm-chest, I stepped into the launch, said a parting word or two to the quarter-master, and then gave the order to shove off; upon which away we all dashed in profound silence for the mouth of the passage.

# Chapter Seventeen
# The Conquest of the Conconil Lagoons

A very short time, some three minutes or so, sufficed to carry us through the channel into the lagoon, which once reached, away we went for the back of the island, under the friendly cover of which we hoped to reach undiscovered within about a cable's length of our foe. Half a dozen strokes of the oars sufficed to carry our little flotilla across the narrow strip of water, during the traversing of which there was a possibility of our premature discovery; and whilst we were dashing across this open space, I made the best possible use of my eyes to take in the position of affairs. I was enabled to note the situations of the three feluccas, which were lying at anchor about a mile distant, and we could see men moving about the decks of each, but there was no movement or sound on board either that we could discern indicative of our presence being observed. I was earnestly hoping and praying that the eyes and the whole attention of the pirates would be turned in the opposite direction, from whence they doubtless expected us to make our appearance, and we subsequently learned that such was actually the case.

The moment we were fairly under cover of the island I ordered the men to ease up on their oars, in order that they might husband their strength as much as possible for the final dash and the ensuing struggle, which I could see would be a severe one, and waving Courtenay to range alongside, the next few minutes were devoted to a final settlement of the plan of attack. I had observed that the two small feluccas were lying inside the larger one, all three of the craft being nearly in a straight line; and it was arranged that our three boats should, on emerging from the shelter of the island, make a dash at the nearest, as if about to board her, Courtenay making for the larboard side of the vessel, whilst Fidd and I made a feint of attacking on the starboard side. The bulk of the crew we considered would naturally, seeing this, muster on the starboard side to oppose the strongest division of the attacking force, thus leaving the larboard side but weakly defended, and so rendering it a tolerably easy matter for Courtenay and his boat's crew to gain a footing upon her deck. Having thus given the gigs what aid we could, the launch and quarter-boat were to pass on and make for the large felucca, leaving Courtenay to gain possession of the first vessel attacked, to secure her crew, and then to further act according to his own discretion.

Shortly after the completion of these arrangements we found that we were getting into close proximity with our foes, the masts of the feluccas opening out simultaneously from behind a high bluff, and showing over a sloping spur or point of the island between them and ourselves. We accordingly got the boats into line, the men braced themselves for a dash, and in another minute or two the boats were unmasked by rounding the point. Even then we managed to get a length or two nearer the vessels before we were discovered, for I had given the strictest injunctions to the men not to cheer until we heard from the feluccas, but the roll of the oars in their rowlocks at length betrayed us, as was announced by a shout of unmistakable dismay from the nearest felucca, immediately succeeded by a tremendous amount of confusion and bustle on board. Then, indeed, our lads *did* cheer once, with an enthusiasm which must have been eminently disconcerting to the enemy, after which they laid down to their oars in a style which, I must confess, fairly astonished me. We went through the water like race-horses over the ground, dashing alongside the first felucca in so short a time that her crew were unable to train their guns upon us, and so greeted us only with a confused volley of musketry which hurt nobody. As we swerved away from her, and headed for the large craft a couple of cable's-lengths distant, I caught sight of Courtenay's head and shoulders over the bulwarks, showing that he, gallant fellow, had already gained a footing on her deck; and a few seconds later, amid the clash of steel and the popping of pistols, another British cheer told us that the gigs were all hard at it, and evidently gaining the advantage.

The crews of the other two feluccas now began to haul on their springs, in order that their broadsides might be brought to bear upon us, but we were too quick for them both as it happened; the second small craft could not be got round smartly enough to do us any harm, and as for the big one, in their hurry to annihilate us, her crew fired too high, and their whole broadside whizzed harmlessly over our heads. We replied effectively with our six-pounder, which was loaded with round and grape, and pointed so high that we were enabled to fire within three fathoms of the felucca's side, and before the smoke had cleared away we were alongside, Fidd tackling them on the larboard side, whilst we in the launch attacked on the starboard.

It was well for us that we had had the forethought to bring the gun with us, for the deck of the vessel we were now attacking was crowded with men, so crowded, indeed, that the bulwarks were closely lined on each side to oppose us, whilst others were seen behind the first line all ready to support their comrades, and but for the confusion created by the timely discharge of our piece, not one of us could possibly have lived to reach her deck. As it was, I slightly altered my plans at the last moment, for seeing that the pirates had mustered strongly in the waist, evidently expecting us to board there, I gave orders for the launch to be allowed to shoot along the vessel's side until we reached her bows, where there were fewer men to oppose us. It proved to be a happy inspiration, for whilst we were busy forcing our way in over the felucca's low rail, several cold shot were hove over her side amidships, evidently with the intention of sinking the boat, but being where we were, they of course all missed and splashed harmlessly into the water. Poor Fidd was less fortunate than ourselves, his boat being stove the instant she ran alongside, and for a few minutes he and his crew were in a pretty pickle, hanging on to the bulwarks and channels, and wherever they could gain a hold, vainly striving to force their way inboard. Indeed, for that matter, none of us were over-comfortably situated, our party being outnumbered in the proportion of fully four to one, with the further disadvantage that we were *outside* the bulwarks, whilst our opponents were *inside*, and with a firm spacious deck to stand upon. It was perceptible at a glance that the case was one wherein a prompt and bold dash was necessary, for unless we could succeed in establishing a footing at the first rush, the chances were that we should fail altogether. I therefore hastily called to my men to reserve their pistol-fire until they were sure of their mark, and, placing my cutlass between my teeth and whipping a pistol from my belt, sprang for the bulwarks the instant we touched. A great brawny fellow, whose ferocious visage I well-remembered having seen among those of the drunken party who boarded the *Pinta*, instantly stepped forward with an upraised axe to oppose me, but I was fortunate enough to send a bullet crashing through his brain ere the weapon descended, and as he staggered and fell backwards on the deck I leapt in over the rail and gained the spot which he had occupied. A dozen opponents at once closed in upon me, but my second pistol accounted for one; another lost his weapon and his right hand together by the first stroke of my cutlass; and by that time most of the launches had gained a footing on the deck, so that we began to make our presence felt. About this time, too, Fidd, with three or four of his best men, were on the right side of the bulwarks; and in another minute the entire party, or at least all those who were not killed or desperately wounded, were on the felucca's deck, and settling down to their work in grim earnest. And now ensued a hand-to-hand encounter of as desperate and sanguinary a character as it has ever been my fortune to witness, our tars on the one hand realising that if we were vanquished very few of us would ever be allowed to escape alive from the lagoon, whilst the pirates, of course, knew only too well that they were fighting with halters round their necks. For fully a quarter of an hour was the hellish conflict waged upon the deck of the felucca, our lads now gaining a yard or two, and anon being driven back by sheer force of numbers until our backs were pressed against the rail, and further retreat, unless over the side, became impossible. And all the while the air was full of the gleam and clash of steel, the crack of pistol and musket, the tramp of feet, the heavy breathing of the combatants, with their muttered execrations and ejaculations, the sharp cries of the newly wounded, and the groans and moans of those who were already down, and whose lives were being trampled out of them in the press and stress of the strife. And, oh! the sickening odour of blood which tainted the hot, still atmosphere, and assailed our nostrils with every gasping breath we drew! The deck planking was slippery with the sanguinary flood, the bulwarks were splashed with it, our hands, faces, and clothing were bespattered with it, the scuppers were flowing with it, for a time it almost seemed to be *raining* blood! Faugh! the very memory of that dreadful scene is sickening; let us say no more about it but pass on. At length our lads—that is to say the launches and quarter-boat's crews—managed to get the pirates fairly jammed in between them, and then the very numbers of our foes were in our favour, for, huddled together as they were in the waist, not half of them could find room enough to strike an effective blow. Moreover, it became pretty evident that they had had enough of it, and were beginning to lose heart; instead of pressing eagerly to the front to meet us, as at first, each man now seemed anxious only to retire into the centre of the crowd, leaving to somebody else the glory of carrying on the defence. Seeing this, I rallied the launches, and with them made a final and desperate charge into the thickest of the enemy, when the rout of the latter at once became complete, some of them flinging away their weapons and leaping overboard, whilst others tore up the hatches and sprang headlong into the hold. Example of this kind is always contagious; if one gives way, another does the same, and is immediately imitated by a third, and so it was in the present case; the panic instantly spread, and before we well knew what was happening the two boats' crews had joined forces, our enemies had vanished, and victory was ours.

The cheer raised by the victors was immediately responded to from the second of the small feluccas, which we now had time to notice had, like the first, been boarded and carried by Courtenay and his gallant little band. My dashing shipmate had, it seemed, on capturing his first prize, promptly clapped her crew under hatches, after which he immediately cut her cables, loosed her canvas, and ran her on board her consort, by which piece of skilful generalship he was enabled to board his enemy upon equal terms, instead of having to clamber in over her bulwarks from the boat. He was just securing his second batch of prisoners, preparatory to bearing down to lend us a helping hand, when our cheer of victory announced to him that his assistance was no longer necessary.

We now set to work to clap the whole of our prisoners in irons, a task in the execution of which I anticipated a considerable amount difficulty; but, fortunately for us, they seemed to have had quite as much fighting as they cared for, and therefore submitted with a tolerably good grace— or, perhaps, I ought rather to say with the apathy of hardened men fully conscious of the fact that further resistance was utterly unavailing. This task completed, and the whole of the captured pirates transferred to the hold of the big felucca—round the open hatchway of which four of her brass nine-pounders were ranged, loaded with langridge, within view of our prisoners, and their muzzles depressed so that they pointed right down into the interior of the hold—our next business was to land a party for the purpose of securing whatever booty could be found, and afterwards to destroy the various buildings and stores of the depôt. As yet we had detected no sign of life anywhere on shore; the pirates seemed, one and all, to have betaken themselves to their craft, apparently confident of their ability with them to achieve an easy victory over us in the—to them—unlikely event of our forcing a passage through the various obstructions which they had prepared for us at different parts of the channel; but notwithstanding this apparent absence of foes on shore I deemed it best to send a very strong party, fully armed of course, under Courtenay's command. The entire force of the expedition, with the exception of six hands which I retained on board our biggest prize to keep an eye on the prisoners, was accordingly sent away in the launch—now, unhappily, in consequence of our numerous casualties, of ample capacity to accommodate the men composing it—and ten minutes later we who were left behind had the satisfaction of witnessing its unopposed landing. The launch, with two boat-keepers in her, was shoved off a few fathoms from the beach; and the remainder of the party, led by Courtenay, headed at once for the buildings which crowned the highest spot in the little island.

They reached their destination unmolested, broke up into parties which entered the various buildings, and, after an interval of some twenty minutes, reappeared, each man loaded with evidently as much as he could carry. The spoil—or whatever it was—was piled upon the sandy beach, close to the water's edge; and a second journey to the buildings then followed. Three of these journeys in all were made, and at the conclusion of the third the launch was hailed to run in and commence taking in cargo. That the articles shipped were tolerably weighty was evident from the fact that the boat repeatedly needed to be pushed further and still further astern to keep her afloat, and from the rapidity with which she settled down in the water. It was no very long job to transfer the goods from beach to boat; after which the men who had been doing the work scrambled on board and took their places, the water reaching above their waists as they waded off to her. A shrill signal whistle was then given from the boat; a lookout on the summit of the hill answered it with a wave of the hand and then disappeared through the door of the principal building. A pause of a minute or two followed, when a little party of four, Courtenay being one of them, emerged from the various buildings and set off down the hill. By the time that they reached the launch thin wreaths of light bluish smoke were seen issuing from the buildings they had just left; and by the time the launch had arrived once more alongside the felucca the smoke had assumed a darker hue, had increased in volume and density, and was seen to be streaked here and there with flickering tongues of flame.

"Well," said I, as Courtenay clambered in over the low bulwarks of the felucca, "you met with no resistance, I was glad to see, and you appear to have taken pretty effectual measures for the destruction of the hornets' nest yonder. Did you see no sign of anybody about there?"

"No sign whatever," was the reply. "We could see all over the place from the top of the hill, and I do not believe there is a living creature of any description on the island. If there is, it will be so much the worse for them half an hour hence, about which time something very like an earthquake will take place, for I have lighted a slow match communicating with a magazine containing about three tons of powder in bulk, to say nothing of perhaps a couple of thousand cartridges. The buildings are all effectually fired, as you may see; and we have brought off a boat-load of plunder which, from its weight, I judge must consist largely of specie, the doubloons, doubtless, of which our friend Carera discoursed so eloquently. Now what is the next thing to be done?"

"Why," said I, "I think you had better take the wounded into the launch, and proceed with her, just as she is, as quickly as possible to the schooner. Turn the wounded over to Sanderson, stow your booty in the hold, hoist in the launch, and then make sail for the mouth of the lagoon, where I hope to fall in with you in the felucca. I shall only be able to spare you six hands to pull the boat, but that will not greatly matter, as I think you are not likely to be interfered with during your passage to the schooner; and I do not wish to start short-handed, as we may possibly have a little more fighting to do on our way down the lagoon. Now, hurry away as fast as you can, please; those two small craft which you so gallantly took are not worth the trouble of carrying away; I shall therefore fire them and then get under way forthwith."

The painful task of moving the wounded was then undertaken; and it was most distressing to see how severe our loss had been. Out of a total of thirty-six, all told, which had left the schooner in the boats, five only had escaped uninjured—Courtenay and I had both been hurt, though nothing to speak of—nine were killed, and thirteen so severely wounded as to be unfit for duty.

Having at length seen the launch fairly under weigh for the schooner, I sent Fidd away with four hands in the gig to fire our two smaller prizes—a task which was soon accomplished, as the vessels were lying alongside each other. The felucca's canvas was then loosed, her anchor was roused up to her bows, and we got under weigh.

We had not proceeded further than a couple of miles down the lagoon before—as I had quite expected—we came upon a battery constructed upon a small projecting spit; which battery, had we been passing *up* instead of *down* the lagoon, could have raked us fore and aft for at least twenty minutes, and peppered us with grape for another ten, without our being able to fire a single shot in return. This battery was a hastily constructed affair of sods, and it mounted only one gun, but that gun was a long eighteen; and had we removed the chain barrier which formed the first obstruction, and persevered in our original attempt to pass up the lagoon, there can be no doubt that this gun would have destroyed the schooner and all hands. The people who manned the battery could not possibly have failed to hear the firing that had been going on at the head of the lagoon; but they seemed to have failed to comprehend its full significance, and, therefore, to have been unable to make up their minds to slue the gun round and point it in the opposite direction. This state of indecision on their part not only enabled us to approach them with impunity but also to take them in flank; and a couple of rounds of grape from the felucca so astonished and demoralised them that those who were not killed or disabled by our fire incontinently abandoned the battery and sought safety in flight to the deepest recesses of the bush which lined the shore.

Fidd, with a dozen hands, then jumped into the schooner's gig, which had been towing astern of the felucca, and shoved off with the object of destroying the battery; and we now had another specimen of the ability with which the defences of the lagoon had been planned; for, on approaching the battery, it was found to be bordered on three sides by a bank of ooze, some ten fathoms broad, which ooze proved to be of such a consistency that, whilst it was much too liquid and too deep to permit of a man wading through it, it was at the same time so thick as to render the passage of a boat through it almost impossible. It took the crew of the gig more than twenty minutes to force the boat through this semi-liquid mass, they exerting themselves to their utmost, meanwhile; so that, had the schooner, in passing up the lagoon, managed to survive the fire of the gun, any attempt to storm the battery with the aid of boats must have resulted in irretrievable disaster. However, Fidd and his blue-jackets managed to reach *terra firma* eventually; and it was then the work of only a few minutes to capsize the gun and all its appurtenances over the edge of the bank into the ooze, where the whole was instantly swallowed up.

Meanwhile, the felucca, slowly drifting down the lagoon, encountered—at a distance of some fifty fathoms below the battery—another obstacle, in the shape of a second chain, similar to the former, stretched across the channel, which rendered our further progress impossible until the barrier had been removed. This—there being nobody to interfere with our actions—was soon done; and we then passed on, meeting with no further obstruction until we came to the first chain. This, like the one previously passed, was removed by casting off both ends and allowing the whole affair to sink to the bottom of the lagoon—where it was doubtless instantly swallowed up by the mud—and in less than half an hour afterwards we found ourselves clear of the terrible lagoons altogether and fairly in Santa Clara Bay, where we fell in with the *Foam*, hove to and waiting for us.

It was by this time within an hour of sunset; so, as I was anxious to get into open water before nightfall, it was arranged that we should go out to sea through the Manou Channel and Cardenas Bay, as we had before done in the *Pinta*; and the passage was accomplished without mishap; Diana Cay being passed on our larboard hand, and the vessels' heads being laid north by east just as the first stars began to twinkle out from the darkening blue above us.

Shortly after this it fell calm; and advantage was taken of the brief period of inactivity preceding the springing up of the land-breeze to apportion the few effective hands remaining to us as fairly as possible between the schooner and her prize, the latter being, of course, put under Courtenay's command, with Pottle, the quarter-master, as lieutenants, gun-room officers, and midshipmen all rolled into one. Courtenay's crew, with their kits and hammocks, were transferred to the felucca in good time to fill on her and stand on in the wake of the *Foam* with the first of the land-breeze; and then, with Pottle in temporary charge of the prize, and Tompion keeping a lookout on the deck of the schooner, Courtenay and I, more firmly knit together than ever by the trying events of the day we had just passed through, sat down to talk matters quietly over together while we discussed the very creditable dinner which the steward had provided for us.

On the following morning the melancholy task of burying our dead was performed, both vessels being hove to, with their colours' hoisted half-mast high, during the ceremony; and I think it was a very great relief to all hands when, the poor fellows—ten in all, including O'Flaherty—having been consigned with all solemnity to their last resting-place beneath the heaving billow, we were able to fill away again and resume our course to the northward and eastward.

Noon that day found us three miles to windward of the Anguilas, situate at the south-east extremity of the Cay Sal Bank; and an hour later the lookout on board the *Foam* reported a sail, apparently a large schooner, on our weather-beam, running up the Old Channel under easy canvas. The breeze was then blowing rather fresh at about east by north, the *Foam* thrashing along with her lee covering-board awash, her royal stowed, and her topmasts whipping about like a couple of fishing-rods; whilst the felucca was about three miles ahead of us and broad on our weather bow, going two feet to our one, and weathering on us at every plunge. We were consequently sailing at right angles to the stranger, and rather drawing away from the line of her course than otherwise; yet such was the speed with which she came along that in half an hour she was hull-up from our deck. It now became apparent that she was manifesting a certain amount of curiosity as to who and what we might happen to be; for instead of gradually revealing her starboard broadside to us, as she would have done had she held on her original course, she was gradually hauling her wind by keeping her bowsprit pointed straight for us. I was at first disposed to regard her as English, but the enormous spread of her lower and topsail-yards convinced me, upon her nearer approach, that I was mistaken. That same peculiarity of rig was a strong argument against the assumption of her being French; and, considerably puzzled what to make of her, I sent for my glass, in order to get a clearer view of her. By the time that the instrument had been brought on deck and put into my hand she was within four miles of us; and a single glance through the telescope sufficed to tell me who and what she was. Yes, there could be no doubt about it; the craft running down so rapidly toward us was none other than Merlani's schooner, the identical craft Courtenay and I had seen hove down on the occasion of our visit to the Conconil lagoons.

Here was a pretty kettle of fish, indeed! The fellow's decks would, of course, be crowded with men, whilst I had not enough hands to man a single broadside, supposing even that I sent every available man to the guns, leaving the canvas to take care of itself! And as for Courtenay, he was even worse off than myself. I was puzzled what to do for the best; for I felt that a single false move at such a juncture, and in the presence of such an enemy, might involve us in absolute ruin. A hurried consultation with the boatswain and gunner, however, decided me to put a bold face upon the affair and "brazen it out;" in accordance with which resolution our ensign and pennant were hoisted, the topgallant-sail was clewed up and furled, and the gaff-topsail hauled down and stowed. Courtenay very smartly followed suit in the matter of showing his colours, tacking at the same time and edging down toward us. This evidently shook the nerves of our unwelcome neighbour somewhat; he seemed to think two to one rather long odds, for he immediately bore away far enough to show us his gaff-end clear of his topsail, when he at once ran up the stars and stripes. With this display of bunting we, of course, feigned to be perfectly satisfied, and each vessel held on her course, Merlani, doubtless, chuckling to think how smartly he had hoodwinked us, whilst we were only too pleased at having got out of the difficulty so easily. On Courtenay rounding to under our stern it appeared that he, too, believed the strange craft to be Merlani's schooner; like me, he had been temporarily thrown off his balance; and like me, also, he had just come to the conclusion that a bold front was the proper game to play, when the sight of our colours and our shortening of sail gave him his cue, and he had forthwith put down his helm and come round to take his part in the game of braggadocio.

This incident of our rencontre with Merlani (for we subsequently learned that it actually *was* he) was the last occurrence worthy of record which befell us on our somewhat eventful cruise; for after losing sight of the suspected schooner we never fell in with another sail of any description until we entered Port Royal harbour, where we arrived, after a pleasant but somewhat tardy passage, exactly one week after our fight in the Conconil lagoons. I may as well here state, parenthetically, that, under Sanderson's skilful hands and assiduous care, all the wounded, myself included, did marvellously well; and though some of the poor fellows, on arrival, had to be removed to the hospital, every one of them eventually recovered. As for me, contrary to all expectation the excitement and exertion to which I had been unavoidably exposed did me no harm whatever; and on the morning of our arrival I was able to dispense with the cumbersome and unsightly swathing of turban-like bandages which I had up to then been compelled to wear, a liberal application of sticking-plaster being all that I thenceforward required until my wound was completely healed.

Our black pilot berthed us, at my request, close under the guns of the flag-ship; and our anchor had scarcely taken a fair grip of the ground before I found myself seated in the stern-sheets of my gig, with my carefully written report in my hand, *en route* for an interview with the admiral I found the old gentleman on the quarter-deck of the *Mars*, up and down which he was stumping in evidently no very amiable mood. Something or other, I forget what, had put his temper out of joint; and he was expressing himself with a freedom, vigour, and fluency of language which I have seldom heard equalled, certainly never surpassed. He was inclined to be ironical, too; for on my presenting myself before him he brought up abruptly, and, surveying me fiercely for a moment, exclaimed:

"Well, young gentleman, pray, who may you be, and what do you want, if I may venture so far as to make the inquiry?"

"I am Mr Lascelles, sir, of the schooner *Foam*, just arrived; and I have come on board to make my report," I replied.

"Oh!" said he, somewhat less sternly, "you are Mr Lascelles, of the schooner *Foam*, are you? And pray, sir, where is Mr O'Flaherty, that you should find it necessary to discharge his functions? He is not wounded, I hope?"

"I regret to say, sir, that he is dead," said I.

"Dead!" he repeated; "tut, tut; that is bad news, indeed. Here, come into my cabin with me, and sit down; you look as pale as a ghost, and have been wounded yourself, if that fag-end of sticking-plaster which I see projecting beneath the rim of your hat has any significance. There, take a chair, help yourself to a glass of wine, and make yourself comfortable," he continued, as we reached his cool, roomy cabin. "Give me your report, and let me have a short verbal account of how you got on and what has befallen you. You brought in a prize with you, I see, and a very fine craft of her class she seems to be. There, now, fire away with your yarn."

I refreshed myself with a sip of the old gentleman's very excellent Madeira, and then proceeded to give him an outline of the principal events of our cruise, my narrative being frequently broken in upon by him with questions of a decidedly searching character in reference to such matters as seemed to him to require further elucidation.

At the close of my narrative the old gentleman rose from his seat and shook me warmly by the hand, exclaiming:

"Well done, my dear boy; well done! You have behaved admirably, and with a discretion far beyond your years. Had I known as much at the outset as I do now I need not have sent Mr O'Flaherty at all. Poor fellow! he was a good officer and a brave man, none braver, but he was rash. He had seen a great deal of boat service, and I thought—well, well! never mind. It is a pity he gave the alarm to those feluccas so prematurely, though. I am very pleased with you, young gentleman, and with your shipmate too—very pleased indeed. You got out of two bad scrapes very cleverly, to say nothing of the way in which you afterwards weathered upon the arch-pirate himself. Ha! ha! that was neatly done, upon my word. You did quite right, my boy, not to turn your stern to him. Never turn tail to an enemy, even though he be big enough to eat you, until the very last moment, nor then, if you think you have the ghost of a chance of thrashing him. Which does not mean, however, that, when retreat is necessary, you are to stay until it is too late and be eaten. I should have liked to see the fellow chuckling to himself as he thought how cleverly he had hoodwinked you. Poor chap! he little dreamed that you were walking off with all his hard-earned savings snugly stowed away beneath your cabin-floor. And it shall not be so very long, please God, before we will have him also and his crew safe in irons. Well, well! Now, be off aboard your hooker again, and see all ready for turning over the prisoners and the plunder; and, harkye, youngster, come and dine with me at the Penn to-night. Seven, sharp! and give my compliments to your shipmate, and say I shall be glad to see him too."

# Chapter Eighteen
# A Dinner Party at the Admiral's Penn

The dinner that evening at the Penn was a very pleasant affair indeed, at all events for Courtenay and myself; for on that occasion we reaped the first-fruits of all the toil and peril which we had recently encountered in the shape of that ungrudging and unstinted praise and commendation which is so welcome and so encouraging to the young aspirant for fame. The party consisted of three post-captains, a commander, four lieutenants, and half a dozen mids, ourselves included; which, with the jolly old admiral our host, made up a nice compact party. The guests, it appeared, had all been invited expressly to meet us and do us honour; we consequently found ourselves to be the lions of the evening. We were, of course, invited to tell our story all over again from its commencement, which we did, beginning with the mutiny on board the *Hermione*, the narrative being frequently broken in upon by questions from one or another of the guests, all of whom, I am bound to record, manifested the utmost interest in what we had to say. These questions, on more than one occasion, took quite the form of a severe cross-examination, the post-captains in particular seeming determined to arrive at a clear and distinct understanding as to the motives which prompted us in many of our actions and decisions. I was somewhat at a loss at first to comprehend the meaning of all this cross-questioning; but it became apparent later on in the evening when the three captains and the commander each formally offered to receive us on board their ships, one of which happened to be a seventy-four, whilst the other three were fine dashing frigates. These offers were all, of course, of a most advantageous character, and had we accepted them I feel sure that, joining either ship with the reputations which we had honestly won for ourselves, our advancement in the service would have been certain and rapid. But something in the admiral's manner caused me to hesitate, so, with hearty thanks to each for his kind offer, I begged the favour of a few hours for consideration; and Courtenay, taking his cue from me, did the same. When at length we all rose to take leave of our host and return to our respective ships the admiral drew Courtenay and me aside, and said, as he shook hands with us:

"Before you decide to accept or to refuse either of the offers which have been made to you to-night come and see me. I shall be on board the flag-ship to-morrow at noon."

We promised that we would do so, and shortly afterwards got under weigh in company with our fellow guests, the whole party being on horseback, for Kingston; our road, or rather the bush path along which we travelled for the greater part of the way, being brilliantly lighted by the rays of a glorious full moon.

The "autocrats of the quarter-deck" with whom we thus found ourselves privileged to ride cheek by jowl all proved to be splendid fellows, very gentlemanly in their manner, yet—having evidently sunk the quarter-deck for the nonce—frank and hearty as I believe only sailors can be. They permitted, or rather they *invited* us by their cordial manner, to join freely in the conversation, instead of relegating us to the rear, as some captains would undoubtedly have done in like circumstances, and held out so many inducements for us to join that I at length got the idea into my head that they actually *wanted* us. This frank and friendly treatment served one good purpose at least; it gave us a clearer insight into their characters and dispositions than we had been able to obtain at the admiral's dinner-table, and helped us to definitely make up our minds under which leader, if either of them, we would serve.

Punctual to the moment Courtenay and I presented ourselves on the quarter-deck of the *Mars* next day and sent in our names to the admiral, who was in his cabin, just as the ship's bell was striking eight. We were at once invited to step into the cabin, which we did, finding the old gentleman busy with his secretary writing letters. He had evidently just completed the dictation of one as we entered, for he remarked to the thin pale young man who was seated with him at the table:

"There, Purkis, that will do for the present. Just transcribe the documents you have already taken down whilst I have a chat with these young gentlemen; and I daresay that by the time you have finished I shall be ready to go on again. Well, young gentlemen," he continued, "good morning. Find a couple of chairs and bring yourselves to an anchor," waving his hand toward some of the articles of furniture in question as he spoke.

When we had seated ourselves he resumed:

"Well, now that you have slept over the offers you received last night, what do you think of them?"

As he looked straight at me during the propounding of this question I took the initiative in replying, and said:

"So far as I am concerned, sir, *unless you have something else in view for me,* I should like to join the *Alecto* and serve under Captain Fanshawe."

"And you?" inquired the old gentleman, turning to Courtenay.

"I should like to accompany my friend Lascelles wherever he goes, if you have no objection, sir," was Courtenay's reply.

"Well," said the admiral, rubbing his bald head in a manner which seemed to denote that he was somewhat perplexed, "I think you have chosen very well. The *Alecto* is a noble frigate and a very comfortable ship, whilst Fanshawe is one of the very best men on the station, or indeed I may say in the entire service. He will be very glad to have you both, I know, if you elect to join, him. But you," he continued, addressing me more particularly, "qualified the expression of your choice by adding the words, 'unless you have something else in view for me,' upon which words you laid some stress. Now, I do not wish to influence either of you in any way; but do I understand you to mean by that expression that you are willing to place yourselves in my hands?"

"Most assuredly yes, sir," I replied. "In any case it would be our duty to do so, but you have been pleased to express such very high approval of our conduct during our recent cruise, and have exhibited such a flattering interest in us and our welfare, that duty in this case becomes a positive pleasure; and for my part, I ask nothing better than permission to leave myself entirely in your hands."

"And I, also," chimed in Courtenay.

"Very well spoken, young sirs; very well spoken, indeed!" exclaimed the admiral, evidently much gratified at our reply. "Well," he continued, "I *have* other views for you both; views which presented themselves as I sat listening to what you had to tell me yesterday morning, and which were strengthened by what I afterwards found in your capitally written report. It is not my practice to flatter or unduly praise officers—especially youngsters like you—for a proper performance of their duty; such a practice is apt to make them conceited—to think too much of themselves, to consider that there is nobody like them, and that they cannot be done without. But you both appear to be modest and thoroughly sensible lads; you have exhibited an amount of tact and judgment quite beyond your years, in circumstances where much older men might have been puzzled how to act; I therefore do not hesitate to say that I am exceedingly pleased with you both, that

I am thoroughly satisfied with your conduct in every respect; and that I think, considering how very short-handed we are at present on the station in the matter of officers, you might be better employed than in the mere doing of midshipman's duty even on board a smart frigate. You have, both of you, interested me very much; I should like to see you getting on in your profession and mounting the ratlines as speedily as may be; and if you like to trust yourselves to me, are willing to work hard and behave well, I'll see to it that you have every chance given you to make your mark. But I am afraid I shall have to separate you. Now, what do you say?"

As the question was again put pointedly to me I replied that, whilst I should greatly regret being separated from so stanch a shipmate and so true a friend as my companion had proved himself to be in many a situation of difficulty and peril, I would not allow the feeling to interfere in any way with the plans of a kind and generous patron; and I felt sure that, in saying this on my own behalf, I might also say as much for my friend. To which speech Courtenay bowed his acquiescence, looking rather glum at the same time, I must say.

"Very well," said the admiral, "I *must* separate you for the present; but I promise you that you shall become shipmates again at the earliest convenient opportunity. Now, listen to me. There have been numerous complaints from the merchants here, during the last two or three months, that cargoes consigned to them have never arrived; and the only conclusion possible is that the ships carrying these cargoes have been snapped up by privateers. I have already sent out all the men-of-war available to cruise about the spots most likely to be haunted by these pests; but there are a couple of cruising grounds which are still less effectively watched than I should like, and I have been thinking I would send you two lads away to them, just to see what you can do. You, Courtenay, I intend to put in charge of that large felucca you brought in from the lagoons; she is just the craft for the work you will have to do—a good powerful vessel, but of light draught of water. Your cruising ground will be from Cape Maysi northward as far as Long Island, giving the Kays in Austral Bay an overhaul now and then, thence to windward of the Windward Passages, down as far south as, say, the Silver Kay Passage, then to the westward as far as Cape Maysi again. But you will have to be very careful, young gentleman, in your navigation of Austral Bay, or you may find yourself cast away on one or another of the shoals. You, Lascelles, I intend to put in command of that schooner, the *Dauphin*, which was brought in by the *Minerva* a few days ago; she is a really formidable vessel of her class, and I think it quite likely I shall be very severely blamed—behind my back—for intrusting her to a mere boy, as you are; but you must look upon this command as an indication of the confidence I have in your gallantry and discretion, and I shall look to you to justify me by your conduct in the choice I have made. Your cruising ground will be round Saint Domingo and as far east as the Virgin Islands, and the duty of you both will be, firstly, to protect commerce, and next to beat up the enemy's quarters everywhere within your bounds, and capture, sink, burn, and destroy everything you can lay hands on which is not too big for you to tackle. The whole coast of Saint Domingo is swarming with French privateers, really pirates under a rather more respectable name; and it is to these fellows I want you to more particularly direct your attention. The *Foam* I shall pay off at once, and I think it will be a good plan if you, Mr Courtenay, will try to secure the hands you now have on board the felucca for your next cruise. If you, Mr Lascelles, have any particularly good men on board the *Foam* that you would like to keep, you had better endeavour to get them to enter for the *Dauphin*, which, by the way, we will re-christen and call the *Dolphin* for the future. And now, good morning both of you; if you want a few days' leave, take it, sending Mr Purkis here your addresses, so that I may know where to communicate with you. Do not leave your ships, however, until the *Foam* is paid off, which will be to-morrow."

Upon this hint to depart we rose, and thanking our kind benefactor as briefly as possible for his really extraordinary kindness to us, bowed ourselves out and withdrew.

As we went down over the side I resolved that I would there and then pay a visit to my new command, and see what she was like. I had already noticed her lying alongside the dockyard wharf, and had admired her, not only for her handsome rakish appearance, but also because she was the largest schooner I had at that time ever seen. We therefore pulled straight away for the dockyard, Courtenay accompanying me in the *Foam's* gig. As soon as we were fairly away from the *Mars* my *fidus achates* turned to me and said:

"Well, Lascelles, this is all very well for you, old fellow, who are well up in your navigation; but I really don't know how in the world *I* shall get on. It is true I did fairly well in the felucca on our trip from the lagoons; but then I was always careful to keep the schooner well in sight, so that I was really trusting to you as much as to myself. But now I shall have to depend upon myself, and if I had not felt certain that you will polish me up during the few days that we may be in port together, I should have been obliged to decline the admiral's very kind offer. What a brick the old fellow is, to be sure; and yet see what a name he has for harshness and severity."

"Depend upon it," said I, "he is only harsh and severe with those who deserve it. Then, great allowances must be made for a man occupying such a responsible position as his; no matter what goes wrong, or who is to blame, it is always he who is called to account for it. He has certainly proved himself a true friend to us, and henceforward I will never sit down tamely and hear him vilified. And as to yourself, my dear fellow, make your mind easy; you are a far better navigator than you think yourself, and what little help you may need to render you perfect I will cheerfully give you; a week's hard study on your part will be quite sufficient to qualify you for going anywhere."

As we rapidly approached the wharf, the noble proportions of the *Dolphin* became every moment more apparent, and when at length the gig dashed alongside and I passed in through the wide gangway I felt as though I had a frigate under me. She measured one hundred and twenty feet in length between perpendiculars, and was thirty feet beam at her widest part, which dimensions gave her a measurement of close upon five hundred tons. Her hull was, however, exceedingly shallow, her draught of water being only nine feet when in her usual sailing trim; her lines were, moreover, without any exception the finest and most beautiful I ever saw; so that, though, in consequence of the curious manner in which tonnage was at that time calculated, she was an extraordinarily large vessel of her class, I do not believe she would have carried a cargo of more than four hundred tons of dead weight. This, however, was all in her favour, so far as speed was concerned, as it gave her large and beamy hull a very small displacement, whilst her long flat floor rendered her exceedingly stiff; this latter quality being peculiarly apparent from the fact that, though on this occasion she had an empty hold—her iron ballast having been all removed and stacked upon the wharf—she scarcely deigned to heel at all to the sea-breeze, though it was blowing half a gale at the time, whilst her spars were all ataunto just as she had come in from sea. She was a truly noble craft, her model was superb, and I fell in love with her on the spot—no sailor could have helped doing so. She had been taken under French colours, but my own opinion, which was supported by that of others who were far better judges than myself, was that she was American built. There was an easy graceful spring in her long spacious deck which no Frenchman could ever have compassed, and there was an American look too about her bows, which raked forward in an exquisite curve, whilst they flared outward in a way which promised to make her wondrously dry and comfortable in a sea-way. Her armament had been, like her ballast, removed to the wharf, and I understood from the foreman in charge that it was to be replaced by one somewhat lighter; but when I stepped on shore and saw the guns—eight long eighteens, with a long thirty-two mounted on a pivot for the forecastle—I inwardly resolved that, since she had been able to carry them so far, she should continue to do so if my powers of persuasion could be made to avail anything with the admiral. She had accommodation for eighty men forward, and a cabin abaft which for size and elegance of fittings would not have disgraced a frigate. Poor Courtenay was so completely overwhelmed with admiration that I really felt quite sorry for him; hitherto there had been nothing approachable in his opinion to the felucca—which, by the bye, I have forgotten to say was called the *Esmeralda*—but now she was dwarfed into insignificance in every respect by the *Dolphin*, and her young skipper quite put out of conceit with her. However, I consoled myself, if not him, with the reflection that, the *Dolphin* once out of sight, he would forget all about her. Having given the craft a thorough overhaul, we sauntered off to the naval hospital, only a short distance from the dockyard gates, to see how our wounded were progressing, and also—to tell the whole truth—that my boat's crew might have an opportunity to take a good look at the schooner, which I felt sure would so favourably impress them that I should have little difficulty in persuading them to enter for her.

We remained in the hospital about an hour, and on our return to the dockyard I just caught a glimpse of my men tumbling over the schooner's side back into their boat, so I had good hopes of finding that they had one and all swallowed my bait.

Shoving off, I put Courtenay on board his craft and then proceeded to the *Foam*, where I was kept pretty busy for the remainder of the day preparing to pay off, as I had no clerk to help me. I allowed the hands to go to dinner without saying anything to them, to give the "gigs" an opportunity to discuss the *Dolphin* with their shipmates, as I felt sure they would, but before they turned-to after dinner I sent for them aft and made my maiden speech, which ran somewhat as follows:

"My lads," said I, "I have sent for you to tell you that the *Foam* will be paid off to-morrow. And I wish to take advantage of the opportunity which this announcement affords me to also thank you heartily for the gallant way in which you have all stood by me, and for the way you have behaved generally from the moment when it devolved upon me, through Mr O'Flaherty's wounding and subsequent death, to assume the command of the schooner. Our cruise together has been a short one, it is true, but it has been long enough to enable me to become personally acquainted with you individually, and to discover both your good and your bad qualities. The latter, I am pleased to say, have been so few and so trifling that they are not worth further mention, whilst the former have been so conspicuous as to render me anxious for a continuance of the connection between us. And this brings me to my final statement, which is that the admiral has been pleased to announce his intention of commissioning that fine schooner the *Dolphin*, yonder, and placing me in command. Now, my lads, I daresay you guess pretty well at what further I have to say: the *Dolphin* is to proceed against the French privateers which are snapping up so many of our westerly-bound merchantmen, so there will probably be plenty of fighting for her to do, but there will also be plenty of captures and recaptures, which mean plenty of prize-money for her crew. And I am most anxious that that crew shall be a good one, as good in every respect as the *Foam's* crew has proved itself to be; in short, my lads, I should like to have every one of you with me again. Think the matter over, and those of you who are willing to try another cruise with me, and to enter for the *Dolphin*, can let me know to-morrow when you are paid off. That will do now, you may go to your duty." Instead of turning-to at once, however, the men clustered together and began to confer eagerly with each other, and with the boatswain, the gunner, and the quarter-master; the result of the confabulation being that in less than five minutes the entire crew, to a man, came forward and announced their desire to enter for the *Dolphin*. This was eminently satisfactory, for I now had at least the nucleus of a thoroughly good crew.

On the following day the *Foam* was paid off, as previously arranged, whereupon all hands re-entered for the *Dolphin*, after which they were granted forty-eight hours' leave.

This business being settled, I sought another interview with the admiral, and told him of my success, at which he expressed himself greatly pleased. "There will be no difficulty in making up your complement," said he, "though I shall have to put on board you a few convalescents from the hospital, but I will take care that you get none but thoroughly sound and healthy men; there are at least a dozen now ready to be discharged, and who only want a mouthful of sea air and a meal or two of salt junk to make them fit for anything. I shall also give you a couple of midshipmen and a master's mate, which, with what you have already, will, I think, make you pretty complete."

This was more than I had dared hope, though certainly not more than was necessary for such a craft as the *Dolphin*; so, finding the old gentleman disposed to be generous, I boldly broached the matter of the guns, and pleaded so earnestly that I at length won his consent to my retention of the schooner's original armament. This concluded my business on board the flag-ship, so, handing my address to the secretary, I jumped into a shore-boat which I had alongside, and made the best of my way to Kingston, where Courtenay had preceded me. We had previously made up our minds to test the sincerity of an invitation which Mr Thomson—who had very hospitably entertained us on our last visit to Kingston—had given us, so we first disposed at the hotel of an excellent meal, which we *called* lunch, but which was quite substantial enough to merit the name of dinner, then hastily dashed off letters to the officers who had proposed to receive us on board their ships, thanking them for their very kind offers, which we explained we were gratefully obliged to decline in consequence of the admiral having intimated his intention of sending us on special service. This duty performed we sallied forth and made the best of our way to our friend's place of business, where, upon our first hint of having obtained a few days' leave, his former invitation was repeated so earnestly and heartily as to leave us in no shadow of doubt as to its sincerity. We found to our great gratification that his family still occupied the country house where we had previously been so hospitably entertained, and to get over the slight difficulty which presented itself as to how we were to convey ourselves thither, our host, with a generous confidence which we certainly had done nothing to merit, urged us to make an immediate start in his keturen, begging us at the same time not to forget to send into town a saddle-horse for his own use later on in the day. The unbounded confidence reposed in us by this gentlemen will be better understood when I mention that we were actually trusted *to drive ourselves*! However, we proved worthy of the trust, I am proud to say, we neither broke the knees nor the wind of the spirited animal which had us in tow, nor did we smash the keturen; on the contrary, we arrived at our journey's end with both in such excellent condition as to extort a compliment upon our skilful driving from our somewhat surprised but by no means disconcerted hostess. We also faithfully delivered the message anent the saddle-horse, and then, feeling that we had done our whole duty manfully, we dropped into the wake of the two black servants who had shouldered our trunks, and followed them to the rooms promptly assigned to us, where we hastily removed our travel stains preparatory to entering the family circle.

Our appearance there was greeted with enthusiasm; for the news of our triumphant return from the lagoons had by this time spread throughout the entire length and breadth of the island; we were regarded as heroes, especially by the juveniles; we were invited to fight our battles over and over again; were made much of; and, had we remained there long, there is no doubt we should have been utterly spoiled. Luckily, perhaps, for us—though we certainly did not think so at the time—our leave was cut short on the fourth day by an intimation from the admiral that our presence on board our respective ships had now become desirable; whereupon we reluctantly bade our land friends adieu once more, and returned to Port Royal; Courtenay, I more than half suspected, leaving his heart behind him in charge of sweet Mary Thomson, our host's youngest and (if such a distinction be permissible) most charming daughter.

# Chapter Nineteen
# We assist in the Capture of a French Frigate

For the next three days I was so busy looking after the thousand-and-one things requiring attention just before a ship goes to sea, that I scarcely had time to sleep, much less to get my meals; but on the fourth morning I was able to report myself as ready for sea, when the admiral gave me my written instructions and ordered me to sail forthwith. We accordingly got under weigh about noon, with a strong sea-breeze blowing; made a short stretch over toward the Quarantine Ground; tacked as soon as we could weather Port Royal Point; passed between Rackum and Gun Cays; and went flying down through the East Channel at the rate of full thirteen knots, with our topgallant-sail stowed. (Courtenay, I ought to have mentioned, sailed on the previous day.) Eight bells in the afternoon watch saw us drawing well up abreast of Morant Point; and half an hour later Mr Woodford, the master's mate, who was doing duty as master, took his departure, and we had fairly entered upon our cruise.

To merely say that I was delighted with my new command would very inadequately express my feelings; I was *enchanted* with her; she worked like a top, and sailed like a witch; she was as stiff as a church; and so weatherly, notwithstanding her exceedingly light draught, that Woodford declared he would be puzzled how to correctly estimate her lee-way. And last, though not least, she was a superb sea-boat, and dry as a bone—save for the spray which flew in over her weather cat-head—notwithstanding her extraordinary speed. The men, too, were in ecstasies with her, slapping the rail with their hands and crying enthusiastically, "Go it, old gal!" as she plunged easily into the short choppy sea and sent the spray and foam hissing and whirling many a fathom away to leeward and astern of her. Then, too, I had a fairly good crew, amounting to eighty-six, all told fore and aft, though several of them were fresh from the hospital. The two midshipmen with which the admiral had supplied me were quiet, gentlemanly lads, aged fourteen and thirteen respectively; Woodford, the master's mate, was a man of about twenty-five, and a first-rate navigator; Sanderson was again with me as doctor; my old friends Fidd, Tompion, and Pottle occupied the same position on board the *Dolphin* that they had held on board the *Foam*; and I had, in addition, a very respectable young man to perform the duty of purser, and a very handy man—a Swede—as carpenter.

As I walked the deck that evening chatting gaily with Woodford and Sanderson I felt, it must be confessed, intensely proud of my position. And was not the feeling pardonable? There was I, a lad who had still to see his eighteenth birthday, intrusted with the absolute command of a vessel so powerful and with so numerous a crew that many a poor hard-working third lieutenant would have looked upon it as promotion had he been placed in my shoes, and with the destinies of nearly a hundred of my fellow-beings in my hands. And to this responsible position I had attained not through the influence of powerful friends—for of such I had none—but solely, as I could not help feeling, through good conduct and my own unaided exertions, with, of course, the blessing of God, about which, I am ashamed to say, I thought far too little in those days. And yet I could not see that I had done anything very extraordinary; I had simply striven with all my might to do my duty faithfully and to the best of my ability, keeping my new motto, "For Love and Honour," ever before my eyes, and lo! my reward had already come to me, as come it must and will to all who are diligent and faithful. And if I had succeeded so well in the past, with the limited advantages which I then possessed, "what," I asked myself, "may I not achieve with my present means?" I felt that there was scarcely anything I might not dare and do; and my pulses throbbed and the blood coursed in a quicker tide through my veins as I told myself that I was now indeed fairly on the highway toward the achievement of that twofold object to which I had dedicated my life.

Shortly after taking our departure from Morant Point, as already recorded, the wind headed us, and the schooner "broke off" until she was heading about north-east, close-hauled. Notwithstanding this, and the fact that we had run into a very nasty choppy sea, the log showed that the *Dolphin* was going through the water at the rate of eleven knots. We stood on in the same direction until midnight, when, having brought the high rocky islet of Navaza far enough on our weather quarter to go to windward of it on the other tack, we hove about, standing to the southward and eastward for the remainder of the night. Daylight next morning found us with Point a Gravois broad on our weather bow and distant about twenty miles. This was most gratifying, as it showed us that we had beaten clear across the Windward Channel against a fresh head-wind in about fourteen hours—a passage almost if not quite unexampled in point of celerity.

It was my intention to work close along the whole of the southern coast of Saint Domingo on our eastward passage; and this we did, looking in first behind the island of a-Vache, where we were lucky enough to descry a French privateer brigantine snugly anchored under the shelter of a small battery. As there is nothing like making hay whilst the sun shines, we at once headed straight for the anchorage, and, trusting to the extreme roguishness of our own appearance to put our enemies off their guard, began to shorten sail in a somewhat slovenly fashion, as though we were about to bring up. Then, passing under the stern of our quarry we luffed up into the wind, shot alongside the craft, hove our grappling-irons into her rigging, and, whilst our boarders were still busy driving her astonished crew below, cut her cable and dragged her a quarter of a mile to sea before the people in the battery woke up and fully realised what we were about. By that time, however, we were in full possession of our prize, and were able to make sail upon her; and although the shot from the battery flew about our ears pretty thickly for the next ten minutes, we actually succeeded in getting out of range without once being struck; and so completely had we surprised the French crew that not one of our men received so much as a scratch.

The *Julie*, for such proved to be the name of our prize, though small, turned out to be of considerable value; for she was pretty nearly full of a rich but heterogeneous assortment of goods which I shrewdly suspected had been taken out of ships which were subsequently scuttled or burnt; we therefore put one of the mids with half a dozen hands on board her, and sent her into Port Royal, where, as we afterwards learned, she safely arrived next morning.

This little slice of good fortune, coming as it did at the very outset of our cruise, was peculiarly gratifying to me, not so much on account of either the honour or the profit likely to accrue to me personally from the transaction, but because it put the crew into good spirits, and infused into them, especially the strangers among them, an amount of confidence in me which my extremely youthful appearance would perhaps have otherwise failed to command.

We devoted an entire week to our projected examination of the Saint Domingo coast, making four more captures during that time; but they all proved to be of so little value that they were set on fire and destroyed. Then, having worked our way as far east as Saona, we stretched across the Mona Passage; looked into the various bays and creeks on the south coast of Porto Rico without success, and finally found ourselves, on our sixteenth day out, with the island of Virgin Gorda and the Herman reefs under our lee as we stood to the northward and eastward to weather the Virgin group.

It was about noon when—having stretched off the land some twenty miles or so, we were about to bear up and take a look at the northern shores of those islands whose southern coastline we had just so rigorously overhauled—the lookout aloft hailed to say that he thought he heard firing somewhere to windward. I was walking the deck at the time chatting with young Marchmont, one of the two mids sent on board by the admiral, and, upon this report being made, the lad volunteered to go aloft and investigate. A couple of minutes later the active youngster was on the royal-yard, peering out eagerly ahead and to windward, with one hand shading his eyes to ward off the glare of the sun. He remained thus for perhaps three or four minutes, when I saw him assume a more eager look, and presently he turned round and hailed:

"On deck there! there certainly *is* firing going on somewhere in our neighbourhood, sir, for I have just heard it most distinctly; and a moment before I spoke I thought I caught sight of something like a smoke-wreath gleaming in the sun away yonder, broad on our weather bow. Ha! there it goes again! Did you not hear it, sir?"

"No," I replied; "the wash of the water under our bows and alongside makes too much noise down here. But that will do; you can come down again, Mr Marchmont. If, as you believe, there is firing going on to windward of us we shall soon know more about it, for, of course, I shall not now bear up until I have satisfied myself as to the matter."

The men forward became at once upon the *qui vive*, as I could see by the animated countenances of the messmen, and the eagerness with which they exchanged remarks as they went to the galley for the dinner which the cook was then serving out; as also by the nimble manner in which the relief lookout aloft shinned up the ratlines. He was one of the keenest-sighted men we had on board; and instead of seating himself, as usual, on the topsail-yard, he continued his upward progress until he reached the royal-yard, upon which he perched himself as easily as if he had been in an arm-chair, steadying his body by bracing his back against the few inches of the slender royal-mast which rose above the yard. He had not been settled more than ten minutes before he hailed to report that he heard the firing distinctly, and had also caught sight of a light wreath of smoke about four points on the weather bow. This was so far satisfactory, inasmuch as there could now be no longer any doubt as to the firing; the next thing was to find out its nature, whether it was in broadsides or by single guns, and how often it occurred. So I hailed him to report every time he heard anything. Presently he hailed again:

"Another gun, sir!"

I took the time. Not quite a minute had elapsed when he again reported:

"Another gun, sir, but not so loud this time. I think it was a lighter piece than the last."

It was nearly five minutes before the next report was made, so I concluded that it must be a running fight—a chase, in fact—which was going forward.

An interval of perhaps a minute passed, when I distinctly caught the sound of a faint *boom!* and at the same moment the hail came down:

"Another gun, sir—a heavier one than the last; and sail ho! three points on the weather bow."

"That will do," I replied; "you need not report the firing any further, but keep a sharp lookout for another sail. What is the one in sight like?"

"I can hardly tell at this distance, sir; the heads of her royals are only just showing above the horizon, but they don't appear to be of any great size."

Some four minutes later a second sail was reported, as I had expected; the lookout now expressing an opinion that the new-comer was probably a frigate, whilst the smaller craft, the leader in the race, was either a ship-sloop or a brig. My other midshipman, a lad named Boyne, was now on deck, having relieved Marchmont at noon, and this youngster, who had taken the precaution to bring his telescope on deck with him, now started forward and, with the agility of a monkey, soon placed himself alongside the lookout. He immediately raised the telescope to his eye, but we were by this time jumping into a short but lumpy sea, which made the motion aloft very considerable; moreover, the position was not one very favourable for observation, so he was rather a long time bringing his glass to bear. At length, however, with the assistance of the lookout, he managed to get both craft, one after the other, into his field of vision, and after a good long look he reported:

"We are raising the strangers very fast, sir; I can see the royals and half-way down the topgallant-sails of both. They are running dead before the wind, with royal studding-sails set on both sides; the leading ship is a brig, apparently British, and the one in chase seems to be a frigate."

"Thank you, Mr Boyne," I replied. "Just stay there a little longer, if you please; keep your eye on the strangers and report anything noteworthy which you may see."

"Ay, ay, sir!" was the answer, and to work the lad again went with his telescope most industriously.

We could now hear the firing quite distinctly on deck, but of course were unable to see anything, though we expected to catch the gleam of canvas on the horizon very shortly.

Presently young Boyne hailed again:

"The big fellow is overhauling the little one very fast, sir!"

"No doubt. How does the frigate bear now, Mr Boyne?"

"About three points on our weather bow, sir."

"Thank you! Keep her away a point," — to the helmsman. "Mr Pottle, take a small pull upon the weather-braces, if you please, and give her another foot or two of the main sheet."

"Ay, ay, sir," answered Pottle. "Lay aft here, you sea-dogs, and check the weather-braces. Royal-yard there! hold on tight, we are going to take a pull upon the weather-braces. Are you all ready there? Now then, lads, steady, not too much; you've rather overdone it. Ease off an inch or two of that royal-brace; haul taut to leeward, well there, belay! Lee to'gallant-brace haul taut; topsail and fore-braces, well there, belay of all. Forecastle there! ease up that flying-jib sheet. What do you mean, you know-nothings, by flattening the sail like that? So, that's better, belay!" And so the old fellow went on, making the round of the decks and trimming every sail until it drew to the utmost advantage.

At length, as the schooner rose upon the crest of a sea, the gleam of the sun upon white canvas was caught for a moment and instantly reported by a dozen eager voices from the forecastle. It then bore two and a half points good upon the weather bow. I again hailed the royal-yard:

"Royal-yard there! can you make out how the strangers are steering, Mr Boyne? We are heading north-east and by north."

"Ay, ay, sir; if that is the case the vessels ahead are steering about west-south-west."

"That will do, Mr Boyne; you may come down, sir! Clear for action, Mr Pottle, if you please, and then let the crew go to quarters."

"Ay, ay, sir. Clear for action, Mr Fidd!"

"*Twee, twee, twee-e-e, tweetle, weetle, tee, tee, tee-e!*" piped the boatswain, following up his shrill music with the hoarse bellow of:

"All hands clear for action. Now then, old stew-pan,"—to the cook—"dowse your galley-fire, my hearty, and stow away all your best chiney down in the run. Tumble up there, you bull-dogs, tumble up!"

It was no very long job to prepare the schooner for action, and in twenty minutes everything was ready—the magazine opened, powder and shot passed up on deck, the guns cast loose and loaded, the pikes cut adrift from the main-boom, arms served out to the crew, and every man at his appointed station. By this time the lower yards of the brig had risen level with the horizon, whilst the upper half of the frigate's topsails could be seen from the deck. The firing, meanwhile, had gone on pretty deliberately, and it was now possible to see from our deck, with the aid of a telescope, that the sails of both pursuer and pursued were suffering pretty extensively from the effects of the cannonade. It was evident that each was firing high, the frigate trying to wing the brig and so arrest her flight, whilst the brig was equally anxious to maim her big antagonist's spars, by which means only could she hope to effect her escape. So far the brig appeared to be getting rather the best of it, for though her canvas showed the daylight through it in several places, her spars and running gear still remained uninjured, and every sail was drawing to the utmost advantage, whilst the frigate had lost her fore royal-mast, which, with its sail, was hanging down over the topgallant-sail and topsail, and the main-topmast studding-sail tack was cut and the sail streaming out loose and flapping furiously in the wind; these little casualties being sufficient to enable the brig to hold her own, for the time being at least, in the unequal race. To encourage the plucky little vessel, by showing her that help was at hand, we now fired a gun and hoisted our colours, allowing the ensign to stream as far out to leeward as possible, in the act of running it up to the gaff-end, in order that those on board her might catch a glimpse of it before it was hidden by our canvas. Approaching each other as we were, nearly end on, we rose each other very rapidly; and at length we in the *Dolphin* had the satisfaction of seeing the frigate, the vessel most distant from us, fairly hull-up. She had by this time cleared away the wreck of her fore royal-mast, had spliced her studding-sail tack, and was in the very act of setting the sail again when the brig's two stern-chasers spoke out simultaneously, and next moment down toppled the frigate's fore and main-topgallant-masts with all attached, the topgallant studding-sail booms snapping off like carrots at the same time, and there the noble craft was in a pretty mess. A ringing cheer, which those on board the brig might almost have heard, went up from our lads at this sight, followed by a hoarse murmur of:

"Lookout! now Johnny Crapeau has lost his temper, and the brig is going to get *loco* in 'arnest!" as the frigate put her helm down and fired her whole broadside at the flying craft. There was not so very much damage done, after all, so far as the brig was concerned. Her peak-halliards were cut and she temporarily lost the use of her main trysail, and we could see a rope's-end or two streaming out here and there in the wind; but that was all, excepting that her canvas showed a few extra eyelet-holes. With the frigate, however, it was different; by yielding to his feeling of exasperation, as he had, her skipper had been betrayed into a very unseamanlike act, in luffing his ship with all her studding-sails upon her, and the result was that he lost the remainder of his booms in an instant, and found himself in a worse pickle than ever.

By this time the brig had passed far enough to leeward of us to be able to clearly distinguish the colour of our bunting; and seeing also that we were indisputably holding our luff so as to close with the frigate, she accepted us as a friend, notwithstanding our decidedly rakish appearance, and at once coolly began to shorten sail, evidently now determined, with our aid, to try conclusions with her big antagonist. It was about time for us to do the same; we accordingly clewed up and furled our royal and topgallant-sail, hauled down and stowed the gaff-topsail and main-topmast staysail, brailed in the foresail, and triced up the tack of the mainsail; which left the schooner in condition to be worked by less than a dozen hands. By the time that this had been accomplished, the running gear hauled taut, rope's-ends coiled down, and everything made ship-shape on board us, we had arrived within a distance of something like two miles of the frigate, at which juncture she fired a shot at us from her bow gun, possibly as a hint to us not to interfere with her. The shot fell short several yards.

"Umph!" remarked Woodford from his post at the helm, "nothing very terrific about that! A twelve-pounder, apparently, and a shockingly poor aim. Our thirty-two will make the Johnnies open their eyes with astonishment, I expect."

"Yes," said I; "we ought to be able to reach her from here, so I'll let 'Long Tom' return their compliment. Forward, there! are you ready with the pivot gun?"

"All ready, sir," was the reply.

"Then just give the frigate a taste of your quality. We will keep away a couple of points so that you may have a fair chance; and see if you can't make the shot tell."

"Ay, ay, sir; if I don't make the splinters fly you may stop my grog for the next month," answered Collins, the captain of the gun, who happened to be a bit of a favourite with me, and was a trifle free in his language in consequence.

The gun was carefully levelled; and, when they were all ready, Woodford gently put the helm up; the schooner gradually fell off from the wind, and presently there was a deafening explosion, accompanied by a jarring concussion which shook the schooner from stem to stern; and as the smoke drove away to leeward we saw a jet of spray a dozen feet high shoot into the air as the ball struck the crest of a wave, and in another instant a white patch of naked wood appeared exactly in the centre of a port-sill, showing where the shot had hulled the frigate.

"Good! if that hasn't crippled one of their guns I'm a Dutchman," ejaculated Woodford, letting the schooner come up "full and by" once more.

"Very good indeed, Collins," I shouted. "Load again, my fine fellow, as quickly as possible. Sail trimmers, ready about! Mr Boyne, see that the muzzles of your larboard broadside guns are well elevated, and fire as they are brought to bear. Take steady aim, lads, and do not throw away a single shot if you can help it. Ha! he is going to rake us! Down with your helm, Woodford. Helm's a-lee! Ease up your jib-sheets, forward, there! Round in upon the main-sheet, smartly, men. Let draw the fore-sheet; braces let go and haul!"

The schooner—what a beauty she was!—worked like a top, and was round on the other tack, presenting her broadside to the frigate, when the latter launched the whole contents of her larboard battery at us. Almost at the same moment we fired the four eighteens in our larboard battery at her; and then, before we had time to note the damage done, if any, her shot came screaming about our ears. There was a crash on board the schooner, but only one; it was caused by a shot passing through our weather bulwarks and striking a ring-bolt in the deck, after which it bounded high in the air and went overboard to leeward. There were a couple of holes in our beautiful mainsail, and one in the flying-jib; but beyond that we were uninjured. One of the men in the larboard battery had his cheek slightly lacerated by a splinter, but with that trifling exception none of us were any the worse. The frigate, however, did not escape quite so easily. When we again looked at her it was seen that we had knocked away her jib-boom close to the cap, and had cut away her flying-jib halliards and stay, with the result that the sail was towing under her forefoot; her fore-topsail tye had also been cut, and the yard was down on the cap, rendering their plight worse than ever.

This loss of head sail occurring at a moment when, having partially luffed to fire at us, the wind was well on her starboard quarter, the frigate now showed symptoms of flying up into the wind altogether; and although it was evident, from the sluggish way in which she did so, that the tendency was being strongly counteracted by her helm, I soon saw that her crew were powerless, and that fly into the wind she *would*, in spite of them.

"Ready about again, lads!" cried I. "Now, Mr Marchmont, it is your turn. By the time that we are fairly round the frigate's stern will be turned directly toward you, offering an excellent mark. Let us see how many of your shot you can send in through her cabin windows, will you?"

"Ay, ay, sir, we'll do our best," answered the lad, in high glee; and then I saw him pass rapidly from one captain of a gun to another, and heard him mention distinctly, in his excitement, something about "bottles of grog."

The men grinned, turned their quids, hitched up the waistbands of their breeches; squinted along the sights of their guns; looked at the frigate, as though measuring her distance, and then adjusted the elevation of their pieces with evidently the nicest judgment and the very best of intentions.

Watching the frigate carefully, the helm was put down at just the right moment; and as our topsail swept round and was braced up—*bang!*—*bang!*—*bang!*—*bang!* roared our eighteens, away skipped the shot, and crash went all four of them slap into the stern of the disabled Frenchman, playing the very mischief with the gilt-ginger-bread work with which that part of the ship was profusely decorated. A rattling broadside from the brig now drew our attention to her, and we saw that she was standing toward us, close-hauled on the larboard tack, under topsails and topgallant-sails; and that she also had taken advantage of the frigate's helpless situation to rake her most handsomely.

The Frenchman, meanwhile, having got himself into what Courtenay would have termed "the centre of a hobble," was very busily doing his best to get out of it again—and in a very seamanlike way, too, notwithstanding his former mistake—by clewing up and furling everything abaft his mainmast and so trimming his yards as to cause the frigate to gather stern-way and gradually pay off again. This, however, was a work of some little time, hampered as the ship was with wreck forward; and before it was done we had passed to windward of her, receiving in so doing the fire of but seven of her sixteen larboard broadside guns, to which we replied effectively with our starboard battery. Having reached far enough to weather her on our next tack we went about, and, crossing her bows, fired our larboard battery and our thirty-two pounder into her again, raking her severely and, best of all, bringing her fore-topmast down by the run. She had by this time paid off sufficiently to have gathered head-way, and her crew actually managed to get her before the wind; but it was only for a few minutes, she soon broached to again; and being by this time almost entirely bereft of head sail—her foresail alone remaining—there she hung, in the wind's eye, helpless, and practically at our mercy. The *Dolphin* was at once placed in an advantageous position on the frigate's starboard bow, and kept there by her topsail being laid aback, whilst the brig took up a corresponding position on the enemy's starboard quarter; and we then both opened a raking fire upon her so effectually that ten minutes later she hauled down her colours and surrendered.

# Chapter Twenty
## The Privateer and the Indiaman

Having satisfied ourselves that the French frigate had actually struck, we filled on the schooner and ran down under the lee of the brig, where we once more hove to; our gig was lowered and manned, and I proceeded on board to see if my services were further required.

On reaching the deck I was met by a man of some five-and-thirty years of age, evidently the skipper of the craft, who held out his hand to me most cordially, and exclaimed:

"Welcome, young gentleman, on board his Britannic majesty's brig *Dido*. You hove in sight just in the nick of time this morning, for, but for your very effective help, we should have been the captured instead of the captors by this time. What is the name of your schooner?"

"The *Dolphin*," I replied, "cruising; sixteen days out from Port Royal."

"The *Dolphin*, eh?" said he. "Well, she is a remarkably fine and powerful craft; carries heavy metal too; and your skipper evidently knows how to handle her. What is his name, by the bye?"

I modestly explained that I was in command of the craft; an announcement which created quite a sensation among the officers who had gathered round.

"*You!*" exclaimed the skipper incredulously. "Well, then, I can only say, young gentleman, that you are shaping well—very well indeed. There is not a man in the service who could have fought that vessel more gallantly, or with better judgment than you did; and I shall take care to say so to the admiral when we get in. You have rendered a very important service, my lad, let me tell you; for you have not only saved the old *Dido* from being taken, and helped in the capture of a fine frigate, but you have also saved some most urgent and important despatches which we have on board. Have you lost many men in the action?"

"Not one," said I; "nor have we, so far as I know, a single man with a wound worth mentioning."

"Ah, you are lucky!" he remarked. "But for that you may thank your heavy metal and the way in which it was served; you were able to cripple the frigate before she could touch you. Well, come down into the cabin and take a glass of wine with me whilst we talk over what is next to be done. Mr Thompson, let Mr Rogers come down to me with his report when he returns from the frigate. Now then, Mr—a—ah—this way, please. By the way, I did not catch your name just now."

There was a very good reason for that, as I had never mentioned it to him; however, I did so then; he informed me that his name was Venn, and that he held the rank of commander, and by the time that we had come to this understanding we found ourselves in the cabin, a much smaller and plainer apartment than that of the *Dolphin*, by the bye.

Wine was produced, we drank a glass together, and then my new friend proceeded to explain to me that, as the brig had suffered rather severely, and had had a great many men wounded in her running fight with the frigate, he would be obliged to draw rather heavily upon the *Dolphin* to make up a crew for the prize, and that, under the circumstances, he considered it would be advisable for us to accompany the *Dido* and her prize into Port Royal.

This arrangement suited me very well indeed, as I thought it just possible there might be letters for me, if not from my father at least from Inez; and I was just about to return on board the schooner to give the necessary orders, when a midshipman, who had accompanied the first lieutenant of the *Dido* on board the prize to take possession, returned with the information that the frigate was named the *Cythère*, mounting thirty-two twelve-pounders, with a crew originally of three hundred and twenty-eight all told; her loss during the action amounting to thirty two killed and sixty-eight wounded, her captain being among the former.

By eight bells in the afternoon watch we had managed to make up between us and transfer to the frigate a very respectable prize-crew, after which hawsers were passed on board the prize from the *Dido* and the *Dolphin*, the brig taking up a position upon the frigate's larboard bow whilst we stationed ourselves on the starboard, when sail was made upon both the towing vessels and we shaped a course for Jamaica, the prize-crew busying themselves meanwhile in getting up new spars and repairing damages in the standing and running rigging. By daylight next morning this was so far accomplished that we were able to cast off the towing hawsers, when the three craft proceeded in company, arriving without mishap or adventure in Port Royal harbour on the morning of the sixth day succeeding the action.

Commander Venn was as good as his word in framing his report of the capture, in consequence of which I rose higher than ever in the favour of the admiral, who showed his appreciation of our services by filling up our provisions and water with all possible speed and hurrying us off to sea again.

As I had hoped, there were two letters for me, one from my father and one from Inez; but as the former was written in the same unsatisfactory strain as those which had preceded it, and as the latter contained nothing of interest to anyone but myself, I shall not trouble the reader with even so much as an extract from either, but pass on to incidents which were destined to very materially affect the happiness of my whole future life, and that of others as well. Having filled up our provisions and water, as already stated, and having received on board again the hands who had helped to take the *Cythère* into port, we sailed once more on the second day following our arrival, and proceeded again over the ground we had already beaten so successfully. We were even more fortunate on this occasion than we had been before, though we found that it was no longer possible to take our enemies by surprise as we had done at first; they had learned wisdom from experience and had become aware of our tactics, notwithstanding which we took four privateers, one of which we cut out from under a battery, and made several recaptures, two of which proved to be very valuable. But as these incidents happened to be mere interludes, as it were, in my story, having no special significance, I shall leave them without further mention and pass on. The reader will therefore please understand that I had been in command of the *Dolphin* rather more than six months when the incident occurred to which I am about to refer.

The time was about half an hour, or thereabouts, after midnight, and our position was about sixty miles south-east of Beata Point, the southernmost point on the mainland of Saint Domingo. The day had been fine, with a very nice pleasant working breeze, but as the sun had declined toward the horizon the wind had shown signs of dropping, gradually dying away after sunset, until toward the end of the first watch it had fallen so completely calm that we had furled all our canvas to save wear and tear, and were, at the time mentioned, lying under bare poles, slowly drifting with the current to the westward. The night was pitch-dark, for there was no moon, and with the dying away of the wind a great bank of heavy thunderous-looking cloud had gradually worked up from the westward, imperceptibly expanding until it had at length obscured the entire firmament, promising a thunder-storm which would doubtless be all the heavier when it broke from the length of time which it took in the brewing. I had remained on deck until midnight; but observing, when the middle watch was called, that the barometer had dropped only the merest trifle, had gone below upon the deck being relieved, and, leaving orders with young Boyne to call me in the event of any change in the weather, had flung myself, half undressed, into my cot, hoping to get a nap before the storm broke, and feeling pretty confident that when it did nothing very serious could happen, the schooner being under bare poles.

But somehow I could not get to sleep, probably on account of the oppressive closeness of the atmosphere, for it was stiflingly hot, although the skylights and companion were wide open; and there I lay, tossing restlessly from side to side in a state of preternatural wakefulness, listening to the lap and gurgle of the water against the ship's side, the creaking of the bulk-heads, the rattling of the hooks which held the cabin doors wide open, the *yerking* of the main-sheet blocks, the *jerk-jerk* of the rudder and of the lashed wheel above it, with the swish of the water under the counter and about the stern-post as the vessel rolled lazily upon the long sluggish swell which came creeping slowly up from the eastward. And if by chance a momentary feeling of drowsiness happened to steal over me, which, carefully fostered, might have eventually led to my falling asleep, it was sure to be put to flight by some ill-timed movement or speech by those on the deck above me, although I will do them the justice to say that, so far as speech was concerned, they spoke but seldom, and then in subdued tones. At length, however, I was going off, the varied sounds I have mentioned had lost their distinctness, had changed their character, and were beginning to merge themselves into the accompaniments of what, a few minutes later, would have been a dream, when I heard Pottle's voice exclaim with startling suddenness:

"Hillo! what was that?"

To which young Boyne replied, in unmistakably sleepy tones:

"What was what, Mr Pottle?"

"Why," replied Pottle, "I thought I saw—Ha! look, there it is again! Did you not see something like a flash away off there on our starboard beam?"

"No, sir," said Boyne, evidently a little more wide-awake, "I cannot say I did. Probably it was lightning; we *must* have it before long."

"Lightning!" exclaimed Pottle contemptuously; "d'ye think I don't know lightning when I see it? No, it looked more like—by George, there it is again!"

At the same moment one of the men forward hailed, but I could not catch what he said for the creaking of the bulk-heads.

"Ay, ay, I saw it," answered Pottle. "What did it look like to you, Martin?"

"I thought it looked like the flash of firearms," was the reply, which I this time heard distinctly.

"So did I," gruffly remarked Pottle. "Depend on't, Mr Boyne, there's something going on down there to the south'ard which ought to be looked into. Just step down below and give Mr Lascelles a call, will ye?"

I sprang out of my cot, slipped my stockingless feet into my shoes, drew on my jacket, and met young Boyne at the cabin door.

"Well, Mr Boyne," said I, "what is the news? I heard Mr Pottle ask you to call me."

"Yes, sir," said the lad. "He says he has seen something like the flash of firearms down in the southern quarter, and the lookout also has reported it."

"All right," said I. "I will be up in a moment."

And turning up the cabin lamp for an instant to take a look at the barometer, which I found to be steady, I stumbled up the companion-ladder, and, blinking like an owl in daylight, made my way out on deck.

"Whew!" I exclaimed, "this *is* darkness, indeed. Where are you, Mr Pottle?"

"Here I am, sir," answered the quarter-master; and turning in the direction of his voice I saw a tiny glowing spark which proved to be the ignited end of a cigar which he had between his teeth.

"Now," said I, as I groped my way to his side, "whereaway was this flashing appearance which you say you saw?"

"Just about in that direction, sir," was the reply; "or stay—we may have swung a bit since I saw it," and he walked aft and carefully raised a jacket which he had thrown over the lighted binnacle. "No," he continued, "that's where it was, just sou'-sou'-west, for I took the bearing of it when I saw it the third time; and I thought that, in case of anything being wrong, it wouldn't be amiss to mask the binnacle light."

"Quite right," said I, peering first at the compass card and then away into the opaque darkness which prevented our seeing even the surface of the water alongside. It was manifestly hopeless to think of seeing anything through such impenetrable obscurity as that which surrounded us; and I was just wondering what steps to take, under the circumstances, peering meanwhile in the direction indicated by Pottle, when I caught a momentary glimpse of a tiny spark-like flash—which the ejaculations of my comrades told me they also had observed—and in another instant a glare of ghastly blue-white radiance streamed out over the sea and revealed to us two vessels alongside each other, the canvas of the one—a large lumbering full-rigged ship, gleaming spectrally in the light of the port-fire, whilst the sails of the other—a brigantine, which happened to be on the side next us—stood out black as ebony against the light. They were about two miles off; and even at that distance we could see with the naked eye that a struggle of some sort was going forward on the decks of the larger of the two craft. The nature of the affair was apparent in a moment to every one of us. The big ship was unmistakably an Indiaman, probably a fellow-countryman; at least so we judged by the imperfect view of his canvas which the flickering light of the port-fire afforded us; whilst, if appearances were to go for anything, the brigantine could be nothing else than a French picaroon. At all events our duty was now plain enough, we ought to investigate the affair without a moment's unnecessary delay; and I accordingly gave orders for all hands to be immediately called, and for the pinnace and the two gigs to be lowered and manned. This was done with an alacrity which I venture to believe would have gratified even my old friend the admiral himself; and in less than a quarter of an hour from the moment of giving the order we were in the boats and well away from the schooner. The pinnace was in charge of the boatswain; Pottle had the command of one of the gigs; and, as there seemed to be no prospect of any worse outcome, in the shape of weather, than a thunder-storm, I did not hesitate to take charge of the other gig myself, leaving Woodford in temporary command of the schooner with instructions how to proceed in the event of a breeze springing up before we were able to rejoin him.

The port-fire on board the Indiaman having long before burnt-out, we had taken the precaution to provide each boat with a compass, the light of which was most carefully-masked; but this precaution soon proved to be unnecessary, the boats having traversed less than half the distance between the schooner and the other two vessels when vivid sheet lightning began to play along the south-western horizon, lighting up the scene with its weird radiance frequently enough to enable us to steer a perfectly straight course. The fight was still going on when we left the schooner; but it appeared to cease soon afterwards, and we came to the conclusion that the crew of the Indiaman had been overpowered and the ship taken. Our chief anxiety now was lest our approach should be discovered in time to enable the Frenchman to make preparations for resisting our attempts to board them when we should arrive alongside; but, fortunately for us, the chief play of the lightning was in the quarter almost opposite that from which we were approaching, and I was in hopes that they would be too busy just then plundering the prize to keep a very strict lookout. In this, however, I was doomed to be disappointed; for when we had arrived within a quarter of a mile of the brigantine a sudden flashing of lights appeared on board her, and before we could get alongside a broadside of four guns, loaded with grape, was hastily discharged at us. Luckily, beyond revealing the fact that we had been discovered, the broadside did us no harm; and, with a cheer, our tars bent to their oars and, with a few lusty strokes, sent us alongside with a rush.

The brigantine, a long and exceedingly rakish-looking craft, sat very low in the water, so that it appeared to be one of the easiest things in the world to scramble in over her bulwarks from the boats; but we found those bulwarks lined from stem to stern with as resolute-looking a set of fellows as one need wish to see, and their reception of us, as regards warmth, left absolutely nothing to be desired. They evidently knew and fully appreciated the advantage they possessed over us in having a good roomy deck to fight upon, and they seemed fully resolved to retain that advantage as long as possible. Three separate and distinct attempts did we make to surmount the low barrier; and as many times were we forced back into the boats, each occasion being marked by the accession of some three or four to the number of our wounded. On the fourth occasion, however, I determined that gain the deck of that brigantine I *would*, by hook or by crook; so calling Collins, the coxswain of my boat, and another man to my aid, I ordered them each to seize me by a leg and *fling* me on board, which they did with a regular man-of-war's-man's "one—two—three—heave!" and away I went in over the bulwarks like a rocket, alighting fairly on the shoulders of a great burly fellow who had already lodged a pistol bullet in the fleshy part of my left arm—and to whom I consequently owed a grudge—beating him down to the deck, only to find myself in the very thickest of the crowd, every man of which seemed more anxious than the others to get a fair blow at me. I was, however, by this time no mere novice in the use of the sword, and I no sooner felt myself fairly on my feet than I made the weapon spin about my adversaries' heads in such good earnest that they were compelled to recoil. Meanwhile my lads had no sooner launched me into space than they sprang after me, and, pressing forward to my side with their cutlasses advanced, we soon made room enough for the rest of our party to follow. But though we had gained the deck we had by no means won the ship, our antagonists rallying time after time as we drove them back, and stubbornly contesting with us the possession of every inch of plank. Meanwhile the storm which had so long been brewing had at length burst almost immediately overhead, the lightning flashing and playing about the mast-heads of the ships with a dazzling vividness which was almost blinding, whilst the thunder crashed and roared and rolled along the heavens absolutely without intermission. The general effect was impressive and appalling in the extreme—or would have been had we been in a mood to properly appreciate it; but just then our only thought—or mine, at least—with regard to it was that it afforded us light enough to fight by and to distinguish friends from foes. And it was by the friendly aid of the lightning that I was, in the midst of the *mêlée*, enabled to identify an object, which I had once or twice kicked from under my feet, as a flannel cartridge. I had already noticed several charges of grape ranged along the shot-racks; and it now occurred to me that one of these discharged into the thick of our enemies might help very materially to mitigate their ardour. So, turning to some of the lads behind, I directed them to run in one of the guns, load it, and slue it fore and aft, with its muzzle pointing toward the taffrail, in which direction we were slowly pressing the crew of the brigantine. This was soon done; when, taking advantage of a momentary lull in the confusion of sound which raged about us, I shouted:

"Back, *Dolphins*, into the waist, for your lives; we are about to treat them to a dose of grape!"

Our lads luckily heard and understood me; we pressed forward with increased energy for a moment, huddling the Frenchmen all up in a heap together just about the companion-way, and then suddenly retired forward, leaving the gun, a nine-pounder, grinning open-mouthed fair at them. The moment that the last of our men was fairly out of danger the topman who had taken charge of the gun discharged it; we immediately rushed aft again, charging through the smoke, found the foe, as we had expected, quite confused and demoralised from the effect of the fire, and, pressing upon them more fiercely than ever, compelled them to throw down their arms and cry for quarter, though not until I had been compelled in self-defence to run their leader through with my sword.

The brigantine was now our own, so leaving Pottle and the boatswain to secure the prisoners, which task they set about without a moment's delay, I rallied my own boat's crew about me and led them on board the Indiaman to take possession of her. We met with no opposition whilst climbing the ship's lofty sides; but on gaining the deck a group of some half a dozen figures were discovered mounting guard over the fore-scuttle. Despatching the coxswain and three hands to secure these, and the remainder of the crew to hunt up any stray Frenchmen who might happen to be lurking about the decks, I turned my steps in the direction of the poop cabin, and calling one hand to attend me, at once made my way thither.

One of the doors was standing wide open, with a brilliant stream of light pouring through it, lighting up the massive mainmast and the gear attached to it for a height of some twelve feet above the deck, and revealing the fact that the quarter-deck guns at least of the vessel had never been cast loose, thus confirming me in the suspicion I had before entertained that the vessel had been taken by surprise. Entering the cabin, a strange scene presented itself. The apartment itself was very spacious, being of the full width of the ship, and extending right aft (the sleeping cabins and the captain's private quarters, I subsequently discovered, were situated below, on the main-deck); and it was very handsomely fitted up with rosewood and maple panels, a great deal of gilt moulding, several mirrors, and some half a dozen very decently executed pictures; whilst a handsome five-light chandelier—with one of the lamps recently broken—swung from the beams overhead. Against the forward bulkhead and between the two doors giving admission to the cabin there stood a very massive and handsomely carved buffet, on which stood a quantity of finely cut crystal, several decanters containing wine and spirits, and some fruit dishes loaded with fruit. A long table stood fore and aft in the centre of the saloon with, perhaps, a couple of dozen luxurious-looking chairs ranged round it; and along each side of the cabin ran a range of wide handsomely upholstered sofa lockers. The floor was covered with a thick Turkey carpet of handsome design. But it was not so much the rich furnishing of the saloon which made it remarkable; it was the aspect and grouping of the people I found there. A dozen or more gentlemen, clad only in their shirts and trousers, and several of them bleeding from wounds, were seated on the lockers, with their feet lashed together and their arms tied behind them. At the far end of the cabin, abaft the table, and crouching on the floor, huddled a number of ladies and children in their night-dresses, all of them pale as death and looking dreadfully frightened, whilst one of the ladies was weeping hysterically over a little chubby, fair, and curly-headed boy of some six or seven years old, who was moaning piteously the while the blood trickled from a wound in his head, matting his golden curls together into a gory mass and slowly spreading out in a great ensanguined stain on the sleeve of his mother's night-dress. Near the door by which I entered lay the apparently dead bodies of two men, who I took, from their dress, to be the captain and chief mate of the ship; and close to them stood a tall, handsome, dark-skinned Frenchman, with gold rings in his ears, a naval cap with a gold band on his head, a crimson silk sash round his waist, fairly bristling with pistols, a drawn sword in his right hand and a pistol in his left, evidently mounting guard over the prisoners.

As I entered the cabin this fellow turned to meet me. The moment he saw me to be a stranger up went his pistol, and, before I had time to realise what he was about, there was a flash, a blow followed by a sharp stinging sensation along the left side of my head, a thud, a groan, and a fall behind me; then came a lunging thrust from his sword, which I had the good luck to parry; this parry I followed up with a lightning-like thrust; my sword passed through his heart, and he fell dead on the carpet close to the two bodies I have already mentioned. All this passed as it were in a moment, with such startling suddenness, indeed, that it left me quite dazed, so that for a few seconds I could scarcely realise exactly what had happened. On recovering my self-possession, my first thought was for the man who had been following me into the cabin. I turned round to ascertain whether the groan had proceeded from him, and there, prone in the passage-way behind me, lay the poor fellow on his back, stone dead, the bullet having crashed into his brain through his right eye.

# Chapter Twenty One
## An Unexpected Meeting

As the man was dead, it was useless to trouble further about him, especially as there were so many of the living to be attended to; I therefore turned again toward the occupants of the cabin and said: "Ladies and gentlemen, I am very pleased to be able to assure you that you have no further cause for apprehension; the privateer has been captured and this vessel retaken by the boats of his Britannic majesty's schooner *Dolphin*, under my command; my men are now busy, on deck and on board the brigantine, securing the prisoners; and it will be my duty—Good heavens—it cannot be—and yet it surely *is*—my father!"

I had, whilst speaking, been gradually advancing nearer to the table, and consequently more directly into the full light of the cabin lamps; and my speech had been interrupted, and the above startled exclamation wrung from me, by seeing one of the occupants of the sofas rise with difficulty to his feet to gaze with an expression of intense eagerness in my direction. My attention had thus, naturally, been attracted toward him, and I could scarcely credit the evidence of my senses when, in the worn and somewhat haggard features of the gazer, I recognised the well-remembered lineaments of my father. Yet so it was, there could be no mistake about it; for as I sprang toward him, he ejaculated my name, "Lionel," and, overcome with emotion, reeled and fell, bound hand and foot as he was, into my arms. As I embraced him our lips met, and I then received almost the first paternal kiss of which I had ever been conscious.

I tenderly reseated him on the sofa, and, throwing myself on my knees before him, busied myself in casting loose the lashings which confined his feet, glad to have so good an excuse for bowing my head, and thus concealing the tears of emotion which sprang to my eyes. My father was even more overcome than I was. I felt his hot tears falling upon my hands as he bent over me; and it was not until I had completely released him that he regained composure enough to ejaculate, as he fervently grasped my hand:

"Thank God—oh! thank God for this most unexpected and welcome meeting, my precious boy, my own Lionel; and still more for your opportune arrival. You and your brave fellows made known your presence just in time to prevent what in another moment would have become a perfect pandemonium of violence, and probably of murder also. You are welcome, my son, most welcome, not only to me, but also, I am sure, to everyone else in this cabin."

This assurance was heartily echoed by everybody present, with the exception of the unhappy lady in whose arms lay the wounded child, and she was evidently too much absorbed in her own grief to notice or be conscious of what was taking place. The sight of her and her misery recalled me to myself, and reminded me of the many duties I yet had to perform; so leaning over my father and pressing a kiss upon his forehead - down which, by the way, the blood was slowly trickling from a slight cutlass wound—I said:

"Thank you, dear father, for your affectionate greeting. I must not remain any longer with you, however, for the present, glad as I am to have so unexpectedly met you; I have many matters yet which *must* be attended to; but I will rejoin you without fail the moment I feel myself at liberty to do so. Meanwhile, have no fear of any further violence; a strong detachment of my crew is in possession of both vessels, and the schooner herself is not far distant. I will send some men in to release your companions from their bonds and to help you all in putting matters straight once more; and, as I see that several of you have been wounded in defence of the ship, I will at once despatch a boat—if, indeed, she be not already gone—for the *Dolphin's* surgeon."

"Many thanks to you, young gentleman, for your kind offer," exclaimed one of the occupants of the sofa, "but if you'll kindly draw your knife across these lashings of mine you need not call your surgeon away from your own men—who, I'll be bound, stand in greater need of his services than we do. I am the doctor of this ship, and if I can only get my hands and legs free I'll soon attend to my share of the patients, and then help my brother sawbones to attend to his as well, if, indeed, he cares to accept my help."

"Thank you, my dear sir," said I, "Mr Sanderson will be only too glad to avail himself of your services, I know; for I fear our casualties to-night will prove to be very heavy when we have time to reckon them up. Allow me."

I at once set to work to cast the worthy medico adrift, my father at the same time performing a like office for those nearest him; and, having released the doctor, I then hurried out on deck to see how matters were progressing.

I encountered the coxswain and several of the gig's crew on the quarter-deck. They were just about to enter the cabin in search of me to report that the ship had been searched and all the Frenchmen on board secured and passed down the side into the brigantine, and to inquire what they should next do. Looking over the Indiaman's lofty bulwarks down on to the deck of the brigantine, I saw that there too the prisoners had been secured and passed below, and that our lads were already busy overhauling the prostrate bodies and separating the living from the dead. I thereupon directed the coxswain to release the crew of the Indiaman—who were at that moment lying bound hand and foot down in the forecastle—to rout out three lanterns, and to hang them lighted one above the other in the ship's rigging, as a preconcerted signal to Woodford that we had been successful; and then to take the gig with eight hands and pull away to the *Dolphin* for the doctor. My next task was to send a couple of trustworthy hands into the Indiaman's cabin to assist the passengers in any way which might be found needful; after which I scrambled down on board the brigantine to see how matters were going there.

I had just gained the deck of the prize when the three lanterns were displayed in the Indiaman's rigging, upon which a hearty cheer came ringing over the water from no great distance, and, though we could see nothing, the lightning having by this time ceased, we soon heard the measured roll and rattle of sweeps, succeeded a few minutes later by the arrival of the *Dolphin* alongside; Woodford having grown impatient and determined to see for himself what was going forward.

This, of course, greatly facilitated matters, as we were enabled to transfer our wounded directly on board the schooner, where Sanderson was all ready awaiting them; and this we made our first task. Our casualties were very heavy, as I had feared they would be, five of the attacking party being killed and seventeen of them wounded severely enough to need the doctor's services; the French loss being twenty-two killed and forty-five wounded; so desperate, indeed, had been their defence that there were only three of them who had escaped completely unscathed. About an hour after the arrival of the *Dolphin* alongside the prizes, the doctor of the Indiaman came down to assist our surgeon, at the same time reporting all his patients, with one exception—but including the skipper and chief officer, both of whom I had supposed to be dead—to be doing well. The one melancholy exception was the poor little boy I had seen lying wounded in his mother's lap, and he the worthy doctor feared would not outlast the night. The brave little fellow, it seemed, from the story told by the doctor, had been cruelly cut down by the wretch I had killed, in revenge for the child having resented with a blow an attempted insult to his mother made by the ruffian after all the crew and male passengers of the Indiaman had been secured. I am not ashamed to say that on hearing this I regretted having slain the villain, I felt that death by the sword was too good for him, hanging in chains being more in accordance with his deserts. And here I may state that it seemed more than probable this would be the ultimate fate of the survivors of the brigantine's crew, for although they claimed that the vessel was a letter of marque, no papers could be found to substantiate that claim, although I allowed the chief officer every facility to find and produce them—if he could.

At length, having seen all the wounded attended to and made as comfortable as possible, and having told off a prize-crew for the brigantine and placed Woodford in command of the Indiaman, with half a dozen *Dolphins* to assist her own crew in navigating the vessel, I returned on board and had another short but pleasant interview with my father, which was broken in upon by Woodford with the report that a breeze was springing up. I therefore bade a hasty adieu to the passengers, most of whom had by this time in a great measure recovered their equanimity, and hastened on board the schooner, when the three vessels were cast adrift, the sails trimmed to a gentle easterly breeze, and a course shaped for Jamaica, it being my intention to escort the prizes into port.

On the following morning, the weather being fine, I had the gig lowered and went on board the Indiaman—which I may here mention was named the *Truxillo*; the brigantine being named the *Clarice*—when I, for the first time, heard an account of the circumstances attending her capture.

She hailed, it appeared, from London, from which port she had originally sailed, having on board twenty-two adult passengers, with five children; specie amounting to one hundred and fifty thousand pounds, and a very valuable general cargo, all for Kingston. She had joined a convoy at Plymouth, and had sailed with it, all going well with the fleet until they reached the neighbourhood of latitude 25 degrees North and longitude 50 degrees West, when a hurricane was encountered which completely scattered the convoy, and compelled the *Truxillo* to run to the southward for three days under bare poles. It was, of course, almost hopeless to think of falling in with the fleet again after the hurricane had blown itself out—the fleet no longer existed, in fact, the ships of which it was composed having been pretty effectually dispersed; as soon, therefore, as he could make sail again, Captain Barnes, the master of the *Truxillo*, determined to shape a course for Jamaica, and take his chance of being able to reach it unmolested. This determination he had put into effect with most satisfactory results up to the moment of his capture, only two sail having been sighted in the interim, neither of which had taken the slightest notice of him. Nor when, on the preceding evening just before sunset, the lookout had sighted and reported the *Clarice*, did her appearance excite the least uneasiness. She was so small a vessel compared with the *Truxillo*, that nobody condescended to honour her with more than a glance of the most cursory description. Moreover, being discovered on the starboard bow, reaching out from the direction wherein land was known to be, with her yards artfully ill braced, her canvas badly set, her running gear hanging all in bights, and her speed — retarded by a topmast studding-sail being dropped overboard and towed from her lee quarter — less than that of the veriest Noah's ark of a north-country collier, she was at once set down as a harmless coaster, and no further notice taken of her. So skilfully, indeed, had the French skipper managed his approach that even when, shortly after midnight, his vessel dropped alongside the Indiaman, the occurrence was regarded as nothing more than an accident of the most trivial character; and it was not until his crew were actually swarming up the *Truxillo's* lofty sides that the alarm was given, and the crew, snatching handspikes, belaying-pins, billets of wood from the galley, or any other weapon which they could first lay hands on, too late bestirred themselves in the defence of their ship. Notwithstanding their total lack of preparation the English made a sturdy and protracted resistance, affording the passengers ample time to arm themselves; and when at length the Indiaman's crew were driven below, the captain and chief mate retreated to the cabin, which, with the assistance of the male passengers, they successfully held for fully twenty minutes after every other part of the ship was in possession of the enemy. It was during this resistance that the two officers named received such serious wounds as prostrated them on the saloon floor apparently lifeless, and it was only with their fall that the resistance terminated.

The fight over, the male passengers were promptly disarmed and secured, and a scene of pillage and violence, the introduction to which was an insult offered to one of the lady passengers and the cruel cutlass-stroke inflicted upon her almost infant son for resenting it, was just commencing, when it was happily cut short by the appearance of the *Dolphin's* boats upon the scene.

The weather continuing fine, I remained on board the *Truxillo* until well on in the afternoon, taking luncheon with the passengers at one o'clock, and many were the compliments and oft-reiterated the thanks which they bestowed upon me for what they were pleased to term "my gallantry" in rescuing them from the clutches of the French desperados. Many of the gentlemen were officers belonging to the various regiments quartered on the island who had been home on furlough, whilst some of the ladies were the wives of officers already there whom they were going out to join, and from what the gentlemen said, I felt sure that my conduct would on our arrival be so well reported as to do me the utmost possible service with the admiral. My father, too, came in for his share of compliments and congratulations at being the parent of such a son, and this gratified me more than all the rest, for I could see that he was both proud and pleased.

As may well be imagined I was most anxious to have a private chat with him, no opportunity for which had yet occurred; so at length seeing that, notwithstanding an obvious wish on the part of everybody to leave us for a time to ourselves, we were constantly being interrupted, I proposed to him a visit to the *Dolphin*, which saucy craft, under her topsail, fore-trysail, and jib only, was sailing round and round the *Truxillo*, notwithstanding that the latter craft was covered with canvas from her trucks down. The proposal was eagerly acceded to; the gig, which had been towing astern in charge of a boat-keeper, was accordingly hauled up alongside, her crew tumbled down into her, and in a few minutes I found myself once more *at home*. How different everything looked here, to be sure, from what it did on board the Indiaman! Our snow-white decks, unencumbered by anything save the long-boat and pinnace stowed upon the booms, the handsome range of formidable guns on either side, with their gear symmetrically arranged and tackle-falls neatly coiled down, the substantial bulwarks topped by their immaculate hammock-cloths, the gleaming polished brass-work of the various deck-fittings, the taunt spars, with their orderly maze of standing and running rigging and their broad expanse of gleaming well-cut canvas, and last, but by no means least, the stalwart sun-burned crew in their neat, clean, fine weather suits, presented a striking contrast to the scene on board the *Truxillo*, where confusion, disorder, and a very perceptible amount of dirt still reigned supreme. My father, however, did not appear to notice the difference, possibly his agitation was too great to permit of his being keenly sensible to his outward surroundings; he knew that the moment for a full and complete explanation of the mystery connected with the strange unreasoning jealousy which he had cherished against my mother had arrived; and whilst I fancied that he was equally eager with myself that the explanation should be made, I could not help seeing that he at the same time shrank from the ordeal.

It was not so with me. I instinctively felt that whatever the nature of the revelation about to be made to me, there would be a sufficiently weak point somewhere in the evidence to cast a serious doubt upon the whole; that I should be able to discover and assail that weak point in such a manner as not only to satisfy myself, but also my father, that he was wrong and I was not entirely hopeless of being also able to discover a clue which, patiently followed up, would eventually lead to a satisfactory clearing up of everything. So I took my father's arm, conducted him below into the cabin, rang for wine and glasses, and as soon as the steward had disappeared, leaned over the table toward him and said:

"Well, my dear father, at last we are alone, and can talk unrestrainedly. Of course I have a thousand questions to ask you, so I will commence by inquiring to what happy chance am I indebted for the pleasure of this most unexpected meeting with you?"

"I will tell you, Leo," said my father. "I am here because I could no longer overcome my longing to see you. That letter of yours, written after your escape from La Guayra, and in reply to several of mine, which, I gathered from what you said, reached you all at the same time, was my salvation, mentally and physically. Its healthy, manly common-sense tone acted upon my morbidly affected mind like a strong tonic mingled with wine; it swept away the mists which had beclouded my intellect, as the keen fresh mountain breeze sweeps the morning fog from out the valleys; it set me thinking, and asking myself questions which had never occurred to me before; nay, more, it caused the sweet blossom of hope to spring up within my heart; and, finally, it aroused within me a belief—or a superstition, perhaps, would be the better word—that if we could unite our forces, what is now dark might be made light, and I could taste of happiness once more. But I must begin my story at the beginning; I see that you are only mystified by what I have already said; you want an explanation, and you shall have it.

"I was twenty-six years of age when I first saw your mother. I was staying at Amalfi at the time, and it was in an old chateau among the hills, some fifteen miles or so in the rear of the town, that we first met. You have seen her portrait; you perhaps have it still, and are therefore able to judge of her appearance for yourself. I fell in love with her at first sight, and having been fortunate enough, as I then thought, to favourably impress the old uncle, her only relative, with whom she was living, I followed up my first accidental introduction to the inmates of the chateau until it had ripened into a close intimacy. And if I was attracted toward your mother in the first instance by her beauty, I was still more powerfully attracted afterwards by her many accomplishments, and above all by the gentleness and amiability of disposition, the charming innocence and truth, and the unsophisticated ingenuousness of character which I thought I had discovered in her. It was with a feeling of indescribable pleasure and exultation that I was soon able to detect in Maria Bisaccia's beaming, yet half-averted eyes and blushing cheeks when we met, the evidences of a growing attachment for myself, which I did everything in my power to foster and strengthen. Her uncle Flavio seemed quickly to guess at my wishes, and with a frankness, yet at the same time a stately dignity, which greatly raised the old gentleman in my estimation, took an early opportunity to acquaint me with the fact that, though some of Italy's best blood flowed through his niece's veins, she was absolutely penniless. That, however, made no difference whatever to me, excepting that it perhaps rather stimulated my ardour than otherwise. I loved your mother for herself; even then I was doing good work, or, at all events, work which was well spoken of, and which fetched a good price, so that the thought of marrying for money did not particularly commend itself to me. At length, when I felt sufficiently certain of my own feelings to justify such a step, I proposed, and was accepted with a sweet half-shyness, half-abandon of manner, which was as piquant and charming in effect, as I afterwards had reason to believe it was a consummately skilful piece of acting—now, do not interrupt me, Leo; wait until you have heard me to an end before you attempt to judge. Well, not to drag out my story to an undue length, after an acquaintance of some six months we were married, and it was about a month after that date that the miniature was painted which I gave you.

"We removed to Rome, taking up our quarters in a roomy but somewhat dilapidated old villa on the outskirts of the city, where, having now someone and something worth working for, I devoted myself in good earnest to the study and pursuit of my art.

"At the outset of our married life, our—or perhaps it would be more accurate to say my—happiness was complete, but a time at length arrived when I was obliged to ask myself whether I had not after all made a mistake. Your mother's manner and demeanour to me was from the very first characterised by a certain shyness, timidity, and reserve, which, charming and proper enough as it might be in a maiden, or even in a new-made bride, I fully expected and hoped would gradually wear off under the influence of such intimate association as that of wedded life. But it did not. She accorded to me rather the respectful and anxiously timid obedience of a slave to her owner than the frank spontaneous affection of a wife for her husband. Not that she was cold or unresponsive to my demonstrations of affection, but she received and returned them with a diffidence which lasted longer than I quite liked, and much longer than I thought it ought to last. Then suddenly, and without the slightest apparent cause, she began to manifest symptoms of restlessness, anxiety, and preoccupation, which she vainly strove to conceal beneath an assumption of increased tenderness obviously costing her a very great effort. Her uneasiness was so unmistakable that at length, finding she did not take me into her confidence, or seek my assistance in any way, I questioned her about it, and was shocked and grieved beyond expression to meet only with equivocating and evasive replies to my questions. Then, for the first time, I began to suspect that when we had married I was only second in her affection, and the result was that, after a severe struggle with myself,

I took measures to have my wife watched. This step soon resulted in the discovery that the woman whom I loved with such extravagant devotion, and whom I had, up to then, believed equally devoted to me, was in the habit of secretly meeting a young Italian after nightfall in a secluded spot at the bottom of our own garden. So great, even then, was my faith in your mother, Leo, that I could not credit the intelligence, to which I indignantly gave the lie, upon which I was challenged to personally test its accuracy for myself, if I dared. After this there remained but one course of action open to me, and Heaven knows with what reluctance I took it I found that what I had been told, was only too true, for I secretly witnessed no less than three meetings between your mother and a young man whom, imperfectly as I could distinguish his form and features in the dusk, I felt convinced I had somewhere seen before. At length, after so prolonged a visit that he was surprised by the rising moon, and his features thus more fully revealed to me, I identified your mother's visitor as a young fellow named Giuseppe Merlani, whom—why, what is the matter, Leo? Why do you look at me like that? One would swear you had seen a ghost! What is it, my boy?"

"Nothing, nothing," I replied; "I will tell you by and bye, father; go on with your story now, and let me know the worst."

"You know the worst already, Leo," answered my father. "You will naturally wonder why I did not break in upon the first interview I witnessed and demand an explanation. I will tell you why I did not. It was because there was really nothing beyond the clandestine character of the interview to which I could fairly object. My place of concealment was, unfortunately, so far distant from the trysting-place that I was only able to indistinctly catch an occasional word or two when spoken in an incautiously loud tone of voice, but I will do your mother the justice to say that there was nothing in her manner to awaken the anger which I felt, and that what I resented as a want of loyalty to me consisted in the mere act of clandestinely meeting and conversing with young Merlani, whom, upon recognising, I at once remembered as having been a somewhat frequent visitor to the chateau Bisaccia when I first made your mother's acquaintance.

"At length an interview took place which proved to be the final one; and at this interview I saw your mother place a package in Merlani's hands, yield herself for a moment to his embrace, and then retreat precipitately to the house in a state of violent agitation.

"It was then that, for the first time, a clear and intelligible explanation of these singular meetings dawned upon me. I realised, all in a moment, that I had been duped by a woman whose chief attraction had, for me, consisted not so much in her surpassing loveliness of person, though doubtless that had had its effect upon me, as in that angelic purity and fascinating simplicity and truthfulness of character which I now discovered to be a mere worthless sham. It was evident enough that Merlani had been her lover—most probably her *accepted* lover—when I appeared upon the scene; and that, dazzled by my appearance of superior wealth, she had in the most heartless and cruel manner thrown him overboard; and, with a cunning and artfulness which even then seemed incredible to me, laid herself out only too successfully to ensnare me, and by becoming my wife to secure for herself those comforts and luxuries which Merlani—poor shiftless scamp that he was—could never have afforded her.

"Now this of itself would not perhaps have vexed me so much—for I never entertained a very high opinion of feminine conscientiousness or scrupulosity—had she, when accepting me, been frank enough to admit that, whilst she was willing to do so, she entertained no very ardent sentiment of regard for me. But what inflicted an incurable wound alike upon my pride and my love was the fact that she had responded to my suit with assurances of reciprocated affection which were assumed with consummate art. And that which to my mind made the worst feature of it all was that, by her diabolical spells, she had won me to love her as I verily believe woman was never loved before. And then, to discover all in a moment that her love for me was a mere fiction, or at any rate a secondary sentiment, although, even with such evidence before my eyes as what I have already described to you, I could scarcely realise it, and that the idol I worshipped was at best the very incarnation of falsehood and unworthiness, was altogether too much for me; I brooded and fretted over it until I could endure it no longer, and then, one day when she seemed striving to weave anew round my heart the fatal spell of her endearments, I broke away from her embrace and suddenly taxed her with her perfidy, charging her with purchasing her former lover's absence and silence by the sacrifice of her jewels, the whole of which I had soon ascertained were missing.

"I hoped for a moment that my sudden outburst, taking her by surprise, would startle her into making a confession; but no, her self-possession, even at that trying moment, was perfect. For perhaps a minute she stood speechless, regarding me with a rapidly changing expression of countenance, in which incredulity, surprise, horror, grief, indignation, and finally withering scorn and contempt, were portrayed with an amount of power and skill which I have never seen equalled; then she retired to her own apartments, locked herself in, and refused to see me for more than a week. And when at length we met, and I endeavoured in a somewhat calmer tone to reopen the subject, she positively refused to listen to a single word until I had apologised to her for what she chose to designate my base and insulting suspicions. 'You, for whom only I have hitherto lived, have insulted and humbled me to the very dust,' said she. 'My conduct admits of a simple and easy explanation, but I will never make it until you have at least acknowledged yourself hasty in bringing so shameful a charge against me without any previous attempt to ascertain the truth.' This, I considered, was, under the circumstances, asking rather too much; and yet, after hurling that defiance at me, your mother's conduct was so gentle, yet dignified, so perfectly self-possessed, that at times I felt myself almost inclined to believe that I had been the victim of some horrible hallucination, and that my wife was innocent of the deceit with which I had charged her. Well, I need not linger over this part of my story. You can easily understand that our domestic happiness was destroyed, and a month later our establishment was broken up and we removed to England. There, in London, in the house you know so well, you were born about six months after the occurrence of the circumstances I have related. It unfortunately happened that urgent business called me into the country just at that particular time; and you may imagine the shock I received when, on returning home, I found the whole house in confusion, and learned that I had been six hours a parent and one short half-hour a widower. Your mother died quite suddenly, and without even time to leave an intelligible message; but I was told that her last words were: 'Cuthbert, darling—cruel unjust suspicion—innocent;' and that as the last word escaped her lips she passed away."

At this point of his narrative my father's voice suddenly broke, and with a wail of uncontrollable anguish and an exclamation of "Heaven, have mercy upon me and heal my broken heart!" he flung his arms out upon the cabin table, laid his head upon them, and sobbed aloud.

# Chapter Twenty Two
# The Foundering of the "Dolphin"

I allowed the first paroxysm of my father's grief to wear itself out unchecked and uninterrupted; but when he had somewhat recovered his calmness I laid my hand upon his shoulder and said:

"Father, listen to me. You have told me your whole story; I have listened to every word of it most attentively; and, though I admit that it is a singular enough history, you have not yet mentioned one single circumstance directly inculpating my mother. For my part I believe she was innocent of the duplicity you charged her with, and that she only spoke the truth when she asserted that her conduct admitted of a simple and easy explanation."

"Do you really believe that, Leo, on your honour as a gentleman?" demanded my father eagerly.

"I believe it, sir, as implicitly as I do the fact of my own existence."

"Well," said my father, sighing heavily, "there have been times when I have felt almost disposed to do so too; what a blessed relief it would be to me if I could believe it altogether! It is these distracting doubts which are wearing both my life and my reason away, and it was those same doubts which prevented my enjoying your company when you were a child, and almost succeeded in destroying my natural affection for you; it was those doubts which caused me to neglect you as I did when you were most in need of a parent's love and care; and it was these same doubts again which—forgive me for saying it, Leo—caused me almost to rejoice when I first contemplated the possibility of your being killed in the mutiny."

"Well," said I, "that is a strange confession for a father to make to his own son—a strange feeling for a parent to entertain toward his own offspring. How do you account for it, sir?"

"I will tell you, Leo," said my father. "Sit down, my son, and do not look at me so coldly; if you had passed through as many years of mental anguish as I have endured, you would wonder, not so much that my ideas have been warped and distorted, as that my reason has not altogether given way beneath the strain. For, Leo, I want you to understand that I loved your mother; *I loved her!*" he repeated fiercely, with a strange maniacal gleam flashing in his eyes. Then, after pausing for a moment and recovering control of himself by a powerful effort, he continued:

"What was the question?—oh, yes, I remember! In the first place, you were, as a child, strikingly like your mother—you are so even now, although the likeness is no longer so marked as it was. Thus you were a constant reminder to me of one who had first raised me to the highest pinnacle of human bliss only to hurl me thence into the lowest depths of grief and humiliation. Then your wonderful physical resemblance to your mother caused me to dread that you would also inherit her character, and that you would grow up deceitful and untrustworthy. Connect those two feelings with the unbalanced state of my mind and you will easily understand the rest.

"This miserable state of things remained with me up to the time of receiving the letter penned by you after your escape from La Guayra; and you will not be surprised to learn that, after so many years of mental anguish, as acute at the end as it was at the beginning, your letter found me with my health undermined, my reason tottering, and myself in hourly danger of dropping into a suicide's grave. That letter, Leo, aroused me; it dispelled the unhealthy vapours from my mind, caused me to see circumstances in a totally different light from that in which I had regarded them before, and, finally, impelled me to take ship and come out here to join you; as the idea suddenly took hold upon me that, with the aid of your young, healthy, vigorous, common-sense intellect, the question which has tormented me all these years might after all be definitely settled one way or the other. And now you have not only the bitter secret of my life, Leo, but the explanation of my being on board the Indiaman."

I warmly grasped the hand which my father extended to me across the table, and said:

"I believe, father, you have done well to come out here; indeed I might almost venture to say that your decision to do so seems providential, as perhaps you too will think, when I tell you that a certain Giuseppe Merlani, an Italian, is a notorious character in these regions. Not that I think it probable *he* can be the individual who has caused you all your trouble, for he is a pirate; and I can scarcely realise the possibility of anyone who has ever enjoyed my poor mother's acquaintance degenerating into such a character as that of pirate. But let that be as it may, now that we are together, and have no longer any secrets from each other, we can talk the whole affair unreservedly over together; and, depend upon it, father, we shall eventually succeed in satisfactorily demonstrating my mother's truthfulness and the groundlessness of your suspicions that you held but a subordinate place in her affection."

"May mercy grant it, Leo!" fervently ejaculated my father. We then sat down and more composedly talked the whole affair over again, I asking questions on such points as seemed to need further explanation, and my father replying to them, until I thought I had gained all the information it was possible for him to give. I was especially particular in my questions respecting the man Merlani; and though my father was unable to tell me much about him, the little I learned sufficed me to arrive at the conclusion that our friend the hero of the Conconil lagoons might, after all, turn out to be the same individual. The only point which puzzled me was, if such were really the case, in what possible way could such a man have ever been associated with my mother!

The weather continued fine; and on the afternoon of the day following our long conversation my little fleet sailed into Port Royal harbour, and anchored not far from the *Mars*.

On going on board the flag-ship to report myself, I learned that the admiral had left for the Penn nearly a couple of hours before; whilst chatting with Captain Ayres, however, the signal midshipman belonging to the *Mars* reported a signal from the Penn, which turned out to be my number; and, on this being answered by the *Dolphin*, it was followed by an invitation to me to join my old friend at dinner, he having evidently noticed our arrival and recognised the schooner on his way home.

I, of course, lost no time in obeying the signal; and, thinking I might venture upon the liberty, took my father with me. We were both received with the utmost cordiality, to which, in my own case, was added many expressions of warm approval of my conduct. I then learned that, had I arrived a day earlier, I should have had an opportunity of once more meeting my old friend Courtenay, who had sailed that morning after having brought in a large French merchantman with a valuable cargo, which he had been lucky enough to fall in with and capture. This mention of Courtenay afforded me a very good opportunity to ask if anything further had been seen or heard of Merlani and his schooner; in reply to which the admiral assured me that, though my gallant young shipmate had most assiduously sought the pirate, nothing further had been seen of him; and it was thought that, disheartened by the destruction of his stronghold, he had left that part of the world altogether.

During the course of the evening the admiral informed me that my return had happened most opportunely, and inquired of me how long it would be before I could sail again, as he wished me to proceed to sea with all possible despatch on an important mission. I replied that if the cruise was to be only a short one, say of a fortnight or so, I could go to sea again next morning; but if it was likely to be protracted beyond that date I should wish to replenish my stock of provisions and water before leaving port. Upon that he ordered me to haul in alongside the dockyard wharf next morning, and if my rigging needed overhauling to see to it at once, as he should endeavour to get me off again in three days at the latest.

My father and I slept at the Penn that night; and next morning, on my way down to the schooner, I established him in comfortable quarters, recommended by the admiral, on the southernmost spur of Long Mountain, where, in addition to a pure and healthy atmosphere, he would have the advantage of a magnificent view of the harbour and sea to the southward, as well as a long range of superb tropical landscape, upon which to exercise the powers of his brush during my absence.

In the course of the morning, after the *Dolphin* had been hauled in alongside the wharf and Fidd had set all hands to work overhauling the rigging, I learned from the admiral that it was his intention to send me down on the Venezuelan coast to cruise, in conjunction with my former acquaintance the *Dido*, on the lookout for a Spanish treasure-ship which, it was rumoured, was about to sail from Cartagena with important despatches. Of such consequence was the capture of this ship considered that I was frankly told a couple of frigates would have been sent to look after her, had such been available; unfortunately, however, there were none in harbour when the intelligence had been received, four days before; the *Dido*, therefore, being the only ship then at liberty, had been despatched forthwith, and I was now to follow her, so that should the Spaniards slip through the hands of one, the other might have a chance to pick her up.

By the afternoon of the third day the *Dolphin* was once more ready for sea; and on reporting this to the admiral I at once received my orders and was directed to be off at once. As I had quite expected this I had run up during the morning to see and say good-bye to my father; I had nothing, therefore, to detain me; and by sunset we were again at sea, clear of the shoals, and standing away to the southward with every stitch of canvas spread that the schooner could stagger under.

My instructions were to first of all proceed to the coast near Cartagena, endeavour, by any means which might happen to present themselves, to obtain information of the date of sailing of the treasure-ship; and, in the event of my being successful, to then cruise to the eastward on the lookout for the *Dido*, on falling in with which I was to communicate to Captain Venn such intelligence as I might have picked up, and thereafter act under his instructions. If I failed to meet with the *Dido* I was to do my best to capture the Spaniard unaided, or, if he appeared too heavy for me to tackle single-handed, to follow him and keep him in sight until I could obtain assistance.

As the information to hand respecting this treasure-ship was very meagre, the admiral had urged me to use all expedition, in the first place, to reach the coast, and secure, if possible, some reliable intelligence; we, therefore, carried on all that night and the whole of the next day, being favoured with such a fine breeze, and making such good progress that twenty-four hours after sailing we had accomplished nearly half our distance.

Towards the close of the afternoon watch, however, the wind showed signs of failing us, which it did so rapidly that by two bells in the first dog-watch our canvas was thrashing itself threadbare against the masts, and the schooner was rolling gunwale under as she headed all round the compass. The atmosphere was hot and close almost to the point of suffocation; the sky, though perfectly cloudless, was thick and hazy; and the sun, as he drooped toward the horizon, glowed like a red-hot ball, whilst the vapour through which he was seen magnified him to at least three times his ordinary dimensions.

"What do you think of the weather, Mr Pottle?" said I to the quarter-master, as he left the boatswain and strolled aft from the waist, where the two had been jogging fore and aft together for the last half-hour, and regarding the sky every few minutes with somewhat ostentatious glances of anxiety.

"Well, sir, I hardly know what to make of it," was the reply. "Mr Fidd and I have been comparing notes together; the boatswain has been a long time on this station, as perhaps you know, sir, and he says he doesn't half like the looks of it; in fact, he remarked to me not five minutes ago that he wouldn't be surprised to find that a hurricane is brewing. Have you looked at the glass lately, sir?"

"Not since noon," said I; "it was pretty steady then, with a slight tendency to drop, it is true, but nothing to speak of. Let us see what it says now?"

We turned to the open sky-light and looked down through it. The barometer was, for convenience, hung in the sky-light so that it might be consulted with equal facility either from the deck or the cabin, and a single glance sufficed to show us that the mercury had fallen a full inch since the instrument had been set in the morning.

"Depend upon it, sir, Fidd is right, and we are in for a blow," remarked Pottle. "And whether or no," he continued, "it seems a pity to let the canvas beat itself to pieces for no good, as it is doing now. Shall we stow it, sir? There is no occasion to call all hands, the watch is strong enough to tackle the job."

I looked round once more at the weather. There was not a breath of wind anywhere; the water, undisturbed by the faintest indication of a cat's-paw, showed a surface like polished steel, and the swell was fast going down. The sun, just touching the horizon, was of a fierce fiery-red colour, and apparently swollen to abnormal dimensions; but save for the angry lurid glare of the luminary, and a very perceptible thickening of the atmosphere, there did not appear to be anything out of the common. Still I was not altogether satisfied, I had a *feeling* that something was about to happen. I took another look at the barometer. The mercury had visibly dropped still further in the few minutes which had elapsed since we last looked at it. "Yes," said I, "clew up and furl everything, Mr Pottle, if you please. Let the watch set about the job at once, and see that they make a close furl of it whilst they are about it."

"Ay, ay, sir," was the answer. "Hands, shorten sail! Haul down and clew up, fore and aft; in with everything. Settle away your peak and main halliards, and let's get this big mainsail snug under its cover the first thing. In main-topmast staysail. Let go the topgallant and topsail halliards, and clew up and furl the sails. Man the jib and staysail downhauls, let go the halliards, haul down. Lay out there, for'ard, and stow those jibs. Shall we send the royal and topgallant-yards down on deck, sir, and house the topmasts whilst we are about it?"

"We may as well," I replied. "If it comes on to blow heavily the schooner will be all the easier if relieved of her top-hamper, and if it turns out to be a false alarm, why we can soon get her ataunto again, and there will be no harm done."

The men, many of whom were thoroughly seasoned and experienced hands, had evidently been feeling anxious, and seemed glad enough to find their officers on the alert, if one might judge by the activity with which they went about their work, and the eagerness which they evinced to get it expeditiously performed. By the time that everything was made snug, the ship under bare poles, the guns secured with extra tackles and what not, it was pitch-dark—darker, indeed, if such were possible, than on the night of our adventure with the Indiaman. Still, there was no sign of a change, so when the steward summoned me to dinner I had no hesitation about following him, leaving the deck in charge of the gunner, with instructions to keep both eyes and ears open, and to call me the moment he had reason to believe the breeze was coming.

Dinner over, I again went on deck. Still no change, the air seemed thick, and hot as the breath of a furnace, but so still that the flame of a candle brought on deck burned straight up, save when the roll of the vessel caused it to waver to port or to starboard as the case might be.

"After all I don't think it's going to be anything, sir, unless, mayhap, another thunder-storm like the one we had," commenced the gunner, as I stood looking round the horizon and vainly endeavouring to pierce the darkness which enveloped us.

"Hark!" I interrupted. "Do you hear that, Tompion?"

A low moaning sound had become audible in the atmosphere, away apparently on our starboard beam, and as we listened it gradually increased in intensity until it had become a rushing roar so loud as to almost drown the human voice, even when raised to its highest pitch.

"Ay, ay, sir; I hear it sure enough," was the reply. "It's coming now. Look out, sir I lay hold on anything you can put your hand upon. Hard a-starboard with your helm! Look out there, for'ard!"

Louder and louder grew the sound until it became absolutely deafening, and then with an awful overwhelming rush the gale burst upon us. It struck the schooner fair on her starboard, broadside, and stout and staunch as was the craft, she bowed beneath it until her larboard gunwale was buried.

"Good heavens!" I thought, "she is going over, she is going to turn the turtle with us!" as I felt the incline of the deck getting steeper and steeper beneath my feet, and I turned and clawed my way aft toward the wheel. On reaching it I found there was someone already there.

"Hard a-weather; over with it, man; hard over!" I yelled as I got hold of the spokes and vainly strove to move the helm.

"It *is* hard a-weather, sir," shrieked Tompion's voice in reply; "but we're done for, sir; if she won't pay off she's bound to capsize."

"Stick to her," I shouted back as I threw my whole weight on the spokes to leeward, "I can feel a tremor in the wheel; she's gathering head-way!"

Such was indeed the case, and after a few breathless seconds, during which it seemed that another inch of inclination would have sufficed to turn her bottom up, the schooner began to right, recovering herself at last with a jerk which filled the decks fore and aft with water, and flying away before the gale like a frightened steed.

The craft always steered like a little boat, and once fairly before the wind Tompion could easily keep her there single-handed, so, letting go the wheel and slanting myself backward against the force of the blast, which pressed upon my body like a solid wall, and demanded all my strength to prevent my being helplessly run forward, I made a snatch at the binnacle and peered into it. We were heading due east, which was a great relief to my mind, as I knew that we had plenty of sea-room in that direction, and could run for days if need were without bringing up against anything. A man came working his way aft, hauling himself along by the bulwarks, to relieve the wheel, and Tompion joined me under the partial shelter of the companion.

"That was a narrow squeak, sir, if ever there was one," he remarked. "When you joined me at the wheel I wouldn't have given a brass farthing for our chance; but we shall do well enough now, at all events until the sea rises; and even then I don't feel particular duberous. This schooner is as fine a sea-boat as ever was launched; and I'd sooner take my chance of riding out a gale in her than in some seventy-fours I've known."

"Yes," I replied, "I think we shall be all right now. I wonder whether we have sustained any damage aloft?"

"Impossible to say yet, sir," returned Tompion. "We shall know soon enough, however. But it was a marcy as them yards was sent down on deck and the topmasts housed; if they'd been on end it would have made more than extra leverage enough to have capsized us. It's to be hoped we've plenty of sea-room ahead of us, sir."

I satisfied his mind upon that point, and the gunner then went forward to see whether the men were all right, returning shortly afterwards with the satisfactory intelligence that they were.

The sea rose with frightful rapidity, notwithstanding that the wind in its furious career caught the crests of the waves as they rose and swept them through the air in a drenching, blinding torrent of scud-water; and in an hour from the bursting of the hurricane we found ourselves exposed to a new danger, that of being pooped and swamped by the mountainous seas which came rushing after us, towering high above our taffrail and momentarily threatening to break on board.

I turned to Tompion, who was standing abaft near the helmsman.

"Tompion," said I, "we must get some canvas of some sort upon the ship or we shall be overrun by the sea. Do you think we might venture to set the foresail, close reefed?"

"Lord bless you, Mr Lascelles," was the reply, "the canvas ain't wove that'd stand a single minute before such a howlin' gale as this here; it'd be blown clean out of the gaskets if we was to cast a single one of 'em loose; indeed, I shouldn't be a bit surprised to find half the sails blown away from the spars as it is, when we get light enough to see how the little barkie has come out of the scrimmage. Still, if so be as you thinks fit to give the order, we—"

"Look out! hold on everybody fore and aft! here it comes!" I shouted, interrupting Tompion; for at that moment I caught sight of an enormous wave rushing after us with its gleaming white phosphorescent crest towering a dozen feet above our taffrail, and curling over in such a manner that I saw it must inevitably break on board. I had just time to spring to the foot of the mainmast and grasp a rope's-end when down it thundered upon the deck, completely burying and overwhelming the schooner fore and aft, filling her decks to the rail, and sweeping forward with such irresistible power that my arms were almost torn from my sockets as I held on for dear life to the rope I had grasped. I had heard a crash even above the howling of the gale and the rush of water as I was swept off my feet, and I made up my mind that the schooner was doomed; nothing, I thought, could withstand the rush and power of so tremendous a body of water as that which had swept over the ship; and if she ever rose again I was quite prepared to find that everything above the level of the decks had been carried away, and that the hull was full of water and ready to founder beneath the next sea which might strike us.

At length, half drowned, I once more found my feet and got my head above water. Either there was a little more light in the sky or my eyes had become accustomed in a measure to the gloom, or perhaps it was the phosphorescence of the sea which helped us, at all events there was light enough from some source to enable me to see that the schooner had relieved herself from the mountain of water which had overwhelmed her, and was still afloat. My first glance was aft, and I must confess that I was as surprised as I was pleased to see that Tompion and the helmsman were still on board, and that the wheel was intact. The bulwarks, however, excepting some ten feet or so on each quarter, were gone throughout the whole length of the ship, so far as I could see. The sky-light was smashed to atoms, leaving a great yawning hole in the deck; the boats had disappeared from the booms, and I could see no sign of anyone moving about on the forecastle.

As I stood, bewildered and trying to recover my scattered senses, Tompion made his way along the deck to *me*.

"Are you all right, sir?" he asked.

"Yes—that is, I believe so, Tompion. Are you?"

"All right and tight, sir, thank God!" answered the gunner. "But I'm afraid it's a bad job with the hands for'ard, sir. I don't see anybody moving about—yes, there is—there's one man—or two. I'll see if I can't reach the fo'c's'le and find out the extent of the damage. And, if there's hands enough left to do it, we *must* get some canvas on the ship at once, as you said, sir. Another such job as that last'd finish us. As it is the ship must be nearly half full of water. We must get some planks and a tarpaulin over that hole in the deck first thing, however. I'll go for'ard and see what can be done."

Watching his chance my companion made a sudden rush along the deck toward the forecastle, which he gained in safety, and from which he returned in about five minutes, followed by the carpenter and several men, with the gratifying intelligence that, so far as he could ascertain, only two of the crew were missing. The forecastle, however, was reported to be nearly three feet deep in water; and the heavy sickly heave of the ship told me but too plainly that, whilst we had already experienced a very narrow escape, there was undoubtedly a great deal of water in the hold, and that we were in a most critical situation.

Without waiting to sound the well, I ordered the pumps to be rigged and manned forthwith, the carpenter, with half a dozen hands, at the same time setting out to get the lumber and tarpaulin necessary for closing up the yawning aperture in the deck left by the demolished sky-light. Meanwhile another gang of men, under Woodford the master, were busy forward trying to loose, reef, and set the foresail.

The carpenter and his gang had found what they wanted, and were busy with their work when the helmsman gave a warning cry, and at the same moment another sea came tumbling inboard, not so heavy as the first, certainly, but sufficient to flood the decks to a depth of a couple of feet; and I heard the water pouring down into the cabin like a cataract. This happened five or six times in succession, the men being each time driven from their work and their labour rendered of no avail. At length another unusually heavy sea broke on board, and when the decks were once more clear the water could be plainly heard rushing about in the hold with the heave and roll of the ship.

"We're foundering! we're foundering! every man for himself!" was now the cry, and the men made a rush to the two boats still hanging to the davits. A groan of despair burst from the poor fellows as, on one of them jumping into each to clear her away for lowering, it was found that neither boat would swim, some of the bottom planking being driven out in each case.

I saw now that the *Dolphin* was a doomed ship; that awful chasm in the deck could never be covered in and made secure in time to prevent her foundering; I therefore rapidly cast over in my mind what would be best to do. In a minute I had the necessary idea, which it seemed had at the same moment presented itself to the carpenter, for he staggered toward me and hoarsely shouted into my ear:

"The ship can't live ten minutes longer, sir. Better cut away the masts so as to leave us something to cling to when she goes from under us."

"Yes," said I, "do it at once. Steady, men!" I continued, "out knives every one of you and cut away every rope attached to the hull; as many of you as can get at the lanyards of the rigging cut them; the masts are our only chance."

The men understood me and at once set to work, most of them going forward and attacking the foremast first, so as to get it down and out of the way before commencing upon the mainmast. The back-stays were first severed, then the lanyards of the shrouds, commencing at the aftermost and working forward; and when the hands had cut through about half of them the remainder suddenly parted and the foremast went over the bows with a crash, being only prevented from going adrift altogether and lost by the circumstance that the topsail sheets and other running gear had not been let go or cut away. The foremast in falling brought down the main-topmast with it; and I fancied that, as it crashed down on the deck, I heard, above the hoarse shriek of the gale, a human cry which led me to fear that some of the workers had been hurt. Leaving Fidd with half a dozen hands to the somewhat delicate task of securing the wreck of the mast sufficiently to prevent its prematurely breaking adrift, whilst at the same time taking precautions against the danger of its being dragged down by the ship when she should founder, the rest of the crew came aft and at once commenced an attack upon the mainmast, which it had now become necessary to get rid of with the utmost expedition, as, owing to the fall of the foremast, the ship was in momentary peril of broaching to and capsizing. The men had reached the main rigging and were in the very act of commencing operations when a huge sea swept unbroken under the schooner; and as the crest passed her and she settled slopingly down on the back of it, I heard the water in the hold come rushing aft, accompanied by a crashing sound below which told me that the cabin bulkhead had given way, and the next instant the water surged *up* through the sky-light-hole in the deck, showing that she was at that moment full to the beams abaft. Her stern settled bodily down with the weight of water in that part of her, whilst her bows, relieved of the burden, rose high in the air. She was now in the trough between two seas, and as the one following her came sweeping up astern with towering foam-capped crest reared high in air, it became evident that, being pinned down as it were with so much water in the after part of her, she would not recover herself in time, and that the approaching sea would run right over her. I knew well enough what would then happen, and so did the men, for at my warning cry they at once dropped whatever they happened to have in their hands and sprang forward. I waved to the helmsman, who up to that moment had stuck most nobly to his perilous post, and he, understanding me, let go the wheel and rushed past me after his shipmates. On swept the wave, the water gathering up round the quarters of the devoted schooner until it began to pour in over the taffrail. Nothing now could save the *Dolphin*— her hour had come. I glanced wildly round the deck and saw, indistinctly through the gloom, the dark blot-like crowd of men all clustered together in the gangway, waiting to spring for the wreck of the foremast; and as the body of the wave came roaring and foaming in over the stern, and I felt the deck canting upward under its weight, I too staggered up the steep incline and shouted, "Jump for your lives!" as one of the men seized me round the waist whilst he thrust a rope into my hand.

Another moment and the great mountain of foaming water had reached to where we stood. I was swept irresistibly off my feet and hurled in among the crowding men; I was jostled and dragged to and fro; and as the sea closed over my head, ends and bights of rope wreathed and twisted themselves about my limbs and body; I received several violent blows from what I supposed were floating pieces of wreckage; I found myself, all in a moment, inextricably entangled in a raffle of cordage which tightened itself about my body until I could move neither hand nor foot; and then there came a great singing in my ears, and I felt that I was being dragged irresistibly downward.

# Chapter Twenty Three
# The Spanish Treasure-ship

Suddenly, with a distinct jerk, the downward dragging sensation ceased; the gear with which I was entangled had broken adrift from the sinking hull; and just as I was upon the point of being suffocated from my long submersion I found myself once more upon the surface. Though scarcely conscious, I still had sense enough to take a long inhalation and so fill my lungs afresh with air; and it was well that I did so, for my head had not been above water more than a few seconds before I was again overwhelmed. I quite gave myself up for lost; for, as I have already said, I was so completely enmeshed by the raffle of loose gear which had wrapped itself about my body and limbs that I was quite powerless to help myself. On emerging the second time, however, somebody seized me by the hair, and in another moment I felt myself being drawn up by the arms upon a spar.

"Blest if I don't believe this is Mr Lascelles that I've just been and fished up," I heard Tom Collins say. "Ay, and it is too," he continued, as he hoisted me still higher on the spar. "Lend a hand here, somebody, to clear the young skipper; he's wrapped up in enough stuff to make a new set of running gear for a seventy-four."

I opened my eyes, and found that I was with a number of others on the wreck of the foremast, which, with all attached, had fortunately broken adrift from the wreck as it foundered, and was now floating, with the yards underneath it, just as it had originally gone over the bows.

"Is that Collins?" I asked, when I had at length recovered breath enough to speak.

"Ay, ay, sir; it's me, safe enough, thank God!" was the answer. "Glad to find as you're alive and hearty, sir."

"Thank you, Collins; how many do we muster here? there's such a network of raffle across my face that I can scarcely see."

"Don't know exactly, sir; it's too dark to count, but we seem to muster pretty strong, all things considered. We'll soon have you clear, sir. Now then, Bill, you stand by to haul Mr Lascelles out of the thick of these bights and turns whilst I holds 'em up. Now then—haul! Is that better, sir?"

"Very much better, thank you," said I, as they dragged me out clear of the thickest of the raffia. "If you are seated firmly enough for me to put my arm round your neck I think I can work myself free altogether. That's it, capital! Now, I'm all clear."

"Is that Mr Lascelles' voice I hear?" asked somebody who was clinging to the topmast, some twenty feet away.

"It is," said I; "who are you?"

"I'm Tompion, sir," was the reply. "Very glad to find you among us, Mr Lascelles. I was afraid you were among the missing at first."

"No, I am here, all right," said I, "and sound, I think, with the exception of a few bruises. Are there any other officers among us?"

"I'm here," replied Pottle.

"And I," said Woodford.

"And I," added Marchmont, the younger of the two midshipmen.

"Well done!" thought I, "this is better than I dared hope." I invited the speakers to join me in my comparatively sheltered position in the crosstrees; and when they had done so an effort was made to ascertain the extent of our loss. This, after a great deal of difficulty, we found consisted of the surgeon, the boatswain, the senior mid, and fifty men, leaving thirty-two clinging to the foremast. This was a very heavy loss; and I felt it so bitterly that for the first half-hour after it was ascertained I almost regretted my own preservation. This feeling, however, was nothing short of impious ingratitude, and so, on reflection, I recognised it to be; with an unspoken prayer, therefore, for pardon to that great Being who had so mercifully preserved me, I strove to divert my thoughts from the melancholy reflections which assailed me, by an endeavour to devise some means for our continued preservation. After a long consultation with Woodford respecting our probable position, it was agreed between us that, as soon as the weather moderated and the sea went down sufficiently, an endeavour should be made to construct some sort of a raft out of the wreckage which was then supporting us, and on it to make our way, if possible, to the southward, hoping to be fallen in with and picked up by the *Dido*; failing which we would try to reach the mainland, and either seize a small vessel or give ourselves up to the Spaniards, according as circumstances turned out.

We had just come to the above-mentioned conclusion when Collins remarked, hopefully:

"The gale seems to have broken, sir; it is certainly not blowing so hard; and the seas don't seem to be breaking quite so heavily; and—look, sir— look, lads, the sky is breaking away overhead; I can see a star. Ah! it's gone again—but there's another. Hurrah, my hearties! keep up your spirits and hold on to the spar like grim death; we'll weather upon old Davy yet, this bout."

It was quite true; the sky was rapidly clearing, and half an hour later it was a brilliant starlight night; the wind, too, was dropping rapidly, and the sea no longer broke so heavily or so incessantly over us as it had done at first. Fortunately for us the water was quite warm; we therefore suffered no inconvenience whatever from the immersion.

At length, after what seemed to us an endless night, day broke; the atmosphere was gloriously bright and clear, the wind had dropped to a fine topgallant breeze, and the sea had gone down sufficiently to allow of our commencing operations; as, therefore, we had no breakfast to get or anything else to detain us, we started at once; and all hands were soon busy cutting adrift the spars, knotting and splicing cordage, and in other ways forwarding the work as actively as possible under the circumstances. We found, however, that we had a long and, from lack of sufficient timber, a difficult job before us; and as the morning wore on it was made additionally so by the appearance of several ravenous sharks close to us, which were only restrained from making an attack by an incessant splashing maintained by all hands except the half-dozen we could spare to get on with the work.

At length—it was getting well on in the afternoon, by the appearance of the sun—when, in despite of all our difficulties, we were beginning to bring our raft into something like shape, we were suddenly startled from our work by the hoarse cry of "Sail ho!" raised by one of the men; and, lifting our eyes from our work, we waited until we rose to the top of a wave, when there she was, sure enough, a large ship apparently, under topsails, approaching us from the southward and westward, and only about five miles distant. A hearty cheer was at once raised by all hands at this unexpected prospect of rescue; and then we went to work once more with renewed vigour and activity to establish a means of making our presence known, as we felt convinced that, though she was heading straight for us, we had not yet been discovered by her.

It will be remembered that, when making preparations for the gale, we had sent down our topgallant and royal-yards. When the project of cutting away the masts to serve as a last retreat for the crew had been carried out, somebody had had the forethought to get these spars overboard and secured to the wreck of the foremast; and in subsequently planning our raft it had been our intention to get the topgallant-yard on end to serve as a mast, with the sail as our means of propulsion through the water. Our plans were not carried out to such a stage of completeness as this when the strange sail hove in sight, and all our energies were now employed to get this part of the work done forthwith; as I felt convinced that, lying so low in the water as we were, we might be passed at a very short distance unobserved, unless we could raise a spar of some sort to attract attention.

But, owing to our very limited amount of standing room, and the aggravating way in which the water still washed over our structure, this particular task of getting the topgallant-yard on end proved most difficult; and we were still struggling ineffectually for success when a loud groan of disappointment, instantly followed by a frantic hail, told me that something was wrong; and, looking again toward the ship, now distant only some two miles, we saw that she had altered her course a couple of points, by which proceeding she would pass to the southward of us without approaching any nearer.

For a minute or two something very like a panic took possession of all hands, and everybody began to shout and gesticulate to the utmost of his ability without reference to the efforts of the rest. At length, however, Woodford and I managed between us to secure silence; upon which we directed that, whilst as many as could do so should stand up and wave jackets, shirts, or any other article most handy, the whole should at a given signal unite in a simultaneous hail. This we did, waiting each time until we rose to the crest of a sea; but it soon became evident that our voices were not powerful enough to reach the ship—I never expected that they would be—for she swept on unheeding, and was very soon to the eastward of us, increasing her distance every minute.

This most disheartening state of affairs continued until she had run about three miles to leeward of us, when we suddenly saw her round to and back her main-yard. I ought to mention, by the bye, that we had ere this discovered her to be a full-rigged ship—and not the *Dido*, as some had at first declared her to be—with her mizzen-topmast and fore and main-topgallant-masts gone, showing that she too must have encountered the hurricane which had proved so disastrous to us. She was evidently a foreigner; many of us pronounced her to be a Spaniard; and I thought that, if so, it was more than probable she was the identical vessel we had been sent out to look for.

"Hurrah!" shouted Tompion, as the stranger rounded to, "she sees us, my hearties; and—look, if my eyes don't deceive me, there goes one of her quarter-boats down into the water. Now, ain't that just like a lubberly Spaniard, to lie there with his main-topsail to the mast and give his boat's crew a three-miles pull to windward when he might just as well make a couple of short boards and heave to within a cable's length of us?"

By this time I had scrambled to my feet, and was with half a dozen others watching with mingled curiosity and apprehension the movements of the stranger, which were certainly not such as I should have expected her to make had her object in heaving to been *our* rescue. A boat had certainly been lowered, but we had not as yet caught a glimpse of it, from the exasperating circumstance that whenever we rose upon a sea the boat happened to be sunk in a hollow. At length, however, we got a moment's view of her, and not only of her but also of something else which looked remarkably like another raft or a piece of wreckage, and it was toward this that the boat was steering and *not* toward us.

"By heaven!" I exclaimed, "they have *not* seen us after all; they are not coming here, and unless we can make them hear us within the next ten minutes our chance will be lost. It is a piece of wreckage—possibly part of the poor old *Dolphin*—that they have stopped to examine. We must shout, lads, and with a will, the ship is to leeward of us and *may* catch the sound. Now then, when we rise stand by—one, two, three, *Ship ahoy!*"

We shouted as we had probably never shouted before, not once but at least fifty times; we shouted ourselves hoarse, and at last had the vexation to see the boat being again hoisted up. We now fully expected to see the ship immediately bear up on her course, but she did not; her topsail remained aback for nearly ten minutes longer, during which we continued to shout and wave for our very lives. At length, however, the ponderous main-yard swung, the square canvas was braced sharp up, and the ship gathered way. A breathless half minute passed, during which every eye among us was unwaveringly fixed upon the distant ship, except when she vanished behind a wave-crest, and then a joyous shout went up.

"*Now* she sees us! she is standing this way, hurrah! hurrah!" And in the midst of it all the boom of a gun came sullenly up against the wind from the stranger, as an assurance of help and rescue.

Oh, how anxiously we watched the noble fabric as she ponderously ploughed her way obliquely toward us over the liquid ridges, now plunging to her hawse-holes and rolling heavily to leeward as she dived into the trough, and anon raising her dripping bows, richly carved and gilt, high in air as she slowly climbed to the surge's crest! Her motion was slow and stately, for the wind had dropped very considerably, whilst, owing to the loss of her upper spars, she was under short canvas, and her approach consequently seemed to us most tediously slow. At length, however, she arrived within a biscuit-throw of us, backed her main-topsail again, and once more lowered a boat, which a dozen oar-strokes sufficed to bring alongside our raft. The bowman laid in his oar and hove us a rope, and as he did so the officer in charge of the boat—a young man in the undress uniform of a Spanish naval lieutenant—rose to his feet in the stern-sheets and, raising his hat to the little cluster of uniforms he saw among us, said in Spanish:

"Are you a portion of the crew of the *Dolphin*, British cruiser, which foundered last night?"

"We are," I answered, very much surprised at the question, and wondering how in the world he came to know anything about the *Dolphin* and her having foundered.

"Then," said he, "you will be gratified to learn that we have already picked up twenty-six of your company which we discovered about three miles to leeward, floating on a portion of the ship's deck; and it was in consequence of the representations made to my captain by one of your officers picked up by us that an examination of the sea was made from our mastheads, resulting in your discovery. But I will not waste time by entering into further explanations at present; have I the honour of addressing the captain of the *Dolphin*?"

"I was her commanding officer," I replied; "and I thank you greatly for the pleasing intelligence you have so promptly afforded us. How many of us can you take at once?"

"I am afraid we dare not venture alongside with more than twelve in addition to the boat's crew; the swell is still very heavy. Will you have the goodness to tell off that number for our first trip?"

I called out the names of the men, one by one, as the boat was brought cautiously alongside the raft, and in a few minutes her complement was complete.

"Adieu, Señor Lascelles," said the young officer, raising his hat again as he shoved off; "we will not leave you in your present uncomfortable position one moment longer than is absolutely necessary."

I mechanically returned the salute, again wondering where he had picked up my name, until it occurred to me that he must have heard it mentioned by some of the party taken off the floating deck. The news that our loss was not as heavy by twenty-six as I had supposed it to be was intensely gratifying, and my spirits rose under its influence to a pitch of almost extravagant hilarity. Twenty-eight poor fellows still remained unaccounted for, and they had undoubtedly gone down with the schooner; but the loss was, after all comparatively trifling, taking into consideration the suddenness and completeness of the disaster, and I was inexpressibly thankful that matters had turned out to be no worse.

The boat was soon alongside again for a second moiety of my companions in misfortune, and a third trip sufficed to clear the raft of its living occupants, I, of course, as in duty bound, being the last to leave the clumsy structure which had served us in such good stead.

As I sat beside the young lieutenant in the stern-sheets of the boat during our journey to the ship—which occupied about a quarter of an hour, she having drifted considerably to leeward during the process of transhipment—he asked a few questions which elicited from me the leading particulars of our mishap; and having learned these he informed me that his ship, the *Santa Catalina*, had sailed four days previously from Cartagena for Cadiz, that she, like ourselves, had been caught in the hurricane, from which, however, she had escaped with only the damage to her spars already referred to. As we approached the ship's side near enough to discern the crowd of curious faces peering at us over the lofty bulwarks, my new friend remarked with a peculiar smile:

"You will find among our passengers two former acquaintances of your own, unless I am greatly mistaken."

We were alongside before I had time to ask him the names of these two former acquaintances, and in another moment, accepting the precedence which the courteous young Spaniard, with a graceful wave of the hand accorded me, I found myself on the side ladder of the *Santa Catalina*.

As I stepped in through the entering port a small, withered-up, sun-dried, yellow-complexioned man in full captain's uniform met me, and, introducing himself somewhat pompously as Don Felix Calderon, the captain of the *Santa Catalina*, bade me, and through me my companions, welcome on board his ship, congratulating us upon our speedy rescue, and expressing the gratification he felt at being the means of saving so many gallant *enemies* from a possible watery grave. I made my acknowledgments as gracefully as I could under the circumstances, and was about to proceed with an inquiry relative to those previously picked up off the floating deck when the ring of people who had gathered round us during our somewhat ceremonious exchange of compliments was abruptly broken through by a female figure, and in another instant my neck was encircled by a pair of lovely arms, a beautiful head was laid lovingly upon my breast, and the clear silvery notes of Dona Inez de Guzman's voice sobbed out:

"Oh, Leo, Leo, my darling! what joy is this to meet you so unexpectedly, when I feared that fate had separated us for ever!"

I was about to reply when, to my horror I must confess, my eye encountered that of Don Luis, Inez's father, as he stepped forward and laid his hand somewhat sternly on his daughter's shoulder.

"There, Inez," said he, "that will do. You are doubtless overjoyed to again meet a friend who possesses so large a share of our regard; but do not allow your enthusiasm to carry you too far. Señor Lascelles is suffering from the effects of a long immersion in the sea; he is doubtless both hungry and thirsty; and he is also undoubtedly anxious to make arrangements with Don Felix as to the disposal of his men. Come, my dear girl, let us return to the cabin for the present; when our young friend has refreshed himself and is at liberty we shall both be glad of an opportunity to renew our acquaintance and to have a little conversation with him. Señor," he continued, turning to me and offering his hand with a stately and somewhat distant bow, "accept my felicitations upon your most fortunate escape."

My beautiful Inez upon this released me and retired, somewhat abashed, with her father; but as she went she managed to throw back a parting glance from her brimming eyes which assured me that my hold upon her affections was still as firm as it had ever been.

This most unexpected meeting with Inez and her father, with the restraint and coolness of the latter's manner to me, coming as it did close upon the heels of several hours of exposure and, what was worse, extreme excitement and anxiety of mind, rather pushed me off my balance, and for a moment or two after my lady-love vanished into the cabin I scarcely knew where I was. Don Felix saw this, and coming forward placed his hand under my arm and very kindly invited me to accompany him to his private cabin, delicately suggesting that I appeared to be much exhausted, and that a glass of wine would do me good. Like most youngsters, however, I was too proud to yield to the weakness which had momentarily overpowered me, so, rallying with an effort, I murmured that it was a mere nothing, and turned the subject by asking his permission to muster my men in the waist that I might ascertain exactly who were the missing ones. The permission was at once accorded, and I then discovered that, of the entire crew of the *Dolphin*, the surgeon, Boyne the senior mid, and twenty-six men still remained unaccounted for.

The question now arose: In what light would Don Felix regard us, and how dispose of us? I thought it desirable that this question should be settled at once; and I was about to submit it to the Spanish captain before dismissing the men, when the individual most concerned forestalled me by calling me aside to the quarter-deck, where he and several of his officers had been in apparently anxious consultation whilst I had been mustering the remnant of the schooner's crew. He informed me, upon my joining him, that, pleased as he was to have been the means of rescuing us, his duty to his government left him no alternative but to regard us as prisoners of war; and, whilst he should be pleased to receive my parole and that of the other officers, he feared he would be compelled to put the seamen in close confinement below—unless I would undertake on their behalf that no attempt should be made by them to capture or otherwise interfere with the *Santa Catalina* and her crew, in which case the confinement should be merely nominal.

I could scarcely refrain from smiling at the suggestion thus thrown out, for the Spaniards mustered twice as strong as we did; and they were moreover armed, which we were not. But, preserving my gravity, I unhesitatingly replied that gratitude alone for the important service rendered us would have sufficed to prevent any such attempt as that hinted at, and that I therefore cheerfully entered upon the required undertaking.

This matter satisfactorily settled, I retired below with the young officer who had had charge of the boat which effected our removal from the raft. His name, he informed me, was Silvio Hermoso Villacampa y Albuquerque; he was second lieutenant of the ship; and being very nearly my size and build he had very kindly proffered me the use of a suit of his clothing with which to replace my own drenched garments. He was a very pleasant, chatty young fellow, remarkably free and unreserved in his manner—for a Spaniard—and whilst I was shifting my rig, and subsequently partaking of some refreshments which had been laid out for me upon the ward-room table, I learned from him a great deal about the ship and her skipper, one item of my acquired information being the fact that the *Santa Catalina* was undoubtedly the identical vessel which I had been despatched to look out for. I learned that Don Felix, though a good enough man in the main, was not very greatly respected by his officers, who found him very deficient in seamanship, and suspected him of being also somewhat wanting in courage. He was new to the ship, it seemed, this being his first voyage in her; and young Albuquerque more than hinted his suspicion that Don Felix owed his command a great deal more to influence than to merit. My meal ended, I returned to the deck, and was then introduced in due form to each of the quarter-deck officers in succession, more than one of whom were polite enough to compliment me upon my Spanish.

When I had time to look about a bit I was greatly surprised to notice that no preparations were going forward to replace the spars lost by the ship during the hurricane; and upon my noticing it to the first lieutenant he replied, with rather a contemptuous shrug of the shoulders, that it was Captain Calderon's intention to put into Cumana to refit, and also to land us Englishmen.

This was by no means pleasant news for me. I was in hopes we should have been carried across the Atlantic, which would have afforded us at least a chance of recapture by one of our own men-of-war; moreover Inez and her father were on board, and though I augured ill from the studied coolness of the latter's reception of me, I thought I should never have a better opportunity than that afforded by an Atlantic voyage for ingratiating myself with him and forwarding my love affairs. I thought matters over a little, and at length hit upon a plan which I thought might serve to render our visit to Cumana unnecessary, at least so far as the spars were concerned. I knew that a quick passage was regarded by the authorities as of the most vital importance, for my friend the second lieutenant had told me so; I therefore awaited my opportunity, and, taking advantage of a moment when Don Felix and several of his officers were chatting with me, I suddenly changed the topic of conversation by thanking the captain for the arrangements he had made for the comfort of myself and my men, which I begged he would allow me to acknowledge in the only way I then could, namely by assisting his crew to replace the lost spars of the ship, which I assured him we could and would do, unaided if necessary, before noon next day. He flushed up a little, stammered something unintelligible, and finally declined the assistance rather curtly.

I saw no more of Don Luis or his daughter until after the commencement of the first watch that evening, when the former joined me and proposed a little private chat on the poop.

I of course acceded to the proposal at once and followed my stately friend to the poop, fully expecting to be severely reproached for having presumed to entangle the affections of his daughter.

I quite looked for an exhibition of righteous anger; but in this I was agreeably disappointed. Whatever Don Luis' feeling might have been he remained, outwardly at least, perfectly calm, speaking throughout our short interview in a low, sonorous, and steady voice.

"Since meeting you so unexpectedly on the quarter-deck this afternoon," he commenced, "I have had a private conversation with my daughter, which has resulted in a full and complete explanation by her of the singular scene I then witnessed, and of all that has led up to it. I will not reproach you with anything that is past, because I feel that it is really *I* who am more to blame than anybody else for it. I have never thought it necessary to provide my daughter with any staid female companion—any duenna—to watch and control her actions; she has been allowed to run wild about the place from her infancy, and to have her own way in everything. I ought to have remembered this, and to have provided against all that has happened, before I ventured to introduce two young men beneath my roof. However, there is no very great harm done, so far—a few love-letters, and so on, but nothing serious. Now, young sir, I wish you to understand me clearly; I am quite willing to forget everything that has happened—but so must you. I am fully aware that, so long as we all remain on board the same ship, it will be quite impossible that you and my daughter should avoid meeting more or less; and after the scene of this afternoon on the quarter-deck I do not choose to excite comment and curiosity by forbidding your speaking to each other. But let me remind you that I am a parent, and that I possess rights which no *gentleman* will for a moment dream of infringing or disputing; in virtue of these, therefore, I must insist that, henceforward, you never presume to address my daughter in the language of love. Nay, do not look so angry, my young friend; I meant not to speak quite so harshly, but I was and am most anxious you should understand that there must be an end to all this business."

"May I venture to ask your grounds for insisting so strongly on what will inevitably wreck the happiness of one if not of two persons!" I demanded, not quite as respectfully as I ought, I am afraid.

"Assuredly," answered Don Luis; "it is the difference in position—the difference of rank—which exists between yourself and my daughter. In every other respect I have not a fault to find. You are a fine, gallant young fellow—your fame has reached even to La Guayra, I may tell you—I believe you to be perfectly honourable, honest, and straightforward, and I feel sure that you will advance rapidly in your profession; but, my dear young friend, you are not *noble*; and you are consequently quite ineligible—"

"Not noble—ineligible!" I interrupted. "Have you forgotten that I am an officer of the British navy? Or is it that you are unaware of the fact that every wearer of our uniform—"

"Is qualified by it to stand in the presence of kings?" retorted he with a laugh. "Oh, yes, I know all this; but it does not alter facts one iota.—There," he continued, "we will say no more about it; we quite understand each other, I am sure; I have demanded that you will respect certain rights of mine, and you *will* respect them, as any other gentleman would. Now let us talk about something else."

"One moment, Don Luis," said I, "and then, if you choose, we will drop the subject for ever. I acknowledge your rights, and will respect them. But—understand me, sir—I will *never* give up the hope of winning your daughter—with your approval—until I learn that she is wedded to someone else. And I shall most assuredly tell her so, before I fall back into the position of a mere ordinary acquaintance to which you wish to relegate me."

Don Luis laughed a little, said that, after all, what I insisted upon was perhaps only fair, and then the subject was dropped and we had a long and quite friendly chat about other matters. I then learned that the poor fellow was in trouble with his government, and was going home, in something almost like disgrace, in obedience to an unexpected and most peremptory message from Spain. He attributed the whole business to the machinations and misrepresentations of certain enemies in La Guayra; and complained bitterly that if he had been allowed a little more time he could have collected an ample sufficiency of evidence to have refuted every one of the charges against him. He explained the whole affair to me in full detail; but as it has no direct bearing upon my story I shall not inflict the particulars upon the reader.

Upon our separating, somewhat late, I was intercepted by a messenger from Don Felix, who, I was informed, wished to see me in his private cabin. I joined him at once; and found that the business was that, after thinking matters over further, he was now prepared to accept my offer of assistance in the replacing of his spars if I would waive his former refusal, which he now endeavoured to explain away, and for which he very handsomely apologised. I assured him that I should still be very happy to be of any service I possibly could; upon which it was agreed that the work should be commenced immediately after breakfast on the following morning; and I then retired, quite worn out, to the quarters allotted to me.

# Chapter Twenty Four
# The Capture and Recapture
# of the "Santa Catalina"

I rather overslept myself that night, so that it was I close upon eight bells before I was ready to go on deck. As I reached the foot of the ladder leading to the upper deck an officer, apparently on the quarter-deck, made some remark which I, being below, did not catch; but I did that of Captain Calderon, who immediately replied quite loud enough for me to hear:

"A schooner in these waters is always an object to be looked upon with suspicion, but the *Dolphin* has gone to the bottom, thanks be to the Blessed Virgin, and I do not think we need fear anything else of her rig that we may meet with hereabouts. Still, I do not altogether like the looks of that fellow yonder."

I smiled as this back-handed compliment to the poor *Dolphin* came floating down the hatchway, and turned back to my berth for a minute or two in order that those on deck might have no cause to think I had overheard a remark which obviously was not intended to reach my ears. Then I went on deck, and found the skipper with two or three officers grouped near the capstan and intently eyeing some object to windward.

The wind, I discovered, had fallen light during the night, and had hauled round from the eastward, in consequence of which the *Santa Catalina* was then heading due north, close-hauled upon the larboard tack, with hardly enough motion through the water to give her steerage-way. The object which was exciting so much interest among the Spanish officers was a schooner broad on our weather-beam, about eight miles distant, and consequently hull-down from the deck. She was steering about west-north-west, and appeared to have every stitch of canvas packed upon her that her crew could spread, including square-sail, topgallant, topmast, and lower studding-sails, which was not at all surprising, considering that the wind was light and dead fair for her. It was apparent enough to me, however, that the Spaniards did not like the look of her.

I was greeted with great cordiality by the little group as I made my appearance on deck; the kindest hopes were expressed that I had passed a comfortable night, and I was promptly invited to take breakfast with the skipper in his cabin. These compliments being duly paid and acknowledged, Captain Calderon remarked:

"We have been looking at that schooner yonder, and wondering who and what she can be. Schooners—unless they happen to be British cruisers, French privateers, or piratical craft—are seldom to be met with about here; and, though we ought to have nothing to fear from the second variety I have named, I have, to speak the plain truth, no very great desire to meet with either of the three."

"Perhaps she is an American from one of the islands, bound up into the Gulf," I suggested.

"Hardly that, I think," answered Don Felix. "Tell me, did you ever see an American trader with such a beautifully cut suit of canvas as that fellow spreads?" thrusting the glass into my hand as he spoke.

I applied the instrument to my eye, taking a good long steady look at the distant vessel; and when I had completed my examination I was forced to admit that I had never seen a trader, American or otherwise, with such a handsome suit of canvas, or with everything so snug and ship-shape about her rigging as was this craft. "Still," said I, "I am disposed to think her American from the enormous spread of her yards, which you have doubtless noticed. But if, Don Felix," I continued, "you are really anxious to ascertain the fellow's intentions, why not wear round on the opposite tack? That will at once make him declare himself; for if he is an honest trader he will continue to hold on his present course, whilst if he is not he will certainly alter it so as to intercept you; you will thus have plenty of time to prepare for him, as he cannot get alongside in less than a couple of hours unless the breeze freshens."

"I was just thinking of that," remarked Don Felix, "and I will do so. For the sake of my—ah—my—passengers, I must be cautious. We will wear ship, gentlemen, if you please, and then go to breakfast."

This was done, the operation occupying nearly a quarter of an hour, in consequence of the lightness of the wind, and we then, a party of four, went below to breakfast.

The steward was only just pouring out our chocolate when the first lieutenant came down to say that the schooner had altered her course about four points to the southward, and evidently intended to intercept us.

Don Felix looked very blank for a moment or two on hearing this, then his brow cleared, and he remarked:

"Pooh! she cannot mean to attack us; she merely wishes to speak. Hoist the Spanish ensign, sir, she will not interfere with us when she sees *that*!"

I must say I had my doubts whether the mere exhibition of the Spanish ensign would have the deterrent effect Captain Calderon anticipated; however, I reflected it could not possibly matter to me—unless, of course, the craft were British, which I did not believe—so I went on composedly with my breakfast. My companions were evidently somewhat perturbed, the news just brought down into the cabin interfered considerably with the enjoyment of their meal, and I could see that they were anxiously waiting for me to finish in order that they might go on deck and see how matters were progressing. I therefore brought my repast to a hurried conclusion, and we all returned to the upper regions together.

The strange sail had by this time reduced her distance to some five miles from the *Santa Catalina*; and, from the course she was steering, it could no longer be doubted that she intended to pass close to us, if nothing more. Captain Calderon lost not a moment in bringing his glass to bear upon her, and so intent was his scrutiny and examination that it was fully five minutes before he removed his eye from the tube. When he did so he handed the glass to me, and I in turn had a look at her. She had now raised her hull clear of the horizon, but owing to the intense heat her outline was so magnified and distorted that it was quite impossible to get a good view of her. Still, as I watched the wavering image, the idea began to grow upon me that I had somewhere seen the craft before; and I tried for a long time to remember where it was, but without success.

"Well, what do you think of her, my friend?" asked Don Felix as I replaced the instrument in his hands.

"I do not know what to think," said I; "but I have assuredly seen that vessel before, though *where*, I cannot for the life of me remember."

"I wish you would allow me to ask you a single question," said Don Felix very earnestly.

"Certainly," I thoughtlessly replied; "what is it?"

"Is yonder schooner one of your cruisers?"

I had not expected such a question as this, and I did not think it at all a fair one for Don Felix to put I scarcely knew what reply to make to it, and in order to gain time I begged the loan of the glass once more, which having obtained I composedly ascended to the main-top, and from that advantageous stand-point renewed my examination. In this situation I obtained a much better view; and as I stood there swaying to the sluggish heave of the vessel, with the glass glued to my eye, my memory suddenly carried me back on board the *Foam*, and I once more fancied myself standing on her heaving deck watching the approach of a strange schooner running down toward us pretty much as this one was now doing; the only difference being that we then had a great deal more wind than we now had, whilst the schooner in sight showed a great deal more canvas than the one we were then so anxiously watching. But the hull was the same; the taunt spars, and especially the excessive spread of her yards it was utterly impossible to mistake; and I hurried down on deck with all speed, feeling that the *Santa Catalina* and every soul on board her was in a very awkward fix, to escape from which would tax our energies and ingenuity to the utmost.

"Well?" said Don Felix interrogatively, as I swung off the rail down on deck close to him.

"Don Felix," said I, "when you asked me that question a minute or two ago I had not succeeded in identifying yonder schooner, though I felt sure I had seen her somewhere before. *Now* I know her; she is the vessel in which that notorious pirate, Merlani, plies his nefarious trade; and I would therefore strongly recommend you to clear for action at once."

"Merlani!" ejaculated the skipper; "the saints defend us! It cannot be true; you are surely joking with us, señor!"

"I was never more serious in my life, Captain Calderon," I retorted; "and to show you how grave I consider our situation, I beg that you will allow my men and myself to assist you in the defence of the ship."

The little gentleman turned almost livid for a moment, and I really thought he was frightened; but after an ineffectual effort or two to steady his voice, he managed to stutter out passionately:

"No, señor, no; certainly not! Your offer is almost an insult—though perhaps you did not intend it as such. The *Santa Catalina* is a Spanish ship, and she is manned by a crew who, with her officers, are quite able to take care of her and to uphold the honour and dignity of yonder flag," pointing as he spoke to the languidly floating ensign at the peak.

"Very good, Don Felix," said I; "you, of course, know the capabilities of your crew far better than I do. But the schooner there is sure to be crowded with men, who, to my personal knowledge, are as desperate a set of ruffians as ever trod a deck. You will have all your work cut out to beat them off; and if you fail, what is to become of us all? I warn you that neither I nor my men will submit tamely and without a struggle to have our throats cut. If the pirates gain possession of this ship we shall fight for our lives, and if we prove victorious I shall consider the *Santa Catalina* my lawful prize."

"And you shall be welcome to her, señor, on those conditions," said Don Felix, with all the hauteur he could muster. "At present I must request that you and your people will retire below and consider yourselves as close prisoners until you hear further from me. And I rely upon your courtesy and sense of honour to relieve me of the necessity for calling upon my crew, in the present critical state of affairs, to enforce my commands."

"You shall be instantly obeyed, Captain Calderon," said I, highly nettled at so very unnecessary an exhibition of warmth. "Come, my lads," I continued to my own people, who were lounging about the decks and looking somewhat wistfully at the guns, "below with you, every man, the *Dolphins* are to have no hand in this fight it seems. Come, down with you; no disobedience; for shame, men; would you disgrace me before all these Spaniards?"

This was enough, and the few who seemed at first inclined to hang back now pressed forward eager to show their obedience by being among the first to pass down the hatchway.

As I turned away with a bow from Don Felix and his little group of officers, the former gave the order to clear ship for action; and at the same moment Don Luis, who, it seemed, had come unobserved on deck and had heard the altercation between Don Felix and myself, pressed forward and placed himself by my side.

"I will come below with you for a moment, if I may," said he.

"Assuredly," said I; "I shall be glad to have a word with you, Don Luis, before the action commences. *Dolphins*," I continued in English, "just look about you as you pass below, and take possession of anything you can find likely to prove handy as a weapon. I'm by no means sure we shall not be yet obliged to fight for our lives, though the dons have so scornfully refused our assistance."

"Is that your honest conviction?" asked Don Luis, who understood English perfectly, "or is it merely the expression of a little bitterness at Captain Calderon's singularly discourteous behaviour?"

"It is my honest conviction," said I. "It may seem a very impertinent thing for me to say, Don Luis; but, from what I have seen of the officers and crew of this vessel, I do not believe they will be able to withstand the pirates' attack longer than five minutes at the utmost. I am glad you have given me the opportunity to say this to you, for I should not like disaster to find you quite unprepared. Would that I could think of some means of providing for your daughter's safety!"

"The saints be merciful to us! Do you really think matters are so desperate as that, Señor Lascelles?" ejaculated Don Luis.

"I do, indeed," replied I.

"Then, supposing the pirates gain possession of the ship, what do you think will happen?" asked my friend, in great perturbation.

"They will undoubtedly ransack the ship and plunder her of every article of the slightest value, in the first place," said I; "but what they will next do is not so certain. 'Dead men tell no tales,' however, and the chances are that every male on board will be slaughtered in cold blood, or thrown overboard, after which the ship will, doubtless, be scuttled or set on fire."

"Stay were you are a few minutes, I pray you, my dear boy," ejaculated Don Luis, in a tone of voice which betrayed his extreme consternation; "I must go on deck and have a word or two with Captain Calderon. I have not yet wholly lost my power or influence, though I *am* to some extent in disgrace."

He hurried away and left me standing on the main-deck. My men, meanwhile, had, in obedience to my instructions, made their way below to the lower deck, and I could hear them now and then—during a momentary cessation in the din on deck and around me caused by the Spaniards' preparations for action—rummaging about below and calling to each other.

About ten minutes later Don Luis rejoined me, with a drawn sword in his hand and a pair of pistols in the sash which girded his waist, showing that he, at all events, fully intended to do his part in the protection of the ship and those within her.

"Where are your men?" he asked.

"Gone below, whither I must now join them," said I. "I can see that your countrymen are already regarding my prolonged presence here with jealous and mistrustful eyes."

"Come, then," said Don Luis, "I will go with you."

We descended to the lower deck, and I saw, by the dim light of a lantern suspended from the beams, that most of my lads had provided themselves with at least *something* in the shape of a weapon. Some had armed themselves with tail-blocks, which they had routed out from somewhere; some carried marlinespikes; and others were balancing crowbars and pieces of old iron in their hands; whilst one or two had dragged to light some short lengths of chain, which, wielded by their sinewy arms, might prove formidable weapons of offence.

Don Luis looked at them, then at me, and smiled.

"You English are a most extraordinary people," he said. "I believe you are never more happy than when fighting. Those men of yours look more like a parcel of schoolboys preparing for a holiday than men making ready for a desperate life-and-death struggle. But I must be brief; there is no time for anything like gossip now; the pirate schooner is within two miles of us, and Don Felix expects her to open fire immediately. I have tried to persuade him that he was hasty and ill-advised to refuse your offer of assistance; but the fellow is as obstinate as a pig; he will *not* listen to reason, albeit I believe he is growing more nervous every minute. Now, first, I want to ask you what had I better do with my daughter?"

"Stow her away as low down in the run of the ship as you can put her," said I. "She will then be out of reach of the shot. It will also be some little time before she can be discovered by the pirates—assuming, of course, that they take the ship—and in the meantime there will be the chance of my men being able to do something. But, for the love of Heaven, Don Luis, let her not fall alive into the hands of the scoundrels!"

"She shall *not*, if I have to slay her with my own hand," ejaculated Don Luis through his set teeth. "There is one thing more," he continued hurriedly. "Your men cannot possibly do any good with those makeshift weapons with which they have provided themselves. Now, if I am willing to compromise myself to the extent of providing you all with suitable arms, will you pledge your sacred word of honour, Don Leo, that those weapons shall not be employed save against the pirates, and only then in the event of my countrymen proving unequal to cope with them."

"Willingly," said I, "but with this proviso, Don Luis: If the pirates conquer your countrymen and gain possession of the *Santa Catalina*, and we, after that, are able to recover her, I shall regard her as my prize and retain possession of her by every means in my power."

Don Luis cogitated deeply for a full minute.

"Be it so," he then said. "That was agreed upon between you and Don Felix, I remember; and after all it would be infinitely preferable that we should be your prisoners than that we should fall by the murderous hands of the pirates. Do you happen to know if there is any other means of gaining the deck above than the ladder by which we descended!"

"Yes," said I; "there is another ladder abaft there which leads to the main and upper decks by way of the after hatchway."

At this moment a muffled *boom* smote our ears, and a crash somewhere above us, which followed a second or two later, showed that the pirate had opened fire and was within range.

This was immediately succeeded by a confused discharge from the *Santa Catalina* of all the main-deck guns of the larboard broadside, one after the other.

"Don Luis," said I, "for Heaven's sake try to persuade Don Felix not to return the pirate's fire. Those twelve-pounder carronades are of comparatively little use except at close quarters, and Merlani is not fool enough to give you the chance to use them to advantage; he will simply heave to out of range and blaze away with his long gun until more than half your crew are killed, when he will dash alongside and carry the ship without an effort. Tell Don Felix to double-shot his guns and to depress them as much as he can, but not to fire. Let the schooner come alongside—haul down your ensign if you cannot otherwise get him to come—and, when the schooner is close under the muzzles of your guns, fire, and your shot will go right through her bottom. The pirates will then be obliged to board, when, with the advantage afforded by the *Catalina's* high sides, you ought to have things all your own way."

"Thanks! thanks! I will see what I can do," said Don Luis. "But now, come this way, and bring your men with you; I will take it upon myself to arm you, and then, if the worst comes to the worst, I shall look to you to save ay daughter."

"And I will do it or perish!" I exclaimed fervently, as I beckoned the *Dolphins* to follow me and made sail in the wake of Don Luis.

He led us along until we reached the after hatchway, through which we ascended to the deck above, when we again turned aft until we reached a bulkhead inclosing a room beneath Don Felix's cabin. Don Luis threw open a door in this bulkhead, and exclaiming:

"There, help yourselves; I providentially noticed this room as I was coming down to you just now," rushed away on deck.

The room disclosed by the opening of the door was of some extent, occupying nearly half the breadth of the vessel; and it had evidently been fitted up as an armoury when the ship had been doing duty as a man-of-war, for though sundry unoccupied pegs and pins showed that the present crew had just been armed from this place, there still remained weapons enough unappropriated for more than twice our numbers. The weapons consisted of muskets, pistols, swords, and cutlasses; but, as there were of course no cartridges lying about, we chose cutlasses only, and, having secured them, hurried back to our former lurking-place. Once safely back there, I lost no time in briefly, yet as fully as possible, explaining the position of affairs to my followers; after which we sat down and calmly waited the course of events, I employing the interval in comparing notes with those of the *Dolphin's* officers who had been taken off the floating deck.

Meanwhile gun after gun had been fired by the pirates, to which Don Felix had persistently replied; but after a time the firing ceased overhead, and I was in hopes that Don Luis had been able to persuade the skipper to follow my advice.

At length, after a somewhat tedious interval of suspense, a sharp order or two was given on deck, quickly followed by the simultaneous discharge of the whole of the *Santa Catalina's* larboard broadside. A terrible din of shrieks, yells, shouts, and imprecations—heard but very imperfectly by us down below—immediately succeeded. A crash of artillery, accompanied by the thud of shot against the ship's sides, and the rending of timber overhead, told us that the pirate schooner had promptly returned the broadside, and a slight but very perceptible concussion a minute later indicated that she was alongside. A rattling fire of musketry was immediately opened from the deck of the *Santa Catalina*, to which the pirates replied with their pistols. Orders were shouted on both sides, the sharp cries of the wounded, and the muffled thud of their bodies falling to the deck, began to mingle with the officers' shouts of encouragement and the fierce defiances of the men. There was a rush, a confused trampling of feet, more pistol-shots, the ring of steel upon steel, and a medley of human voices raised high in the excitement of mortal combat which told us that the pirates were boarding.

"There they are!" exclaimed Woodford, springing to his feet, his example in this respect being followed by the whole of the men. "Now, what do you say, Mr Lascelles, are we to go up and tackle them?"

"Not yet," said I; "I have pledged my word that we will not interfere unless the pirates absolutely gain possession of the ship, and that pledge must be scrupulously observed. By the way," I continued, as an idea flashed through my brain, "I wish you all to understand, my lads, that I am particularly anxious to secure the pirate captain alive, if possible; and I will give fifty pounds to the man who effects his capture. And I suppose I need not remind you that if we have to fight at all it will be for our lives. Those fellows on deck are not likely to give any quarter if they get the best of the tussle."

"Never fear, sir," answered Collins, one of the smartest of the crew; "we'll give 'em a second taste of what they got from us away over there in the lagoons."

"Ay, ay; we will. Trust us for that," etcetera, etcetera, murmured one and another; and as I looked round at them standing there like hounds in the leash, their eyes gleaming, their feet shuffling impatiently on the deck, their cutlasses tightly grasped in their sinewy hands, their every movement betraying their excitement and eagerness to join in the fray, I felt that they most assuredly would.

Presently hasty footsteps were heard approaching, and in another moment several of the *Santa Catalina's* crew came helter-skelter down the ladder, and, taking not the slightest notice of us, rushed off and disappeared in the darkness.

"Steady, lads; not yet!" said I, as the *Dolphins*, like one man, pulled themselves together and braced themselves for a rush.

More footsteps, and Don Luis appeared, bareheaded, in his shirt-sleeves, his right arm bleeding profusely and dangling useless and broken at his side, whilst his right hand still convulsively grasped the hilt of his broken sword.

"Quick, Don Leo," he panted; "up with you, for the love of God! Captain Calderon's courage failed him half an hour ago, and he left the defence of the ship to the first lieutenant, who was killed a moment ago fighting gallantly, and the crew, panic-stricken, at once gave way, scattering all over the decks like frightened sheep, and huddling by twos and threes into the first corner they could find, where they are now being savagely slaughtered by those fiends of pirates. Quick, my dear boy, or you may be too late—my daughter—oh, God, have mercy!—"

"Collins," said I, "off with your neckerchief; quick, my man; tie it tightly about this gentleman's arm, *above* the wound, mind, and stay here in charge of him until you are relieved. Now, lads, away on deck we go. Follow me; hurrah!"

The brave fellows responded with a single heart-stirring cheer as they bounded after me up ladder after ladder, and in the twinkle of a purser's dip we found ourselves on the upper deck.

A glance sufficed to show us that Don Luis' statement was literally true. The pirates were scattered all over the upper deck, killing the unresisting Spaniards as if they had been so many rats.

I hastily detailed the gunner with a dozen men to enter and explore the cabins, to defend them against all comers, and to capture any strangers they might discover therein; and then, Woodford leading one division and I the other, we swept the decks from the after hatchway right forward, cutting down everybody who attempted to oppose us. The pirates thus unexpectedly found themselves all huddled together in the eyes of the ship, where, their freedom of movement being seriously interfered with by the presence of the heel of the bowsprit and all the gear which so frequently hampers a ship's forecastle-head, they were placed at a very serious disadvantage; and, though they fought desperately, we overpowered them without much difficulty, gaining possession of the ship in less than two minutes from the time of our first appearance on deck.

# Chapter Twenty Five
## "All's well that ends well"

Leaving Woodford to attend to the securing of the prisoners, I hastened aft to see how Tompion and his little party were faring in the cabins. I found them in the saloon under the poop, with four prisoners who had been discovered ransacking the cabins, and in one of these prisoners, a fine handsome middle-aged man of swarthy complexion, with dark hair clustering in close ringlets all over his shapely head, dark piercing eyes, small ears, from the lobes of which depended a pair of plain gold ear-rings, and a somewhat slim yet wiry and athletic-looking figure clad in a picturesque but somewhat showy costume, I thought I identified the man I was so anxious to meet, Giuseppe Merlani. The man was badly wounded, having been run through the body by Tompion, who had been compelled to inflict the wound in order to save his own life. The fellow looked hard, almost wildly at me, and muttered something which I could not catch, as I was at the moment speaking to the gunner; and when, a minute afterwards, I found myself at liberty to interrogate him, I discovered that he had swooned from loss of blood. I directed Tompion to have him taken below, undressed, and placed in a hammock, despatching one of our men, meanwhile, to hunt up the surgeon of the *Santa Catalina*, and then made my way below to the spot where I had left Don Luis. I found him still in charge of the man Collins, who had managed in an effectual if somewhat clumsy way, to stanch the bleeding of his wound; and it is scarcely necessary to say that he was overjoyed when I informed him that we had succeeded in recapturing the ship. He at once staggered to his feet, and upon my assuring him that there was nothing further to fear from the pirates, announced his intention of going immediately to his daughter's hiding-place, begging me to accompany him thither. We accordingly started on our way to the main-deck, Collins supporting Don Luis by placing his arm round the latter's waist. But we were barely half-way up the ladder when a sudden hubbub and confusion arose on the upper deck, and I was compelled to hasten away to see what it meant. I found that it was caused by the discovery, suddenly made, that the pirate schooner was sinking alongside, and I reached the poop only just in time to see her heel over and founder stern first, the broadside of shot which had been fired into her when she ranged alongside having passed through her deck and out through her bottom, thus occasioning so fatal a leak that the only wonder was that she had floated so long.

The excitement and confusion attending this incident had not subsided when the surviving Spanish officers and crew made their reappearance on deck. The former were very profuse in their compliments and thanks for what they termed our invaluable assistance; having tendered which they manifested a disposition to resume their former status on board. But I was quite determined not to allow this. The ship had passed completely out of their possession into that of the pirates, and had been recaptured by us. She was therefore our lawful prize, and I was resolved to retain possession of her, as I had informed Don Felix I would. I pointed this out to the Spanish officers, and requested them to surrender their swords, which, very sensibly, they did. Don Felix, however, who had hidden himself away below somewhere, and who did not reappear until some time after the others, stormed and blustered and reviled us, calling us everything but gentlemen, and demanding to know whether we considered we were making him a proper return for his kindness in having rescued us. This, of course, was all very well; but he had refused our offer of assistance, as I pointed out to him, and had had his ship taken from him, not by us, but by the pirates. He was, of course, obliged to deliver up his sword; but he would not listen to reason, retiring to his cabin and sulking there until our arrival in Port Royal harbour, for which, on gaining possession of the ship, I had at once shaped a course. Previous to this, however, I had secured his despatch-box and had put it in a place of safety, otherwise I have no doubt he would have promptly dropped it overboard out of the stern windows.

I was anxious to treat my prisoners with the same generosity and consideration which they had accorded to me; and I hastened to set their minds at rest upon this point. But whilst the officers were perfectly willing to give their own parole, they reluctantly admitted that they felt it quite impossible to guarantee the good behaviour of their men; I was therefore compelled, in self-defence, to confine the latter below. All this took up a great deal of time; it was consequently not until after the men had had their dinner that I was able to set the watches and start the carpenter upon the task of getting new spars ready for sending aloft. I had been informed by the Spanish surgeon, when we all sat down to luncheon together, that Don Luis' hurt was not of a serious character, and that he was likely to do well enough if the fever resulting from his wound could be kept under; but with regard to the pirate captain the case was different: his wound, I was assured, was mortal, and whilst the man might possibly linger for several days, he might, on the other hand, expire at any moment. The surgeon further informed me that Merlani—for he it really proved to be—had manifested quite an extraordinary inquisitiveness respecting me, and had at last requested that I might be informed he would like to speak to me.

As soon, therefore, as I found myself at liberty, I, without delaying even to wait upon Don Luis and Inez, made my way below to the sick-bay, where, in a little corner which had been separated by a screen from the part occupied by the other injured men, lay Merlani in a hammock, with one of my men to attend upon and at the same time stand sentry over him.

He was ghastly pale, and evidently suffering great pain, as I could see by the occasional twitching of his facial muscles, as well as by the perspiration which bedewed his forehead and trickled down upon the pillow; but he seemed to be quite free from fever, and he was perfectly steady and collected in his mind.

He looked long and eagerly in my face as I stood beside his hammock, and his countenance brightened up with pleasure. At length he said in Spanish:

"This is kind of you, Señor Lascelles. I wanted to see you, because in the moment that I first looked upon your face I was reminded of one who in my younger days I almost worshipped; and when, during the dressing of my wound, I learned your name, I could not resist the temptation of believing that you must be related to her—that you must, in fact, be her son. Tell me, am I not right? Are you not the son of Maria Bisaccia?"

"That was indeed my mother's name," I said, greatly disconcerted. "But I find it difficult to understand how it could possibly have happened that you and my mother should have—"

"Known anything of each other?" he interrupted. "Yes; and well you may. But it is easily explained. I have not always been the blood-stained villain that I now am; when I knew your mother I was, I need scarcely say, wholly innocent of crime. Idle, perhaps; wayward; and a trifle wild I undoubtedly was; but crime and I were strangers, and strangers we should have continued to be," he added somewhat wildly, "if I had but listened to and heeded the warnings and pleadings of my sweet foster-sister."

"*Your foster-sister!*" I ejaculated, a great light bursting in upon me in a moment. "Was my mother your foster-sister?"

"Ay was she," replied Merlani. "Her mother died half an hour after giving her birth; and my mother—who was at that time nursing my sister Bianca, now dead, woe is me!—was summoned in all haste to the chateau to take the place of a mother to the new-born infant. I was at that time a youngster of seven years old, and as my mother became a permanent inmate of the chateau for the first four years of your mother's life, I saw a great deal of the dear child, and have played for hours with her and my sweet Bianca on the sunny terrace in front of the chateau, ay, and have dragged them in a little chariot, made by my father, many a weary mile up and down the rough steep road leading to Amalfi."

"So, then, you and my mother were friends?" I remarked, in the hope of leading him on to talk further upon the subject. "Friends!" ejaculated Merlani; "well, yes, we were; but that expression is hardly the right one. She was the guardian angel; I the poor, weak, erring mortal over whom she watched. Always listening to her advice and admonitions with the profoundest and most respectful attention, and always anxious to do right, whilst I was in her presence, I had no sooner withdrawn myself and mingled once more with my usual associates, than my natural weakness prevailed, and I found myself involved in some scrape or other, from the consequences of which your mother, with a patience more than mortal, rescued me as often as she could. Had I but heeded her counsels I should never have been what I now am."

"I can readily believe that," said I, "little as I know of my mother. But do you intend me to accept that remark as *literally* true, or—"

"It is literally true," answered Merlani. "You must know, señor, that at the time to which I refer, like many more young men of my own age, I became greatly interested in politics; so much so that after a time I united myself to a secret society, the object of which was to compass the freedom of our beloved Italy. I was on sufficiently intimate terms with your mother to confide freely to her all my hopes and aspirations, this among the rest; but, whilst she thoroughly sympathised with me in the particular matter to which I have referred, she had penetration enough to be fully sensible of the danger to which I was exposing myself; and she earnestly sought to dissuade me from having anything to do with active politics. But I was proud of being looked upon as a patriot, and blind to the fact that my country was not then ripe for the freedom which I, among others, burned to give her; I, therefore, as usual, went my own headstrong way, and eventually got into very serious trouble. I was obliged to fly; and learning that your mother—by this time married—was in Rome, I resolved to seek her in the first instance, and beg of her that pecuniary assistance which my other friends were incapable of affording me. I did so, found her, and, after considerable difficulty, succeeded in obtaining a private interview with her. I represented to her the danger of the position in which—"

"One moment," I interrupted. "What, may I ask, was your object in making the interview *private*?"

"It was on your father's account," answered Merlani. "I know not what he may be *now*, if he still lives, but he was then an exceedingly proud, haughty, and overbearing man, very impatient and hasty of temper, as I had had many opportunities of noticing; and he had, moreover, no sympathy with the movement with which I had associated myself. I happened to know, also, that though he was unaware of the relationship—if I may so term it—which existed between your mother and myself, I had been unfortunate enough to attract his unfavourable attention whilst he was prosecuting his love suit with your mother. I was therefore anxious, above all things, to avoid compromising the wife in the eyes of her husband by letting him know that she possessed so disreputable an acquaintance; and finally, I felt convinced that if he became acquainted with the facts of my case he would consider it his duty to deliver me into the hands of the authorities. Hence my desire for secrecy.

"Well, as I have said, I found your mother, represented to her the peril of my position, pointed out to her the imperative necessity for absolute secrecy, and besought her, by all she held dearest, to help me once more and for the last time. She was deeply distressed when I told her in how serious a scrape I had involved myself, the more so as she could see no way of helping me without appealing to her husband for the necessary funds, which I bound her not to do, assuring her that such a step would inevitably bring about my ruin. At length she promised to think the matter over and do what she could for me, promising to meet me again the next evening.

"It so happened, however, that the pursuit after me was so hot that I was compelled to be closely hidden for nearly a fortnight, during which I have reason to believe that your mother suffered the keenest anxiety on my account. When at length I dared venture out again I found your mother's distress more keen than ever because she had been unable to obtain even the modest sum of money I had named as necessary to secure my safety. She bade me meet her again. I did so, only to find her still in the same pitiable state of helplessness and distress. I met her again, and yet again—seven times in all; and at our last meeting your mother pressed into my hand a small package of money—the proceeds of the sale of her own private jewels, as a hastily-written tear-blotted note inside informed me. The assistance, however, came just too late. I was arrested that very night and cast into prison, where, without even the pretence of a trial, I was confined for seven long years among the vilest of the vile. I should probably have been there still had I not succeeded in effecting my escape. But those seven years of misery unutterable had done their work upon me; I entered the prison a harmless enough young fellow, save that I was the victim of a mistaken enthusiasm; I emerged from it *a fiend*, my heart full to overflowing of hatred for the entire human race, with which I have warred, in one way or another, from that day to this.

"Such, Señor Lascelles, is my story; my only excuse for telling you which is the tender memories of your sainted mother, evoked by your extraordinary personal resemblance to her. You have listened to me with a patient kindness which you must surely have inherited from her, and I thank you; the thought of her has made me once more human; I feel the better for having been permitted to take her honoured name once more upon my lips; but now, señor, with your permission I will rest a little; I am weary, and oh, so very weak."

I withdrew, and making my way to Albuquerque's berth, begged permission of the owner to occupy it for an hour or two; which permission being obtained, I sat down then and there, and, whilst Merlani's story was still fresh in my memory, put the whole of it in black and white.

This done, I thought it high time to look in upon Don Luis, who would, perhaps, otherwise think I was slighting him. I accordingly made my way to his private cabin and knocked softly. The door was opened by Inez, who no sooner saw me than she flung herself into my arms—full in view of her father, who was reclining upon a couch—kissed me rapturously, and exclaimed:

"Oh, Leo, my dearest, how glad I am to see you once more, and unhurt, after all the dreadful occurrences of to-day; come in, *mio*, and sit down; papa and I have both been longing to see you, have we not, you dear, proud, good-natured darling of a father?"

"Yes," said Don Luis smiling, much to my astonishment, for I quite expected that his displeasure would have been kindled by his daughter's demonstrative reception of me—"yes, we have; but not from *precisely* the same motives, I fancy. However, let that pass. Come in, Leo, my boy, come in; why, you look as frightened as if it were you, and not that wilful headstrong daughter of mine, that I ought to be angry with. Sit down, and let Inez pour you out a glass of wine whilst you tell me how affairs have been progressing since I saw you last. But first," he continued, offering me his left hand—his injured limb being tightly swathed in bandages, and therefore unavailable—"let me express to you my heartfelt gratitude for the prompt and effective response you made to my appeal for help and deliverance at the moment that we were about to fall irretrievably into the hands of those piratical desperados. You and your gallant followers have saved us all from death—and, in my daughter's case, from a fate so much worse than death that I shall never be able to think of it without a shudder. You will find that I am not ungrateful—but I will speak of that anon. Now tell me, how have you managed with that miserable poltroon, Don Felix, and his officers and crew! Tell me in detail all that happened from the moment you were obliged to leave me."

Seating myself by his side, with Inez close to us both, I gave my friends a full and detailed account of everything that had transpired, omitting, of course, the particulars of my interview with Merlani; and I wound up by saying:

"Of course, Don Luis, I cannot say how the admiral may deal with the matter of my seizure of the ship, or how he will dispose of her officers and crew; but in any case I think that, as you and Dona Inez are civilians, he will not attempt to detain you; and even should he think of doing so, I do not believe I am overrating my influence with him when I say that I think he would, at my intercession, restore you your freedom."

"Thank you, Leo," said Don Luis heartily; "this is good news. I have been feeling a little anxious on that point since I have found time to think about it; for detention, at the present crisis in my affairs, might affect me most seriously. But if I can only succeed in making my way back to La Guayra, I have no doubt that, in a fortnight at most, I can collect evidence enough to completely frustrate the machinations of my enemies and set myself perfectly right again with the authorities in Spain.

"Now, with respect to yourself and this foolish—well, no, I will withdraw the word 'foolish'—this love affair between you and Inez. There is no doubt but you and your brave fellows have been the means of preserving us both from a very terrible fate; and, as I have said, you shall not find me ungrateful. I am not going to give my unconditional consent to Inez's marriage with you—not yet at least, that would be rather too absurd. You are both—and you, especially, Leo—far too young to seriously contemplate marriage for some years to come; moreover, you are at present merely a midshipman; you still have your way to make in the noble profession you have chosen to follow. I have not the slightest doubt that you *will* make it in due time; you have already established something more than a merely local reputation as a most gallant officer and seaman; you have distinguished yourself in a most remarkable manner for so young a man, and your superiors would be worse than ungrateful were they to fail to duly acknowledge and reward such distinguished merit. I have no doubt they *will* reward it, and I fully expect that when once you have 'served your time'—I believe that is the correct expression, is it not?—your rise in your profession will be rapid, and that it will not be very many years before you gain your post rank. When that day arrives, if your present regard for Inez remains unchanged, come to me, and you shall find me perfectly willing to incline a favourable ear to your proposals. In the meantime I completely withdraw my veto as to your intercourse with her; you may have as much of each other's society as you wish during the short time you are likely to be together, and you may afterwards correspond as voluminously as you please; but—understand me clearly—I will not accede to or in any way countenance anything approaching to a betrothal, or, as you English term it, an engagement! And now, my dear children, I hope you are both satisfied."

My story is ended. Is there any need that I should say more? Well, perhaps some of my readers may object to so abrupt a termination to this veracious history; and, to please them, it may be as well, perhaps, to briefly state a few additional facts.

I will add, then, that we succeeded in carrying the *Santa Catalina* safely into Port Royal, after a fine but somewhat slow passage, though I suppose I need scarcely say that to Inez and myself the days sped only too fast. I duly reported myself to the admiral, and was by him received most favourably, notwithstanding the deplorable *contre-temps* of the loss of the *Dolphin*. The *Santa Catalina* was duly declared a lawful prize; and though objections to this proceeding were raised by the Spanish government, and her surrender was formally demanded of us, she was never given up; and after even more than the usual delays, all concerned in her capture duly touched the prize-money due on her account—a very considerable sum, as in addition to a valuable cargo she had on board a large quantity of bullion. I do not know what became of her officers and crew, as I was almost immediately appointed to a dashing frigate fresh out from England; but no objection was raised to the departure from the island of Don Luis and his daughter, who managed, after some delay and difficulty, to secure a passage to La Guayra in a neutral vessel; and once there, he soon found means to set himself right with his government. Contrary to all expectation, Merlani survived long enough to be able to tell my father all he had told me, and more; thus completely and for ever setting at rest those harassing doubts and suspicions as to the sincerity of my mother's affection which had gone so far towards making a wreck of my father's life. My father's remorse and regret for his cruel treatment of my mother were keen in the extreme, and most painful to witness; but he faithfully strove to make what compensation he could by lavishing upon me all the love of his really warm and affectionate nature.

I remained on the West Indian station long enough to complete my time as a midshipman; and my old friend, the admiral, lived long enough to bestow upon me my post rank, which he did with almost indecent haste—at least, so said some of those who chose to feel jealous at my rapid advancement, which, however, the admiral stoutly maintained I had faithfully earned.

I presume it is scarcely necessary to add that, this coveted rank once gained, I lost no time in pressing my suit for Dona Inez's hand, which was then yielded to me with a very good grace—and with it a handsome fortune—by Don Luis, who only stipulated that we should live with him, he shortly afterwards resigning his post and removing to England to enable us to do so.